Praise for
TALL, DARK AND DEADLY

"The best book I've read this year!"   —*New York Times*
bestselling author Lora Leigh

"O'Clare writes edgy suspense with tough-as-nails characters who endure more than most can imagine and come out stronger on the other side."—*Romantic Times BOOKreviews*

"A gripping novel."   —*A Romance Review*

"Ms. O'Clare has written a gritty, dangerous, ~~and~~ sexy story. The action starts on the first page and d̶ ̶ ̶ ̶ ̶ ̶ up until the last. *Tall, Dark and Deadly* is a pag̶ ̶ ̶ ̶ ̶ ̶ ̶ with sensuality and suspense. You won't ̶ ̶ ̶ ̶ ̶ ̶ ̶ ̶"
                                                                    ̶s

Praise for Lorie O'C̶ ̶ ̶ ̶ ̶ ̶ ...

"O'Clare [writes] pag̶ ̶ ̶ ̶ ̶ ̶ ̶ ̶ ̶ ̶ell-developed characters, and sparkl̶ ̶ ̶ ̶ ̶ ̶ ̶ ̶ dialogue…and attraction so strong you ca̶ ̶ ̶
                                        —̶ ̶ ̶c *Times BOOKreviews*

"Intriguing [and] highly stimulating…a fantastic blend of mystery and suspense."   —*All About Murder*

"The passion and steamy sensuality are great, as are the action and emotion."   —*Romance Reviews Today*

St. Martin's Paperbacks Titles by
LORIE O'CLARE

Tall, Dark and Deadly

Long, Lean and Lethal

Strong, Sleek and Sinful

Strong, Sleek And Sinful

LORIE O'CLARE

St. Martin's Paperbacks

This is a work of fiction. All of the characters, organizations, and events portrayed in this novel are either products of the author's imagination or are used fictitiously.

STRONG, SLEEK AND SINFUL

Copyright © 2010 by Lorie O'Clare.
Excerpt from *Play Dirty* copyright © 2010 by Lorie O'Clare.

Cover photograph © Shirley Green

For information address St. Martin's Press, 175 Fifth Avenue, New York, NY 10010.

ISBN: 978-0-312-94344-8

Printed in the United States of America

St. Martin's Paperbacks edition / April 2010

St. Martin's Paperbacks are published by St. Martin's Press, 175 Fifth Avenue, New York, NY 10010.

10 9 8 7 6 5 4 3 2 1

Chapter 1

"Is this a joke?" Chief Murphy Radisson wasn't laughing.

"Hardly." Lt. Perry Flynn couldn't sit facing the Chief any longer.

"Tell me where you found these again." Rad hated anyone pacing in front of his desk. Perry didn't care. He walked over to the window and returned to loom over the Chief's desk.

"I sure as hell wasn't looking for a date." Perry focused on the printed Internet pictures that Rad held in his hand.

"I'd like to think not," Rad bellowed, his expression hardening fiercely. His immediate outrage was proof enough that he was taking this seriously. "Do you want to tell me what your sudden fascination with kiddy porn is doing on my desk?"

Flynn blew out a breath. It had been a long day, and it was far from over. He nodded to the pictures scattered across the Chief's desk.

"I did some searching earlier. And only printed the ones that I would swear are legitimate."

Rad glanced once again at the pictures before dropping them on his desk and then leaning back in his chair, lacing his fingers together and clasping them behind his head. He relaxed although still managed to look ready to pounce, and stared at Perry for a long moment. "There's no such thing as a goddamn legitimate pornography Web site. Why the hell did you print these? Start making some fucking sense or get the hell out of my office."

Flynn ignored the crass tone. "You know damn good and well what I mean. These come from Web sites—in fact, four of them from the same site—where you can buy these children off an auction block if you want."

"And you've got proof?"

"No, I don't have proof other than what is printed on the site. You need to subscribe to these sites, and register with a fair amount of personal information."

"And you did that?"

"I've saved the links if you'd like to take a look. I used the same credit card I got over a year ago when I worked that casino case. Someone would have to do a fair amount of digging to link the card to me as a cop." He couldn't look at any of those pictures without seeing his nieces, all of whom were about the same ages as the girls in those pictures. It made him sick, pissed him off. He would kill any bastard with his bare hands who tried doing anything demented or perverted to any of his sister's girls. "In the past year two high school girls have disappeared." He stalked over to the window again and tugged at the collar of his uniform, more than ready to get out of it and chill in front of the TV for the night. Like that would happen at this rate. "Yesterday we bring in a sixteen-year-old, Sally Wright, who was convinced she was talking to a boy her age over in Topeka. If she didn't have overly protective parents, as she called them, who watched out for her and followed her to the rendezvous point, we might have had three missing girls." Perry rested his fist on the edge of Rad's desk and stabbed at the pictures with his index finger. "And the worst part is the ISP for those goddamn sites is right here in Mission Hills."

That grabbed Rad's attention. "You've verified that?"

"I looked into it myself. But just to make you happy," he added, offering a wry grin, although he was anything but amused by this conversation. "I've contacted a Web site expert and am verifying it."

"There is nothing to pin Sally Wright's interrupted rendezvous to anything as serious as child pornography."

Perry dragged his fingers through his short dark hair and took his time choosing his words. Rad was a damn good Chief of Police, but he was a hard-ass, too. Present his argument right and he'd get a chance at this. Fuck it up and he'd get his wish at watching TV all evening. He wasn't going to win either way on this one.

"The MO is wrong for runaways. You've agreed with me on that on more than one occasion. When Sally Wright was in here yesterday with her parents, we saw a mother and father frantic over the fact that they almost lost their daughter. If Charlie Wright hadn't followed his daughter to the mall and spied on her, some prick would have snagged her up. Mr. Wright brought your proof to you."

Rad didn't move but continued resting his head against his hands while eyeballing Perry carefully. "So what's this all about? You think snooping around on porn sites will help you nail some online predator?"

"You never know. But I think possibly creating a trap might draw our perp out from behind his Internet shield." Perry moved the pictures around with his finger, making it easier to see all of them. "We create a fictitious teenager, start chatting online, and get ourselves lured in. Our perp is here in town, Rad. And quite possibly he's the same man who killed Maura Reynolds last October. We documented proof on that case that she was talking to someone online who claimed to be a teenage boy. She'd arranged to meet him the night she disappeared."

"And if you catch a sixteen-year-old boy what are you going to do?"

"It won't happen like that. There are things you say, ways that you talk to a predator, and of course ways to behave online that attract a sexual predator."

"So suddenly you're an expert on online sexual predators." Rad lunged forward in his chair aggressively enough that it almost snapped him into a stand. "You don't have any experience tracking an online stalker. Don't insult me and pretend that you do. Unless of course there's something you need to tell me." He raised one thick, shaggy brow, silently challenging Perry.

"I know how to cruise the Internet at least as well as anyone else in this department, maybe better than some of your married cops."

"You want to bet on that?"

"I have four nieces, all teenagers."

"Not the same as having your own," Rad rebuked.

Perry ignored him, sick of hearing how he didn't know kids just because he didn't have any. "And I know the sites where the teenagers hang out online. It's like learning which is the in mall to go to. Any teenager will tell you there are Web sites that they check out daily and others they wouldn't be caught dead going to."

Rad stacked the pictures and shoved them across his desk toward Perry. "In your downtime if you want to follow children around online, feel free. I'm not taking you and your partner off your beat so you can glue yourself to a computer." Rad stood slowly, pushing his chair back and straightening his large frame. He stood well over six feet and was in pretty good shape for going on fifty. A bad knee forced him to work behind a desk, and Perry respected the man for sticking it out and working his way to chief of police instead of throwing in the towel like so many did when injured badly enough on the job that it got them yanked off the streets. He pressed his fist against the top of his desk when he came around to face Perry. "Take some advice from an old man," Rad began. "Chill out on this for a while. You're one hell of a good cop. But you don't have any proof at all that the teenager who died last fall and our teenager last night almost meeting a stranger off-line are in any way connected."

Perry reminded himself he wouldn't snap when the Chief rejected his proposal. "When Charlie Wright brought his daughter into the station last night, I saw myself with one of my nieces. For all I know, Sally Wright might know Dani or Diane. They're about the same age. I felt his rage, the desire burning in his blood to take out the asshole who almost snagged his daughter."

"There's often rage in victims," Rad said, stacking the photos and handing them to Perry. "You aren't going to find a connection between these Web sites and a father and daughter who had a close call. You don't have any proof."

Perry didn't want the photos. It was all he could do not to let his frustration boil over to anger from Rad's indifference that the possibility existed they had a serious problem. "The only way you gather proof is to investigate," Perry growled, his teeth clenching together in his effort to keep his emotions under wrap. "If we've got a sexual predator feeding off young girls, we need to investigate and find out. I will not allow some creep to feed his fetish on innocent children. My nieces are online all the time chatting with their friends. I'm not going to have some asshole pretending to be a boy their age luring them into a trap like this." He stabbed his finger into the pages Rad still held in his hand.

"And the last thing I'm going to have is anyone breathing down my throat if they think your good intentions are directed more toward you and not the force."

Perry wasn't ready for that one. "What the fuck?" he hissed. "Who in the hell would suggest that I went to porn sites for any reason not related to work?" he growled, feeling his temper rise in spite of his efforts to keep it under wraps.

"I didn't say that anyone would do that. Bring me proof these sites are here in Mission Hills, and who is running them, and we'll talk." Rad walked over to his office door and opened it. "Call it a night, Flynn. Your partner appears to have headed home. You should, too. We'll discuss this further when you have more solid proof for me."

Perry threw out his last offer. "Give this case to me," he said quietly, ignoring the open door. "I'll make sure we don't lose any more girls."

"Go home." Rad was done discussing it. He pressed his lips into a thin line as he let go of the door handle, leaving the door open. "You did a good job with the Wrights. Hopefully their daughter's incident will get around to the other kids her age. You claim to know how teenagers are. But let me tell you something. By tomorrow everyone at her school will know that she fell for the wrong guy online. It will make the other girls think twice before agreeing to meet someone when they can't verify that kid is for real."

Perry grunted, which was all the response he cared to give. Rad was wrong, but Perry wouldn't imply the Chief didn't remember how his kids had behaved when they were that age. More than likely his wife did most of the raising anyway. And the Chief's kids didn't grow up using the Internet as their main source for communicating with their peers.

Perry got damn sick and tired of the assumption that since he'd never fathered a child he therefore was clueless about them. "You should call it a day, too," he said as he headed out the door. He didn't wait for the Chief's response.

Carlos Ramos, Perry's partner, had already headed home for the night, not because he hurried home to a wife and children. Like Perry, Carlos took wearing his uniform very seriously. It left little time to find that perfect soul mate. That didn't make him any less of a man. Unless they were hot and heavy in a serious investigation, Carlos always cut out at quitting time. His mother was elderly and suffered from dementia. He didn't have the heart to put her in a home, and for that Perry respected him even more. Carlos owned a duplex and his mother still lived in her own home, maintaining her pride, and managing for herself for the most part. But Carlos was right there for her always.

"You headed home?" Lieutenant Barker looked up from a stack of files and pulled her glasses off that had already slipped to the edge of her nose. "What's wrong?"

Perry forced the scowl from his face and shook his head. "Long day."

"I heard you had a hell of a mess with that kid yesterday. Thank God for overprotective parents, huh?"

"No shit." He paused at his desk, which was at an angle from hers and focused on the files she'd stacked in the corner facing him. "What are you doing?"

"Just catching up on paperwork." She didn't elaborate.

Jane Barker was a good cop, had been on the force for four years, and was married to a good man who could barbecue up a mean steak. The rumors that she was one hell of a good fuck didn't make Perry receptive to her flirtatious smiles. He didn't do married women. "You're stressing pretty hard over this teenage thing, aren't you?" she asked, brushing a sandy brown wisp of hair behind her ear.

"What are you stressing over?" Lt. Pete Goddard, who'd been on a beat almost as long as Perry, seven years, strolled over to the desk and crossed his arms, glancing from Perry to Jane.

"Nothing," Perry grumbled. Neither one of them understood how delicate a matter it was raising teenagers. Ever since his brother-in-law had died in the line of duty, Perry had stepped up to bat, helping his sister raise her four daughters. No one understood teenage girls as well as he did. "I'm heading out."

"You stressing over that Wright girl?" Pete continued, obviously having overheard more of the conversation than he originally let on. "Did you know her?"

"Nope." Perry met Pete's curious stare but kept his own masked. "She was one of the lucky ones. Proof there are parents out there who really care about their kids."

"There're some sick bastards in this world," Pete grunted.

Perry glanced at the clock. Diane would be done with her classes at junior college and would be heading home to fix supper for her sisters. Ever since his sister took on a second job, the girls had been forced to step up to bat and take on more responsibilities to keep the house running smoothly. It was good for them, and for the most part everything got done. Perry would still touch base, make sure supper was on the table and homework was being done.

All four of his nieces were as near perfect as young girls could be. Maybe his life didn't allow for a wife and children. He knew his job was dangerous, and the last thing he would ever do to a woman was make her a widow and force her to raise a family alone. Not that David Vetter, his sister's husband, hadn't been a damn good cop and head over heels for

Megan. David couldn't have seen his own death coming so soon. But it was a lesson, and a tragedy, Perry took to heart. Megan and the girls wouldn't make it without him. He wouldn't put a lady in the same predicament. A personal long-term relationship wasn't in the books for him.

"Sometimes kids create drama for attention," Pete continued as Perry reached for the door. "Don't stress out over a ghost."

"Fucking ghost, my ass," Perry growled under his breath, and let the door close behind him as he headed toward his car. An attitude like that would slow the action in nailing the prick who was stalking teenage girls. They weren't dealing with a ghost. Ghosts weren't traceable through ISP addresses.

Heading out of the parking lot in his own car, a two-year-old Thunderbird he'd picked up for a pretty good deal off one of the lots in town, Perry pulled out his cell phone and scrolled through his names. Then punching the number, he adjusted his Bluetooth and listened as it rang on the other line.

Maybe he didn't have a connection between the Web sites he'd found and a teenage girl disappearing after talking to a boy online and then being found dead several days later. Right now, there wasn't anything to piece that crime with the Wrights' coming in last night after too close of a call with their daughter trying to meet some jerk off the Internet. But there was a connection. He could feel it. And he wasn't some rookie cop. Half the time hunches were what he worked off of, and turned into cold, hard proof.

Perry listened to the phone ring in his ear a third time as he slipped behind the wheel to his car. He would get proof in bits and pieces, starting with the Web sites. But damn, if a predator was stalking teenage girls in Perry's town, he was on that case, whether Rad liked it or not. Even if Perry didn't bring them into this world, his nieces were everything to him. And it was his responsibility to ensure they had a safe environment to grow up in.

"Kayne here," a deep male voice finally answered.

"Noah, it's Perry Flynn." Perry gripped the wheel and

headed out of the parking lot and toward the ramp for the interstate.

"Hey, Flynn. What the hell is up with you?" Noah sounded unusually cheerful.

"I hear you're settling down and accepting a leash and collar these days," Perry teased, hardly in the mood for it, but he couldn't remember the last time Noah didn't snap over the phone if Perry pushed the right buttons. It was a tradition they'd upheld since college, berating and insulting each other but always there for the other when needed.

"Fuck you, man. There's not a goddamn collar around my neck." There was a lady's laughter in the background and Noah grumbled something inaudible before sounding a bit more like himself when he snapped, "You call for a reason?"

"Actually, I did, but giving you crap sounds a hell of a lot more fun than talking shop. Who's the unlucky lady?"

"She's the luckiest woman on the planet, and she will tell you that herself." Noah sounded happy again.

A small twinge of jealousy tightened Perry's gut, but he ignored it. He was glad his old college buddy was happy. Noah deserved a good woman. It wasn't the life for Perry, though, and that was something he had accepted years ago. It wasn't jealousy he felt for the leash and collar, but more so the fact that his old friend sounded less stressed because he was getting some every night. They didn't make women Perry could stand living with, though, only having sex when schedules matched up and then amiably parting ways.

Perry grunted. "Trained her well, did you?"

"You know it," Noah said.

"You sound so happy that I hate bringing up why I called," Perry added, and accelerated on the interstate toward his exit. A drive-through would be his usual stop, but for some reason tonight he didn't have an appetite. After interviewing the Wrights last night and then spending hours on the computer afterward searching and finding Web sites that possibly were the reason some jerk was stalking Sally Wright, Perry couldn't eat or sleep. He needed his head on straight, if he was going to find whoever it was who was stalking teenage girls. Maybe after taking a shower and changing he'd get a burger and a twelve-pack.

"What's up?" Noah asked.

"Just thought I'd see if you've heard anything through the grapevine."

"About?"

Perry knew Noah wouldn't tell him anything confidential. But there were times in the past when a case had turned haunting and knowing an old buddy who was FBI helped out. Occasionally, Noah had tips that cracked a case wide open.

"We've got a sexual predator in town," Perry began.

There was silence on the other end of the line, which meant he had Noah's attention.

"There've been two cases so far," Perry continued. "Two teenage girls, lured in by someone they thought was a boy from their school. They chatted online, agreed to meet, and then the girls disappeared. We've found one of the girls, but not the other." He took a breath and heard Noah curse under his breath. If anything, unloading on his old friend helped Perry focus. The attitude at the station that he might be chasing ghosts, or that this wasn't something that merited anyone being assigned the case full-time, pissed him off. "Last night a third girl snuck out of her home to meet a boy she'd been chatting with online. Her father followed her and watched his daughter park the family car at a pizza place. As she started toward the restaurant a man got out of his car and went after the teenager. If the father wasn't there to run after his daughter, he would have lost her."

Noah cursed again. "I haven't heard anything. You been assigned the case?"

"Nope." Perry ground his back teeth together, forcing himself not to unload his frustrations over his conversation with his Chief. "Keep your ear to the ground for me, though. Will you?"

"Will do," Noah said seriously. "Keep me posted as well. If there's anything I can do, let me know."

"There is something," Perry said, and turned at his exit,

then slowed on the off-ramp as it rounded and merged into the main street of his neighborhood. "I found some Web sites."

"Oh yeah? What kind of Web sites."

"Pornography. The kind where the girls are barely legal, if that."

"They're a dime a dozen, my friend."

"Tell me about it," Perry growled, images of the pictures he had printed for the Chief turning his stomach and twisting it into a ball of pissed-off rage. "These Web sites are a bit different, though. They're worded carefully, as most of them are, but they look as if you could bid on these girls, buy them off the auction block. I need help understanding ISPs and domains and crap. Because from what I can tell, and if I'm right, the Web sites were created here in the Kansas City area."

"No shit." Noah must have put his hand over the phone at his end, because he mumbled something too muffled for Perry to hear. More than likely Noah was explaining to his new lady, who Perry knew was a cop up in Lincoln, Nebraska, what the conversation was about. "Let me get back to you on that one. I might be able to e-mail a file I have on a flash drive that explains domains and web hosting."

"Appreciate it, man," Perry said. "Sure hope that lady of yours doesn't come to her senses."

"She's got it bad for me, what can I say?"

"Lost cause," Perry mumbled, again feeling that pang of jealousy before hanging up.

The police radio installed under his dash beeped and chirped just as Perry pulled into his driveway. He put the car in park but didn't cut the engine as he listened to the dispatcher send two cars to a disturbance over at a nearby mall parking lot. Dispatch reported a female, age sixteen, was reported missing by her friends and they were trying to get into her car to retrieve their belongings when passersby grew concerned the teenagers were breaking into the car. Perry listened a moment longer to see who was dispatched and where they were right now. Then grabbing his phone, he auto-dialed dispatch, the words *teenage female missing* ringing in his head.

"Cliff, this is Flynn. I'm ten forty-two but just a couple blocks from the Shawnee Mission mall."

"Unit Six is already ten ninety-seven," Cliff said while other dispatchers talked in the background. "Apparently he was a couple blocks away."

"Franco up to bat again." Perry shifted into reverse and backed out of his driveway. "I've got a personal interest in any teenage disappearances right now. Do you know how long she's been missing?"

"Negative," Cliff said. "You know Franco isn't going to take lightly you stepping in on his call. I'm sure it's something he can handle."

Perry snorted. Franco Romero didn't like any case that wasn't high profile. If he couldn't make the news with an arrest, he'd let the perp go. The arrogant prick cared more about how he looked in his uniform than he did about crimes going on around him.

"I'll just do a drive-by." Perry knew Cliff didn't care one way or the other.

"Ten four," Cliff said, ending the call.

Perry headed around the corner toward the mall parking lot. He gripped the steering wheel, his insides hardening with predatory rage as he took in the familiar surroundings. Pulling in the first entrance, he drove to where Franco was already parked, his lights flashing on his squad car as he walked around the front to where a handful of teenagers looked more nervous than angry. Perry had picked up his nieces and their friends too many times in this parking lot after they spent a day at the mall. This was more than home turf. This was where his girls hung out, where they laughed and played, flirted and shopped. He exhaled, making it sound as if he growled. There had better be a rational explanation why these kids were locked out of their friend's car and unable to get their things. Whoever the girl was who drove them better be inside the mall, her cell phone dead, or possibly distracted by a boy from her class. If the online predator was sniffing around this mall, Perry's nieces weren't safe. He'd turn this goddamn town upside down finding the prick whether the Chief liked it or not.

Perry parked behind the squad car, checking out the group of kids who huddled close to one another, watching Franco warily. He wasn't sure whether he recognized any of them or not. His nieces weren't here, but that knowledge offered him only a small amount of relief. Every kid standing alongside the car in question looked about Dani and Diane's age and very well could be friends of his nieces.

He didn't get out of his car right away, taking his time absorbing the surroundings. Franco was busy barking at the kids, playing it out as if he were rough and tough and every one of those boys and girls was up to no good. Perry wanted to send a right hook to Franco's head for being a prick. The kids were obviously nervous as hell, didn't appear to be ready to run, and shifted nervously, each of them growing paler and wide-eyed the longer Franco ranted loud enough for Perry to hear inside his car.

There were other cars parked down the long row, each stall marked with fresh, bright white paint. The car with the missing driver parked on the outer edge of the lot, with most remaining cars parked closer to the mall entrance. Perry watched two ladies, probably about his age, walk through the lot with their purchases in various-sized bags that each lady held in her hands. They strolled slowly, curious as they watched the scene, but stopped at a minivan and loaded their bags, then headed out.

Another lady strolled through the parking lot in a short dress that showed off leg clear up to her thighs. Her waist was so small he bet he could wrap his fingers around it. She paused, as if hesitating, possibly not remembering where she parked. When she leaned against a parked car several stalls down, Perry got the impression it wasn't her car. She looked like she stopped just to watch Franco yell at the kids.

Perry acknowledged that many of his nieces' friends were too hot for their own good. And at their age, they were so excited with their brand-new sensual bodies and no longer being awkward little girls, they went out of their way to show off what they had. More than once Dani's and Diane's friends had flirted with him. It was vaguely amusing. Not once had Perry ever been aroused by any teenage girl, even when they stretched out in his sister's backyard, tanning in little more than string bikinis. They were children, goddamn children, no matter what their bodies looked like.

Something about the young woman leaning against her green hybrid, her arms crossed against her waist and her full breasts partially exposed under her low-cut neckline, did more than distract him. He grew hard watching her, focusing on her pouty lips when her tongue darted out and moistened them. She never once looked his way, but if Perry didn't know better he'd swear she knew she had an audience and posed, offering one hell of a view of her hot, perfectly shaped body.

If one of his nieces dressed like that, he'd march her right back to her bedroom to change into something more decent. In spite of the lady leaning against her car giving all appearances of being a teenager from her attire down to the way she leaned against her car, her body language screaming attitude and a saucy nature that would probably be hell to take on, Perry guessed her to be probably in her early twenties. He wondered if she dressed to appear younger than she actually was on purpose.

As he took his time getting out of the car, his attention was torn between the conversation now playing out between Franco and the group of teenagers and the young woman leaning against her hybrid. Her short blond hair was tousled, possibly gelled, like some of the teenagers wore their hair. If it weren't for the curves, the way she filled out her sleeveless minidress, and how her slender legs were crossed and very much on display, he might have guessed her a bored teenager trying to stay out of the scene yet very much a part of it. Perry walked toward the group of kids. Franco spotted him and straightened, intentionally looking away from him and deepening his voice as he addressed the kids.

"Whose car is this?" he demanded.

"She's not here." A freckle-faced boy stepped forward. "Olivia gave us rides here, but we can't find her. We thought she ditched us, but here's her car and it's locked. Our stuff is in there."

Perry glanced again at the young woman leaning against her hybrid while Franco called in the tag and continued questioning the teenagers. It was obvious she was attentively watching the teenagers who loitered around the car Franco was calling in. As Perry watched her, she shifted her attention to him. She had blue eyes, bright blue eyes that were sharp and focused and widened when she realized she did in fact have an audience.

It hit him that a sexual predator might watch a teenage girl the way he was staring at this woman right now. If Perry were determined enough, he could approach the woman, engage in a conversation, and leave with her. Even if she went with him against her will, there weren't enough people around for anyone to notice, especially if he were to gag her, or even drug her. No one would give them a second glance if Perry were a predator, and if he were confident in his moves.

The thought made him sick, hardening his insides and pissing him off. A quick survey showed there weren't any other people loitering around them. Perry stood in front of his car, staying put, and squinted at the parked cars nearby. No one sat inside any of them.

The teenagers moved, leaving their huddle, when another car pulled up and a woman got out, hurrying over to Franco and not bothering to turn off her engine.

"That's my daughter's car," she announced. "Where is she?"

Perry glanced again at the woman leaning against the hybrid as the teenagers, who apparently knew the lady who'd just arrived, all started talking, quickly informing her when they'd last seen her daughter.

The woman with the hybrid appeared to be listening attentively to the anxious chatter that escalated in tone to worry and panic when it became apparent that her daughter, Olivia

Brown, was missing. Franco was on the phone with Dispatch confirming who had called in the disturbance. Perry headed toward the woman, deciding it wouldn't hurt to learn what she might have seen.

As he walked around the teenagers toward her, Perry stared at the woman and those bright blue eyes of hers flashed defiantly. She straightened and then the material of her short dress swayed over her perfectly shaped ass as she jumped into her car.

"Hold on a minute," he called out.

There wasn't a car parked in front of her hybrid and the woman started hers and peeled out. As she drove away, Perry repeated her tag number out loud to himself. If she was a witness to anything, he would find out.

Chapter 2

Kylie Donovan would nail the son of a bitch to the wall.

"Look at her," she hissed, staring at the pictures of Maura Reynolds her parents had provided the FBI. "She barely got a taste of life."

"Which is why you were called in." Paul Hernandez sat at the computer, clicking his mouse repeatedly while biting his lower lip. "All right. I've sent the files I pulled off her hard drive to this flash drive." Paul tapped the small drive plugged into the USB port in the tower next to him. Then pushing his glasses up his nose he stared at her over the thick brown rims, looking very much the computer geek that he was. "She chatted with a boy named Peter for three months and last October agreed to meet him at the movie theater."

Kylie stared at the pictures, barely hearing what Paul said. For a moment she didn't see the pretty young teenager. A half buried, naked body broken and twisted in an impossible position, Karen Donovan, Kylie's older sister, appeared in her mind, also dead, her legs and arms bent the wrong way.

She knew why she was called in, for the same reason she was flown from city to city any time the local police ran into a snag with online predators. Especially when their prey were teenage girls. Kylie wouldn't say why, and she wasn't convinced she knew the reason herself, but she was good at tracking assholes who fed off of innocent teenagers. For some reason, it came naturally to her. It wasn't something she was proud of, understanding the minds of twisted bastards who fed off of innocent teenagers. She saw the beauty of young girls, how virgins inexperienced in the art of seduction yet provocative in their willingness to flirt and explore could be more of a turn-on than a fully grown woman who was already jaded from life's experiences.

That was how Karen was, her older sister, cocky and a flirt, flaunting her perfect body and teasing and torturing every boy in their high school. Karen loved every minute of it. And Kylie, being younger and not yet as developed, envied the hell out of her beautiful, perfect sister, who managed to get every boy at school to stumble over his own feet to do anything for her. Kylie couldn't get any of them to give her the time of day. Of course all of that ended the day her sister died.

Kylie pinched her nose, blowing out an exasperated breath, and put the horrible memory out of her head. Someday she would quit seeing her sister every time she took on a new case. "You've tracked the ISPs?"

"That's why you're working solo, kiddo." Paul probably wasn't more than five years older than Kylie, possibly in his mid-thirties, yet he spoke like an old man.

He looked like a nerd, but there was an easygoing side to him Kylie immediately liked. She'd spent the day with him, after flying into Kansas City and renting a car to drive to the suburb of Mission Hills. And in that short time she already knew he would be volumes of help in gathering data for this case.

"I'm still working on narrowing it down to a specific computer. Our perp is jumping around. But whoever is chatting with these girls is using city computers. The Mission Hills, Kansas, Law Enforcement Center for one, and other city offices, but I'm narrowing it down, and it's not looking pretty."

"You think he's a cop?" she asked, keeping her emotions at bay.

Someone who'd taken an oath to uphold the law, to protect and serve, to watch over the youth of their city and make sure they were safe, was tested and put through rigorous courses in order to earn his, or her, badge. Any signs of being fucked up should have been detected long before he donned that uniform. It wouldn't be the first time she'd arrested someone in uniform, though. A bad seed could pop up anywhere. Unfortunately, working in law enforcement could make a man, or a woman, believe he, or she, was invincible, above the laws he enforced on everyone else. It didn't happen a lot. But it did happen. Kylie wouldn't hesitate in making her arrest, no matter if her perp wore a uniform or not. It wouldn't take her long to gather intel, scope out the town, and find her guy.

And anyone capable of doing this to a young girl was a hell of a lot more than mental—he was insane, not worth saving or wasting tax dollars on to rehabilitate. As far as Kylie was concerned, he should be made to suffer a horrendous death worse than what he put his victims through.

"What I think doesn't matter," Paul said, as if he followed her line of thinking and came up with the inevitable conclusion. He was still clicking his mouse repeatedly and staring unblinking at his computer screen. "It's our job to find proof. Just the facts, ma'am."

Kylie turned to study Paul. Although still light outside, heavy shadows stretched across the small office. Light from his monitor cast different shades of color over his hard, dark face as he continued jumping from screen to screen. There were streaks of silver in his black hair and crow's-feet stretched to his temples, more visible through the lenses of his glasses that he stared over as he focused on the computer. He was a gaunt man, but not grossly unattractive.

The thick gold band on his ring finger and the heavy gold chain around his neck stood out against his brown skin, making them look more like intentional bling-bling than jewelry he'd probably worn for so many years he forgot they were there. Something told her, in the week or so she'd spent communicating with him prior to arriving here in Mission Hills, that her opinion of him summed up his nature: the computer geek taken for granted and often forgotten by agents in the field until they needed his talents. Special agents like him were overlooked in the heat of the action, yet Kylie wouldn't be as ready to jump into this case if it weren't for the profile he'd already created on her perp.

Paul pulled the flash drive out of the USB port and held it in his hand, palm up. Kylie walked over to his desk and took it.

"What you think does matter. I want your opinion, Paul," she said quietly, and moved so she could see the screen he stared at through the lenses in his glasses. She pressed her lips together, hiding her smile when she realized he was playing a computer game. "Any gut reaction or thoughts that come to mind, whether you can prove them at the moment or not, matter to me and I need to hear them," she added, walking around his desk and staring at his monitor.

"Okay, sweetheart," he said, clicking his mouse repeatedly while moving a starship into orbit around a glowing red planet. "Peter is a city employee, paid by the hardworking citizens of Mission Hills and sitting at a computer right now somewhere here in town, trying to beat my high score."

An instant message box popped up in front of Paul's starship, and he moved the cursor to minimize it so quickly Kylie barely managed to read what it said.

"You're battling against our perp right now?" she asked, shocked.

"Don't know," he said, and sent a stream of laser fire toward an approaching ship until it exploded on the screen.

The next evening Kylie pulled into the narrow driveway of the rental house provided by the FBI and hung up her cell phone. Everything was in place. The tag on her car was registered to Kylie Dover, her undercover name. She'd signed a month-to-month lease and picked up all of her new identification for her undercover work. Her aunt in Topeka owned the house, as the cover story went, and anyone who did a background check would learn that much. The FBI was very good at protecting their own.

She'd answered to many names over the past five years. Although a lot of her cases were handled in her home office in Dallas, once she showed an ability to narrow in on this particular type of perp, her supervisor, Susie Parker, started sending her around the country, helping out local law enforcement agencies to nail online sexual predators.

At least this time she would use her real first name, except when she was online. She might not be attacking starships in distant galaxies, but her battle would definitely go down on the Internet. The online predator stalking and killing teenagers in Mission Hills would die from worse than laser file, at least if she had anything to say about it.

Paul Hernandez turned the corner in his Ford F-150 and pulled in behind her rental car. This wasn't her favorite part of a case, all the prep work, and she was grateful he'd agreed to stop by and help her get organized. Kylie pushed the button to release the trunk and then hopped out of her car.

"Holy crap," Paul said, and then let out a low whistle between his teeth. "How much for the goods?" he drawled, strolling up her driveway and eyeballing the skimpy outfit she'd worn while scoping out several of the teenage hangouts in town.

"You couldn't afford me," she told him smugly, and walked around to her opened trunk. "There's more stuff inside. We've got this computer, and then a camera system that needs to be installed. Without your help, this would take me all night."

"You stay in that getup, we might be here all night anyway." Paul reached in and lifted out the box holding her new computer, then wagged his eyebrows at her before heading toward her house. "That or I might have to persuade the wife to put her cheerleading outfit on tonight."

"I'll change," Kylie called out after him, and smiled when he groaned.

Slamming her trunk closed, she looked up and down the street before heading inside. She'd been here a couple days and had stopped at quite a few different businesses where kids tended to hang out, the fast-food chains in walking distance of the high school, the mall, the bowling alley, as well as the library. Only once did anyone pay attention to her, and that was while she watched the kids trying to get into their friend's car outside the mall. It didn't take much to learn the man who'd tried approaching her was an off-duty cop, and she hadn't seen him since. She couldn't let her guard down for a second, though, especially with their perp possibly being a cop.

Her work was cut out for her, getting to know who'd been friends with Maura Reynolds and Sally Wright, as well as learning enough about the kids in town to find out if any one of them might be chatting with someone named Peter. Kylie would need to go online and try to lure her perp out of hiding. The toughest part of her job would be getting to know the local cops. Anyone comfortable enough to rape and murder while donning a badge daily would be shrewd, incredibly confident, and also capable of obtaining inside knowledge about how close she might be to closing in on him.

Kylie changed into comfortable shorts and a T-shirt, ordered pizza, and worked with Paul until the house was secure and wired thoroughly.

"No one will set foot on your lawn without you knowing." Paul finished screwing the plate into the wall and stood back adjusting the cameras in the smaller of the two bedrooms that now looked like a high-tech surveillance room. "Any chat conversations will be saved using this program here. Every keystroke is monitored as well. It's all saved to this flash drive."

All the equipment now installed in her small two-bedroom rental house was standard-issued equipment. "I'm familiar with the programs," she assured him, but continued listening since Paul seemed intent on explaining how everything worked.

As it grew dark, she closed blinds and turned on lights. It had been a long two days. She pinched the bridge of her nose, her eyes dry with exhaustion.

"Okay, kiddo." Paul packed up his tools in a small leather case and looked at the room like a proud father. "My work here is done. Get some sleep. I've finished the easy part. You've got the hard part of the job, catching this asshole."

"We'll catch him." Kylie patted Paul's shoulder while walking behind him down the hall to her front door. "But you're right; I'm ready to crash."

She would soak in a hot bath and then see how many hours she could get online before she couldn't stay awake any longer.

"Where are you headed tomorrow?" he asked, pulling his cell out and glancing at the screen before shoving it back in his pocket.

"Tomorrow is Friday. I can hit the bowling alley after school and there are a few house parties I heard about while hanging at the McDonald's across from the high school today."

"You're going to house parties?" Paul reached for the front door but turned and raised an eyebrow.

"No," she said quickly. "That won't be necessary. I need to be around the kids in order to learn if any of the girls are chatting with someone online they don't know. From what I heard today, the group I was following will be at the bowling alley tomorrow and Saturday. Then there's another group that camps out at the movie theater by the mall both Friday and Saturday."

Paul stepped around her and scooped up one of the remaining pieces of thin-crust pepperoni pizza slices. She watched him stuff half the slice into his mouth. "I'll need to log into your local network," she told him.

Paul nodded and grunted, his mouth full of pizza. Wiping his hand on his jeans, he reached into his back pocket, pulled out a worn wallet, and then freed a card, which he handed to her. She stared at the plain business card, one similar to the kind she had—somewhere.

"Call me tomorrow and we'll get you set up with a screen name and password. That's my cell," he said, pointing with his thumb at the card. "I'm going to head out. The wife's already called twice."

Kylie smiled. Everyone in her world had someone to answer to except her. "I'll call if I need anything."

Once Paul was gone, she set up her police scanner, turned

it up so she could hear it, then headed back for a hot bath. An hour later she sat in front of the computer, ready to create her profile as a teenage girl. Her assignment: nail the son of a bitch who was raping and killing girls in Mission Hills, Kansas. Her focus: the Mission Hills Police Department. No city employee or official in Mission Hills, or anywhere in the Kansas City area, knew she was here; no one other than the handful of people working at the field office here in town.

Kylie clicked on the Internet Explorer icon, typed in "Yahoo!" and then proceeded creating a screen name. She typed in a few variations, working until she found one that wasn't already in use. Grabbing one of the flash drives out of her purse, she plugged it in and then opened the first file. She'd taken pictures of herself with her digital camera before arriving here. Not professional. Some of them goofy. And looking very much like pictures that she'd seen on the many teenager profiles she'd browsed through over the past few days. It never ceased to amaze her how much information she could always gather about high school kids in whatever city she worked simply by going to Twitter and Facebook.

Sticking to the life she'd created for Kayla, her online persona, she worked with her new profile—Kayla2010. She was sixteen, graduating from high school in 2010, and from Wyoming. She was in Kansas City, not Mission Hills, so kids online wouldn't question who she was, staying with her grandmother. Using the pictures on her flash drive and searching the Internet for backgrounds and songs to finalize the profile she made, Kylie finally sat back and let her head fall.

"That was work," she said out loud, and straightened, realizing it was almost midnight. It sucked sometimes not being able to use the same profile as she moved from city to city, chasing down the bastards who made the Internet their lair for sick behavior. If there was one strong consistency about online predators, they were intelligent, usually very Internet savvy, and if her profiles didn't appear 100 percent legitimate she wouldn't be able to nail them.

But the basic traps were set. Tomorrow she'd start working the profiles, hitting chat rooms, blogs, and YouTube.

Kylie crawled into bed, leaving the scanner on for background noise, and cuddled under her new blankets. Another town, another bedroom, another case. She was damn good at what she did. One of the best.

As she closed her eyes, images of the many profiles she'd been to that evening swam around in her head. She faded away, hitting a deep, hard sleep quickly. There visions of her older sister, so perfect and popular, until the day she was found naked and beaten, and very dead, tortured Kylie's dreams.

Kylie stared at the open coffin, watching her older sister for the longest time, willing her to move. She'd been fourteen, her older sister, Karen, seventeen, and that funeral was the day Kylie's life ended. Their happy family destroyed, changed forever, as dead as her sister.

Her father, who'd never missed a day's work in his life, suddenly seemed sick all the time. Kylie remembered watching her mother grow old before her eyes, as if time were sped up and in a week she'd aged twenty years. The laughter ended. Their home turned into a shell. Where once there was continual chatter and TVs on in every room and her mother's radio always buzzing in the kitchen, the moment they returned home from the funeral all that seemed forgotten. The house was quiet, continuous, non-ending silence, like the tomb where Kylie's sister lay. Kylie didn't grow up, she passed through time, until she, too, left the shell that once was her family.

Now Kylie kept it on autopilot, determined to make up for her sister dying so unnecessarily. It was more than a full-time job. It was Kylie's life's work.

Today she didn't allow social life, or family, to get in her way. Her family was destroyed with the death of her sister. But if Kylie worked her ass off, other families wouldn't be destroyed like hers was.

She twisted the sheet around her body, waking up from the painful dreams and staring at the ceiling. Her mom had called before Kylie had left Dallas. She still had the voice-mail message on her phone and needed to return the call soon. Suddenly Mom wanted to be friends, as if so many painful years hadn't passed between them. She told Kylie living like this wasn't healthy, pointing out she had never dealt with the sorrow of losing her sister. Kylie could handle her mom believing that about her. It was better than her mom thinking Kylie worked her ass off to prevent loving anyone. Never again would she know the pain and deal with the sorrow and healing process of losing someone she loved.

The noise in the bowling alley was comparable to a dull roar. Kylie managed to ignore it as she sat at a table, nursing a Coke and focusing on her laptop. She glanced up when a group of kids, four boys and three girls, entered the building and headed toward the arcade connected to the bowling alley. They were the same group of kids she'd followed around the mall yesterday.

One of the girls looked Kylie's way and smirked. Maybe it was a smile. The girl's long brown straight hair covered part of her face, which looked intentional. She wore a tube top, hip-hugging jeans that showed off her concave tummy, and an oversized plaid shirt that was unbuttoned and flowed behind her like a cape.

The girl next to her grabbed the long-haired girl's arm, and she looked away from Kylie focusing across the lanes as her friend whispered in her ear. Kylie watched the two girls follow their friends through the opened doors into the arcade.

Another group entered from the doors behind Kylie. A bunch of guys, feeling a good buzz, it appeared from their loud and obnoxious behavior, traipsed past her toward the counter.

"This isn't the library, shorty," one of them sneered at her.

"I got something you can study," his buddy offered, stopping in front of her and letting his gaze travel down her and then back to her face with an open invitation.

Kylie smelled alcohol on them and knew from experience

that any comment would be enough to egg them on. She glanced toward the arcade room, no longer seeing the teenagers.

"Don't tell me you like little boys," the first one sneered, following her focus toward the other room.

"I don't," she said, standing. "Which is why I'm not talking to you."

She couldn't help herself. Although barely five feet, five inches, and 135 pounds of lean muscle and little body fat, Kylie lived with being thought younger than she looked. Her physical appearance aided in her line of work, though. She was the perfect bait for any online predator. Unfortunately, there were too many lowlifes who weren't criminals but would pick up any woman, including her. Kylie didn't mind using her physical appearance to help lure scum of the earth out from under their rocks. Occasionally she yearned for a real man, someone who was intelligent, gorgeous, and could carry on a conversation while looking at her face instead of her breasts. In her line of work though, those weren't the type of men she spent time with.

Closing her laptop and getting up from the table, Kylie ignored the laughter of the men and the rude comment the guy she'd just insulted threw at her. It was getting into late Friday afternoon, and she only had an hour or so of the teenagers being here before they would head out for the next hangout spot.

She shoved her laptop into her leather case and zipped it up while working her way around the growing group of people lingering behind the lanes. The noise level dropped drastically when she entered the arcade. So did the lighting. The group of teenagers sat on a long cafeteria-length table in the corner of the room. Legs draped over bodies and they all managed to touch one another somehow as they twisted and crawled over each other, laughing and sharing cans of Coke.

Kylie walked up to a game that looked similar to the one Paul was playing on his computer the other day. Dropping her laptop case in front of her, she dug into her pocket for coins. It was important to become part of the environment in order to learn more about the prey of the predator she stalked. No matter how many times she tried playing these games, she sucked at them. But she stood close enough to hear the kids talking and hoped if they mentioned chatting online she'd learn if any of them were talking to a Peter, or anyone whom they possibly hadn't met in person yet. Fortunately, she was an expert at understanding teenage lingo, which was a language in and of itself.

"Are you a spy?" The girl with the long brown hair leaned against the side of the arcade game, sizing Kylie up.

Kylie stared into her gray-green eyes. Black eyeliner accentuated her clear, attentive eyes, and dark lipstick gave her full lips a pouty look. The teenager would be pretty without all the paint on her face.

"No. Are you?" Kylie answered without hesitating.

The teenager snorted. "You were at the mall yesterday. Then in the parking lot when the cops showed up at Olivia's car. And here you are now. Mighty coincidental, don't you think?" There was a challenge in her tone.

Kylie wouldn't insult the girl's intelligence. In fact, Kylie commended her for being alert to her surroundings. "I'm not a spy. My name is Kylie." She held her hand out to shake the teenager's hand.

The girl quit leaning against the game and shifted her gaze to Kylie's hand but didn't take it. "How come you're suddenly everywhere?" the girl demanded. Her posse remained on the table in the corner but no longer crawled all over one another. Instead they were still, watching curiously as their spokesperson gathered the info she would no doubtedly return to inquiring minds.

Kylie had endured interrogation from a lot worse than this assertive teenager. "I'm working on my thesis at the University of Kansas," she offered, ready with her cover she'd prepared for when she became interactive with this community.

"Then why are you here? That university is in Lawrence."

Kylie shrugged. "There's more action here," she said.

"I'm studying the interaction and subculture known to the world as that of the American teenager."

The girl stared at Kylie a moment longer before her eyes widened. Understanding apparently kicked in and her surprise made the gray flecks in her green eyes grow. It was a very pretty eye color.

"That is fucking cool as hell," she said quietly. "So you're like trailing us around and watching how we act and shit?"

"Something like that."

"Dude, that is so cool." The girl turned around and left Kylie, her long brown hair flowing down her narrow back as she hurried back to her group of friends.

Kylie flipped coins in her hand and searched the arcade game for the slot where the money went. The teenagers were talking in the corner, watching her, and once again crawling over one another. Kylie strained to listen while dropping quarters into the machine, and then proceeded to lose miserably in several games of war against battleships in some remote galaxy. Fortunately, the volume on the game was so low she couldn't hear anything it said. If she cared about winning, that would probably annoy her. She pushed the buttons, barely paying attention to what happened on the screen, and focused on the teenagers' continuous chatter. The kids never discussed the Internet or meeting anyone they'd never met before. Instead they talked about her and what they would do when they went to college, or if they were going to college.

Kylie listened, learning more about the group of kids. They were normal, healthy children, all of whom appeared to come from decent homes from what she could tell by their conversations. They were living the life she never had the chance to live. And if she did her job right, all of them would continue growing up normally and healthy and not be robbed of their youth like her sister and Kylie were. She knew better than anyone how an online sexual predator destroyed more than just his prey. But she was here, protecting them. None of them would be deprived of life. She would see to it.

Once it was dark, the movie theater, which was about a mile from Kylie's rental house, turned into a teenage jungle. She really had submerged into a world that didn't exist anywhere else. And to these young people there was no world other than their own. It was the same from city to city, a subculture of teenagers, preoccupied with their sexual hormones and unaware of the evil that lurked, watching them prance around, wearing next to nothing. Not that children of her own were in her future, but Kylie would never allow her daughter to leave the house dressed the way some of these girls were dressed.

Kylie stood in a bathroom stall, listening while three girls discussed whether they should stay at the movie theater or head over to the McDonald's parking lot, apparently another popular location for the in-crowd. There wasn't any mention of seeing a movie.

Heading across the parking lot to where she'd parked her car, Kylie strolled slowly, aware of the long-haired girl who'd approached her earlier. The teenager sat on the curb, under a streetlight, possibly waiting on a ride. She spoke quickly and quietly on a cell phone. Kylie paused, hovering between two parked cars, out of sight but not out of earshot.

"I told you, dude, that's just stupid." There was a bossy, commanding edge to the girl's voice. Maybe she was the leader of her group of friends, the one who called the shots, told everyone else how to dress and act. Kylie had always envied and been a bit mystified by girls like that when she'd been in school. Karen had been a leader, but Kylie hadn't even been a follower. She'd never figured out how to be part of any of the in-groups. "Everyone knows you don't go meet some dude off-line you've never met before. And no, I don't sound like my uncle. I'm just smart. Now if you take me with you, I might be cool with it."

The girl laughed and jumped up from her perch on the curb, hurrying across the parking lot.

"Shit," Kylie groaned, turning for her own car. All evening she'd listened to nonsense hoping to hear something to help her move this case forward. Finally a bite, and the girl took off sprinting across the lot. "So head home and surf around online. We've got the beginning of a lead on the prey; now we look for the predator." Kylie rolled her eyes, wondering when she had started talking about herself like she was fucking royalty or something.

"That's her, Uncle Perry," a familiar voice said behind Kylie.

"Who?"

"That college girl I told you about. The one studying teenagers."

Kylie slowed, realizing the teenage girl she had just watched run across the parking lot now walked directly behind her. If she didn't turn around, she would appear rude. And gaining the trust of some of the teenage girls in town was imperative if she was to solve this case.

"Studying teenagers, huh," the uncle said, sounding gruff.

Kylie glanced around her as she turned, taking in her surroundings. It was a large, dark parking lot with bright streetlights creating enough light to make it easy to see from one end of the lot to the other. There were kids everywhere, some huddled in small groups while others threw a football over parked cars. It was like walking across a large playground instead of a public parking lot. It amazed her that teenagers did the same thing, no matter which city she was in, when they didn't have a clue what was going on in the world around them and focused only on their friends.

Turning a half circle, she met the amused look of the long-brown-haired girl, her eyeliner applied even thicker than it was that afternoon. There were two other girls with her, one of them tall and lanky, with curly auburn hair, and the other about the same height as the brunette, with hair almost identical. They could be sisters.

"Learn lots of good stuff to write in your paper?" the teenage girl asked.

"Getting some ideas." Kylie smiled at her and the other girls but then shifted her attention to the man with them.

It was the man who'd shown up at the parking lot yesterday and tried coming over to her. She didn't get a good look at him at the time, but now, in the darkness with streetlights accentuating shadows, the tall, dark-haired man staring at her, his expression unreadable, was damn near the best-looking guy she'd ever laid eyes on in her life.

"My uncle is a cop," the teenage girl said smugly, grinning broadly.

Kylie matched the girl's smile, unwilling to lose what little trust she'd managed so far. Since she already knew he was part of the local law enforcement, she at least maintained her cool with that piece of knowledge.

"How neat." Sounding calm when absolutely sinful eyes gazed down at her proved a hell of a lot harder to do than it should have. Her heart pattered too fast in her chest, and her palms grew damp, making her itch to rub them against the sides of her short dress.

Kylie fought not to show any signs of being affected under his incredibly scrutinizing stare. Heat flamed to life inside her, but she held her ground, not doing as much as even shifting her weight from one foot to the next. "I never did get your name," she said, turning her attention to the girl and meeting those alert gray-green eyes head-on.

"Dani," she said.

"Let's go, girls," their uncle growled, and quickly herded them away from Kylie; then glancing over his shoulder, he pinned her with dark, intense eyes that sent chills over her enflamed body. "I didn't know college students drove around in rentals."

"You do now," she offered, and turned away from him toward her car before she lost her composure. He'd run her tag after seeing her in the mall parking lot. Interesting.

Chapter 3

"Unit Seven, what's your ten twenty?"

Perry grabbed the two-way radio from the clip where it hung on his dash.

"I'm headed back in," he said on the radio. "I just passed the Eighteenth Street Expressway."

"We've got a head-on collision at Forty-seventh Street and Fontana. Possible drunk driver. He ran from the scene of the crime."

"I'll be ten ninety-seven in minutes. What direction is our suspect headed?" Perry switched lanes and accelerated toward the accident scene.

"Northeast and on foot."

"I'm heading into that neighborhood now." Perry put the radio on its hook on the dash and turned right at the next intersection. The small tract homes lining either side of the street were predominantly rentals, some duplexes and others single dwellings. It was a neighborhood mixed with college students and families with small children, affordable housing for those starting out in life.

The radio chirped on his dash: "Suspect is reported heading northeast on Elledge Road."

Perry pulled his Jeep to a stop on the neighborhood street and stuck his Bluetooth in his ear. He forwarded his private cell to the earpiece and jumped out of his car, heading down the block on foot. His phone rang and he pressed the small button to acknowledge the call.

"Flynn, where are you?" It was Barker, and she sounded out of breath.

"On Elledge. Do you have a visual?"

"He ran in between a couple houses. I'm calling in for more backup. He's a white male, late teens, blue jeans, and red baggy T-shirt. Dark hair, shoulder length."

"Ten four." Perry walked quickly up the street, looking in between each house. "East or west side of the street?"

"West."

"Roger that. Where are you?"

"I see you. I'm on the corner. He disappeared about four houses up from me. He runs a lot faster than I do."

Perry snorted. Barker was in pretty good shape. He continued glancing in between houses as he worked his way up the block and spotted a cruiser heading slowly down the next street. Pausing at a double driveway, he thought he saw something move behind overgrown hedges that ran the length of the property line. At the same time, the sound of children laughing grabbed his attention.

"Shit, Barker," he hissed under his breath. "Kids in the yard. And I think I see our guy."

"Crap. Not in the same yard?"

"How intoxicated is our man?" Perry asked, glancing at both homes on either side of the double driveway.

"I arrived at the scene and walked up to his car when he bolted. The man in the other car that was struck said the kid never got out of his car. He stayed in his car, too, and dialed nine-one-one." She wasn't at the end of the block anymore, but her voice was clear in his ear. "Do you see him?"

"Stand by," Perry whispered, reaching the end of the hedges and moving behind them. A chain-link fence lined the property line, and the unruly hedge grew along it. There wasn't much space to crawl behind the bushes, and the hedge grew on both sides of the fence. It offered a natural blockade to prevent neighbors who lived on top of each other from seeing into each other's private lives. Perry dropped to his knees and squinted past branches and leaves. "I see him," he whispered. "He's toward the backyard and we've got children at play." Perry stood and glanced at the front of the house. "The address is Sixty Ten. Get down here and have those kids pulled inside. I'm going after him."

"Ten four."

Perry palmed his gun at his waist. He didn't want to use it. Not with children laughing and playing. Their young voices sounded happy and innocent. He moved silently, coming closer toward where the suspect squatted behind the hedges, and where the children played. Before Perry reached the back of the house, he heard a car pull up on the street. He glanced over his shoulder, noting the squad car before returning his attention to the hedges. He bent over, caught sight of the man's shoes and legs at the same time that a woman appeared from the back side of the house.

"Oh God," she screamed, surprised to see Perry and clasping her hands over her mouth.

"Get your kids inside," Perry ordered, pointing to his badge on his belt.

The woman dropped her attention to his waist and her eyes widened as she froze and turned pale.

"Do it now," he ordered.

At the same time the man leapt out from behind the bushes, racing toward the children, who immediately started screaming. The woman screamed, too. Backup raced up the driveway behind him. Perry leapt at the man.

He grabbed the man at the waist, but his wiry frame twisted in Perry's grip.

"Get your kids inside!" Perry yelled at the woman. He didn't focus on the cops who appeared in the yard and hurried toward the children, or on the woman as she started screaming and crying at the same time, adding to the noise the children were making. The young man slid out of Perry's grip and shifted his direction, no longer running toward the kids but instead racing toward the back of the yard. "Police!" Perry yelled. "Stop now!"

Perry watched the punk leap at the privacy fence bordering the backyard and then manage to pull himself up and fall over the top to the other side.

"Son of a bitch," Perry hissed under his breath, following suit and hoisting himself over the fence. Goddamn. He wasn't as young as he used to be.

The man fell in a crablike position but managed to pull himself to his feet, tripping twice as he bolted toward the house facing the next street.

"You're making it worse for yourself," Perry yelled at the man. "Stop, now, or you'll face more charges." He wasn't surprised that the man ignored him.

Perry dropped to the ground on the other side of the fence. He wracked all the muscles in his body as his hands and knees scraped over the uneven, hard-packed ground. The coolness against his palms did little to stop the stinging that zapped up his arms and from his legs to his hips. He would lecture himself later about staying in shape. Right now, he'd be damned if this punk would get away. Nothing pissed Perry off more than terrifying small children when moments before they'd been laughing and yelling at one another without a care in the world.

The man raced toward the driveway between houses while dogs barked furiously inside each house. A car turned and pulled into the driveway. Perry watched the driver's expression contort with terror. He accelerated instead of hitting the brake and the man couldn't turn around quickly enough. Perry grabbed his phone as he watched the guy leap backward and fall on his back when the car hit him. The guy driving found his brake and slammed it hard enough to lock his tires. The driver stared in shock out his windshield while white-knuckling his steering wheel. Immediately a squad car pulled up behind the idling car in the driveway.

"Take it easy," Perry said quietly, placing his hand on the guy's shoulder when he tried rolling over.

"Fuck you!" the man grumbled, and then moaned when he again tried rolling over.

"Suspect is down," Perry informed Dispatch, and then stood, walking toward the front of the house to find an address. "We're going to need an ambulance."

Barker walked around the side of the house and grinned

smugly as she moved to his side. "You're pretty impressive for a man close to forty," she said under her breath, and glanced up at him with an invitation in her eyes.

It was an invite he'd never accept. "You need help getting statements from everyone?" He didn't bother telling her he was thirty-three, not close to forty. There wasn't any reason to dwell on personal information with her, or anyone on the force.

She squeezed his biceps and gave him a quick once-over. There was definitely approval on her face. "What? And let you do all the work?" She met his gaze and lowered her voice. "I have no problem jumping in and getting dirty to get the job done, darling."

Perry nodded. Anything he said would simply encourage her. There were as many cops on the scene now as there were civilians. This time Perry walked around the block back toward his Jeep, nodding to the ambulance driver when he came around the corner. Perry paused at the middle of the block, spotting the mother of the small children, who now stood talking to her neighbor at the end of the hedge dividing their yards. She sounded shaken but okay. Perry picked up pace toward his Jeep.

He paused when he reached for his door handle, frowning and staring over the roof. A green hybrid was parked across the street in a narrow driveway. Perry instantly recognized the tags—those registered to Enterprise. Dani had told him Kylie was a college student at KU, working on a thesis about teenagers as a subculture. He imagined that would make for an interesting paper; his nieces definitely lived in a world of their own.

Perry opened his car door and leaned against it, taking his time studying the hybrid, the narrow driveway, and the small home. Although it wasn't quite evening, the blinds in the house were all closed. The yard was neat, though, with patches of dirt breaking up thick clumps of grass, typical of the many yards on this street. The house was probably a rental. Most on this street were government housing or rented to private individuals. It was an affordable alternative to living in an apartment and not unusual for college students to be found living here, although not many who attended KU, which was half an hour drive from here.

There was something about her, though. He'd spotted it the moment he laid eyes on her the previous afternoon in the mall parking lot. Dani was a pretty perceptive kid, and she'd noticed something about her, too. Enough so to approach a stranger, which he should have lectured Dani about doing, and ask what she was about. Obviously Dani didn't confront her—Kylie—because she was distractingly pretty. Although his niece did comment that Kylie was a sharp dresser, he didn't conclude from that statement that Dani approved of her appearance.

Perry wouldn't describe her as a sharp dresser, more like alluring, tempting, as if she slipped into that minidress she'd worn the night before knowing it would turn the head of every man who passed her. Her blond hair wasn't long, but long enough to give a man something to grab hold of, to yank her head back and enjoy the slender arch of her neck and back.

There was a compelling spark in her bright blue eyes, noticeable even at night. But the way her dress hugged her figure, showing off perky, decent-sized breasts and narrow hips, made it damn hard for him not to physically respond when he first laid eyes on her. It was more than the challenge in her eyes, the cool way she had responded to him when he let her know he'd pulled her tags after seeing her at the mall the other day, which made him ache to know more about her. In spite of how young she looked, there was intelligence in her eyes, wisdom and something else. Something that told Perry there was more to the young lady than just a college student going all out to write an incredible thesis.

Perry focused on each of the front windows, seeing no movement inside. Maybe a bit more investigation was in order here. It was right there, kicking in, causing his insides to harden while predatory and protective instincts burned inside him. And maybe something else. He appreciated that curiosity warred with other emotions, with the desire to learn what a beautiful woman was about. Years on the force had taught him that danger appeared in all shapes and sizes. Although he doubted anything about Kylie the college student was dangerous, he still fought the compelling urge to get to know her better.

His radio beeped inside his car. "Unit Seven, what's your ten twenty?"

Perry slid behind the wheel and slowly closed his car door. Grabbing his radio, he cupped it in his palm while continuing to watch Kylie's home. "I'm here; go ahead."

"Request ten eighty-five."

Perry frowned as he reached for the radio on his dash and switched to a different channel. Cliff Miller, the dispatcher, didn't often ask Perry to move to a secure channel, unless there was trouble.

"Roger that," he said, and released the button, waiting for Cliff to enlighten him as to what was so serious that they needed to move to a different frequency.

"The owners of that car at the mall yesterday just came in and visited with Rad. Appears their daughter is officially missing."

"Shit," Perry hissed, dragging his fingers through his hair. "Get me everything you can on her. I'll hit the streets."

"Ten four." The silence ran for several minutes while Perry stared at Kylie's home. Something told him he would see the hot, sexy college student again.

But for now, school was out. His nieces would be home. Maybe he'd start with them. He hated dragging them into this, but the reality was that teenage girls were disappearing. Whether his sister approved of him scaring her daughters or not, awareness would protect them.

Cliff came back with Olivia Brown's home address, the name of her high school, and a list of several girls who were considered her closest friends. "Rad just told me to send you over to the Browns'. They should be receptive to you going through her computer."

"Ten four. I'm on my way."

* * *

It was after seven when Perry's sister, Megan, called and asked if he'd pick Dani up at the library. Those first few years after David's death were hard as hell on the entire family. Megan was young, and left alone with four girls to support and raise on her own. Perry jumped in right away, to the point where he helped support all five of them while Megan struggled to find work that paid enough to keep a roof over their heads. Perry was pretty fucking proud of his kid sister. Many women would have crumbled under the life she'd been dished out, but Megan remained strong and brought up four beautiful young ladies. Diane had started junior college last fall, and now if they could get Dani through high school and not have her turn into a wild child like she seemed determined at times to become, Perry was sure they'd be able to get the other two through high school as well.

"There a reason why you're not answering your mother's calls?" Perry said in a low, deadly whisper when he approached Dani from behind.

She sat in an oversized chair in the middle of the library and jumped noticeably, spinning around, when he spoke. Her eyes were wide with fear but narrowed quickly when she stared at her uncle.

"You scared the crap out of me, Uncle Perry."

"Watch your mouth." He continued staring down at her, letting her know with his hardened look that he expected an answer to his first question. Whenever he was certain Dani would do both him and Megan in with her willful nature, Megan would assure him that Dani was simply incredibly intelligent and would make them both proud someday.

"I got us a computer," Kylie said, speaking in a soft whisper, as she appeared out of the first aisle of books. She froze, lifting her attention from Dani, who still sat in the chair, to Perry, who stood behind her. For a moment something dark passed over Kylie's gaze. It disappeared in the next moment and her features softened. "Oh, shoot. Do you have to leave?"

"Apparently visiting hours are over." Dani stood slowly

and kept her back to Perry as she said something that he didn't hear to Kylie.

Kylie's sleeveless dress ended at mid-thigh and showed off slender tanned legs that weren't muscular but appeared toned enough that she could wrap them around a man and squeeze the life out of him while he drove deeper inside her. Her pink fingernail polish matched the color on her toes, which were visible through black open-toed sandals. And her blonde hair, which didn't quite reach her shoulders, looked soft, like silk, and made his fingers itch to find out if it was.

Kylie lifted her gaze to his and he swore he saw awareness in her bright blue eyes, as if she knew that he wanted her and hadn't decided yet whether that knowledge appealed to her or not.

More than likely, dressing like that, Kylie was propositioned on a regular basis. That didn't sit well with him for some reason. There were people with strange kinks out there. It was enough worrying about protecting his nieces all the time. He didn't need an incredibly sexy college student distracting him and creating carnal needs that were torn between fucking the shit out of her and protecting her as well as his niece.

"Dani, we're leaving now," he said, sounding gruff enough that his niece turned around and studied him. "Let's go."

"Just a minute," she said, sounding exasperated. She turned and looked at Kylie as if apologizing with her eyes. It was a quick glance, one he'd miss if he weren't focusing on the body language between both of them and noting the intense similarities. "Uncle Perry, I'll be out in like ten minutes, okay?"

"No," he said firmly.

Kylie interrupted him. "It's okay, Dani," she said, her soft voice soothing, incredibly sultry sounding. "We can do this another time. Your uncle is in a hurry."

"No, he's not," Dani grumbled. "He's just bossy."

"Dani," he warned her. His sister might tolerate public mouthiness, but he sure as hell wouldn't.

"You don't even want to know what we were going to

do?" Dani's tone turned sweet when she faced him and stared up at him with eyes that remotely resembled the beautiful, intelligent eyes he remembered before she insisted on covering them up with all that black eyeliner. "You've got to be just a little bit curious, Uncle Perry."

"Dani, it's okay." Kylie shook her head at him and laughed softly. "There's nothing to be curious about."

Perry easily noticed his niece was working him. That didn't spark any curiosity. What did intrigue him was how suddenly Kylie didn't want him to know. In fact, to the point where she made eye contact with him for the first time and held it, while he focused on her bright blue eyes. They were intense, almost the color of sapphires, and they didn't change color the longer he held her gaze, no darkening or lightening or anything that often happened when moods changed in people. It hit him that she might be wearing contacts—the kind that changed a person's eye color.

"Uncle Perry is one of the best cops in the Kansas City area," Dani bragged, shifting her attention to Kylie. "He's always curious about everything."

"Is that so?" Kylie's voice returned to its soft, alluring, come-fuck-me tone.

He'd give her this: she was one unique woman. As much hesitation and trepidation as he swore he read in her body language, there was something else there, too. In the way she watched him, the tilt of her head, the way her hands moved from clasped in front of her to her palms brushing over her thighs. Perry made his living reading people, and this woman either didn't know her own mind or was intentionally covering up sexual interest with other emotions to throw him off guard.

Dani shifted her attention from him to Kylie and then back to him. "Kylie's never seen how people chat on You-Tube, you know, in the comments section?"

"Dani, your uncle doesn't care about this," Kylie whispered.

He cared now. "Better show her before someone else takes your computer," he said.

Dani looked surprised and Kylie wary. All the more reason to witness this little scenario play out. "You can show me, too."

"You already know," Dani grumbled, and turned, grabbing her backpack off the table and then leading the way through the stacks toward stairs that took them to a row of computers set up for public use.

Kylie glanced at him and he gestured for her to follow his niece. He brought up the rear, and didn't mind the view of her miniskirt swishing back and forth and her ass swaying in front of him. He didn't doubt for a moment that she gave him a show intentionally. And he found it interesting that as he watched, he imagined what Kylie would look like in tight-fitting jeans, high heels, and found that image much more arousing.

Dani hopped down the stairs and Kylie followed, her sandals slapping against each stair as she ran her painted fingernails over the banister like she was stroking it on her way down.

"Why do you care about comments on YouTube?" he asked her before they reached the bottom of the stairs.

"For my thesis." Kylie didn't look at him until she reached the bottom of the stairs. "It helps hearing Dani explain in her words."

"How so?" He walked alongside Kylie now but focused on his niece, who was several paces ahead. "She really knows something about YouTube that you don't?"

"I'm about to find out," Kylie said, glancing up at him with a sly smile before moving around Dani, who'd already plopped into a chair at a computer. Kylie pulled the chair from the table behind them over and sat next to Dar.i. "I really appreciate you doing this, Dani," she said quietly.

"It's no big deal," Dani said, shrugging off the gratitude. "I just wish Uncle Perry weren't making it feel as if it was."

He stood behind them, fixing his attention on the computer screen, and crossed his arms. His niece and the college lady sat close, heads almost touching, and whispered to each other. He managed to catch almost everything they said.

"You've been to YouTube before, right?" Dani asked Kylie, turning her head so the two of them stared at each other briefly.

"Of course," Kylie said in that soft, sultry tone of hers.

"What videos do you watch?"

Kylie's grin was almost apologetic. "I check to see if episodes I like are on there. Sometimes there are news reports or different angles on current events."

Dani rolled her eyes. "Boring," she drawled, and then shook her head while making a tsking sound with her tongue. "You have so much to learn about being a teenager," she began.

There was something akin to a satisfied smile on Kylie's face, her expression pulling more curiosity out of Perry as he studied her while she focused on Dani.

"What would I watch?" Kylie asked.

"Music videos, dude." Dani opened the main page to You-Tube and then clicked so the cursor blinked in the search bar. "And the videos linked to our Facebook profiles or Twitter."

Perry growled and Dani quickly waved her hand dismissively in the air. "I don't have a profile of me on either site. But I can show you one we all made up and use it to link to You-Tube videos. Personal videos are the bomb, though."

"Personal videos?" Kylie asked.

"Yeah. Some of them are so obviously bogus."

"Okay," Kylie said slowly. "What are personal videos?"

Dani looked over her shoulder at Perry and then leaned back to survey Kylie. "Dude, you know what personal videos are. Everyone knows what personal videos are."

"Show me," Kylie suggested, nodding to the screen.

"Okay." Dani placed her fingers over the keyboards and then her fingers moved expertly, proof again that teenagers these days seemed to be born with secretarial skills intact. A new page opened and then the video began. "I don't know these people, so don't throw a fit, Uncle Perry," Dani said, and pointed at the screen. "Some guys I know know the people who made this."

"These are the kids' names in the video?" Kylie pointed

to a description of the video on the side of the box where a group of boys and girls danced in a parking lot to a rap song.

"Beats me." Dani shrugged. "But this is what I was talking about."

She scrolled down the page while the video continued playing. The sound was low enough that Perry couldn't quite catch what was being said. He had a feeling he didn't want to hear it, though. He moved closer, resting his hands on the back of Dani's chair, and leaned over her to read what she pointed to. "See, people talk on YouTube."

Underneath the video, there were posts, individuals making comments about the video and commenting on what other people said in response to the video. It was similar to reading a printed conversation, although the posts were typed in slang with intentionally incorrect grammar and spelling. Several of the comments came from people who appeared to know those who made the video. There were several others, though, that seemed to come from strangers, with comments typed that suggested how they would love to do sexual acts with some of the girls in the video. Perry fought a growl as he read through some of the lewd and incredibly inappropriate comments made toward high school girls who were most definitely underage, judging just by the looks of them.

"Learn something new every day," Kylie said, and then moved her chair to the side, away from both of them. "Thank you, Dani."

"No prob." Dani X'd out of YouTube and turned sideways in her chair, sliding her backpack over her arm. "I guess I'll see you around."

Dani slid out of her chair and walked into Perry. He backed up as she grabbed his arm and started guiding him to the stairs.

"Bye, Kylie," she said over her shoulder.

"Suddenly in a hurry to leave?" he grumbled under his breath, noticing how obvious his niece was being in dragging his ass out of there.

"You're in the hurry." Dani didn't let go of him when they reached the stairs.

But Perry stopped her and then turned to see Kylie slowly raising the strap to her purse up her shoulder. She looked up, meeting his gaze, and for a moment he saw how lost in thought she was. Her expression relaxed almost immediately. The easy smile she gave him would make most men think she didn't have a care in the world. He knew better.

He understood how time-consuming and difficult it would be to balance keeping grades up along with working enough hours to survive and pay bills. Even though he only spent two years and got his associate's degree before entering the police academy, he remembered the all-nighters studying for exams. He'd also helped his sister finish her college degree and respected the hell out of her for sticking it out. There was more than drive and confidence in those bright eyes that took him on without blinking. Perry saw interest. Whether it be simply that he was the apparent guardian of a teenager Kylie was interested in or something else, something erotic and enticing, he didn't want to speculate.

He waited until Kylie approached them. "Did you learn everything from my niece that you needed to know?" he asked, keeping his voice quiet and pleasant sounding.

Dani glared at him and then stomped up the stairs.

"Your niece is a wonderful young lady." Kylie held his gaze for only a moment and then followed Dani up the stairs. "I'm sure there is so much I could learn from her."

"Oh, really." He opted to follow a few paces behind.

The view was mouthwatering. That short dress Kylie wore showed off slender legs all the way up to her thighs. If her dress were less than an inch shorter, he'd have one hell of an ass shot. As it was, he found himself wondering what kind of underwear she wore underneath it.

"What else is there you hope to learn from her?" he asked, once he and Kylie hit the main floor.

"As much as she'll share with me."

"About what?" He glanced ahead as Dani pushed open the glass doors and disappeared outside.

"About being a teenager." Kylie didn't elaborate.

Perry held the door open for her and searched the dark

parking lot until he spotted Dani heading for his Jeep. He pulled out his keys and pushed the button, causing his Jeep to beep and unlock. Dani didn't flinch at the sound but reached his Jeep, pulled open the passenger door, and plopped down inside.

"How many other teenagers are you interrogating?"

Kylie paused at the curb and turned to look up at him. "Is there some law you're concerned that I might be breaking?"

"I have a feeling you would know if there was."

"You think so?"

"If you're doing your job right, yes." He searched her face and was impressed that nothing changed in her expression.

Kylie laughed softly and then ran her fingers over her blond hair, brushing a strand behind her ear. "There are days when writing a thesis feels like a job. I'll leave Dani alone if it bothers you that I'm talking to her," she offered. Her lips curved into a small smile, one that he swore appeared victorious. "But you'll have to explain to her why I'm not seeking her out anymore."

"And what if I told her the sensuality seeping from you might be more than I want her exposed to at her age."

Kylie's smile didn't fade. "I have no doubts she'd give you an earful regarding her opinion on that matter."

Chapter 4

Kylie suggested she would leave Dani alone but never actually agreed to do it. Perry didn't take her up on the offer. Therefore, she wasn't harassing the teenager. Dani agreed to meet her after school. Kylie was anxious to talk with her. Especially after spending the day surfing from profile to profile, matching kids she'd met so far with comments she found online. She glanced down at her handwritten notes and then back at the main door to the library. Dani would be arriving any minute.

"Crap," she hissed when the library doors opened and Perry sauntered inside.

He was damn near the sexiest cop she'd ever laid eyes on. There was a badass look about him, and a dangerous glint in his eyes when he studied her. Every inch of her screamed caution whenever he graced her with that intense stare of his, and it wasn't because he might blow her cover. It was more because she could so easily fantasize blowing him.

Which was insane. Perry was a cop. Whoever their online predator was, more than likely he was a police officer, or at least worked at the Judicial Center in order to have access to the computers there. With as little evidence as she had right now, Perry could be her perp.

He paused at the entrance, scanning his surroundings. The look on his face was confident, as if he knew all he saw was his domain, his world to command. His dark eyes moved over her, and every inch of her heated to dangerous levels. No way could she allow herself to react to him like this. Young lives were at stake. Until she confirmed his innocence, he was a suspect. She had to look at him as such.

Kylie closed her notebook and slid it under the books she'd pulled from the stacks. She stared at the cover of the romance novel she'd thought about checking out, but the cover barely registered on her. She didn't need to look up to know he approached. So much sex appeal, such raw, unleashed male ego and confidence, made the air sizzle as he walked to her table.

"Working on your thesis?" His deep voice caressed her body and forced her heart to pound faster in her chest.

"Taking a break." It would be hard to convince anyone she was studying with the books that were spread out in front of her.

"What do you do in your downtime?" Perry pulled the chair out next to her and sat, his long legs stretching out under the table.

She pulled her feet under her seat, knowing if he touched her in any way it would be even harder to stay focused. Perry had danger written all over him.

"I don't have a lot of spare time." She studied his face, the well-defined cheekbones and long, straight nose. His skin was blemish free, although she noticed a small scar that was on the side of his jawbone. He'd recently shaven and she guessed a day or so without a razor and a dark shadow would cover that small scar. His black, thick lashes matched the color of his hair, and he looked at her face, piercing her with green eyes that had flecks of brown in them. "Is this what you do in your downtime?" she countered.

Those green eyes darkened while she watched. Anger, fascination, maybe confrontation. She wasn't sure what emotion she triggered with her question.

"I'm not on downtime," he drawled. His facial expression didn't change but remained hard, unreadable. It was those eyes, though, intense, deep, challenging.

She could drown in that heated gaze if she wasn't careful. "Is that so?" She matched his lazy voice inflection and leaned back in her chair, crossing one leg over the other under the table, and focused on her pen, stroking the side of it with her thumb. "Am I part of some dangerous investigation?"

When she looked up at him, intentionally trying to sound amused, she caught him looking at her pen. He took his time returning his attention to her face, as if everywhere he directed his attention was intentional. Most cops used their uniforms and their badges to boost up the dominating persona they liked to present to the world. This man didn't need a uniform. She assumed he was packing something somewhere, but there weren't any obvious signs that he carried a gun. Overall, Lt. Perry Flynn used his body as his deadliest weapon, and she imagined it had gotten him far in investigations in the past.

"You tell me." He rested his arms on the table and leaned forward, allowing her to see the brown in his eyes grow until there was hardly any green left. His eyes could go from an attractive green to a dangerous dark shade that sent shivers down her spine. The longer he stared, the darker they grew. "Convince me the only reason you're spending so much time with my niece is school-related and not for possibly a more personal reason. You can write this thesis of yours on the opinions of one child?"

"Hardly," she grumbled, sighing intentionally. She would have to play him carefully. She saw that. His assets and qualities were very nicely fine-tuned. That didn't make him innocent. Kylie had been surprised more than once when discovering who her perp was after extensive investigation. Maybe that made her leery, but better safe than sorry. "Dani appears to be the leader of her friends, so it's been easy to talk to her. But I hope to spend time with other children from all ranks of their social ladder, so to speak."

"What are you going to write about them?"

"The truth," she answered easily. "Teenagers are really incredibly fascinating. They're a species among themselves, moving around in our world, on our streets, in our stores, yet so engrossed in themselves they don't see anything the way we do. Nor do they care to. When they transform from teen-agers to adults, as we all do eventually, the behavior and attitudes of youth disappear and are forgotten. We begin our lives." She paused, catching him watching her, fascinated. "This carefree, innocent part of our lives isn't always that innocent."

"Which is why I'm here to protect them," he growled, his eyes turning almost black.

Kylie shivered: She got a rise out of him, which was what she wanted. Now to interpret his reaction. Whatever he felt right now, it was hitting him strong. She imagined a bit of anger mixed with curiosity, and possibly a bit of aroused interest. Were the emotions surging to life inside him strong enough for him to rape and then murder a teenage girl?

"You're here to protect all of us," Kylie whispered, and let her gaze drop to his mouth. His lips weren't too full, or too thin. A man like him, rugged, carrying a badge, and so damn dominating and protective, would have a docile woman tucked away somewhere.

Kylie returned her attention to her pen, forcing herself to quit focusing on his sex appeal and to just make mental notes of what characteristics seemed engraved in him. A sexual predator quite often preferred only one type of woman or, in this case, girl. If Kylie played the part of an experienced seductress and Perry was her man, it would turn him off. He might like a cocky, and pretty, flirty female, but teenage girls very seldom had worlds of experience tucked under their belts.

"I'm fascinated at how many teenage girls have the freedom to meet me in public places, yet I seldom see the parents. These young ladies are apparently at an age where they're mature enough to go where they want after school and not get in trouble for not heading straight home. Do you agree?" She glanced up in time to watch him straighten and knew she'd hit yet another nerve. But it was an easy strike. That subject was an open nerve in her as well. It amazed her how many teenagers came and went as they pleased and had parents who didn't have a clue where their children were when a horrendous crime was committed. "Many teenagers appear to know everything, as in Dani's case. She puts on a show of understanding all the world has to offer her, and doesn't ask questions. But in truth, is she simply parroting her adult role models, or has she gathered her beliefs through life experiences?"

"Are you seeking my opinion on this topic?"

"You're here," she said, shrugging. "And you pose as a father figure to your niece."

"Dani's talked to you about her father?" He raised one eyebrow, suddenly looking and sounding skeptical.

Kylie shook her head, realizing there was history here she didn't know about and wondering if she needed to know. "It was mentioned that he was dead."

It was as though she could see Perry bristle when he growled the one word. "Mentioned."

"I didn't ask for details," Kylie told him, seeing immediately the truth would send him through the roof. The level of protector's instincts in this man was strong even for a cop.

"My guess is that would be out of character for you." Perry watched her, the smoldering dark shade of his eyes resuming a forest green color.

Kylie's heart skipped a beat, a mixture of excitement, at taking him on in a battle of wills, and sexual energy creating a pressure that swelled in her chest. The main door to the library opened, causing her to shift her attention from his face as four girls entered.

Dani hesitated when she saw Kylie sitting with Perry, and the three girls around her stopped as well and a group huddle formed as they started whispering among each other.

"I'm sure your investigative skills are in tune well enough for you not to jump to conclusions about anyone's nature," Kylie said dryly.

The girl who led the group to Kylie's table looked a lot like Dani, except older. "Are you making the moves on our uncle?" she demanded, and slowly crossed her arms over her chest.

"God, Diane," Dani groaned, rolling her eyes and then

shoving herself in front of Diane. "Kylie, I thought bringing my sisters might help give you more information. You said different-aged teenagers would have different attitudes about stuff."

"What is going on here?" Perry slid his chair back and stood, glaring at the four girls while he pressed his fists into his sides.

"Hi, Uncle Perry," the youngest one said, and scooted around her sisters to give her uncle a hug. "We came here to tell the woman about teenagers."

"Denise, shut up," Dani ordered.

"Dani," Perry growled.

"What's the deal, Uncle Perry?" the oldest, Diane, asked, giving Kylie the once-over before raising one eyebrow and focusing on her uncle. "If I'd known you were coming, you could have hauled everyone here."

Kylie looked over at the information desk where two older women glanced at their small group. There weren't a lot of people in the library, but it was a Saturday and more would probably arrive as the day progressed. "Maybe we can move our discussion to a place where we don't have to be quite so quiet," she suggested.

Everyone looked at her and quit talking.

"You aren't driving my nieces anywhere." Perry put his hand protectively on the youngest.

Kylie stood, smiling. "That's fine. You can drive them," she said, guessing they would talk his ear off about catching him sitting with her. "Where is a good place to go?"

"How about your place?" Perry said, his gaze growing intense as he stared at her.

If he wanted to get inside her house to check her out further, she didn't have a problem with that. Her temporary home was up and running and ready for visitors. "That's fine, but I don't have any munchies or anything."

"You can order pizza," Dani offered, grinning broadly.

Kylie stared at the expectant faces of the teenagers and at Perry, whose dark expression wasn't readable. "Okay," she said slowly. "We can meet over at my house."

She gathered her things and then walked with the girls surrounding her to the door. None of them commented on her not giving Perry directions. She didn't doubt he remembered where she lived after chasing the perp in her neighborhood the other day.

Kylie pulled up in front of her house, with Perry parking right behind her, and led the way to her door. After unlocking it, she pressed the keypad just inside her door on the wall to turn off the alarm system.

"Pretty elaborate alarm," Perry commented, pushing the door open all the way and entering in front of his nieces. He stopped in the middle of her living room and turned slowly, taking in his surroundings. "That come with the rental house?"

"I paid extra for it. But my aunt owns the house, which is a blessing. Otherwise I'd be paying too much rent for a really small apartment." She smiled at the girls, refusing to let Perry interrogate her further about her home. "Sit down. Where's the best place to order pizza?"

All the girls spoke at once and almost immediately were arguing. Perry made himself comfortable on her couch, stretching his legs out in front of him and placing one arm across the back of the couch. He appeared to ignore his nieces while continuing to study her home with an attentive eye. There wasn't anything in her living room to give away her nature, lifestyle, or career. He could memorize every inch of the room and the most she guessed he'd conclude was possibly she was a shitty decorator or, better yet, she was a college student who didn't have time, or the money, to decorate.

"You girls decide where you want to order and what you want to order," Kylie announced, speaking over their loud chatter. "I'll go get some cash."

She headed down the hallway, stopping at the middle bedroom and pulling the door shut. She reached around the door, turning the lock on the doorknob, then closed it. Any incriminating evidence, including her badge and gun, was locked up securely. The house was wired, and everyone's actions in the living room would be recorded. Coming here was a good idea. Any information she could pull out of them would be on tape for review if needed.

Kylie hurried into her bedroom and over to her dresser. She pulled out some cash from her top drawer and then turned to head back to the ruckus still going on in her living room.

"Do you have enough money to feed the girls?" Perry asked quietly, standing in her bedroom doorway.

Kylie stopped, unable to leave the room with him standing there. "I can manage," she said easily, and stepped forward, hoping he'd move.

He didn't. "What questions are you going to ask them?"

She pointed past him. "My notebook is in the living room with all of my notes."

"What university are you attending?"

She looked up into those deep green eyes. He studied her intently, his brooding expression impossible to read. "I'm working on my Ph.D. at KU. I thought you knew that already."

When he reached for her, Kylie stepped back without giving it thought, immediately wary of his actions. He didn't hesitate but cupped the side of her head and tangled his fingers in her hair, then held on tight. Pulling just hard enough that she felt a quick sting, he forced her head back and lowered his face to hers.

"You'll keep your questions off any sexual topic," he whispered. "You aren't as good at hiding your personal desires as you might think. And if this is some game to determine how innocent my nieces may or may not be, you can find someone else's kids to interrogate."

"It's not a game." She hated how her voice suddenly sounded husky, and how her body reacted to his aggressive actions. Tingles rushed over her flesh while her insides tightened, a quickening swelling in her womb and traveling fast enough that she struggled to keep her breathing from growing ragged. "They're going to wonder what you're doing if you continue to stand in my doorway, trapping me in my bedroom."

"No, they aren't," he said, his voice too damn calm. "They'll know I'm making a move on you."

Now she couldn't breathe, let alone speak. Which she told herself played well into the woman she needed to portray to make her cover believable. But if he accused her of being more experienced than she wanted him to see, it should be a part of her he didn't like. Especially since he had just demanded she not press his nieces about anything sexual.

Her sexual predator would be turned off by a worldly woman. He would crave beautiful girls who were sexy but had a clean slate, were easily manipulated and overpowered. Perry seemed even more aroused when she didn't flinch as he damn near pounced on her.

"You aren't, though, right?" she whispered, continuing to stare into his incredibly dominating gaze.

Perry let his fingers slide through her hair and let go of her, straightening and backing out of the doorway so she could pass. She let out a sigh and stepped past him. When she dropped her gaze, she noticed the bulge in his jeans. Her heart started pounding so hard that it was suddenly too damn hot in her hallway. Closing her eyes for a moment and forcing herself past him, she blew out an exasperated breath of air.

Fuck him anyway for getting a rise out of her like that. Even if it did affect him, Perry was messing with her head. He demanded she not discuss anything sexual with the girls, yet the only way she'd learn anything was if they touched on the subject of boys and dating. Although if he were her man that would explain him not wanting that topic brought up. She entered the living room, all eyes on her as she forced a pleasant smile on her face, knowing she wasn't any closer to eliminating Perry as a suspect.

"Figure out where we're ordering pizza?" Kylie asked, stuffing the bills she'd pulled out of her dresser into her purse that she'd left on the coffee table.

"A long time ago," Dani said dryly. "What we're trying to figure out now is what you two are doing back there."

"You and me both," Kylie grunted, and rolled her eyes at Dani, who continued giving her a hard stare. Dani might not mind talking to her, but apparently Kylie's getting too close to Dani's uncle was a different story, and one she wasn't too sure she approved of. One look at the other girls told Kylie they all were of the same mind. "I think your uncle wants to make sure my intentions with you, Dani, and all of you," she added, looking pointedly at each one of them, "are on the up-and-up."

"He gets like that," Dorine said, looking past Kylie toward Perry and narrowing her eyes. When she looked back at Kylie, she straightened and tucked loose brown hair that was pulled back into a long braid behind her ear. "What is it that you want to know?"

Kylie pointed at Dorine. "First one of you order the pizza, and then I want to know how old each of you are. You're all sisters?"

"God, it's that obvious," Dani groaned.

"Yes, we're all sisters." Diane nodded at Dorine. "Order the pizza."

Then, moving to the single overstuffed chair next to the couch, Diane pulled the youngest girl out of the chair, sat down, and then tugged her back down on her lap. "I'm Diane, eighteen, in college and moving out really soon."

"Sounds exciting," Kylie whispered.

Diane's eyes were green like her uncle's but more almond-shaped. She was definitely pretty, gorgeous in fact, with straight brown hair like her sisters, except hers fell just past her shoulders and wasn't pinned back but fell straight.

"Danielle—," Diane continued.

"Dani," Dani snapped, correcting her sister.

"Who likes to go by 'Dani,'" Diane added, "is sixteen. Dorine is fourteen, and Denise is twelve."

"Eighteen, sixteen, fourteen, and twelve," Kylie mused, and walked around the coffee table. She sat on her floor facing the two girls on the couch. Perry didn't sit this time but instead walked toward the back of the living room that opened into her kitchen area. "Your mom must be a saint," she mused.

"She's the best in the world," Denise agreed quickly.

"We're really lucky," the others chimed in.

Perry didn't turn around but clasped his hands behind his back and stared out Kylie's sliding glass doors at her backyard. Apparently he wouldn't be part of this discussion, although it was clear he intended to hear every word said.

As the pizza was ordered, Kylie glanced at the notes she'd taken so far.

"I want to ask you something," she said without looking up. "And any of you or all of you can answer. What's the most common way you talk to your friends? On the phone? Text messaging? Instant messages?"

"All of those are the same," Dorine said, laughing.

"She means instant messaging on the computer," Diane offered. "Like AIM or Yahoo! And for me it's probably mostly on my phone."

"We don't have a computer at home anymore," Dani said. "But you can text-message or instant-message on the phone."

Kylie nodded. "I actually knew that one," she said, pulling her cell phone out of her purse and holding it up before dropping it back into the bag again. "So you think most kids between the ages of twelve and eighteen use their phones to talk to their friends? But do most of them talk on them? Or do they type on them?"

"I never thought about that." Denise turned on Diane's lap. "I think we text-message more than talk. And Diane can text-message without looking, even when she's driving."

"No. She can't," Perry growled from across the room, his back still to all of them.

Diane slapped her sister's leg. "No, I can't," she stressed to Denise, who looked appropriately chastised.

"How many people do you talk to by texting on your phones?" Kylie asked, putting her notebook on her lap and writing: *Check ISPs; if there aren't any, then phone records.*

"Dani talks to so many that Mom had to put unlimited messages on our phone plan. But Dorine never talks to anyone because she doesn't have any friends."

"Speak for yourself, brat," Dorine snapped. "Not all of my friends have cell phones like Dani's rich-bitch friends."

"Watch your mouth, Dorine," Diane snapped, and glanced over her shoulder at her uncle.

"Okay. Okay." Kylie held her hand up in the air with her pen between her fingers. "I want to talk about online relationships. How many of you have met guys you've talked to online?"

The room got quiet and each girl glanced down at her hands. Perry turned around, watching them as well, a frown planted on his face. Kylie shook her head at him, silently willing him to stay quiet. He had demanded she not discuss anything sexual. Kylie would simply argue that relationships at their ages, or at least of the ages of the younger three, probably weren't sexual. Either way, she prayed he wouldn't interrupt her line of questioning.

"It's okay, girls. Everyone does it today, right?"

"Have you ever met anyone you've chatted with online?" Dani asked.

"Sure have," Kylie said without hesitating. She didn't add that they were fellow agents and the discussion was work-related. Her private life was just that. But gaining the girls' confidence would let them open up to her and help her gain more knowledge of what they knew. "So let's assume that each of you has."

"I haven't," Denise offered.

"And you'd tell on any of us if we agreed to meet anyone," Dani snapped, chastising her younger sister.

"I would not," Denise denied the charges, but focused on the ground, her long hair streaming over and partially covering her face.

Kylie smiled at the twelve-year-old. She was very thin and in a year probably at the most would start filling out. If she followed suit like her sisters, she would be drop-dead gorgeous in no time.

"How do you know the person you're chatting with is who they say they are?"

"And not some pervert," Dani said, nodding. "They've

talked to my friends, or there are pictures of them on Facebook that are taken around town and you can tell that they are from around here."

"Have you ever talked to anyone who's chatted with someone that they think is not for real?"

Dani and Diane leaned forward. Diane pushed her little sister to the floor and rested her elbows on her knees.

"A friend of mine has," Dani said.

"Yeah, same here," Diane offered, lowering her voice. "He said he was going to school with us, but when we read his messages there were things he didn't have right."

"So what did you do?" Kylie asked.

Diane turned and gave her uncle a pointed look. "I'm not going to answer her questions and risk you yelling at me," she said, sounding cross.

Perry turned from the group and pulled open the sliding glass door. Kylie managed to keep her expression relaxed. She'd fought with that damn door forever this morning and wasn't able to make it budge. He opened it as though he did it every day. Without saying another word, he disappeared into her backyard.

"He's so moody sometimes," Diane said, looking at Kylie and sighing.

"Mom says he just needs to get laid," Dorine offered.

Kylie quickly cleared her throat and refused to allow the image of Perry's buns of steels to form a clear picture in her head. All that mattered was gathering intel from these girls that could help her clear a path toward the pervert stalking children online.

Someone knocked on her front door and her alarm buzzed. Perry was back inside in a second, proof he hadn't wandered too far. Kylie stood, grabbing her purse, and walked over to the peephole she'd drilled herself when Paul had set up her computer system. The pizza guy stood there holding a large black bag in front of him.

Opening the door, she grinned at the young, pimply-faced kid. "How much do I owe you?"

"Forty-three dollars," he said, pulling the Velcro strap and then sliding out several pizza boxes.

Kylie pulled the bills from her purse and paid the kid as the girls came to the door to help. "Looks like you all ordered a lot of pizza. Sure hope you're hungry."

"Starved," Dorine said, eagerly taking a couple of the boxes.

Diane stood in line to take the third pizza. Kylie watched the girls hurry to the table with three large pizzas and a couple smaller boxes that she guessed contained bread sticks.

"Hey, Jimmy," Dani said, offering a limp wave. "She tip you good?"

"Hi, Dani." Jimmy blushed so brightly his acne stood out. "Yeah. She did."

"Good." Dani walked to the open door and stood next to Kylie. "Any more word on Olivia?" she asked.

"Nothing, dude," Jimmy said, lowering his voice. "She's like totally disappeared. Word is she is like dead or brutalized or maybe sold into slavery."

"God, Jimmy. Don't be sick," Dani said, sounding serious. "She probably flipped on her parents and skipped town."

"Without her car?" Jimmy challenged. "Dani, grow up. You're as hot as she is. Someone stole her cute ass, and you could be next."

"Yeah, right." Dani seemed to have lost the fight in her. She turned noticeably pale and didn't say anything else, nor did she move.

"Man, sorry, Dani," Jimmy said, and backed up down the sidewalk. "I've got your back, though."

"That's what we all have to do," Dani decided, her spunky, confident tone returning. "If someone stole her and he wants to steal one of us, we've got to stop him."

Jimmy looked at Kylie, and Dani did, too. "I'll see you at school," she said, backing away from the door.

Kylie closed the door and turned to look at Dani. The teenager scowled as she walked over to the boxes of pizza with her sisters and Perry. Kylie followed, her mind spinning with the conversation she'd just been privileged to hear.

"Do you know someone who is missing?" Kylie asked.

Kylie shrugged. "We were in the same grade. She was my ride home. Mom threw a fit until Uncle Perry vouched that she'd disappeared."

"Who are we talking about?" Perry asked.

"You said her name was Olivia?" Kylie focused on Dani. "She didn't get along with her mom?"

"God, no!" Dani shoved half a slice of pizza in her mouth and then spoke with her mouth full. "Everyone knew she hated her mother. But her mom was as uncool as they came, demanding to know everything her daughter did and reading her text messages and just smothering her, you know?"

"Do you have other girlfriends like that?" Kylie asked.

"Like what?" Dani frowned.

"Whose mothers, or parents, are smothering them." Kylie was very aware of Perry watching her but kept her attention on Dani.

"Like everyone, dude. Most adults don't have a clue."

"If her mother read all her messages, though, she probably wouldn't complain to her friends in chat messages about it, though, would she?"

"Why not? It wasn't her fault her mother was a prude. Might do her mom good to read that she needs to back off."

"Okay. So she would." Kylie didn't like the picture forming in her mind. "And a sympathetic guy, like Jimmy out there, would offer to protect and help her out of her misery when her world is caving in on her."

"Jimmy's harmless. Besides, he works two jobs. He'll be a millionaire by the time he's twenty." Dani stuffed more pizza in her mouth and waved her hand dismissively toward the door.

"That is the kind of guy you want," Diane pointed out.

"You can have him." Dani snorted and reached for more pizza.

Kylie walked into her kitchen. The profile of her victims was the same as it always was. Her online predator hunted teenage girls who weren't happy with their home lives, and who were pretty, and who somehow had the ability to get out of their houses on their own. The girls who'd disappeared so far were sexy, had an independent nature, drove their own cars, and were intelligent and leaders among their peers.

Her stomach twisted painfully and the smell of the pizza was nauseating. She'd only known Dani a short time, but the girl was very easy to like. She didn't have her own transportation, but that didn't stop her from getting around town without the help of an adult. Other than that, she fit the MO perfectly. Kylie needed to narrow down her list of suspects quickly. The thought of Dani being lured in by a sexual predator wasn't a thought Kylie wanted to dwell on.

Chapter 5

Kylie finished putting dishes in the dishwasher and started it. The instant humming sound it made was rather comforting. Made the place feel like home. It was the first time she'd started it, and she took a moment to soak the new sponge behind the sink and then wipe down the countertops and then the coffee table. She might have run a vacuum, gotten all the little pizza crumbs off the floor, but she didn't have one. The temporary housing provided for her compliments of the Bureau was designed only to make her rental appear like a college student's home. She wasn't here to play domestic goddess.

"Lord," she groaned out loud. God forbid she ever felt a strong craving for that role.

Although as she dried her hands on the sides of her dress and headed down the hallway to the middle bedroom, she admitted to herself it was nice having all the girls here, even with Perry in the background, his brooding expression dark and distracting.

Usually when she handled a case, the opportunity didn't arise for her to get close to the victims. Kylie got to know the town, walked the streets where the victims had lived, and then stalked her predator, enticing him to make her his next victim. Then she struck, taking the perp down and putting him where he belonged, behind bars, where no teenager would be hurt again by his disgusting brutality.

Kylie went to the last bedroom, her bedroom, and opened

the top drawer to her nightstand and pulled out the small key that unlocked the doorknob to the middle room. After unlocking it, she returned the key and made herself comfortable at the desk Paul had helped her set up the day before.

"He's going to come back," she whispered, chills rushing over her flesh at the same time a heat swelled inside her. "Even if he doesn't have the evening off, or possibly it will be tomorrow, but you know he's going to show up here again."

She knew this beyond any doubt for two reasons. The first made her fingers trip over keys when she allowed the knowledge to sink into her brain. The physical attraction she felt for Perry was mutual. If he returned alone, she really needed to be on her toes. There wasn't any evidence confirming his innocence or guilt yet.

"I need to know he's innocent." Which meant spending more time with him. Let that be the reason she wanted to see him again.

Swallowing the lump of apprehension that rose to her throat, she forced her attention to the computer, and to her task. An hour later, she was chatting with several kids and updating her Facebook page, making the kids she was chatting with her friends. At the same time, she had several other windows open to help her with knowledge of bands, movies, and other current events the kids were talking about.

She chatted with different kids from different schools, and after an hour she'd talked about everything from music and movies to sex.

Kylie worked to keep up with the fast-paced chatting without getting a headache as the kids, who ranged in age from thirteen to eighteen, openly talked about oral sex, French kissing, and whether or not they were virgins. It never ceased to amaze her how easy it was to get kids to talk openly online. And finally, when asked by a boy who was eighteen and enrolled at a local high school, she typed that she wasn't a virgin and that sex was great.

As another private instant message box popped up in front of her, startling her with its popping sound, Kylie realized it was now dark outside. Her blinds were still open, and headlights trailed down the street when a car slowed and then parked in front of her house.

"He's back," she whispered, standing and closing the blinds while butterflies fluttered in her stomach. She glanced back at the computer screen and at the instant message box now sitting in the middle of her screen. "Oh, shit," she hissed, sliding back into her chair.

The screen name at the top of the box was PeteTakesU. She stared at the message in the box: *Do your parents know you like sex?*

Kylie stared at the small flash drive where all her chats were being saved. Perry was walking up her sidewalk. Crap. Talk about bad timing.

Returning her attention to the instant message box, she typed: *duh.* PeteTakesU typed: *LOL.*

There was a firm knock on her door. Kylie stared at the far wall, as if she could see through it and take in the man standing outside her front door. The instant message box chimed again: *You sound hot. Where are pictures of you?*

On my Facebook profile. My profile is Kayla2010, same as my name here. G2G parents are near. She finished typing and minimized the chat box. Even though the program on the computer would save and log every chat she had, Kylie worked better saving her own chats. She liked being able to review them on her own, without having to head over to the field office to request seeing the logged files.

Her heart thumped in her chest when she turned off the light, locked the door to the middle room, and headed down the hall to the front door.

"Yes?" she said, placing her hand on the door handle and leaning against the front door.

"Open the door, Kylie." Perry's deep voice sounded all business—or pissed.

She slid the chain into place on the door and unlocked the dead bolt. Opening it as far as the chain would allow, she flipped on her porch light and watched him squint as she blinded him.

"What do you want?"

"Open the damn door and let me in," he growled.

It was tempting to spar with him, but she closed the door, slipped the chain free, and stepped out of the way when he pushed the door hard enough that it swung open. She grabbed it before it hit the wall, staying clear when he stalked into her home.

"What were you doing?"

"When?" She watched him when he stopped in the middle of her living room and turned to face her.

"Just now. When I knocked on the door."

She was toying with him just a bit. It was so easy to do, and she kind of liked how she could make his eyes darken with her comments.

"What do you think I was doing?" she asked, turning from him and closing the door. "I was studying."

"Where are your books?" he asked, his demanding tone pushing as he continued watching her, slowly crossing his arms. Apparently he had the night off, as he was still dressed in his T-shirt and jeans. God, he made simple clothing look deadly.

Kylie took her time answering, unwilling to spar with him full force. Already she felt the charge in the air, the sexual energy radiating off him. It was best to keep her head clear, stay focused on the fact that she quite possibly had just communicated with their killer. Although that would mean Perry was innocent, it also meant if her man was online right now, she needed to take this opportunity to get to know him.

"You heard me interview the girls. What else do you want to know?" she challenged, crossing her arms over her chest and watching Perry's expression harden.

Perry walked toward her. If she didn't move, he would have her cornered.

"I think you're avoiding the answer to a simple question." He grabbed her arm when she tried walking past him. "Where are your books?"

"I do most of my work on my computer," she said honestly, and looked down at her arm. "Is there a reason you're restraining me?"

His hand was large and his fingers long. His skin was tanner than hers. She watched his fingers wrap around her forearm and then his grip loosened and slid down to her wrist.

"This isn't restraint, darling," he drawled. "When I restrain you, you won't be able to move."

"That is what restraining means." Kylie laughed, walking away from him and pulling her arm free as she headed toward her kitchen. Perry let go of her but followed when she walked around the open living room that turned into her small kitchen. "You haven't told me why you're here," she said, keeping her back to him.

She grabbed a plastic cup from her cabinet and filled it with ice from the ice maker in her refrigerator. There hadn't been time to grocery shop, so other than the leftovers from the pizza, of which all fit in one box and took up a shelf in her refrigerator, there wasn't any food in her kitchen.

"Because I know what you're doing."

Kylie put her cup under the faucet and let it fill with tap water.

She took her time turning around and brought her cup to her lips, watching him while sipping. No way would he get her frazzled.

"Why are you questioning me if you already know what I'm doing?" An ice cube brushed against her lip and she savored how cold it was. Anything to help keep her grounded.

"Questioning you?"

"You asked me what I was doing when you walked in the door, yet now you say you know what I'm doing." She smiled, sipped again, focused on the cold water soothing the fire burning inside her. "Did you learn this by my actions after entering my home?"

"No." The hungry look in his eyes made them brighter. But it was the way he pressed his lips together, not frowning or smiling, that made him look dangerous, like a deadly predator who ruled all around him, and contemplated making her his next conquest. "Who is your professor?"

Kylie rolled her eyes, although she needed to play out her next card very carefully. If and when she nailed her guy, it would come out that she was FBI. She wouldn't insult Perry too much for questioning her.

"You don't believe I'm a student." She put her cup down on the counter and sighed, sounding frustrated as she started to move around him.

Once again he grabbed her arm, this time turning her to face him with enough force that she slapped her palm against his chest to balance herself. Tingles shot through her hand when she touched muscle that was solid like steel.

"Where are you going?" he growled, searching her face.

"I don't have my professor's information memorized." She gestured with her free hand. "I was going to get you his phone number so you can call him and prove to yourself who I am."

"And will this professor also confirm what it is you're writing your thesis about?" he asked.

"You can ask him, or believe me," she said, softening her tone and looking up at him through her lashes.

"Here's what I think. You might be the student you claim you are, and you might be working on a paper or thesis." He let go of her arm but then gripped her neck, his long finger pressing under her jaw until she tilted her head back farther. "I also think you've stumbled onto something, crimes that intrigue you, and now you think you're Agatha Christie."

"You see me as an old woman with a British accent?" she retorted, pulling free from him and hurrying out of her kitchen. She needed him to leave, and the longer he kept his hands on her, the harder it would be to get him out of her house.

He was behind her faster than she imagined he would be. "Hardly," he growled, flipping her around to face him once again and this time pulling her into his arms. When he kissed her, the savage hunger he displayed had her insides boiling feverishly within seconds.

Kylie tried moving her hands to his chest. Maybe he thought she meant to push him away, and in some part of her brain she knew that she should. Get him to leave. Return to work. Her thoughts grew more muddled the longer he devoured her mouth. Not to mention the way he tightened his hold on her, pinning her with his arms against his rock-hard body, turned her on a hell of a lot more than she should let it.

There was something about a man who got a bit rough. Something about how a demanding nature, taking and controlling and leaving no room for any reaction other than submission, got her so hot she swore she'd be a puddle at his feet in moments.

"Perry," she gasped, managing to turn her head and break the kiss. Her lips tingled and a pang of regret hit her when she sucked in a deep breath. If she moved her face, looked into his intense eyes, she would initiate the next kiss. And she couldn't do that. "Why are you doing this?" Her voice was no more than a raspy whisper.

"To get it out of the way." His voice was rough.

"And that was necessary?"

He moved his fingers through her hair and then brushed them across her face. She needed distance, for him to quit touching her, and then her thoughts would return to normal.

Kylie stared at her hand, resting against his chest, and moved her fingers. Roped muscle quivered under her touch. A sense of control rushed over her. Maybe he could turn her brain to mush and create desire inside her stronger than anything she'd felt in years, but she was doing the same thing to him. He wasn't the rock of solid determination he wanted her to believe he was.

"You tell me." He gripped her chin, forcing her to look into his eyes.

"I think it was necessary for you. Maybe you worried your rock of resolve might crumble if you didn't taste me."

"Are you always this stubborn?" he asked, chuckling and then letting his fingers stroke her neck, move lower, and brush the swell of her breast before he quit touching her.

"I'm being stubborn?" Kylie felt control once again and sucked in another fresh breath, strengthening her resolve. "You should go, Perry. I've got work to do."

"Show me this work."

That was the last thing she wanted to do. "I'll show you

when it's done, if you really want to see it." She headed to her front door and rested her palm against the doorknob. It was cool and made her realize how hot and damp her hand was. "And I'm not going to get it done if you don't leave." She offered him a smile she hoped reassured him she wasn't getting rid of him, although that was exactly what she needed to do.

"I think you promised me a name and number to call." He didn't budge.

"Oh, yeah." Kylie turned, padding barefoot down her hallway to her bedroom. Paul had made business cards for her in case she needed to back up her story, but they were in her briefcase. That wouldn't be a problem if she could keep Perry at bay long enough to fish them out.

She squatted in her dark bedroom and unzipped the side pocket to her briefcase as her bedroom light turned on. "Tell me you're not trying to play detective and I'll be satisfied," Perry said, leaning in the doorway and crossing his arms.

"I'm not," she said, taking in how his jeans molded over long, muscular legs. He made T-shirts look like body armor, the way they sculpted his broad chest and the sleeves hugged well-defined biceps. "Eye candy" barely described how tempting he looked. "What has you so worried though?" she asked, deciding turning the tables and putting him on the defensive would keep her head clear, in control, and probably make him leave sooner. "Are you on some investigation right now?"

She knew the look people gave her when they asked about what crimes she might be fighting to solve. That look of excitement, eagerness to hear the inside scoop. It caused people's faces to light up, their eyes to spark with curiosity. Kylie looked up at Perry from her squatting position and knew she gave him that exact look when his expression turned wary.

"No," he said simply, surprising her, but it was something that clouded over his gaze that grabbed her attention.

"Oh," she said, not needing to pretend to sound disappointed. "Then what are you worried about?"

She fished through the pocket of her briefcase, which

leaned against the side of her dresser until she found the card she needed.

"My nieces think the world of you."

The admission startled her.

"And they're my responsibility to protect. If you're using them in any way to gather information because you're trying to find a criminal, no matter how good you feel your intentions are, you're going to stop right now. I'm not going to let you put yourself, or them, in harm's way."

Kylie stood and ran her hand down her dress, straightening it while she watched Perry's attention shift down her body. She moved toward him slowly, holding her hand out with the card in it.

"I'm going to let that comment slide," she began, and his gaze snapped to her face. "Because you don't know me that well. But you'd better believe that I would never do anything to harm your nieces, or any other child, ever."

He took the card and slid it into the pocket on his chest without looking at it. She worried he'd trap her in her bedroom, but he turned and started down the hallway. Kylie was right behind him, but he stopped, causing her to almost run into his backside. He grabbed the doorknob to her middle bedroom and turned, then frowned when it was locked.

"Why do you keep this room locked?"

"It's where I work."

He looked down at her. He was easily over six feet tall, with his broad shoulders and thick chest aiding in him looking fierce. His dark eyes and short, almost black hair, not to mention that tiny scar on the side of his jawbone, made him appear dangerous. Kylie could hold her own, with the self-defense classes she was required to take, a black belt in karate, and years of experience handling criminals who were twice her weight and body size. Nonetheless, she felt the danger radiating from his pores. His body was a weapon, and if she wasn't careful, she'd be his target practice.

"Unlock the door," he ordered.

She smiled easily. "No way. It's locked for a reason. My work is private until I'm done. If I allow anyone to give their opinion on what I'm writing, it distracts me," she added for good measure. Then, keeping her expression light, she added, "You really should go now, Perry."

He turned on her and she barely had time to raise her hand in protest before he pushed into her, proving how solid and invincible that body of his was.

"No, don't," she managed to get out before he knocked the wind out of her when he shoved her against the wall and pounced on her mouth.

God. She loved it rough. And obviously Perry did, too. He impaled her mouth, devouring her before she could catch her breath. His fingers scraped over her shoulder, pushing the strap of her dress down so that she couldn't raise her arm. He squeezed her breast and growled into her mouth.

Kylie swore her world turned sideways. She had one free arm and she grabbed his shoulder, fighting to stay grounded as she opened to him, taking what he insisted on giving her and drinking him up as fast as she could.

She kept her fingernails short yet filed and painted, her personal vanity. And with what nails she had she dug into his shoulder, feeling how solid he was and rubbing her fingers over the swell of roped muscle. Then wrapping her fingers around the side of his neck, she lost herself in the solid, repetitive beat of his heart as it pulsed through his vein in his neck.

"Don't tell me no again," he hissed into her mouth, moving his lips over hers.

Her eyes were still closed and she relaxed between the wall and his virile body. "Don't do anything that I wouldn't want," she challenged, and then blinked several times, her vision blurring when she gazed into his face.

His eyes pierced her soul. "I haven't so far," he growled.

"Perry, leave." There was no insistence left in her, but she made the words come out nonetheless.

And she hated it when he backed up, leaving her against the wall. He headed down the hall toward the front door and opened it. She felt drunk when she followed him and gulped in a few soothing breaths to regain her composure so that when she reached the door she hoped there was some appearance of control in her expression.

"Your nieces are good girls. I won't let them get hurt," she promised him.

Perry didn't comment but walked down her sidewalk to his car. She watched him climb in and start his engine before she slowly closed and locked her door.

Chapter 6

Perry adjusted the earpiece, listening carefully while he drove out of Kylie's neighborhood. He heard the sound of a doorknob turning and then footsteps. Kylie had unlocked that middle room and was once again in there. For good measure, he drove around the block, confirmed what he'd heard when he saw the middle light on through the window and kept going. Something that sounded as if a chair slid across the floor. Damn, his bugging equipment that he'd placed in her hallway, and just inside her front door, was sensitive as hell. It might not be what some would consider scrupulous, but no one would harm his nieces. Perry would know beyond any doubt that Kylie's intentions were good before he allowed anyone to get closer to her.

His cell phone rang as he ran his tongue over his lips, still tasting her. No, he wasn't getting too close to her. It didn't matter how good she felt or smelled. Or how damn aroused she got him. Her intelligence and beauty were compelling, and he'd see her again, and soon. But he had to know beyond any doubt that she wasn't indulging in any foul play.

"Hello," he said, noting the number calling as he yanked the earpiece for his equipment that allowed him to hear into Kylie's house.

"Hey, little brother," Megan said, sounding cheerful yet tired. She always sounded tired these days. "Word on the street is that you might have found a hot little number."

"What?" he hissed, rolling his eyes. "Hold on a minute."

He dropped the earpiece that had a cord attached to a black box in his passenger seat. Then grabbing his Bluetooth out of the cubby on his dash where a CD player or some other modern contraption could be installed if he were so inclined, he shoved it in his ear. "Do I even want to ask what you might have heard?"

Before Megan, his sister and mother of his nieces, spoke he was positive he heard amusement in her sigh. "It appears the girls spent the afternoon with a Kylie Dover. I admit freaking on it a bit, even with Diane there, too, until they told me you were part of this gathering as well. Mind filling me in on what's going on?"

"What did the girls tell you?"

"You know I hate it when you answer my questions with questions."

He knew. He also was curious whether the girls had told Megan a different story about Kylie than what they had told him. When he didn't respond, Megan sighed again, sounding slightly less amused, and continued. "Dani met her first at the bowling alley earlier this week. They tell me she's working on her thesis over at KU but came here to get a different perspective from teenagers. Apparently she's going to several different towns before writing her thesis and turning it in. They tell me she's a cultural anthropologist and is focusing on teenagers as a subculture within our social structure. From what I heard, it sounds as if she actually has some interesting data gathered."

"She told the girls what data she's gathered?" It wasn't jealousy or envy that stabbed at his insides. Just because Kylie wouldn't let him see her work but shared it with his nieces didn't mean shit. He did barge in on her and accuse her of playing investigator. And the jury was still out on that one.

"Dani told me she saw some of Kylie's notes. She's convinced that fourteen- to sixteen-year-old girls are more daring on the computer than seventeen- and eighteen-year-old girls. Apparently, although all girls in that age group seem to have no problem meeting people they don't know after talking to them online, girls in the fourteen- to sixteen-year-old bracket are more inclined to meet boys for dates than teenagers in other age brackets." Megan paused and sipped at a drink.

He pictured his sister gripping her glass of iced tea, drinking and then getting that faraway look in her eyes like she always did when she digested information. "What was Dani's take on all of that?"

"Are you kidding? Dani tell me what she's thinking?" Megan laughed. "So anyway, the girls think it would be great to have Kylie over for dinner. And I admit I'm a bit curious about her. How does next Wednesday night sound to you?"

"Why are you asking me?" Perry scowled, already guessing the outcome of the conversation. He hated his sister trying to match him up with anyone. "If you want to meet Kylie, that's your business. I'll be busy."

"You will not," Megan snapped. "And I expect you to invite her over. Let's say six thirty. That gives me time to get home from work and I'll have the girls focus on supper."

Perry turned onto his street and slowed, hitting his brights before he reached his driveway. "Megan, you know I hate it when you get your hopes up about something."

"Perry. I'm a widow with four teenage daughters. I work two jobs and have no life. Let me do this. It will be fun and something to look forward to," she said, pausing as her tone turned serious. "Or are you telling me that there is absolutely no chemistry whatsoever between the two of you?"

He didn't mean to hesitate with his answer. Perry glanced in his rearview mirror and then across his yard when his headlights swooped over his large, neatly mowed corner lot. It was habit, confirming that no one lurked waiting for him to get out of his Jeep. Years of being on the force, knowing he was personally responsible for more than one criminal going to jail, made it habitual to watch his ass coming and leaving his home.

"That's what I thought," Megan said smugly, as if he'd responded. "Then next Wednesday at six thirty. Be sure and tell me when she confirms."

"I'll see what I can do," he grumbled, and parked the

Jeep outside his garage door, which was closed. "Talk to you later, Sis."

"Love you, little bro," she chirped, and hung up the phone.

Perry grabbed his monitoring equipment and cell phone and then headed inside. He showered, something that usually helped him unwind after coming home, but tonight he was wound just as tight after slipping into his sweatpants and padding barefoot to his kitchen for a beer.

He opened his refrigerator, staring at the bleak contents before leaning over and pulling out one of several long-neck beers. Twisting the cap off, he tossed it in the trash and grabbed the monitoring equipment.

Perry's den faced the front of his house and oftentimes served as his bedroom as well as a computer room. After closing his blinds and placing the small black box next to his computer, he changed the settings so he could hear everything without earphones and slumped into his chair behind his computer.

His desktop appeared on his monitor when he moved his mouse and at the same time the audio started crackling on his monitoring equipment. Perry strained to hear what was picked up on the bugs in Kylie's home.

"You're still up, sweetheart," he whispered, staring at the nondescript black box.

Before tonight, his interest in Kylie was physical. He hated thinking that a grown woman wearing such innocent-looking yet incredibly seductive minidresses could get him hard as stone when so many other women had tried and didn't hold his interest. Granted, listening and watching her over the past couple of days had piqued his curiosity, and more than physically. Although any time he got anywhere around her his cock grew harder than steel.

But there were things about her that bugged him. The simplicity of her house, no knickknacks, no pictures, barely any furniture, seemed odd. It also bugged him that being in her company brought forth more than just a craving to sink into her hot little pussy. She questioned his nieces like a pro, using a pattern, building her line of questioning like a professional. And then so easily blew him off, using the lame excuse that she couldn't show him her schoolwork until it was done.

Things didn't add up, but that didn't make her a criminal or an amateur detective. Regardless of his inability to figure her out, Perry was a patient man. He would learn what she was about. And there was more to Miss Kylie Dover than just being a student.

Reclining in his chair, he picked up his sweating bottle of beer and guzzled half of it while moving his mouse over the icon to check mail. Nothing came over the monitoring equipment other than occasional static popping, probably the result of some small noise in her home that the device barely registered. When he opened his mail, the chat feature automatically signed in as well. Immediately Dani popped up with an instant message box.

Did you ask her? She put a silly smiley face at the end of the question.

Chatting online wasn't one of Perry's strong points. He didn't like a means of communications that eliminated body language.

No. He typed the answer, which was immediately followed by a frowning face.

Mom says she wants to meet her if we're going to spend time with her. Now Dani presented her argument in an effort to corner him into doing the dirty deed. *So you've got to ask her*, she added before he could even think about what to say to her previous comment.

The monitoring equipment crackled and Kylie's voice came through the small microphone. Perry's insides tightened, a rush of adrenaline hitting him as he growled at his computer when it chimed from another message from his niece. Turning down the speaker volume on his PC, he leaned closer to the small black box.

"What did you say, sweetheart?" he whispered, and checked to see if a microcassette was in place. "Talk to Papa," he said, and pushed "play" to start recording what would be said.

"Any idea which department?" Kylie's usually soft, alluring tone sounded crisp, firm, all business. "Okay. Well, I'm going to have to get cuddly with local PD then."

"Get cuddly, huh?" Perry brought the bottle of beer to his mouth again, swallowing the last half of the brew and tossing the bottle into his trash can. "How much of the police department do you plan on getting close to, and why?"

A flash of light reflected against the front window and grabbed his attention. Perry stood, frowning, when a car pulled into his driveway. People didn't come over without calling first to see if it was okay. They just never had.

He headed out of his den and stopped in the living room, watching as the Chief pulled into his driveway and parked.

"What the hell?" Perry returned to his den and scowled at his monitoring equipment, a device that would definitely be a tough one to explain to Rad. "Goddamn it," he growled, turning the thing off and shoving it into the top drawer of his dresser. His gut told him something was off with Kylie. He was so damn close to learning what the hell it was and then this. "Why the hell are you here?" he snarled under his breath, slamming the drawer closed and making it bang.

Perry reached the back door, which opened off his driveway, as Rad knocked firmly. "Rad," he said, not caring if irritation sounded in his tone.

"Sorry to interrupt your evening." Rad didn't look or sound apologetic. "I need to talk to you, Flynn."

His serious manner didn't sway Perry. "What's up?" He had enough decency to stand to the side and allow his Chief to come inside. The bugs were hovering over his outside light anyway, and the longer they stood like this, the more bugs would get inside.

Rad entered but didn't turn around in the dark kitchen. Instead, he walked into the living room and focused on the den, the only room in the house with a light on.

"What were you doing?" he asked, frowning at the open door like he was itching to head in that direction.

"Having a beer, checking e-mail." Perry joined him, standing in the middle of his dark living room. "What's up?"

"Mind if we go in there?" Rad asked, but instead of waiting for Perry's consent headed into the den.

"Something on your mind?" Perry followed Rad into his den and walked around him to his desk. Remembering that his beer was empty, he turned and headed back through the dark living room. "You want a beer? Anything to drink?"

"I'm good."

Perry grabbed another longneck from his fridge and headed back to his den. Rad was standing behind his desk staring at his computer when Perry entered. The Chief looked up at him, concern lining his face. Perry frowned, twisting the cap off and moving around the desk so that he saw the screen that Rad saw. "What's got you bugged?" he asked.

"I've got a question for you. I need you to be straight with me." Rad turned and faced Perry. He stared at him with shrewd gray eyes.

"Ask," Perry said. Although he was six foot one and Rad had a bad knee and was damn near twenty years older, he stared the Chief straight on, eye to eye.

"This case with the girls coming up missing, with them being stalked online, what do you know about it?"

"About as much as you do." Perry tried reading Rad's intent expression but wasn't getting anywhere with it. "You going to give me the case now?"

"No," Rad said, not hesitating. "Are you working on it on the side? Possibly going after anyone in chat rooms or posing as someone you aren't?"

"Hell, no," Perry snapped.

"Mind pulling up that chat box?" Rad asked, pointing at the monitor.

Perry cursed under his breath, pressed his palm against the back of his office chair, and used his free hand to move the mouse and pull up the chat box with Dani.

"Who is that?"

"My niece. My sister Megan's daughter," Perry growled. "What the hell is this?"

The chat box showed Dani's last two messages with her insisting Perry ask her. It didn't say who he was supposed to ask, or why. But Dani's comment referred to "Mom," which added simplicity and innocence to the chat. Perry looked away from the screen and at Rad's profile as he stared at the large green font and finally nodded.

Perry took another drink and walked around his desk. Rad joined him, moving around the desk and sitting on the edge of it, crossing his arms and still scowling.

"I assigned a partner to you last month, but the two of you aren't riding together. Why is that, Flynn?"

"Don't know. Why?"

"You two got issues?"

"I don't have issues with anyone," Perry snapped. "And if any occur, they're worked out before I call it a day. Did you come out to my home to ride my ass about not spending enough time with my new partner?"

"You know we work cases with partners for a reason."

"I know how to do my fucking job."

Rad didn't say anything but studied Perry, which aggravated the hell out of him.

"You didn't come over here to remind me that I have a partner. You could have done that down at the station. Whatever it is, spit it out," Perry demanded.

"I want you and Ramos to start running together, got that?" Rad said coldly. "Watch your ass and make sure everything you do is accounted for." The Chief pushed away from Perry's desk and headed out of his den.

Perry stopped him, grabbing the Chief's arm and forcing him to turn and face him. No one entered his home, no matter who the hell they were, and threatened him without offering an explanation as to why. And it had better be one fucking good explanation. The Chief knew Perry didn't like working with a partner, and it had never been an issue before. He worked best alone, whether it was investigating crime scenes or getting reports turned in. Call him anti-social, he didn't care. But someone else tagging along simply slowed him down.

"Why do I need to cover my ass?" he demanded, unable to control the anger growing inside him.

"Hopefully you don't." Rad suddenly sounded relaxed, like a calm before a storm.

Perry's guts twisted from nerves, but he wouldn't be intimidated. He hadn't done anything wrong, and had a hard time believing Rad thought otherwise.

"I don't and you damn well know it," Perry hissed. "You're not walking out of my house without explaining why you show up off-hours, unannounced, and imply there's a situation when there isn't one."

"I didn't say there wasn't a situation. Account for your time and your actions and it won't become your situation." Rad looked down at his arm where Perry still held him and then started across the room, yanking his arm out of Perry's grasp.

To grab the Chief again would be a sign of aggression, one Perry would take if that was what was needed.

"Rad," he said, trying this tactic first. He didn't doubt for a moment that he could physically restrain the Chief, but he'd never had a beef with the man, and didn't now, at least not at this moment. "You'd better tell me what's going on or I'll be forced to learn on my own."

"I'm not at liberty to say." Rad turned around, his stressed-out expression lined with aggravation. He stared at Perry for a long moment, and when the Chief spoke again the coldness in his tone was enough to put a chill in the room. "Watch your fucking ass and if you're confronted, ordered to show your reports, or," he added, lowering his voice and pinning Perry with a brutal stare, "if your personal computer is subpoenaed, your ass better be clean. I've already gone out on a limb for you. And I'm here to tell you now, there are a lot of holes in your time sheets. Start keeping your log sheets current. You take a fucking piss, log it."

"What the fuck?" Perry hissed.

Rad walked through Perry's house and opened his back door, leaving it opened as he headed toward his car. Perry didn't bother shutting it, either, as he stormed after the Chief.

"Are you implying that I'm under investigation? Tell me who's trumped up charges against me."

"No one has," Rad offered easily. "Yet. Keep it that way. You hear me?"

Perry heard him but didn't have a fucking clue what he was talking about.

Chapter 7

Perry had the eeriest feeling that someone was watching him. The back of his neck prickled as he parked, taking up two stalls, and then headed up the broken sidewalk toward one of five duplexes that surrounded the small parking lot. Rubbing the back of his head and trying to get the sensation to go away, he knocked on the door and then glanced up and down the busy side street.

The front door to the adjoining duplex opened and an elderly woman, wearing a full, long paisley dress that hung to her skeletal figure, peered out at him.

"What do you want?" she demanded as if he'd just knocked on her door.

Perry knew Carl Ramos' mother only through her son but knew her mind wasn't what it used to be. "Good afternoon, Mrs. Ramos," he said. "Do you know if Carl is home?"

"He's out back playing ball." Mrs. Ramos closed the front door before Perry could say anything.

More than likely so she could hurry through her house and announce to her son that he had company before Perry could walk around the duplex. When he reached the back side of the duplex Perry heard laughter and bantering and wondered if he'd inadvertently stumbled onto a Sunday afternoon party. A large gathering was the last thing he was in the mood for.

"Playing ball" was an understatement. Perry paused in between duplexes, feeling the cool breeze in the shade from the buildings, as he stared at the aggressive game of football going on in the open field between the homes and a row of trees that hid the industrial park spread out beyond it.

"Perry!" Natalie Anderson waved as she announced his presence, calling to him from the other side of the field. "You're just in time. Just don't take Carl's side. His team is getting their ass kicked."

"Fuck you, Anderson." Marty Taul worked in Records at City Hall with Natalie. He leapt into the air, pulling off a decent interception, but then tumbled over Carl, who bulldozed into him. Both men went sprawling to the ground.

"I don't do sloppy seconds," Natalie hollered, laughing as she started around the field toward Perry. Over a year ago, Perry took Natalie out, which ended up with both of them drunk and naked. He seldom drank and sure as hell wasn't used to tying one on like he had that night. From what he remembered, the sex was incredible, but neither spoke to each other much after that for at least several months.

"The game is probably over," she said when she approached him. "And it should have ended long before now," she added, grinning easily as she stared up at him with soft blue eyes.

"Looks like it." Perry shook his head, watching the men help each other up and then laugh at how they weren't as young as they used to be. "I'd say I showed up at the right time. I'm the only man standing upright."

"They don't hold a flame to you no matter how they stand," Natalie said under her breath. Over the past few months she'd started flirting openly with him. Rumor was that she'd recently broken up with her boyfriend and was on the prowl for a new man.

Perry wasn't going to be that man, but he didn't mind humoring her. "Flattery will get you everywhere," he drawled, and then walked into the backyard, reaching down to grab the football that had rolled away from the guys.

"Flynn. If you'd showed up forty-five minutes ago . . . ," Marty said, breathing heavily as he pressed against his lower back. "Carl, I'm going to have to head out, man. The wife will be home from shopping soon and we're supposed to go to her mom's tonight."

"Fun, fun," Carl said, rolling his eyes and slapping Marty on the back. "Tell her you threw your back out trying to beat me at football and so can't go."

"She wouldn't believe me." Marty winked at Natalie and then started toward the path between the duplexes.

"What brings you over this way?" Carl asked, catching the ball when Perry tossed it to him. "Seems a weekend for company."

"Anyone else shown up from the station?" Perry asked, trying to sound indifferent.

"Yeah, actually. The Chief, if you can believe that."

Perry met Carl's gaze and his expression hardened, appearing almost wary. "Oh, really," Perry said, trying to sound curious when he ached to grab Carl by the arm and force him to a more private location. Something wasn't right, but worse yet, Perry sensed things were worse than he thought.

"I'm heading down to Lucy's for a drink and to stare at the big screen in the company of strangers," Natalie said, wrapping her arm around Perry's. "Dare to join me?"

He hadn't been to Lucy's in ages but had dared enter the club since taking Natalie there on their date. He smiled down at her knowingly. "Sounds like a challenge."

"Never," she said, looking shocked. "Just more fun to zone out on the boob tube with a crowd around than alone in my apartment, unless I know that company will be showing up soon."

"I hear you," he said, deciding not to fall for the bait.

"I might head down to Lucy's after a shower," Carl offered.

Natalie turned the same welcoming smile to Carl. Possibly she was simply looking for company during drinks and watching the prime-time lineup. Or maybe she was horny and didn't care who she took home with her as long as he fell into her criteria of "decent." Either way, Carl's offer was good enough for Natalie.

"Both of you come down. I'll see you there." She let go of Perry and took off around the duplex toward the parking lot.

Carl tossed the football into the air a couple feet and then caught it, heading toward his back door. "You going to head down there?"

"Wasn't planning on it," Perry told him honestly. "I really showed up here to talk to you for a few."

"No problem. Come on in." Carl pulled his screen door open and held it, allowing Perry to enter first. "You want a beer?"

"Sounds good."

"Rad come pay you a social call, too?" Carl pulled a couple cans out of his refrigerator and handed one to Perry. "Are we being written up on some bullshit or something?"

"I doubt it." Perry followed Carl into his living room and reclined on the comfortable couch, relaxing into the corner and watching Carl do the same on the other end, kicking his shoes off before resting his sock-covered feet on his coffee table. Perry felt like doing anything but relaxing. "Something's going on, though. If he came to see you and me, I'm betting he visited a few other cops on the force as well."

"What the fuck for?" Carl gulped down a fair bit of his beer and belched.

"What exactly did he say to you?" Perry decided to ask the question before Carl could. He would rather form his conclusions after hearing what was said, and knowing nothing Carl told him would be altered based on anything he heard from Perry.

"He told me to start working with you, that we were partners and to start acting as though we were."

"Said the same thing here."

Carl frowned, staring at his beer for a moment without saying anything. Perry allowed the silence to grow, wanting to make sure Carl said everything on his mind, or that he had to share, before Perry added anything to it.

"If you came over because you think I complained about us not working together, I didn't do that." Carl looked at

Perry, searching his face as if needing to see his reaction to his comment.

"Actually, that never entered my mind," Perry told him honestly. "You're the best partner I could ask for," he added, guessing Carl needed reassurance and not minding giving it to him. Carl was a good cop, quite a bit younger than Perry but molding well and learning the ropes quickly. "You've never bitched that I head out on my own, and are always there when I've asked you to run with me."

"Hey, whatever works, man," Carl offered, shrugging and returning his attention to his beer. "Maybe his ass is on the line for something. It might not even be us. Could be that he got his butt chewed and wants us all prim and proper to save his own hide."

"Could be," Perry said, leaning forward and watching his beer can perspire. "What else he tell you?"

"Not a lot. He came over unexpected—scared the crap out of me. It was late last night and I was about to crash. To tell you the truth, it wasn't so much what he said but how he acted."

"Like he was checking your place out?"

Carl looked at Perry, his black eyes not blinking as he stared at him for a long moment. "Yup. Exactly what he was doing. He was checking the place out, searching for something. Flynn, you think we're under investigation for some bogus charge?"

Rad didn't chase ghosts. Perry had worked with the Chief long enough to respect the man. Something was going on. Whatever it was, he wouldn't figure it out sitting here bullshitting and speculating with Ramos.

"I honestly have no idea what the Chief is up to."

After leaving his partner's house, Perry did a drive-by past Kylie's house, not surprised but feeling a bit frustrated when she wasn't home. He hit the mall, bowling alley, and library and didn't find her car at any of those locations. Then heading over to the station, he decided to see if Rad was pulling some overtime. Perry was on edge, needed to burn off some steam, and returning home wouldn't help him find answers.

As he entered the station and then walked down the hall toward the "pit," the large room where all their desks were lined in rows, paired off and facing each other, the smell of coffee hit him, which didn't alert him as much as the whistling. The "pit" held onto way too many smells from years of exhausted cops working overtime. He paused, though, listening as someone tried carrying a tune.

Goddard stopped in his tracks, quickly raising his cup and holding it away from himself so the steaming brew wouldn't spill. "You scared the crap out of me," Goddard said, and then blew on his coffee.

"Anybody here?" Perry asked, heading toward his desk and passing by Goddard's. His computer was booted up, but he'd been away from it long enough that the screen saver had kicked in.

"What? I don't count?"

"It depends on what you're doing."

"Looking for pussy on the Internet."

Perry stared at Goddard, who returned the serious look for a moment before laughing easily. "Goddamn, Flynn. Look at me like I'm serious. Shit." He rolled his eyes and then slumped into his chair, moving his mouse and then focusing on his screen. "What brings you down here, anyway?"

"Have you heard anything new on the Olivia Brown case?"

"You get assigned to the online predator case?" Goddard clasped his hands behind his head and leaned back, studying Perry. "And no. I don't know a thing."

"Nope. Not assigned to anything. I tried to get Rad to let me head it up, but no dice." He'd get the Chief to agree to him having the case, though. No one else would take it. His nieces' lives were at stake with the bastard hunting girls in Mission Hills. That didn't sit well with Perry. But even more so, he wouldn't stand for the Chief giving the case to one of several cops on the force who would love to have it just for the publicity. The case wasn't about publicity. It was about putting one of the lowest forms of life behind bars, or killing him. Perry would love to be the one to pull the trigger.

"No one is assigned to those cases. And you would think someone should be, yes?" Goddard didn't wait for Perry's response but leaned forward, playing with his mouse again and then typing. "Seems to me if someone was assigned to play around online a bit, they could find the guy."

"Yeah, maybe." Perry booted his computer up and waited for the icons to appear on his desktop. He wanted to read over the reports of all the cases they had on file so far. And to hell with anyone if they questioned him researching a case not assigned to him. Data needed to be gathered. The sooner he learned as much as there was to know about each teenage girl, the faster he could create an MO on the perp who was stalking them. If he was going to be written up for doing that, then someone had too much damn time on their hands.

Olivia Brown had disappeared the other day, not showing up at her car at the mall and leaving her friends stranded and in need of rides home. The police report didn't offer anything he didn't already know. Olivia's parents were panicking, calling the police department hourly. The notes after the report stated that the parents had hired a private investigator. All of Olivia's friends were interviewed. Two of her friends knew she had been chatting online with a guy she had the hots for. Neither interview offered anything conclusive that could be followed up on.

Perry pulled up Maura Reynolds' file next. She had disappeared over three months ago and there were no new leads. Interviews conducted right after she disappeared confirmed she had talked with her friends about meeting a boy who went to school in Independence, a town over thirty minutes away and across the state line into Missouri. The police had her hard drive from her computer as evidence, and chats were documented showing she'd arranged to meet a boy named Peter. They were going to see a movie together. Maura never came home, and interviews with theater employees that night stated that no one remembered seeing her pay for a movie. A current picture was shown to all theater employees. No one recognized her.

Then there was Sally Wright, whose dad had saved her life. Perry reread the interview that he'd gone over several times already, along with the other files he'd just browsed through. Sally confirmed the boy she was supposed to meet was Peter. He was a junior attending a high school in Overland Park, a town ten minutes away from Mission Hills. Although there were three Peters living in Overland Park who were juniors, the officer who'd interviewed each boy stated in the report that none of the boys knew Sally and they hadn't been chatting online with any girl who lived in Mission Hills.

Perry scrubbed his head with his fingers, reading the interviews with the Peters in Overland Park again. One of them was one hell of a good liar. Either that or whoever Peter was, he wasn't a junior in Overland Park.

The doors outside the "pit" opened and loud voices echoed off the walls. Barker and her partner, Richey, headed down the hallway toward the holding stall with several unique-looking characters, probably prostitutes, judging by the skimpy clothing on the two teenage girls who teetered on their incredibly high heels. The boy with them ranted the usual mantra about how they had picked him up by mistake.

Barker glanced his way and winked, holding the arm of one of the teenage girls, who also looked his way.

"Why couldn't we get picked up by a cop who looks like him?" the teenager asked Barker.

Lt. Ann Richey brought up the rear, rolling her eyes at him and grinning. He didn't return the smile. Instead he turned his attention to the screen. There were people in the world who lived with others continually dropping comments, either crude or meant as sincere praise, that let that person know they were sexually appealing, good-looking, eye candy. Perry had lived with comments like that most of his life, and as he sat there thinking about it, he realized he didn't usually bat an eye.

Nor did he give much thought to getting a date—if he wanted one. Maybe he did in his earlier days. Today dating didn't enter his mind, whether it was because most women seemed to be the same no matter how they looked or it had become more work than it was worth to cut through the red tape for a piece of ass, he wasn't sure. If there was quality in a lady, to get her to believe he was more than a piece of ass was too much work. The whole single, dating, "he's one hot piece of eye candy" thing got old ages ago.

But what if a person never lived life like that? Maybe they married young and never played the field. Or possibly they weren't physically appealing and so were never pursued. Their desire for that pursuit or for companionship wouldn't be any less.

Stretching his legs under his desk, he stared at the files, imagining an individual who craved attention, ached to be noticed, flirted with, and desired. The Internet would offer that means for satisfaction.

And if that wasn't enough?

"Penny for your thoughts," Ann said, and moved behind his chair.

Perry wasn't sure when she reached his desk. When she started massaging his shoulders he didn't flinch but moved to close the file he'd been reading.

"Trying to piece together the puzzle on those teenage disappearances." Ann didn't make it a question.

She was one of those ladies who weren't attractive but didn't realize it. She flirted easily and was outgoing, sometimes even friendly. Like most on the force, though, she was out for herself, although he hadn't known her to step on too many toes in the few years he'd worked with her.

"Yeah, I guess." Perry closed out the program on his computer, leaning forward and away from her touch.

Ann took her hands off him and moved to sit on the edge of his desk. Her dark hair held on to a few red highlights and he guessed that when she was younger it was a lot redder. The way it curled, she was probably accused more than once of being Little Orphan Annie. She crossed her muscular arms over her chest, causing what breasts she had to press against her uniform.

"I think we're dealing with the same perp on each of those cases, if you ask me." She chewed her lower lip and her gaze shifted over his face, making it look as though she sought his approval of her statement. "I mean, don't you think? All of them got out of the house and went to meet some guy who was talking to them on the computer."

"Not Olivia Brown," Perry pointed out. "She was out shopping with friends."

"The archives on her computer were loaded with chats she'd been having with a boy named Pete."

"That's not in the report." Perry leaned forward, reaching for his mouse. "Who told you that?"

"Stan went over to the Browns', right?" Goddard asked.

Ann turned around to acknowledge Goddard when Jane walked in. "That little fucking brat has an attorney already posting bail for him," she said, scowling as she joined Ann.

"Where the hell did he get money for a lawyer?" Ann asked, then turned to Perry. "And yeah. Stan told me about her archives. It's the same song and dance as the other girls."

"Apparently he's got a rich daddy." Jane stood next to Ann, facing Perry, and crossed her arms, matching Ann's pose. "We brainstorming on the missing girls?" she asked.

"Just comparing notes," Perry offered. "Anything else not on file going on with these cases?"

"It's not your case," Goddard reminded him.

"It's no one's case," Perry pointed out, keeping it cool. If there was more info running around, he wanted to hear it. "But we've got a serious situation going on here. If there are any other similarities, we all need to know about them and keep our eyes open."

"Since we're doing the open communication thing here," Jane said. "Did Rad stop by anyone else's house this weekend?"

"He went by your house, too?" Goddard asked, lowering his voice.

"He pay you a visit, Perry?" Ann asked.

"Yup. Sure did." Perry scrubbed his hair with his hand and stared at his computer screen. "I'm sure we'll find out why," he added, and although he was as curious as the rest of them as to why the Chief had paid each of them house calls, he wanted to keep the conversation on the teenage girls.

"It was weird," Ann mused before he could pick their brains further on the girls. "He was way too obvious about wanting to see what I was doing on my computer. I teased him about getting rusty with his detective skills and he got all bent out of shape."

Perry stared at her, focusing on one dark curl that twisted down the middle of her forehead. Rad was at his computer, too, when he returned to his den after getting a beer. Turning his attention to his monitor, he remembered the Chief asking him about who he was chatting with.

"Maybe he was just trying to find out who knew how to chat online." Goddard laughed.

Perry looked at Goddard, musing over the possibility. Rad wouldn't give a rat's ass about chatting online. But it was a very big issue with this case. What if Rad was taking on this case himself?

Perry scowled, staring across the room but not focusing on anything while he pondered the possibility. It pissed him off. This was a big case, high profile. That wasn't why he had asked for it. Perry had seen the pattern and wanted the creep off the streets. Every day he was allowed to chat with girls online was one more day that a teenager might lose her life. Rad didn't strike Perry as a media chaser. He wasn't out to earn brownie points. But if he took this case himself, that meant he didn't feel anyone in his department was competent enough to handle it.

That possibility irritated Perry even more. Everyone chatted around him, allowing the conversation to jump from topic to topic. Perry didn't pay any attention to any of them and it didn't appear to bother them that he ignored their bantering and jokes. He wanted to know why Rad had taken the case, and he wanted to know why the Chief felt no one else could handle it. Perry wasn't a conceited man, but damn it to hell. He could find the perp faster than Rad could. And maybe it was time to prove that he could, in spite of not being specifically assigned the case.

If anyone said good-bye when he stood and left the "pit," he didn't notice. Heading out to the copy room, Perry used the computer in there to pull up the files on Brown, Wright, and even Maura Reynolds, who had disappeared three months before. Her case matched the profile of the other two. He copied their files and then headed home. It was time to do some snooping online, and for that he'd use his own computer. The only way to catch this guy was to play in the perp's territory.

While at it, he would figure out what Rad was all about. But the more he pondered that matter, the more determined he got to dig deep into this case and show the Chief he was the man for the job.

Chapter 8

Kylie entered the FBI field office in Kansas City Monday morning. She wore comfortable jeans and a sleeveless blouse, and although they were not an extreme variation from the wardrobe she'd donned over the past few days and made a habit of wearing every time she worked an online predator case, it had felt good to wear her everyday clothes over the weekend.

After spending time in Dallas at her apartment, clearing her head of the case for a day or so while taking care of matters at home, she hurried into the field office, grabbing coffee and listening while a couple secretaries complained about Monday mornings sucking.

It had been good having lunch with her mother, chatting about things that were important to her. Deirdre Donovan, who went by "Dee," was aging before Kylie's eyes. Suddenly it seemed more important than it had in years past to give her mother more attention, to consent to conversations about Kylie's sister, and maybe to consider there was still mending to do. Kylie was more than willing to accept that her relationship with her parents was strained, but accepting that her relationship with her dead sister needed to be repaired, as her mother put it, was something Kylie hadn't considered.

She sure never thought she blamed her sister for dying. But when her mother accused Kylie of chasing after all of these online predators because she wanted to punish a man who'd never been caught, or possibly because deep inside

Kylie believed the man who had killed Karen might be one
of the men she arrested, that brought her pause. She didn't
like hearing that she was chasing ghosts and that nothing
she did would ever bring Karen back. And it bugged the
crap out of Kylie that she couldn't get it out of her head when
her mother told her to let Karen go and to start living with
the living and not with the dead.

No matter what her mother said, Kylie didn't believe she
was living on autopilot, simply rehashing the same crime in
her mind over and over again, determined to replay it until
finally she saved every teenage girl out there. Kylie knew
she wasn't Superwoman. She knew girls would be sexually molested, tortured, and killed no matter how hard she
worked. But she was good at what she did, very good. If she
wasn't, the Bureau wouldn't continually assign her to every
sexual predator case when local authorities contacted the
FBI for help, or when the agency determined a case merited
their intervention.

For a moment she felt her mother's arms around her, hugging her good-bye before she'd headed back up here from
Dallas. Her mother was so much smaller, almost frail. Kylie
had held her for several minutes, feeling the warmth and the
love. And in spite of not agreeing with everything she said,
Kylie had promised to visit again as soon as possible. She
meant it, too. This weekend had reminded her that her family wouldn't be around forever. Someday she would have to
cope with losing more family members, and she wanted to
spend every minute she could spare enjoying time with both
of her parents before that day happened.

"Kylie, good, you're here." John Athey ran his fingers
down his tie as he stood, walking around the table and ex-
tending his hand to Kylie when she paused in the doorway to
the briefing room. He patted her arm, a fatherly gesture, instead of shaking her hand.

"I hope I'm not late." She knew she wasn't although there
were already several men sitting around the rectangular
table in the meeting room. "There was construction all along
the highway this morning."

"This town is always like that," John said. "And no, you aren't late at all. Let me introduce you. You already know Paul, of course."

"Yes." She smiled at Paul, who nursed a hot cup of coffee.

"This is the chief of police for Mission Hills. Murphy Radisson, this is Special Agent Kylie Donovan. While here, she's working undercover as 'Kylie Dover.' "

The chief of police was a large man, who stood slowly from the other side of the table and extended his hand. "It's a real pleasure to meet you, Ms. Donovan," he said in a deep voice.

Kylie took his hand, feeling his warm, strong calloused fingers grip hers in a firm handshake. "Please, call me Kylie," she insisted. "And it's good to meet you, too, Chief Radisson. I look forward to discussing this case with you."

"Which is why we're here," John said.

"Call me Rad," the Chief said, playing old school and sitting when Kylie did. He placed his hands, palms down, on two stacks of manila file folders. "And I appreciate your coming to Kansas City to help us out on this case, Kylie." He turned his attention to Paul and John. "I've gathered additional information since I first sent over what we had so far on this case."

His knuckles were large and he didn't wear a wedding ring. There wasn't even an indentation where a ring usually would be. He was either a confirmed bachelor or too much of a man to be bothered with such trivial jewelry as a band on his finger to confirm his love to one woman. Kylie would put him somewhere around fifty, in good shape, although a bit weathered around the edges. She wondered what his opinion of Perry was, and mulled over whether or not to bring up meeting with his nieces and having them, as well as him, over to her house for pizza last Friday.

She would hear the Chief out and then decide what information she would offer. Getting comfortable in her seat, she pulled her notebook out and opened it. The first thing that caught her eye in her scribbled notes was the block letters

PETETAKESU. He'd been silent all weekend, which meant he was either on the prowl or unable to use a computer without getting caught over the weekend.

"We're concerned with the information we have so far that our perp might be a city employee," Paul began, speaking up as he put down his coffee cup. He opened the laptop in front of him and stared at it while continuing to talk. "More to the point, we could be looking at our perp being one of your cops."

Rad's expression hardened and he looked angry enough to attack, but when he spoke his tone was as calm as it had been a moment ago during introductions. "I checked out each of my officers over the weekend. I got a look at most of their computers and several of them were chatting on them when I stopped by. Which doesn't prove shit."

"It shows you're willing to cooperate," Kylie said, reassuring him.

"We've got several ISPs," Paul said slowly. "The alleged boy that Olivia Brown and Sally Wright were chatting with online used different computers at different times during their chats. None of them were home computers, and most were public computers. But with Olivia Brown," he continued, and then paused, tapping keys on his laptop and then looking back up wide-eyed, excitement making his eyes bright. "On two different days Peter uses a computer that is located inside your police station."

"When? What days?" Rad snapped.

Paul looked down at his laptop. "March third, ten thirty A.M. He spoke to her on her cell phone. We've got a specific address on the computer that sent the messages to Brown." Paul jotted something down on a piece of notepaper and then slid it across the table to the Chief. "Confirm with your own IT department. Here's the IP address."

Kylie saw the numbers scribbled on the piece of paper and an uncomfortable knot tightened in her gut. "How strict are you on your officers only using their own computers?"

"Not everyone has their own computer," Rad said, staring at the paper as if he could decipher the numbers and determine which computer it was in his department. "But we're going to implement policy effective immediately stating no one can use anyone's computer without my personal consent."

"Where were the other computers located?" Kylie asked Paul.

"We've got documented online chats dating back to last October," Paul said, making eye contact with each of them and then resting his intense gaze on Kylie. "He used the library, several different coffee shops, and a few bookstores." Paul pushed a few more keys on his laptop and then pushed his chair away from the table. "I'll give you a printout so you'll have potential locations. But since our guy isn't using the same computer twice, it's like trying to track a guy who is using a pay phone. We don't know where he's going to be next."

Paul stood and left the room. When he returned he gave Kylie a printout of different businesses. Most were places she hadn't been to yet, but then she'd focused on the teenage hangouts so far. Unlike other sexual predators she'd hunted down in previous cases, apparently this perp didn't care where his prey hung out. He focused on public locations with semi-private computers to hunt for his next victim.

"Check out those locations," John told Kylie, and tapped his ballpoint pen against his legal pad. He glanced at her over his glasses, the top button of his white shirt undone and his tie loose and slightly crooked. He made it look as if it were Friday afternoon instead of Monday morning. "You have anything for us so far?"

Everyone watched while her gaze dropped to the bold letters in her notebook—*PETETAKESU*. "I've spent this past week in the shopping malls, the bowling alley, and a few other local hangouts," she began, not looking up. Something told her not to let go of the screen name she'd made contact with. She didn't like the knot that tightened in her gut, but years of working case after case had taught her to pay attention to her physical reactions to her surroundings, even when she didn't understand the message. "My focus has been where these kids spend their time socializing and I've gotten to know a few of them already."

"Who have you gotten to know?" Rad asked.

"Just a handful of kids." She decided to be evasive. "I'm using the cover of being a cultural anthropologist working on my master's and doing a thesis on teenage interaction."

The others nodded, obviously satisfied with her story. Each of them played their own part in capturing this guy and Kylie knew none of them cared about details from her, unless it was about a bust.

"It's shocking as hell how easily they will give you their online screen names," she added, deciding to show them she'd accomplished something this past week.

"Not really," Rad said. He focused on her with gray eyes that seemed to be searching, trying to learn as much as possible about her. His focus wasn't leery, but at the same time she saw little trust. He was the typical jaded cop, years on the force making it impossible for him to accept anyone for who they were without analyzing them first. "Kids these days live on computers. It's becoming incredibly common, and the accepted norm, for people, not just children, to meet online and start dating. Smoke-filled bars that once were meat markets are becoming a thing of the past."

"And good riddance," she said, smiling easily at him. Then inching her chair backward, she glanced over at John. "We don't have a clue what Peter looks like, do we?"

"The girl who went to meet the boy who was supposed to be from Topeka," Rad began, and looked down at one of the files he'd spread out in front of him while blowing out a breath. He ran thick fingers over closely shaved gray hair and didn't look up when he continued speaking. "Sally Wright, that was her name. Her father, Charles Wright, reported seeing a Caucasian male get out of a car and then jump back into it when he approached his daughter."

"I saw that," Kylie said. "But he couldn't give a solid ID. We don't know what he was driving?"

"Nope." Rad raised his gaze to her, his brow wrinkling,

giving his face the look of a bulldog. "That's all we've got so far."

Kylie nodded. It was nothing to go on. Pushing her chair back farther, she gathered her notes and shoved them into her briefcase.

"Well, I've got a job to do," she said, anxious to get out of there.

"Keep me posted daily on what you do," John told her.

She didn't answer to him, but it was a courtesy she was expected to give the local agency. Nodding once, "Of course," she said, as she lifted her strap to her briefcase over her shoulder and headed toward the door.

"And Kylie," John said. "Remember, until we narrow this down further, you can't rely on the cops in the area."

She noticed Rad's expression tighten, his face pinch with aggravation, but he didn't say anything. There wasn't anything worse than the possibility of someone close to you, or an individual whom you've trusted over the years, turning out to be a criminal. And a child molester—the worse kind.

"Got it," she said, and headed out the door.

Stopping at the first Starbucks she spotted, she spent time on her computer using MapQuest to locate each of the businesses her perp used. Mission Hills wasn't a big town, although it ran into other suburbs surrounding Kansas City. Sitting in her car, sipping on her coffee, she used her wireless printer from her trunk and quickly printed directions to help her around town. Today she wouldn't play the teenage scene but would instead focus on every location with public computers, starting with the ones their perp had already used. Something told her she wasn't dealing with an idiot. She was probably miles behind her guy and she seriously doubted he'd retrace his steps. But this guy had several months on her if he was responsible for the deaths of all the girls she had files on. His level of comfort would be pretty high right now. Quite possibly, if he had found a comfortable location and was content with the knowledge that he wasn't being tracked, he would use a computer more than once to set up a meeting with his next prey. If she was lucky, his next "victim" would be her.

Her cell phone rang as she pulled into the parking lot of a locally owned bookstore and coffeehouse. She parked, focusing on the squad car idling along the curb by the entrance, as she answered her phone.

"Hello," she said, adjusting her earpiece and then taking in the busy-looking bookstore.

"Peter struck again."

"Huh?" She looked down at the number on her phone.

"It's Paul. Don't even try to keep up with all of the numbers down here," he said, as if he could see what she was doing at that moment. Computer geeks made her nervous. For all she knew, he very well could see what she was doing. "PD just got a call in at Raney's. It's three blocks north of you."

"You can see me," she accused, and glared at the navigator on her dash that stared ominously back at her with its one blank eye. "What's the call?"

"A fifteen-year-old female," he began.

Kylie looked up when Perry hurried around the squad car and got in on the driver's side. Another man climbed in on the passenger side and the car pulled away from the curb.

"Apparently a Raney's employee found her when he was collapsing boxes in the Dumpster."

"Found her?" Kylie's stomach twisted.

Perry drove past her, pinning her with a possessive stare that he held her with until he was forced to look ahead and focus on his driving. Chills rushed over her at the same time that a sickening sensation grew in her gut.

"Yup. Police are arriving on the scene now. I'll have a name here in a few moments."

Kylie pondered continuing with her project of checking out the locations on her list or heading over to Raney's.

"Raney's is a grocery store?" she confirmed, pretty sure that was the name of the store she'd driven past a few times since she'd been here.

"Yup. It's at Sixty-second and Indian Lane. I'll have more

details for you here in a few." He barely paused before adding, "You're practically across the street right now."

"I'm going to check out this bookstore first. Maybe our Peter enjoys watching his victims being discovered," she added. "Then I'll head over and check out the crime scene."

"Are you going to let the cops see you?" Paul asked.

Kylie wouldn't ask him if he had watched Perry and her in her house last week. She wasn't sure she wanted to hear the answer. "I'll wait and see how much of a crowd of spectators forms around the scene. Call me back when you have more info."

There were three public computers inside the bookstore and no one was on any of them. After spending a few minutes browsing on the side of the store where windows offered her a view of the grocery store across the street, and taking in the other customers in the store, Kylie decided Peter probably wasn't in the store. The only guy there worked behind the counter and didn't pay any attention to the police cars that entered the busy parking lot across the street. She didn't rule out the possibility that Peter could be a woman, but the two customers in the store were intent on browsing through books. Kylie nodded at the salesclerk, who gave her a half-interested nod in return, then headed back to her car.

It wasn't the first time Kylie had worked under distracted circumstances. Paul hadn't called back, and Perry's intense look was burned into her mind. Evidence was mounting in favor of a cop being Peter. She wanted those ISPs confirmed and fingered her phone inside her purse when she slid into her car. What if Perry was Peter?

Perry's obsessive nature, his dominant behavior, and the way he was intent on knowing what she was doing would be justified if he believed she might be trailing him. But, if PETETAKESU was her perp, he'd talked to her online as Perry had knocked on her door.

Dragging her fingers through her hair, she blew out an exasperated breath. "You'll know soon enough," she told herself, and headed out of the parking lot to the grocery store across the street.

There were several cop cars, an ambulance, and obvious unmarked vehicles parked alongside the grocery store. A handful of civilians stood alongside the building as well, curiosity besting them as they watched the crime scene in action.

She decided to call Paul instead of waiting for him to call her when she pulled into the busy grocery store parking lot. "Paul Hernandez, please," she told the receptionist who answered. "This is Special Agent Kylie Dover," she added, not wanting to be on hold long. "It's important."

Paul snickered when he came on the line. "It's always important or you wouldn't be calling me," he said, a smile in his voice. "And I don't have any more information for you."

"That's cool. Let me know as soon as you do," she told him as she parked in the middle of the parking lot in front of the grocery store, which was on a nice side of town. "I really want those ISPs confirmed at the police station. Any way you can take care of that and not wait for the Chief to get us the info?"

"John has me working on another project, but I'll see what I can do for you," Paul said.

"I appreciate it." Kylie stared out her window at the scene in front of her.

Yellow tape already secured off the crime scene on the back side of the building. From where she parked she could partially see the activity going on behind the store. But she didn't see Perry or any other officers.

"I'm at Raney's."

"Why doesn't that surprise me?"

"I didn't want the Chief to know this morning, but last week I had a few teenagers over for pizza and plugged them for information on the cases. The girls' uncle is Lieutenant Perry Flynn."

There was silence on the line only for a brief moment. "One of the cops here in town?" Paul guessed.

"Yup."

"And the pizza party was purely business?"

"What the hell kind of question is that?" she snapped.

"So, it wasn't," he decided, that damn smile still obvious in his jovial tone.

"Hernandez," she growled, getting out and leaning against her car as she studied the scene predominantly hidden by the brick and mortar building and emergency vehicles. "Teenage girls are disappearing and being murdered."

"I'm very aware of that," he interrupted, the smile no longer in his tone. "I've also heard of Lieutenant Flynn."

"You have?" She didn't mean for the catch to sound in her words, or for her tone to turn raspy. There was something about Perry, though, something she didn't have a label for yet. Maybe it wasn't anything more than incredible sex appeal and a dominating nature that seriously turned her on. And maybe he turned her on because he bordered on dangerous. If he were her guy, though, "danger" didn't begin to describe him.

"He's handled some high-profile cases here in town over the years. Word is he's quite the womanizer, which, if it's any consolation, would make him less of a candidate to be Peter."

She understood Paul's line of thought, the simple premise being that a man who could get it easily wasn't as likely to be a serial rapist, although she forced herself to accept that wasn't always the case. People with sick minds came in all shapes and sizes.

"I'm not ruling out anyone this early in the game," she told Paul. "I don't have any established profiles yet. But I need them not only on Peter, but also on the local law. So, I'm headed over to this scene and going to play the curious onlooker. See what I can find out."

"I'll call you as soon as I have more info." Paul's tone remained serious. "Watch your ass."

"Always." She said good-bye and snapped her phone shut, then pushed away from her car.

Kylie wouldn't try counting how many times she'd walked along this side of a crime scene, playing the curious bystander, while analyzing the scene from a different angle than those on the other side of the tape. She walked around those who stood alongside the building, trying to learn what was going on, and stopped when she reached the back side.

Four officers in uniform moved around the Dumpster behind the store. Kylie stared at the outline drawn on the ground, where the body was found. The ambulance hadn't left yet, but she figured the body was already inside. She would get a good look at the girl down at the morgue.

Perry and the Mexican man with him, who she guessed might be his partner, weren't in uniform. The two of them stood talking to three store employees along with two other men and a woman who possibly were also store employees, maybe management.

Kylie focused her attention on the cops in uniform, two men and two women. They moved around the crime scene, snapping pictures, talking among themselves, and taking in all the details. Their actions were by the book, which made it easier to follow what they did. If anything, that spoke highly of their department, and she understood better why the Chief got his dander up so easily when it was suggested that one of his own could be their perp. Kylie noted a well-trained unit, recording and documenting a terrible crime. She also noted that none of them appeared to show any peculiar behavior.

Tingles raced over her flesh the moment Perry spotted her. His dark, ominous gaze damn near made her shiver in spite of the warm sunlight on her back. He looked away first, saying something when one of the store employees finished speaking. Kylie edged around the people standing around her, paying attention to their comments and speculation but not hearing anything suspicious. Then backing away from the crowd of spectators, she took in the crowd, studying each face and putting it to memory. Everyone looked horrified and disgusted.

Her cell phone rang and Kylie turned toward her car when an officer ordered the onlookers to disperse. She walked faster, answering as she reached her car.

"Kylie, it's Paul."

"What do you got?" she asked, glancing over her shoulder and then unlocking her car.

"Female, age fifteen, student at Holy Mary's, a private high school in Mission Hills. Her name was Kathleen Long." He continued with her address, parents' info, and then paused. "I'll e-mail all of this to you. Obviously this is pending the autopsy, but the immediate diagnosis was rape and sodomy. It sounds as if she was pretty beaten up. They don't have a clue why her body was there."

"Was she dead before she was put there?" Kylie asked, knowing Paul wouldn't know, but it was the first question that came to mind.

"I'm sure our Chief will have those answers for us soon."

"You know, you could have filmed that crime scene for a textbook demonstration video," Kylie commented, moving behind her wheel and closing the car door. "I didn't notice any odd behavior from any officer working just now."

"That's good to know," Paul said.

"Yeah."

The ambulance left and another unmarked car followed. Kylie started her engine but kept her fingers on the keys when Perry drove toward her. The squad car stopped, taking two stalls when he put it in park at an angle. He got out of the car, leaving his partner in the passenger seat, and approached her with long, determined strides. It crossed her mind to lock the doors the second before he reached for the door handle and yanked her car door open. Kylie hung up her cell and tossed it to her passenger seat just as strong fingers wrapped around her arm and lifted her out of the car.

"What did I tell you about playing private detective?" Perry growled. He looked pissed, but there was something else smoldering in that dark gaze that heated her insides to a dangerous level so quickly that she couldn't think of a good answer. "This isn't a game."

"I'm not playing." Her voice cracked when she spoke and she cleared her throat, daring to stare him down in spite of his intimidating glare. "What happened to her?" she asked before she could stop herself. For a moment he looked as though he would growl. A small muscle twitched along his jaw next to that hairline scar of his. "I was across the street. You saw me. I was curious just like everyone else," she added quickly.

"Someone raped a young girl and beat her so badly that it will be hard for her family to recognize her, I'm sure," Perry told her, his voice rough with emotion while his gaze moved slowly across her face. "We're not positive yet, but it appears she collapsed where she was found and possibly laid there for a few hours before she died."

Kylie saw that he told her these details to terrify her. He didn't speak as one professional would to another. But then, he didn't see her as a professional. She bit back the foul taste of frustration that she couldn't question him the way she wanted, and instead found herself staring at his mouth. If he had killed Kathleen Long, describing how she died, what was done to her, might possibly get him off as much as the act of raping and sodomizing her had. That would make him one hell of a despicable man, and Kylie wondered for a moment if she'd become too jaded from so many crime scenes, so many deaths.

"Who would do something like that to a child?" Kylie heard her mother's words, arriving in her mind at a rather inopportune moment. If she were searching for her sister's murderer, she'd searched for too long. Because as she stared at Perry, at his hardened, brooding expression, fire ignited inside her even when she reminded herself she could be staring at a killer.

"A sick and dangerous person."

"Obviously."

"Why are you here?" he asked again, and let go of her arm. Instead of stepping back, though, he touched her neck and pushed under her chin with his thumb, forcing her to tilt her head back and stare more directly into his eyes. "This isn't the closest grocery store to your house. Tell me the truth, Kylie."

"I already told you. I was across the street at the bookstore," she told him honestly. "I saw you head over here. I saw the lights and the crowd and was curious," she said, trying to shift her attention past him to see who might be watching them, other than his partner. She hoped Chief Radisson still wasn't on scene.

His fingers tightened around her neck until she couldn't suck in a breath. Staring up at Perry, unable to swallow, she grabbed his hand, scratching to get her fingers between his and her flesh.

"Promise me that's the last lie you'll tell me," he growled, and released his grip but moved so that his lips brushed over hers. "I'd rather hear that you don't want to tell me than hear a lie."

"What makes you think I'm lying?" she asked, feeling the roughness of his unshaven face under his lower lip. "I saw you and I followed you."

"Do you always chase flashing lights?" This time, instead of making her come up with an answer to a ridiculous question, his fingers tangled in her hair and he kissed her.

He parted her lips with his tongue and dipped inside, filling her and turning her world sideways. With her eyes closed she still sensed his strength, incredible domination, and a predatory possessiveness. His hands moved to her back, and strong arms wrapped around her, becoming her world.

Kylie had never known a man who could so easily sweep her off her feet and demand her submission. Worse yet, his style, technique, made it damn simple to let go, allow him the control he demanded. Even though her eyes were closed, she sensed his aggressive, dominating, and predatory possessive nature seeping deeper inside her, wrapping around her. If she didn't break the kiss, he'd be holding her up, because her legs were damn near giving out under her.

His hands moved over her back, and powerful arms enclosed her tighter. He pinned her with muscle, strong like steel. Her insides quickened, his sensuality creating a heat that burned deep in her womb. It was a fire she knew wouldn't simmer out anytime soon.

And that sucked. As easy as it would be to let go, there

wasn't any way she could let down her resistance. Years of training barely allowed her to hold on to her resolve. But something deeper, engrained in her soul, let out a warning. Let go, and she'd never be able to return to where she stood right now. In his arms or not, Kylie was still in control. She had to be.

Kylie couldn't let go of the hard, cold fact that Perry could be her killer.

Turning her head, she broke the kiss and sucked in a breath. She filled her lungs with the smell and taste of Perry Flynn. A mixture of danger and domination made for an alluring and way too tempting combination. One that would destroy her if she allowed it.

"Your partner is waiting for you." She tried sliding away from him.

Perry straightened but gripped her arms, refusing to let her move out from between him and her car. "I'll be at your house at five this evening. We'll talk more then."

"Talk?" She dared him with a sharp gaze. It was imperative that he see, right now, that she wasn't an idiot, and although letting him see how strong she really was might not be her best move at the moment, staring him down was impossible not to do. "If I'm done by five, I'll be there."

"We'll talk, and anything else you want to show me, you can." He leaned forward and brushed his lips over hers, sealing his words with a promise that surged through her like an electrical current. "And you'll be there."

Chapter 9

Perry headed out of the station around six. It didn't bother him that he wasn't at Kylie's at five. She wouldn't have been there. He saw it in her eyes after he kissed her. Kylie felt power in knowing she held on to some sense of control in her mind. The way she stared at him, determination and resolve lining her pretty face, gave him more insight into her nature than she probably intended for him to see.

"We should have autopsy results tomorrow," Rad said, catching up with Perry in the parking lot. The worry lines were deeper than usual around his eyes. "This makes girl number four."

"We'll get him." Perry wouldn't bother pitching for the case. Whatever Rad's agenda, Perry knew what he needed to do to work the case, and he had every intention of doing it. "That autopsy will hopefully give us more on our perp. We're building a psychological profile and that's more than we had yesterday."

"No more deaths," Rad insisted, as if Perry could make the call on that one.

But he nodded once and turned toward his Jeep. "Works for me." Then glancing at Rad, Perry decided to suggest, since he hadn't heard that anyone had done it yet. "I'll interview the family and her friends."

Rad studied him with shrewd gray eyes. There was something more in Rad's attentive stare than what Perry normally saw. It almost looked like hesitation or lack of trust.

He was a pretty good judge of character but knew he was as tired as Rad probably was. And what Perry saw could be the exhaustion, mental and physical, that he felt as well. "O-kay," Rad said slowly, drawing out the one word. Rad seriously hesitated, but he gave his consent.

Perry didn't blink. Hiding his surprise wasn't easy. Rad hadn't been himself the past day or two. But having a rapist in town was enough to wear on anyone's convictions. And one preying on teenage girls made the situation even more draining. They couldn't waste one moment. Perry's girls moved in the same circles as the victims who had been abducted, beaten and tortured, and then killed had moved in. No one would touch his nieces. No one!

"I'll contact the family tonight for a list of her friends." Turning to his car, he parted ways with the Chief without saying good-bye. Whatever had crawled up Rad's ass, Perry wouldn't challenge it. Not tonight. He had Rad's permission to pursue the investigation and that was what Perry would do.

When he headed across town half an hour later, after visiting with the Longs, the list of numbers he needed to contact was already on his clipboard next to him. Ramos had headed home to have dinner with his mother. A cop didn't get to do that enough and Perry would give his partner the next hour or so before calling him. Rad was all over them all of a sudden to work together. As well, the new policy about logging in with passwords every time they used a computer so that everyone's actions online would be kept track of bugged Perry, too. It appeared there was suspicion in the department over something, which would also explain the wariness Perry was certain he saw in Rad's eyes earlier.

There was something else that annoyed the crap out of Perry and had since he saw Kathleen Long lying crumpled behind the Dumpster earlier this afternoon. He wasn't sure if she was one of his nieces' friends, but the young girl looked familiar. Her parents had shown him pictures of a very pretty girl, who was in the same grade as Dani.

The image of the child, and yes, damn it, a fifteen-year-old girl was a child, lying on the ground, abused to the point of death, curdled his stomach. It also pissed him off. That teenage girl would never know the wonders of life, of adulthood, of falling in love, going to college, getting married, having a family and a good job. All of that was robbed from her by a motherfucker Perry couldn't wait to get his hands on.

He turned onto the street where Kylie lived and slowed in front of her house. Parking, he bounded up the sidewalk toward her house, trying to put the case out of his mind for a few minutes at least while he spoke to Kylie.

He walked past her green hybrid and touched her hood. It was warm. She hadn't been home long. He wondered where she'd been as he climbed the one step and then stood at her front door, rapping his knuckles against it.

Kylie was quickly making a habit of not answering her door right away when he knocked. It could be that she did it on purpose to get under his skin. Something told him that she didn't think about him enough for that. He stepped away from the front door, glancing both ways at the front of the house, and then headed away from the drive, taking in the outside of her home and the windows.

Blinds were closed over each window. The white siding was slightly dirty but in good shape. The small bushes along the house had been trimmed back, probably a landlord's doing before she moved in. She hadn't said, but he put money on the fact that she hadn't lived here long at all. Her house barely looked lived in and wasn't homey. Kylie struck him as the kind of woman who would make a place her own given time. It was part of her need to feel in charge of her life.

Power lines extended from the street pole to the house, and it looked like someone, at some point, had drilled cable into the house to accommodate different rooms. Perry turned slowly toward the front door and squinted, noting a small wire under the roof overhang just above the door. Walking closer, he followed the wire with his eyes to where it disappeared inside the home. He traveled the length of it, looking up as he moved closer, and then stopped, gawking at the small, barely noticeable camera that was secured at the edge of the overhang.

"Fuck me running," he muttered under his breath, moving past it to the front door and paying close attention to every detail of the rest of the house. "I wouldn't have guessed this about you."

He made a show of knocking on the door again, although there really wasn't any point. Kylie knew he was out here, knew it without looking through her peephole. She had her entire home wired with some incredibly expensive-looking spy equipment. Studying the back side of the tiny camera, noting that it didn't move but remained focused on the side of the home he'd just walked down, he turned around slowly, prickles attacking his spine, as he already felt the sensation that he was being watched carefully.

"There you are," he whispered, spotting the other camera down the length of the house, just underneath the guttering. "Damn."

He ran his hand over his hair, taking this new bit of information in about Kylie, and turned his attention to the doorknob when the lock inside clicked.

The door opened and he stared at her flushed face. Sleep had made her eyes slightly puffy and her lips were full, moist, and reminded him of how much he enjoyed kissing them. But it was her hair, tousled and turning in small waves that caressed her slender nape, that made him instantly hard.

"You're late," she murmured, her voice scratchy, further proof that possibly she hadn't been inside watching him but instead asleep.

"You weren't here at five," he said, and knew instantly by the slight twitch of her lips that he was right.

She licked them and then raised her baby blues to his eyes, looking a lot more alert than she did a moment before.

"And I can't stay," he added.

"What do you have to do?" The scratchiness in her voice was gone and she moved around her door, pulling it open farther so he could enter.

Her curiosity didn't surprise him. He knew he'd pegged her right when he'd listened to her question his nieces. Possibly she was working on a thesis. But there was another side of her, a side that craved action, adventure, and even a mystery. More than likely when she had picked up on teenage girls being abducted and showing up dead she decided to become a private detective.

His protective instincts kicked into overdrive as he stepped inside and let his gaze drop to the swell of her breasts, accentuated by how her oversized T-shirt draped over them. The fact that she didn't wear a bra and if she had shorts on underneath the large shirt they weren't visible made it damn hard to keep his cock from getting hard as a rock. Her long bare, slender legs and no shoes or socks somehow made her even sexier.

"Work," he said, knowing not elaborating bugged the crap out of her.

"What are you working on?" She combed her blonde hair with her fingers and pulled her attention from him, looking into her home.

Her living room looked exactly like it did the last time he was here. Not as much as a cup on the coffee table, pillows in the corner on each end of the couch, and no media on anywhere. She spent all of her time back in her bedroom, and probably in that middle room she kept locked. He took a moment to glance toward her hallway, betting that room probably held the equipment for those cameras outside. No wonder she kept it locked.

"I get to go talk to the family of the young girl we found earlier today."

"Oh." Pain registered on Kylie's face as if she actually knew what it was like to talk to parents of a child who'd just died. "Do you want something to drink before you go?"

"No time right now." He looked down the hall. Both bedroom doors were open. "I stopped by for this."

Kylie fascinated him, sexually and otherwise. There really wasn't room in his life for any kind of serious, long-term relationship, but he was compelled to pull her in close, tighten the reins he decided needed to be put on her, and keep a close eye on her.

"What?" she started to ask, returning her attention to him.

He didn't let her ask anything else. Grabbing her arms, he pulled her to him and then attacked her mouth with savage need that unleashed the moment his fingers moved over her flesh.

She cried out into his mouth, which brought out even more of a craving to possess her, have her, taste every inch of her warm, sensual body.

Perry cupped her ass, enjoying the soft curve and smooth, round shape of it, and lifted her against him, deepening the kiss. Kylie dragged her nails down his chest, not holding on but definitely not pushing him away, either.

But when she opened to him, parting her lips and tilting her head to give him full access to the moist heat surrounding her feisty little tongue, a growl tore through him that he didn't anticipate.

Kylie didn't do anything special to try to lure him in, which was part of her appeal. Her oversized T-shirt and bare legs and feet made just about the sexiest picture he'd ever seen. He pictured her coming home, stripping down, and then crashing without a care in the world about her appearance. Along with that, as he moved his hands over her rear it became apparent that she wasn't wearing anything underneath. And she knew he would be coming over.

Damn.

"You can't," Kylie whimpered, turning her head but leaving it tilted perfectly with an arch that was an open invitation to feast.

"Can't what?" he growled, raking his teeth over her skin and feeling her shiver against him. Lifting her shirt, he ran his hands over her bare ass and then enjoyed the way her curves ended at her slender waist.

"What can't I do, Kylie?" he asked again, and nipped her flesh at her collarbone.

Her breath caught, stifling a small cry as she dug in with

fingernails that pinched his skin through his shirt. "This," she hissed.

Perry dragged his fingers up the sides of her body, feeling her ribs as she arched farther against him. If she was trying to tell him no, she was doing a damn lousy job of it. And although it crossed his mind to lift her into his arms, head down the hallway to her room, he wouldn't push matters. One, she was trying to tell him to stop even though she didn't want him to any more than he did. And two, he would wait to fuck her when he had time to enjoy everything he knew she had to offer him. He lifted his head and caught her with her head tilted, her eyes closed, and soft strands of blonde hair draping over the side of her face. Cupping her breasts, he ran his thumbs over her nipples, which were hard like pebbles. His cock fought against the constraints of his jeans while all blood drained from his brain.

Damn it. She'd told him no.

"I have a feeling you're going to be a lot better at making love than you are at saying no."

Her eyes snapped open and those bright blue eyes flashed with emotions that made them glow. A mixture of lust and defiance created the perfect shade. Something else he put to memory as he reluctantly let his hands slide down her shirt.

"I was trying to be nice," she said, and pressed those moist, pouty lips of hers into a firm line.

"To you, or to me?" he asked, and tapped her nose before she could swat his hand away and turn from him.

She let out a loud sigh. "Perry."

He didn't want to listen to her lie to him and tell him she wasn't interested. "What did I tell you about lying?" he growled, and decided he knew how to change the subject.

With her back still to him, he headed down her hallway.

"No!" she yelled, and shocked the shit out of him when she raced faster than he thought she would.

Kylie flew around him, pushing him hard, so that he almost fell against the wall. Grabbing the door to the middle room, she yanked it closed with enough force to shake the house.

"You need to leave," she said with enough conviction that if she'd spoken like that when he'd kissed her his dick would have gone limp.

"I know," he said, not fazed by the sudden hard, almost cold look she gave him. The sensual creature he'd caressed a moment before was now all business. Possibly she protected her work, but more than that, he now believed she didn't want him seeing the elaborate camera system she'd rigged around her house. And if she was digging deep into the case of the teenage girls being abducted, it didn't surprise him if that created a bit of paranoia in her. "But I'm coming back."

He turned before she could say anything, or tell him no, and headed toward the door. "It will be a couple hours possibly, but when I do, I'd love for you to show me that surveillance equipment you've got set up around your house."

Perry opened the door and let himself out quickly, closing it behind him, and regretted that he couldn't have enjoyed the expression that he knew was on her face right now.

Kylie pressed her hand against her hallway wall. The coolness of it did little to soothe the fire burning inside her, not just from that damn kiss but also from his parting words.

"Fuck you, Perry," she snapped, hitting the wall and pulling her hand away when her palm stung from the frustrated slap.

Heading to the front door, she locked it and turned around, staring at her living room. Perry's interest was physical. Damn, was it physical. If he came back later tonight she would be in trouble. Her interest and desire were as strong as his.

And if he was her killer?

"He's coming back," she said, knowing it was true. Just the thought of it created a heat inside her that swelled quickly until the moist flesh between her legs pulsed feverishly. "Shit," she hissed, and combed her hair out of her face with her fingers.

Returning to the middle bedroom, she pushed open the door, chastising herself for forgetting to lock it. She'd only put her head on her pillow for a minute and had been out like a light in no time. But she was awake now.

Paul had told her Perry had a good track record as a cop. From what she'd seen when she watched several officers from his force working that crime scene, they were all well trained. It was time to dig deeper, learn more about every police officer, and every other employee, who worked at the station.

"It's going to be a night at the computer," she conceded, still talking to herself as she moved the mouse across the mouse pad and cleared the screen. Then plopping down in her chair, she stared at the chat box that had appeared since she'd taken her nap.

You there? The message was from PeteTakesU.

The message came in half an hour ago. If Perry had made it into this room and to her computer, out of curiosity about her thesis and research, he would have seen this message. Also, this was the second time he'd shown up at her house when a message had appeared on her computer, which meant he couldn't have sent them, not unless he was incredibly good at sending messages from his phone while walking. The chat program she was using would have told her if the message came from a phone though, and it didn't. Wherever PeteTakesU was, he was on a home computer. If he was even her guy. If he was her guy, then Perry was innocent.

"It's time to find out," she said out loud, and then pulled up the buddy list that showed PeteTakesU was online but idle. She typed a message: *I'm here now*, and clicked "send."

She scrubbed her head furiously with her fingernails, scratching her scalp and glaring at her knees as she pressed them together. Teenage girls were dying, another one earlier today, and it was Kylie's job to stop the perpetrator before someone else's daughter lost her life. It was more than Kylie's job, it was her responsibility, no one else's, to put an end to this monster's madness.

The pressure of her job didn't bother her. Taking the heat for another death was something she would live with. But slipping because a cop was too damn sexy for his own good wasn't something she could live with. Jumping up from her desk, she moved through her home, making sure all lights were out, doors and windows securely locked, and the alarm was turned on. She flipped on the light that would shine outside the front door and make it easier to see anyone approaching her home through the cameras.

Cameras that obviously Perry had noticed. She blew out a breath, wondering whether a shower would do her any good or if running soap over her body and touching herself would only increase the fire smoldering deep inside her that refused to go out.

She paused in her hallway, torn between showering and returning to the computer to work. "You know you want to shower for when he returns." Which was argument enough not to shower. There was work to do, and she'd be damned if she wasted time primping for a man just because he created sensations inside her that she hadn't felt in years, if ever.

Her computer chimed and she hurried into the computer room, sliding into her chair. PeteTakesU had answered her. She stared at the bold, black font, pursing her lips together while her heart started beating quickly.

I know who you are.

The thin-line cursor blinked eagerly in the response box while she focused on the words until her eyes burned. Blinking several times, she sucked in a breath. Her fingers posed over the keyboards. Her heart raced in her chest while adrenaline pumped through her and made her palms wet. This was what she did, what she was known for. Now was the time to narrow down her list of suspects, starting with PeteTakesU.

She needed the perfect, saucy, no-cares-in-the-world response. It was time to clear her head of everything in her world and think like a teenager. It was time to find out if PeteTakesU was her killer.

Who are you? she typed, and clicked "send."

Pete Rubble.

As in the Flintstones? she typed.

You know old cartoons, too?

She smiled. "If you're my guy, you're quick." Well, she was quick, too.

Kylie clicked on the large smiley-face emoticon and then clicked "send." This was how it was done. This was how the perp snared his victims. Pick a comfortable topic, start chatting, and the unsuspecting victim would relax until she didn't feel like she was talking to a stranger anymore. Kylie entered into the mind of her killer, thinking like he would, directing the conversation the way he would. She could make him relax and unsuspecting, too.

You are prettier than any girl in my school.

She stared at the next message, contemplating her best response so he would ask her to meet him. The sooner she knew whether he was a teenager or not, the better.

Thank you. What do you look like? She clicked "send" but then quickly typed: *What school do you go to?*

I'm not in Mission Hills. There was a brief pause and then the next message appeared in the box: *Doesn't it scare you that I know who you are?*

He wanted her to ask how he knew who she was. She decided to take the bait. Give him what he wanted and get him to ask her to meet him. Teenage girls these days were forward. They knew what they wanted and didn't hesitate. An image of Kathleen Long, her gray, dead body lying straight on the cold table at the morgue where Kylie had gone earlier, was the ruthless truth as to what happened to girls who thought they knew what they were doing and acted without parental consent. Kathleen Long had been forbidden to meet the boy she'd been talking to online. Kylie read the faxed report that had been typed up by Perry after he interviewed the parents before coming to see her. His report was inconclusive and he stated follow-ups were pending, which was probably where he headed after leaving her house, to interview Kathleen's friends and learn more about who she went to meet.

Kylie typed and sent her next message, guessing that waiting a minute before sending it would feed her perp, if she was indeed talking to the killer, and make him believe she was wary. *How do you know who I am?*

I've been watching you.

Oh yeah? You don't live here. LOL.

Is the green hybrid yours?

She frowned, her heart thumping hard in her chest while she fidgeted in her chair. He had been watching her.

He sent a large smiley face and then followed it with a kissing face. *My grandmother lives in Mission Hills*, he offered. *When can I meet you?*

"Bingo." Kylie grabbed her earpiece to her cell phone and quickly scrolled to the saved number for the FBI field office. Listening to it ring, she decided to go for broke. "You're going down, buddy," she said, feeling the adrenaline charge to life inside her. Unfortunately, it accentuated the pulsing that still throbbed between her legs. She rubbed herself against the chair, which only made the craving worse, and posed her fingers, deciding on her response.

"FBI. How may I direct your call?" a man's voice said in her ear.

I can probably get out tonight for a few, but I can't leave town. She clicked "send" at the same time as she spoke. "Paul Hernandez, please," she said.

"I'm sorry. He's not in the office right now. Can someone else help you?"

"This is Special Agent Kylie Donovan." She quickly rattled off her ID number. "It's very important that I speak with him now."

"I can have him call you."

"That works." She stared at the message that appeared in the box.

It will take me half an hour to get to the bowling-alley parking lot in Mission Hills. Be there and don't be late.

"It's imperative I speak to him right now. I'm going to need backup."

"Roger that. Return the call to this number?"

"Yes."

"You'll have a callback in five minutes." The dispatcher said good-bye and the line went dead.

Kylie started to type: *What car do you drive?* PeteTakesU signed off before she could click "send."

"Crap," she hissed, her heart still thudding in her chest. She wiped her damp palms against her shirt that partially covered her thighs and then quickly saved the chat to her personal file, where she could access it later. Then jumping out of her chair, she hurried to change clothes.

Her cell rang as she was pulling jeans up her thighs. Fidgeting with the zipper and button, she pressed the button on her earpiece and answered on the third ring.

"This is Paul. What's up?"

"We've got a meet."

Chapter 10

One of the worst parts of Perry's job was talking to parents who'd lost a child. It was just as hard stopping in at the victim's friends' homes and interviewing terrified teenage girls while their parents paced nervously behind them. The circumstances around Kathleen Long's death were heinous. He didn't bother with e-mail, knowing there was no way he could focus on answering any of it, let alone standing on the delete button to get rid of junk mail. Instead, he went straight to his saved Web sites.

"Son of a bitch," he hissed, staring at the Web site page he'd shown Rad last week. "It could be her."

The young girl who pouted at the camera, her hands resting on her knees as she sat on a bare hardwood floor naked, looked a hell of a lot like Kathleen. He printed the page, slipped it into his file, and reached for his cell. Rad's phone went straight to voice mail.

"Damn it." Waiting until morning seemed an eternity. Every minute that ticked by could mean another teenage girl might be facing the same terrifying death Kathleen had endured.

Perry paced his den for a few minutes, realizing there wasn't anything that linked Kathleen to the Peter girls. The Longs had told him they'd forbidden their daughter to meet a boy she'd been talking to online and wanted to meet. When their daughter disappeared, apparently leaving home without their consent, they'd immediately feared the worst.

Perry hoped they would be willing to let him search Kathleen's computer. If he confirmed Kathleen spoke with Peter and had snuck out to meet him, they would have a definite pattern. But Mr. Long had asked Perry to leave when Mrs. Long grew hysterical. They'd been through so much, and now Perry needed to push them to allow him to search into Kathleen's personal life.

Yet something else he'd have to wait until tomorrow to accomplish.

Hyped up and frustrated, Perry dropped his file on his desk and headed back out his door. He didn't make a habit of using sex to release adrenaline, but he wanted to see Kylie again. Somehow he needed to convince her to quit trying to play private detective. Kylie wasn't a teenager, but she was young. He wouldn't have her sniffing around crime scenes any longer out of mere curiosity.

Taking the exit to Kylie's house, Perry slowed at the first intersection as another car went through it, heading westbound. He scowled at the green hybrid, squinting in the dark at the license plate. "Where are you going at this hour, sweetheart?" he whispered, turning to follow Kylie.

He kept his distance, trailing her as she stayed off the interstate and took one of the main streets into a commercial district.

"Late-night munchies?" he mused, glancing at the clock on his dash. It was barely ten, definitely not too late to order delivery. Did she intentionally not want to be home if he stopped by again?

He contemplated the possibility that she might intentionally avoid him. There were several reasons that came to mind why she might, but one he couldn't get his head to wrap around was lack of interest. Kylie was on fire when she returned his kiss earlier. In fact, if he'd pressed matters when he'd been there earlier, he probably could have fucked her.

Maybe he wasn't a pro with women, but he knew interest when he saw it, and felt it. Yet here she was, several cars in front of him, out on the town when she knew he was coming back over. Was she heading out to interview another teenager? It was a school night, and rather late. But possibly someone had given Kylie consent to do an interview and she needed to jump on the opportunity to do so.

He slowed when she switched lanes and signaled right before she turned into one of the shopping malls. Several cars were between them and he searched for her car when he pulled in a minute later.

The only store still open here was the donut shop and of course the bowling alley. Kylie had pulled into a stall on the far side of the parking lot, away from the floodlights that lit up the parking lot, and turned off her headlights.

"A rather odd place to meet someone for an interview," he said out loud, and scowled in the darkness when he slowed, not wanting her to spot him.

Perry pulled into a stall in the middle of the parking lot and turned off his car. Then getting out, he walked slowly past the few parked cars. At this hour, on a Monday night, business was slow and the few cars in the lot were parked in front of the donut shop or the bowling alley.

"Why aren't you getting out of your car?" he asked, frowning when she remained shielded by the darkness in the far corner of the parking lot.

A black Suburban came at him with its brights on and Perry squinted, looking down but quickly returning his attention to Kylie as soon as the car passed. When Kylie still didn't get out of her car, he crossed over to the bowling alley, deciding he would make it look as though he were entering through the main doors to see if she'd spotted him and that kept her from getting out.

At the doors, he pulled one of them open, immediately hit with the noise from inside, but then turned, standing just inside, and watched the Suburban circle the lot and slow, not parking but not leaving the lot, either.

Perry stepped back outside. Kylie continued sitting in her car. From this distance he couldn't tell whether her car was running or not. She'd engulfed herself in the darkest part of the lot.

The whole thing didn't sit well with him. He watched the

Suburban start to accelerate, heading toward Kylie's car. Was she meeting someone here?

Something tightened inside his gut. Maybe he didn't know her really well, but his protector's instincts kicked in big-time. Kylie didn't strike him as a stupid woman. But if she was sitting over there in the dark, waiting to meet someone in a public parking lot, it might be smart to make his presence known.

Not to mention, she didn't tell him no thanks when he said he'd be back over. Whatever she was doing, he bet she didn't have it planned when he was over there earlier. An impromptu meeting in a dark parking lot meant something was up.

Kylie wasn't stupid enough to meet someone off the Internet, was she? She was a single, gorgeous, intelligent woman. Perry knew there were people who met and formed relationships from the Internet. It wasn't as if he'd tried starting anything with her. But that kiss they'd shared earlier clearly showed mutual interest. If Kylie was the kind of woman who would come on to one man and then prance off with another, Perry would find out right now.

Perry glanced across the parking lot. Kylie's car hadn't moved. In the darkness, he couldn't tell from this angle whether she was still in her car or not. That damn Suburban pulled around the parking lot, circling it like some fucking bird of prey. It turned at the end of the row of stalls, flashing its brights on Kylie's car. She still sat in the driver's seat.

The Suburban stopped, its lights remaining on Kylie until she raised her hand over her eyes. Perry took advantage of her being blinded and walked along the sidewalk that ran the length of the bowling alley. The floodlight above him hummed loudly and another car came along the back side of the bowling alley.

"Do I know you?" Perry met gazes with the driver in a small Honda, who slowed as he hesitated, trying to decide whether to turn into the parking lot or head straight.

The driver looked away from Perry first and put a cell phone to his ear. Perry returned his attention to Kylie, who now looked down at her lap. Her soft blonde hair fluttered around her face, and he guessed she continued avoiding the bright lights, which remained trained on her.

He stopped at the end of the parking lot and the Honda turned into the lot, driving past him toward the front of the bowling alley. Perry focused his attention on the Suburban driver. The man behind the wheel appeared to be watching Kylie, who for whatever reason sat like a sitting duck in her car.

Whatever the scenario playing out in front of him was, Perry didn't like it. Worse yet, standing and watching, unsure what he witnessed, bugged the crap out of him. The driver of the Suburban was being more than rude simply sitting there blinding Kylie. Perry wished he had a flashlight so he could return the treatment. Studying the man for a moment, Perry noted the strong profile of a Caucasian man, his relaxed expression proof of the narrow-minded attitude of someone who thought nothing of anyone other than himself. More than likely some prick waiting for his kid to come out and indifferent to the fact that he blinded Kylie while she was playing sitting duck.

Perry glanced back down the parking lot, noting the parked cars, his own sitting halfway down the lot, and the Honda that had turned the corner moments ago, now pulled into a stall not too far down. That driver cut his lights but also didn't get out. Perry didn't have time to focus on everyone's agenda tonight. He returned his attention to Kylie.

As he stepped off the sidewalk, Kylie opened her car door. At the same time the black Suburban started toward her.

"What?" Perry grunted, scowling at the back of the Suburban when it approached Kylie.

Was she here to meet the man in the Suburban? And if so, did she sit there docilely while he checked her out with his high beams to see if she met his criteria? Like any man would be disappointed with a woman like Kylie.

Perry took in the tag number, XLS519, Johnson County tags. But his attention shifted back to Kylie when she closed her car door and stepped away from her car. The Suburban headed toward her, and Perry picked up his pace. He was about to bust her party wide open.

"Kylie!" he bellowed.

The Suburban's brakes came on, the red lights glowing in the dark. The truck hesitated long enough for Perry to get close enough to touch it. The windows were tinted, not a lot, but the night added to the hindrance, making it hard to see the driver. Perry walked up alongside the truck and it turned, accelerating and headed out of the parking lot. Perry watched it leave quickly before he turned to face Kylie. Anger spiked inside him, raging out of control before he could stop it.

"What the hell was that all about?" he demanded, yelling as he started toward her.

She didn't answer but climbed into her car, gunned the engine, and squealed out of the parking lot, leaving him standing there looking after her.

"Son of a fucking bitch," he spit, turning and sprinting across the parking lot to his car. He jumped in as the Honda pulled out in front of him, also leaving. There was still only one person in the car. "What in the hell is going on here?" he roared, the vein in his right temple pounding as hard as his heart.

Perry hit the steering wheel when he drove past Kylie's house and she wasn't there. He felt his blood pressure boil and knew he needed a grip now or he wouldn't be thinking clearly soon. It wasn't too often his outrage reached the point of wanting blood, but Perry knew himself well enough to know calming down was imperative and any other poor sap who might get in his way before he did chill out would regret it seriously.

He headed back to his house, made it across town, cut back, and did another drive-by. Kylie still wasn't home.

"Enough." The tires squealed on his Jeep when he took her corner too sharply. "Not my problem anymore."

If she was pissed at him for interfering with her meeting someone in a dark parking lot when she knew he was coming back over, he was best off without her. All he needed to do was get the taste of her off his lips, the soft feel of her warm flesh out of his memory. He balled his hands into fists, remembering their kiss earlier and how good she had felt when he'd caressed her body. And how well she'd responded to him.

"Just be okay," he muttered, scrubbing his head and pulling into his driveway fifteen minutes later. God. Going home didn't seem like the right thing to do.

It wasn't just the protector's instinct still simmering way too hot inside him, it was the cop in Perry that needed to know she was fine. He reluctantly got out of his car, fingering his keys and heading toward his back door. The silence around him, the peaceful and serene surroundings, annoyed him even further.

Perry paced his living room floor, not bothering with lights, as he replayed what he saw play out at the parking lot. On an impulse, he headed to his computer and wrote down the tag number to the black Suburban. Underneath it he wrote the words "green Honda"; then he stared at the block letters he'd just printed on the notepad.

"What are you up to, Miss Kylie Dover?" His stomach knotted; anger, concern, and not having any answers making for a cruel combination in his gut. If she was a player, then she was a pro. He hated feeling he'd busted her trying to meet another man and forced himself to remember there was nothing between them. "Nor will there be if this is how she plays."

Perry slipped the paper with the tag number into the file where he'd put the printed picture of the Web site page. He stared at the young girl, looking so innocent and anything but happy, as she stared naked at the camera. He needed more puzzle pieces to fit this case together. The best thing to do right now was bury himself in this investigation and put Kylie out of his mind. Her life was her own damn business.

Carl Ramos studied the picture from the Web site and compared it to the pictures Kathleen Long's parents had given Perry. "When did you get pictures of her?" Carl asked.

Perry glanced at the pictures Carl compared, and returned his attention to the road. "I went over to the Longs' last night after you went home."

Carl shot him a quick glance. If he was hurt, he didn't show it. Perry doubted that was his reaction.

"You want me to put it on my log sheet that I went with you?"

His question surprised Perry. Carl was a good man, and a good cop. "You don't ever have to lie for me," Perry told him, studying Carl only for a moment to see that his question was sincere. "You'd headed home to be with your mother and that is important. I didn't know I was going over there until I left the station and ran into Rad in the parking lot. It was an impromptu visit, but we need more information."

He turned onto the Longs' street and slowed to 20 miles per hour as he headed down the long, quiet, shady side street. Large well-kept homes lined either side and there wasn't a car visible anywhere. People in this neighborhood parked in garages, and most were at work.

"The Longs know we're coming?" Carl asked.

"Yup. Eileen Long said Kathleen had a computer in her bedroom. She knows we're coming with a subpoena for the hard drive and didn't have a problem with it." Perry had been distracted all morning at the station, especially when he ran a check on the Suburban's tags and came up with nothing. The tag was fake, a crime in itself. "Sorry I didn't tell you about this before we headed out. These teenage girls meeting some prick off the Internet and then ending up dead is hitting a bit too close to home, I think."

"Are you worried about your sister's kids?" Carl stuffed the pictures back into the file and placed it in Perry's open briefcase on the floor at Carl's feet. "She's got all girls, doesn't she?"

"Yup. And about the same age as these girls. When I get time I'm going to find out if they knew Kathleen."

"I'm sure you've had enough involvement raising those girls for them to know better than to meet some stranger off the computer."

Perry nodded and pulled up in front of the house. They

weren't quite up the walk to the front door when it opened and Eileen, a woman not much older than Perry, and fairly pretty, nodded to the two of them. She looked as though she hadn't slept and leaned heavily on the doorknob when she stood to the side so the men could enter.

"How are you doing today?" Carl asked, always the concerned cop.

"Not very well," she answered honestly, offering both of them a small smile and then taking the copy of the subpoena Carl handed her. "This way. Her computer is in her room."

They followed Eileen up the stairs and down a wide hall to a bedroom, whose door was closed. She pushed it open and walked in ahead of them. There were clothes on the floor and the bed wasn't made, giving all indications that someone had slept here the night before and headed out that morning in a hurry. Perry guessed Eileen hadn't touched it since her daughter disappeared by the somewhat musky smell in the room.

"Do you know what chat programs she used?" he asked, pulling out the wooden chair from the desk and sitting in front of the home computer.

"We all use AOL," Eileen said. "But I think Kathleen used Yahoo! Messenger sometimes, too. I'm sorry I don't know her passwords or anything. I guess I should have made her give those to me." She sounded defeated.

"From what you've told us, it sounded as if Kathleen was a good girl," Carl offered.

"She was the best." Eileen choked and covered her hand with her mouth. "When she approached us and talked to us about meeting a boy who went to another high school but whom she'd been chatting with online we had a long discussion about it. Mitch and I thought Kathleen understood the danger involved in meeting someone from the Internet, even when the situation appeared harmless. We even offered to invite him over to the house so they could meet that way." Her voice cracked and she covered her mouth with her hand. "I'm sorry. Do you need me in here? I'll let you two do whatever you need to do."

Carl walked out of the bedroom, offering words of support and asking if Eileen and her husband had considered counseling for dealing with the loss of their daughter. Perry let Carl console Eileen and studied the contents of the desk while the computer booted up. His instructions were to remove the hard drive and return to the station, but he wanted to search the computer for what he could find before doing that.

He stood, walking over to the briefcase Carl had placed on Kathleen's bed, and pulled out a ziplock bag and gloves. Then returning to the computer, Perry gently removed the pictures that had been taped around the monitor, pictures of Kathleen and her friends, different poses, different friends. A few of them were class pictures. Either way, they created a profile on her, helping him know who her group of friends were.

He went through the programs on her computer, took a look at the list of songs that were on it, and opened a few files that seemed to be nothing more than homework assignments.

"Find anything?" Carl entered the room. "Mrs. Long is downstairs if we need her."

"Nothing yet," Perry said, closing the ziplock bag and handing it to Carl as he slid back into the chair in front of the computer.

"She gave me a list of pet names, birth dates, anything she could think of to help us with passwords." Carl didn't bother handing the list to Perry but pulled out another bag and slipped the paper inside.

When they took the hard drive down to the station, passwords wouldn't be an issue. They could crack into any password-protected program once they hooked the hard drive up to the computers there.

Perry clicked on Yahoo! Messenger, knowing it was his nieces' preferred chat program. The long, slender box appeared on the screen, Kathleen's screen name and her password already saved into it.

"We're in luck," he said, and Carl moved to his side. "We

find a screen name with Pete, or Peter, and we might have to add pornography charges to kidnapping, rape, and murder."

"Do you think Kathleen is connected to the other girls who've disappeared?"

"I'd bet my life on it," Perry muttered, and watched as Kathleen's buddy list appeared. He scrolled down a long list of screen names and then back up again. Not one of them used any form of the name Peter.

"Maybe she talked to him on AOL," Carl suggested.

Perry was already on it, although he said nothing. While signing onto AOL, which also had the password saved, he went through Yahoo! Messenger again, hitting the preferences and changing her settings so that the actual screen names were displayed instead of each person's name. Still, there was nothing. It was the same with AOL. Not one screen name came close to Peter.

"Maybe she used another screen name," Perry mused out loud.

"They'll be able to tell down at the station. Ready for me to pull out the hard drive?" Carl reached into the briefcase and slid a screwdriver out of the side pocket.

No, Perry wasn't ready. He wanted to tear into the computer himself and not turn it over to Rad, who in turn would probably ship it out to Kansas City's larger police department or, worse yet, the FBI field office. Since this wasn't officially his case, he would have to sift through red tape just to learn what they found.

"One more minute." He clicked the drop-down box on AOL to view the other screen names. Then flipping open his notebook, he jotted down the names. "How many brothers and sisters does she have?"

"Just a younger brother."

Perry guessed the screen names on AOL all belonged to family members. More than likely, the account holder was Eileen or her husband and they would authorize any new screen names. Since there were only four names, Perry doubted Kathleen used AOL for a lot of chatting.

He looked through the programs on the computer, pulled up IE, and then typed in: *MySpace*. This time the password wasn't saved. Doing the same with Facebook, he ran into the same snag. And there was no way to tell what other names she might have on Yahoo! Messenger. Frustrated, he stood and let Carl do his thing. "There's a connection here. I know there is."

He thought about how Dani showed Kylie the way people chatted using Web sites.

"Your hunches are usually right." Carl stepped around him and then unscrewed the back of the tower.

Perry wished Rad felt the same way. He was a damn good cop, one of the best on their force. And it wasn't bragging rights that allowed him to say that. The facts spoke for themselves. In his years on duty, he'd brought in more criminals, solved more cases, than any other man, or woman, in his department. Yet for some reason, Rad wouldn't assign the case to him. That in itself bugged the crap out of him, too.

Dani and Kylie's conversation kept popping into his head as well. There were other ways to talk online. He wanted to be the one figuring this out and not some IT geek.

When they arrived back at the station, Perry headed straight for Rad's office, keeping the hard drive in his possession. Rad looked tired when he glanced up from paperwork and gestured for Perry to enter.

"I got something to show you," Perry said, closing the door to the Chief's office. He swore Rad's expression turned wary as he leaned back and watched Perry approach. "Remember those Web sites I showed you last week?"

"Yeah." Rad leaned forward on his desk, resting his elbows over paperwork, and plopped his chin in his hands. "What about them?"

"Take a look at this." Perry opened his file and pulled out the printed page and then slid a picture of Kathleen Long out next to it.

"Son of a bitch," Rad hissed.

"Yup. A match."

Rad let out a loud sigh and leaned back, keeping his focus glued to the two pictures and not saying anything for a minute.

"Did you get her hard drive?"

"Yeah, it's right here." He pulled out the ziplock bag and held up the black hard drive. "Where are you sending it?"

Rad focused on him with intense gray eyes that today looked more tired than usual. Reaching across his desk, he took the hard drive from Perry. "I'm sending it over to the FBI field office."

Perry blew out his frustration. "Rad, give me this case. You know I can work alongside the FBI. We've done it before."

"Yup, we have." Rad set the hard drive on the side of his desk. "I thought you wanted the Peter case."

"It's the same case."

Rad raised one eyebrow. "You've got proof that Kathleen Long was pursued by Peter?"

"Not yet. I couldn't dig into her hard drive at her house other than glimpsing at where she'd saved her password."

"And you didn't see anything?"

Perry shook his head, frustrated. "Give me the case. I can prove their connections, or learn who kidnapped Kathleen Long."

Rad slid the hard drive across his desk toward Perry. "The case is yours," he said, but then pointed a finger at Perry. "Keep Carl with you when you're doing your investigating. Promise me you won't spend one minute on this case without him by your side."

Perry grabbed the hard drive and stood, turning toward the door. "No problem," he said, getting the hell out of Rad's office before he changed his mind.

"Flynn!"

Perry turned, studying Rad's hard gaze as the Chief stood slowly. "I'm serious about this. Watch your ass, Flynn. You hear me?"

Perry rested his hand on the doorknob, hearing the Chief

loud and clear but not liking his tone. "What the hell is that supposed to mean?"

"You're a good cop."

"I'm a damn good cop."

Rad nodded. "Keep it that way. Don't fuck me over."

Perry let go of the doorknob and walked toward Rad's desk, squaring off with the large man who stood opposite it. "You mind telling me what you're trying to say?"

"This is my town, Flynn. Not a goddamn thing goes on here that I don't know about. We've got a criminal on the loose and he's going to go down. And when he does, it's going to be bad and ugly." Rad pierced Perry with a fiery glare. "I'm going to see to it."

"Wait in line," Perry hissed. "This is my fucking town, too. And if you think I'm going to tolerate a monster preying on teenage girls one minute longer than I have to, then you disappoint me, Chief."

"I'm giving you this case because I think you're the man for the job," Rad said, his voice taking a low, calm tone that was almost unnerving. "But I'll have some explaining to do."

"What?" Perry hissed.

"That's all I'm saying." Rad pressed his lips into a paper-thin line and wrinkled his brow when he scowled. "You're a good cop and I believe that, which is why you just got this case. Don't make me regret giving it to you."

Perry didn't have a fucking clue what Rad was talking about and was getting pissed off listening to him ramble. But he had the case and that was what mattered. He headed out of the Chief's office, forcing himself to relax his grip on the hard drive before he snapped it in two.

"Flynn!" Rad bellowed when Perry had barely reached his desk. "Take that hard drive over to the KCMO 3rd precinct. I'll call and tell them to be ready for you."

Perry nodded, not trusting himself to speak at the moment. He didn't like being told to watch his ass and not being told why. Worse yet, there was obviously something wrong, or Rad wouldn't have spoken to him that way. If someone had told the Chief something about Perry, he had a right to know what it was. But Rad wasn't asking him to justify his actions, just watch himself in the future. Perry didn't like it. But he didn't have a problem taking the hard drive to the KCMO precinct instead of the FBI field office. At least this way, he could get answers faster.

Carl walked over toward Perry, a question in his eyes although he didn't say anything. Perry preferred running alone, but whatever was bugging the crap out of Rad, if he pushed him Rad looked wired enough to yank him right back off the case, just to cause a fight.

"Let's go," he grumbled, not bothering to elaborate. He'd credit Carl for having enough sense not to ask questions but simply follow him out of the station.

He'd run over to the Kansas City, Missouri, precinct, hang there while they tore through the hard drive, then drop Carl off at his car. They'd have some answers today. One way or another Perry would know if Kathleen had been involved with Peter.

After he had that information, Perry planned to seek out one hot little blonde. Player or not, she had a right to know the man she had tried meeting was running in a car with illegal tags. Perry wasn't seeking her out to fuck her but out of his sworn obligation to protect his community. If Kylie wanted to be an idiot and meet men in dark parking lots, that was her business. He wouldn't be able to live with himself if she got hurt and he didn't warn her. And that was the only reason he would seek her out.

Chapter 11

"You know what, go to hell!" Kylie shoved her chair back from the table, pushing hard enough with her legs that it squeaked loudly across the floor. She couldn't hold her anger in any longer. "Don't ever suggest that I don't know how to do my fucking job," she hissed, gritting her teeth together so hard her jaw hurt.

"What I'm suggesting is that you keep a safe distance from anyone who might be viewed as a suspect," John Athey said. He remained seated at the opposite end of the long, narrow conference table, his tone as cool as his expression. "Especially in light of what happened last night. It seems rather odd to me that Lieutenant Flynn just happened to be at the exact location you agreed to meet this Peter."

"Last night I verified that PeteTakesU is not a teenager, that he drives a black Suburban. Sitting here going over everything that didn't go right, instead of seeing what did go right is a waste of my time."

"How do you know your guy was in that Suburban?" John demanded, his cool tone almost more annoying than his idiotic line of questioning.

"He sat there in his car with his brights on me for several minutes before approaching." Kylie shoved her chair back further from the table in the meeting room at the FBI field office. It made a loud screeching sound against the floor.

"What proof do you have that Flynn wasn't the one there to meet you?" John demanded, ignoring her comment. "Why the hell would he just happen to show up in that parking lot at the same time you were supposed to meet someone?"

Kylie had no idea why Perry was there last night. But the next time she saw him, he would get a piece of her mind, and his ass kicked if he pulled any macho crap on her.

"Are you sure you got the tag number right?" Paul held his hand up defensively, stopping her before she could bite John's head off. "If you did, it's fake."

Kylie slapped the table with her palm and glared at John. "More proof, if you ask me, that we've got our guy. I'll flush him out again. At least we know we're on the right trail."

"Kylie," John said when she turned toward the door, making her name sound like a warning. "We already know our guy is a cop. Flynn was there. Maybe you should think twice before you believe you are chasing some black Suburban that just happens to have illegal tags. That's hardly the same level of crime as raping and killing young girls."

She ignored him, stepping out of the conference room at the FBI field office. The last thing she would tell any of them was that Perry probably had followed her to the bowling alley, since he had promised her he would return last night. More than likely he saw her leave her home. But offering that bit of information would open a can of worms. And she wasn't going to go there. It was bad enough getting chewed out because her meet didn't go down right.

There wasn't anything to tell John anyway. Perry knew her because of her involvement with his nieces. End of story. She blew out an exasperated breath, knowing there would be a confrontation with him soon and unable to quit speculating as to how that meeting might turn out.

She wanted to beat the crap out of Perry, knock some sense into him, show that dominating, aggressive man that he couldn't push her around, or follow her and yell at her from across a parking lot. That's what she wanted to do. Pound some kind of acknowledgment into his thick, sexy skull and make him see who he was messing with.

Kylie stopped at her car, pinching the bridge of her nose and closing her eyes. Blowing out a frustrated sigh, she fought to get her temper under control. Daydreaming about taking her fists and beating that steel chest of his wasn't doing a damn thing but getting her hot and bothered. Pissed and horny was a bad combination.

"Kylie," Paul said, hurrying out the door. "Wait up a minute."

He hurried toward her, his straight brown hair falling in thin strands over his forehead. Paul pushed his glasses up his nose and offered a weak smile.

"John's got a hot temper. He's not a bad guy, though. He'll simmer down quickly."

"I've got a temper, too," she said, not apologizing. "And I don't like being told how to do my job."

She turned from Paul, unlocking her car, and threw her purse over to the passenger seat.

Paul held her car door when she slid behind the wheel. "I've got the live feed running surveillance on your home," he began, suddenly sounding awkward.

Kylie remembered Perry telling her he wanted to see her surveillance equipment. "Yeah? And?" she said, knowing where this was heading.

Paul sighed. "If it's any consolation, when John questioned Chief Radisson about Perry Flynn the Chief got all hot under the collar, too. If there's a bad seed in his department, the Chief is putting his neck on the line swearing it's not Flynn. Apparently he gave him the Kathleen Long case today."

"Okay," Kylie said, managing to sound indifferent. If Perry was assigned the same case she was, though, they were going to start crossing paths a lot more often. She hated not being able to come forth with him. "If he did that, why is John all bent out of shape about him? You'd think if the police trusted one of their men enough to put him on this case, we could work together."

"You could suggest it to John. He seems hell-bent and determined not to trust anyone down at the station, though. He damn near got into a screaming match over the phone earlier with the Chief for putting Flynn on the case." Paul shook his head, letting go of her car door and taking a step backward. "If it's any consolation, from what I'm seeing, Flynn seems to be more in your corner than out of it."

When she looked up at Paul, he looked away, apparently unwilling to admit he'd seen her kiss Flynn. She needed to find out if every room in her home was bugged. "I've got a criminal to catch. Is there anything else?"

"Actually, there is. What are you doing now?"

"I thought I'd get online and see if I can't get Mr. Pete to give me a rain check."

"Good. When you get him online, call me. I'm going to run a check through all city office computers and find out who is online when he's talking to you."

"Good idea."

"Some advice?"

"What?" She glanced up his slender body, not built up at all like Perry was, although Paul wasn't a bad-looking guy. She smiled, still feeling irked over her lecture from John, but seeing Paul was doing his best to be diplomatic.

"Go somewhere other than your house so that you aren't . . ." He hesitated, staring down at his shoes. "So you aren't interrupted."

She fought not to smile when Paul blushed. "Maybe I'll find a good coffee shop and set up camp there for a while and work off my laptop. But I'll call you once I'm online."

Kylie leaned back in the black metal chair while nursing a damn good mocha latte. The richly flavored aroma drifted around her face as she licked her lips. She stared at her laptop and her buddy list. PeteTakesU wasn't online.

In spite of the years she had behind her on the job, sitting and waiting and doing nothing was damn hard. More than likely John also viewed the live feed from her house. He saw her kissing Perry. And it was more than just a kiss. She raised her gaze to the street in front of the coffeehouse Paul had suggested. Kylie was the only one sitting on the brick patio in front of the small café. Across the street, a new-wave bookstore seemed to do a decent amount of business. There was a buy, sell, and trade record and game store next to it. On the corner, cars drove in and out of a gas station. Business as usual for a growing, progressive town and suburb of an even larger city.

Where were the cameras in her house? She knew there was one in the living room and two out front. But she wasn't aware of any that were installed in the back end of her home. It actually surprised her that she didn't pay closer attention to where Paul had installed them. In her defense, she'd been busy as well that evening, working to get her computer going and setting up passwords and screen names. It had been a normal day preparing for undercover work, and one she would do exactly the same if she were to do it again. But then she didn't anticipate Perry sweeping her off her feet.

Was that what he'd done?

Kylie scowled. She was a professional, one of the best in her line of work. Her record was impeccable. There wasn't an online predator she'd gone after that she hadn't nailed to the wall. A local cop sniffing around her wouldn't hinder her investigation.

"Damn," she sighed, blowing out her frustration with a loud sigh. She was thinking about Perry as if he were lower on the totem pole than she. Yet picturing him, remembering how he grabbed her, damn near swept her off her feet with a kiss more powerful than anything she'd experienced in a long time, made him seem anything but inferior. The way he kissed her, touched her, got her off more than sex had with some of the men she'd been with in her past. She fidgeted in her seat, feeling her jeans rub between her legs, and closed her eyes, imagining Perry touching her there.

The chime from her laptop made her jump and she damn near spilled her latte in her lap. Not the kind of heat she was looking for, she thought, scowling at her computer screen.

You are so sexy.

Kylie stared at the words that appeared on her screen. She bit her lower lip, switching gears quickly, and posed her fingers over the keyboard. Nothing pissed her off more than getting her ass chewed, especially when she was doing her job. She didn't like how John had brushed off the Suburban, indifferent to it having illegal tags when that appeared to her to add suspicion to her guy. She'd had cases in the past where her perp hunted young girls using an alias as well as being illegal in almost every aspect of his life. It was common for a sexual predator to live somewhere where his name wasn't on a lease, the car he drove was not registered, and all efforts were made to keep his identity hidden. If John refused to acknowledge that, possibly he wasn't doing his job right.

She stared at her computer screen, forcing herself to calm down and think only about being the bait this sick monster fed off, and bringing him in.

My mom might see you talk to me like that. Kylie clicked "send" and then glanced at her buddy list, which was empty since his was the only name on it. She added quickly: *Why can't I see you online?*

I can see you, but you can't see me.

She typed a quick, *LOL*, and then sat back, forcing a calming breath into her lungs, and reached for her latte. Glancing toward the small parking lot next to the café where she sat and then up and down the busy street, she saw life was as usual around her. She returned her attention to the screen. PeteTakesU wasn't typing.

Maybe a bit of encouragement was in order. *I didn't get to see you last night.* Then thinking quickly, knowing she needed to offer some kind of explanation for Perry, she took a sip of her latte and licked her lips as she grinned. *I'm sorry about my friend's uncle.*

I saw you, though. You're hot as hell. The bait worked. He accepted her explanation.

She watched the bottom of the box where it said: "PeteTakesU is typing a message." *May I ask you a question?*

Sure.

Are you a virgin?

Kylie ground her teeth, outrage covering her with a feverish rage. Instead of dwelling on how this bastard preyed on innocent girls, she forced herself to focus on how Dani might talk to him. With her flippant, know-it-all attitude, she wouldn't take crap off anyone.

Are you?

No. Sex is the best thing in the world. Do you know that?

Kylie envied Dani and her sisters. They were so socially adjusted, with one another to help out. Kylie imagined they fought. For a brief moment she remembered fighting with her own sister. Karen used to yell at Kylie for how she dressed, telling her repeatedly no one would ever ask her out if she refused to brush her hair and take care of herself.

Did her sister know how much worse Kylie looked after Karen died? No one noticed Kylie, and if they did they sure didn't talk to her. She coasted through high school like a ghost, ignoring everyone around her and doing her best not to do anything to draw attention to herself. It wasn't until college that she pulled out of that shell, once she left Dallas and decided she would rather live attacking life than running from it.

Pinching her nose, she checked her surroundings once again and watched as a couple of girls gave her the once-over and then sat at a table on the other side of the patio. They immediately started talking with each other and sipping their drinks.

Kylie forced her attention to the screen, wondering if going home wouldn't be better. The hell with Perry and whether he showed up or not. She needed to be able to concentrate on saying the right thing to PeteTakesU.

Where do you hang out? She decided to change the subject knowing there were times when she would have to chat for hours with a perp before he asked to meet her.

At the mall here in town, he answered quickly, but then sent another message: *Want to hang this weekend? Give me your number and I'll text-message you.*

Her heart skipped a beat. But she was ready for this. Already she knew statistics showed that teenagers text-messaged as their main means of communicating. In fact, most texted on a phone more than they talked on it. She quickly typed in her cell phone number, a number that would be traced to K. Dover in Mission Hills, Kansas. Even the best investigative programs wouldn't narrow her phone down any further than that. It was hard to search for information on someone using programs that her side had devised in the first place.

Kylie leaned back, took a long drink of her still-warm latte, and glanced at the women facing each other at the nearby table. They were deeply engrossed in a conversation about their husbands. It wasn't the first time Kylie had watched the world around her feeling like the outsider but knowing she was right where she belonged. It was her job to make sure women like those two could sit, relax, and not worry about anything other than catching up on gossip. Kylie was the protector.

Karen never got the chance to grow up and be the gorgeous woman she seemed destined to be. Granted, back then there wasn't the Internet and her abductor hadn't seduced her out of her home. Sexual predators used many different means to seek out their prey. Kylie would use whatever means to track them down and stop them.

Her cell phone buzzed and she glanced at her screen, seeing she'd received a text message. *Where do you hang out?* it said.

Kylie sucked at text messaging. Although she believed the statistics, she didn't understand for the life of her why people preferred this means of communicating when the buttons and screen were so small. She worked quickly to type: *With my girlfriends, usually the bowling alley or mall.*

At least talking to him like this, she could head home and not miss out talking to him. Closing down her laptop, she finished her latte and then headed to her car. Kylie didn't speed but hurried the best she could, praying he wouldn't text her while she was driving. No way would she text and drive. Not only was it against the law, but she also knew there was no way she could pull it off.

He didn't send another text message, though. And after

talking to Paul, giving him the phone number PeteTakesU sent his text message from, she entered her middle bedroom and stared at the monitors for her security system. She could see outside from two different angles, front and backyard. There were also cameras trained on her living room. Were there more cameras in the house that she didn't have monitors for? She walked through her home, peering into air-conditioning vents but finding only the cameras that matched what the monitors showed in the bedroom. Her phone rang as she debated ordering out for supper or going to the store.

"If you're really dying to know," Paul said when she answered, "there aren't any cameras in the bedrooms."

Kylie rolled her eyes. "I was just curious." She couldn't hide her grin and was glad she spoke on the phone and was alone in her room so he couldn't see how terribly she blushed. "Don't you have a high score to beat somewhere?"

"Sure do. Oh, and that number he texted you from is a track phone. No way of knowing who purchased it or from where. Annoying little contraptions."

Kylie thanked Paul, not too surprised, and hung up the phone. She was staring out her living room windows when a Jeep pulled up to the curb and parked in front of her home. Confrontation time. Maybe she should beat the crap out of Perry on the street. She was pretty sure the cameras didn't go that far.

As she glanced down at her phone, a thought hit her. Not waiting to watch Perry get out of his Jeep, she headed back to the middle bedroom. She hurried inside, and her heart started pounding as she walked over to the equipment monitoring the surveillance around her home.

"Okay, let me see," she said, tapping her finger to her lips and glancing at the control panel. She would catch hell for this, but damn it, she needed to keep her cover and it was no one's damn business what she did on her own time. "You're going to have to get your jollies some other way, Paul."

She flicked the switch, shutting off the cameras. Then placing her cell phone facedown on the desk, she placed her briefcase over it, which would work in stifling any sounds it made. She didn't want to turn it off and risk missing any text messages that might come through.

Perry knocked solidly on the front door as she left the bedroom, pulled the door closed, and then made sure it was locked. She glanced down at the jeans she wore today and sleeveless vest with its V-neck collar. Tugging on it offered a better view of what cleavage she had to offer.

"Good grief," she grumbled, suddenly disgusted with herself. Damn good thing she turned off the cameras. Her plan was to kick his ass, not jump his bones.

She cringed, feeling the heat swell deep inside her when she reached for the doorknob just as Perry knocked again.

"I heard you the first time," she said dryly as she opened the door. Goddamn, Perry looked better than any man she'd ever laid eyes on in her life. His eyes were exceptionally dark. And his almost black hair, windblown and probably longer than protocol stated his hair should be for his line of work, added to his bad-boy looks. Kylie pulled in all levels of training and kept her expression hard, not letting her gaze sway from his face. The last thing she needed to do was dwell on all that packed muscle that filled her doorway.

"What the hell were you doing at that bowling alley last night?" he barked, entering her house without invitation. "And you heard me yell at you. Don't tell me you didn't. I'm dying to hear your explanation for taking off like that."

She was forced to move out of the way so he wouldn't bulldoze over her. "Come on in," she grumbled dryly, keeping her tone flat but unable to prevent her focus from dropping to his hard ass before he turned around. "I guess I missed the meeting where I learned I answered to you."

Perry spun around, having made it to the middle of her living room, and slowly stalked toward her. "Cut the crap. Right here, right now. Because I swear, if you're playing me—"

"You swear what?" she snapped, interrupting him. "What I do on my own time is none of your goddamn business. Are we clear on that?"

It wasn't the first time in her life she had moved in on a

man who stood almost a foot taller than her and endured that slight tilt of the eyebrow, the pressing of the lips together. With his fatal expression, she saw all she needed to see. Perry didn't care about any demands she made on him. He wanted it his way or the highway. She couldn't have that in her life. No matter the physical attraction or his continual attention, an overbearing man would mess with her head, and her job. Kylie ignored the stabbing pain to her gut and pointed to the door when he didn't answer her.

"Get out. Now," she said, keeping her tone cool even though she felt like yelling. It was almost impossible to swallow; her mouth was suddenly too dry. She clenched her hands into fists at her sides to keep herself from shaking and did her best to find a calming breath. As she refused to look away or break eye contact, it was almost too much to bear when the discomfort in her gut swelled around her heart.

Why the fuck did he have to be so damn bossy? He was gorgeous, absolutely fucking sexy as hell, even while staring her down. His broad shoulders and muscular, tall body seemed to grow before her eyes. When a moment ago she couldn't swallow, suddenly she licked her lips, scared she would drool in spite of anger washing over her and determination warring with lust while she continued glaring at him.

Perry crossed his arms over his chest, and roped tendons flexed that were impossible not to watch. "Not yet, Kylie."

He was calm, way too calm. She looked into his eyes, blinking when they were green, almost flat. She needed to be very careful. Perry could close down his emotions as well as she could, which meant he would be harder to read.

"If I want to sit on a street corner in a fucking blizzard," she said, grasping for the bizarre to throw him off his guard, "I'll damn well do it, and without needing to explain myself to anyone."

He dropped his arms and walked toward her. She didn't budge. This was too damn important. But when he moved past her and closed her door, then tripped the lock into place, she took her time letting her focus travel over his hard, flat gut, the way the T-shirt he wore stretched over his perfect body and disappeared into faded blue jeans.

Perry didn't have too thick of a neck, in spite of how built he was. Focusing on his physical perfection didn't stop the fact that he was preparing for a battle of wits. It was more than obvious when he turned around; his expression, intense and powerful, made her heart skip a beat.

"You will explain yourself to me," he said with conviction as he stared hard into her eyes. "Tell me right now why you left your house when you knew I was coming over, drove to a parking lot and parked out of the way in the dark where you weren't safe, and then got out of your car when that Suburban approached you. And while you're at it, tell me how this helps you understand how teenagers act. Are you writing a section on how they can be idiots?"

"Go to hell, Perry."

"You're going to throw everything away out of stubborn determination to prove to me you're a tough guy." Perry moved closer, within inches of her, his body heat making her flesh tingle, her insides swell with a need so violent that even if she attacked, forced him out of her space, the act of touching him would prove more dangerous than trying to physically make him do what she wanted.

"There's nothing to throw away." She crossed her arms, refusing to move. It sucked that he stood close enough that she had to tilt her head to see his face. "And I'm not proving anything because I choose to keep my affairs private."

Perry moved so fast that she squealed when he grabbed her under her arms and lifted her off the floor. All air flew out of her lungs and she grunted loudly when he forced her against the wall. The one picture she'd hung, a print of a mountainous landscape, rattled dangerously next to her head.

"There's nothing to throw away, huh," he growled, his tone so deep and gravelly that it damn near made her toes curl. "Are you sure about that?" he demanded, using his body to keep her pinned, and every inch of steel muscle throbbing while his cock swelled and grew as he pressed it against her.

"Perry." She would have to attack brutally to get him to release her from the trap he'd just sprung.

"Are you panting and your face flushed because I just pissed you off?" he asked, dropping his voice to a dangerous guttural whisper. "Tell me you didn't leave your house to meet another man when you knew I was coming back over."

"Put me down." She willed him to meet her gaze instead of focusing somewhere around her mouth.

"Answer my questions." His cock pulsed between them while his fingers moved slightly against the sides of her breasts. "Tell me why you went to meet someone in a parking lot where there was no one around to protect you."

Kylie twisted, feeling the cool, hard wall against her back and all that bulging, hot muscle pressed into her front. She grabbed his shoulders, pushing, and narrowed her gaze. "Don't push me, Perry."

"Then answer me."

If she offered him any answer at all, he would push even harder the next time he wanted information from her. Perry's aggressive, dominating nature might make her swell with need. But in spite of the throbbing between her legs, or the way her nipples puckered and her breasts swelled and were heavy, creating an ache she would be forced to live with after she taught him a lesson, Kylie had to do just that.

She brought her leg up quickly, feeling corded muscle in his inner thighs brush against her jeans as she neared her target. Fighting dirty didn't usually appeal to her, but lesson number one, if a man twice her weight and size overpowered her, it wasn't time for manners or playing fair. At the same time she raised her hands, straightening them, and aimed for his neck.

"I told you," she hissed, bringing her knee up with aggressive force and ready to rack him. She sliced her hands through the air, knowing she could make him release her but believing in spite of how she might hurt him, he wouldn't attack. Once he let her go, she'd make him leave.

Not only did she not reach her target, but she cried out when she suddenly flew away from the wall and across her living room. For a moment she thought he had tossed her across the room, and tensed her body, preparing herself to land and gear up for her counterattack. But Perry didn't let go of her. He held on to her, his fingers pinching her flesh as he gripped her rib cage hard enough that for a moment she wondered if he would hurt her. Already she'd seen signs of a temper, of strong emotions and a dominating, aggressive personality. If he was the kind of man who would hurt a woman, she'd get her ass reamed big-time for shutting off the cameras. And for being ready to defend him when John suggested none of the cops should be trusted.

Perry kept his grip on her when he lowered her to the couch, damn near dropping her. Her breath flew out of her lungs and then he was on top of her.

"Play with fire, sweetheart, and you will get burned," he growled, pressing her flat on her couch and resting half of his body over her.

Once again she felt the hard length of his cock, but at the same time she realized he could have hurt her and didn't. If anything, he cradled her fall and, even now, only applied half of his body weight on top of her. His face was inches from hers, though, and the powerful dark green shade of his eyes captivated her, which dimmed the outrage she should be feeling right now for being manhandled like this.

"You were in that parking lot trying to see if you could pick up someone off the Internet, and I spoiled your game." He spoke with such conviction as his expression relaxed and his hands moved, caressing her breast and then moving to her neck. "If I'd wanted to hurt you right now, I could have."

"And if I thought I were in danger prior to letting you in my home, I wouldn't have let you in."

"So you know before meeting a complete stranger if he's dangerous or not?"

She wouldn't win this argument, predominantly because he was right and she agreed with everything he said wholeheartedly. "You're too smart for me, Perry. There's nothing I can do but agree and thank you for the lesson."

His fingers snaked around her neck and he squeezed, bringing his face closer to hers and then brushing his lips over hers. His breath was hot, the kiss a steamy promise of what he could do for her. Keeping her eyes open, holding up her façade of indifference, proved damn near impossible to do.

"Yes, Kylie, there is something else you can do," he whispered, and bit her lower lip.

She sucked in a breath hard enough that she hissed. His gaze was confident satisfaction, that of a victor, taking his time pulling in his win and enjoying every moment of dominating and gaining submission.

There was no way she would ask what he wanted her to do.

"Promise me right now you won't pull a stupid stunt like that again." Apparently Perry believed he'd learned the truth even though she never confirmed it. His confidence probably got him far in life, and if she wasn't careful it would get him too far with her.

Creating even a fraction of a romance during an investigation would be a serious mistake. "What?" she said, whispering as he did and making her tone husky and as sultry as she could manage. Which didn't take much effort with all that solid muscle touching her everywhere. "Let you in the door? Is that the stupid stunt you're referring to that I shouldn't do again?"

Perry growled and pounced on her mouth, pressing his tongue between her lips and parting the way inside. He impaled her with a savage hunger that sent the fever that already tortured her insides to the boiling level so fast she swore the room tilted.

Once again he grabbed her, keeping the kiss going, hot and heavy and so damn demanding there was no room for argument. He dragged her over his body as he moved on the couch. Then sitting, with her draped over him, he wrapped his arms around her, cradling her against his chest.

As rough as he'd been a moment before, his actions turned

gentle, enticing, his lips pressed to hers, and he moved slowly, with meticulous detail. The man could kiss better than anyone else she'd ever met. He turned her on more by just kissing her, his hands barely moving, while he devoured everything she offered. And if he didn't stop soon, there wouldn't be much she would say no to.

Goddamn him for putting her in this position. She wanted to fuck him. No, right now she needed to fuck him. The pulsing between her legs created a swelling that spread throughout her body, making every inch of her incredibly sensitive to any move he made. The gentle caress of his fingers up her arm until he reached that sensitive spot just above her collarbone had her melting in his arms. The muscles that twitched in his legs when she adjusted herself on his lap made her pussy throb. And his cock, hard, thick, and long, promising every time it twitched to satisfy her in ways she was sure she'd never dreamed possible, damn near made her come.

She could fuck him and not allow any further involvement to occur. After all, even after he damn near brutalized her, she hadn't told him a thing. And he wasn't pressing for information. Perry was satisfied he had all the answers. She knew he could satisfy her.

"The stupid stunt that you won't pull again," Perry began, tracing a moist trail from her mouth to her neck, "is putting yourself in danger without letting me know so I can watch your back."

Kylie let her head fall back, arching into him, and laughed. "I doubt you'd be watching my back. And if I suggested doing something dangerous, you'd throw out that macho act of yours and demand I behave and submit."

His hands slid up her back while he held her, keeping her from falling backward. She relaxed, giving him the opportunity to show how he would hold her, keep her from falling. A rather odd thought tripped through her mind. She imagined working with him, Perry truly watching her back, while they took on her perp together. It was a sobering thought, and ridiculous, too. John had the power to pull her off the case if she blew her cover.

"I'm not an act, Kylie," Perry said, his tone serious enough that she lifted her head and stared into his smoldering gaze. "While you keep up your act, and after you drop it, I will watch you. And protect you," he added, pressing his lips over the swell of her breast exposed above her vest. "Even against yourself."

Chapter 12

Kylie laughed, wondering if it was possible to protect herself from herself. The thought had its appeal at times. Right now, if she really had a protector, he would yank her off all of this hard-packed muscle and shake her silly until she came to her senses.

Even when Perry stood, still holding her in his arms, and walked down the hallway to her bedroom, thoughts warred in her mind over the ramifications of what she was about to do.

Damn it. She wouldn't think about how long she'd gone without sex. There were offers every now and then. Offers easily tossed to the side. Nothing about Perry was easy, though. And one thing she knew would be true over anything else: fucking him wouldn't make him easier to handle.

He entered her bedroom and adjusted her, allowing her to slide down his body until she stood in his arms, her breasts pressed hard against his muscular chest.

"Fucking you isn't going to make you trust me any more than you do now." He stared down at her with those penetrating green eyes while brown flecks floated around his pupils, giving him more sex appeal than a man should be allowed. "And I'm curious why you don't trust me yet were willing to meet someone in a dark parking lot. Did you know the man in the Suburban?"

Kylie sucked in her lower lip, enjoying the power she held over Perry when his gaze dropped to her mouth. She fought the smile at the realization that he voiced her thoughts, but wouldn't give him the satisfaction of knowing what he'd done.

"I'm not going to discuss that with you." She stepped backward, slipping out of his arms. "If you don't drop it, you know where the door is," she offered, refusing to allow the conversation to stray toward trust, or to admission of her personal life.

"Take off your clothes." He moved next to her, sitting on her bed, and took off his shoes.

When she didn't move, he grabbed her waist, those strong hands of his large enough that he easily wrapped his fingers around her. Then turning her to face him, he slipped his fingers under her vest and reached up to cup her breasts.

"I'm going to fuck you."

"Do you ever lack confidence?" Her voice was raspy, the need inside her so strong she almost shook from it.

"Do you ever let your guard down?"

"Never."

Perry pulled her to him, falling backward on the bed and bringing her down on top of him. "My God. I think you just told me the truth for the first time."

"Fuck you, Perry."

"Yes, you will."

He displayed amazing skills when he removed her clothes, kissing her flesh as he exposed it. When he unzipped her jeans, she slipped out of her shoes, letting them fall to the floor with a gentle thud. He peeled the denim down her legs, rolling her to her back and bending forward, kissing her pelvic bone with soft, warm lips.

She was already dangerously close to the edge and grabbed his head, groaning her desires as his mouth moved lower.

"I think your brutal confidence is a cover-up for a desire to please," she suggested, preferring they dissect his nature instead of hers.

She couldn't tell if the dark gaze he gave her was a warning or he simply thought her comment preposterous. He didn't stay focused on her face for long, though. His knuckles scraped the outsides of her legs as he pulled her jeans the rest of the way off her and tossed them to the floor.

"I don't plan on covering up anything." The corner of his mouth twitched, a movement she was learning meant he hid his smile from her.

"What is your plan then?" she asked, leaning on her elbows when he grabbed her legs.

When he lifted her legs, Kylie grabbed her bedspread and willingly opened for him. He crawled closer, releasing her so her ankles landed on his shoulders, and then brought his face to her, bending her in two.

"You're the little detective. You figure it out."

She hoped her expression looked hurt, but didn't have time to worry about it when he nipped at her lip. His hands moved over her breasts, cupping and tugging and then capturing her nipples between his fingers. When he pinched, electrical shocks surged through her, igniting the heat smoldering between her legs.

"This doesn't take any detective work," she whispered against his lips. "You're making your intentions very clear."

"You would do well to look beyond the obvious," he said, his voice a husky growl.

She blinked, trying to focus, but his face was too close. Those dark eyes glowed with charged energy matching the need surging inside her.

"What makes you think I'm not already doing that?"

Perry rose to his knees and grabbed her legs when she tried sliding them off him. Then yanking her toward him, he tugged hard enough that her hair dragged underneath her and her back burned against the covers. She grabbed his wrists, digging her nails into his flesh. His eyes darkened when she pinched his skin. Her heart raced as she stared into the thunderhead that brewed in his gaze.

"If you were, you wouldn't be hiding the truth from me," he growled, and pressed his swollen cock against her soaked entrance.

It was thick, throbbing, and sent her senses into an overheated frenzy. He was playing dirty, demanding and manipulating while using the most dangerous weapon he possessed, his body. And she sensed he knew that.

"You're looking for something that isn't there," she whispered, and shifted her ass against the bed.

Maybe his body was primed and ready to attack, but she had a few weapons of her own. Kylie knew desire when she saw it. He wanted her, and the game he played wasn't a new one. She'd mastered it years ago.

"I've found what I'm looking for, for now," he growled.

"For now?" she gasped, digging deeper into his wrists, which she couldn't even get her fingers around.

"Are you on birth control?" He didn't answer her question, and his changing the subject threw her a curve.

"Yes," she answered without hesitating.

Perry continued staring at her, holding his position while his gaze seemed to focus deep into her soul.

"And I don't have any diseases. Have you ever been tested to make sure you are clean?" She needed to stay alert. She would most definitely enjoy this, but letting her guard down for a moment would give him the upper hand.

"Yes," he said, and sunk deep inside her with a smooth, aggressive thrust.

Perry hissed, gritting his teeth while his expression hardened with what she guessed was concentration. There wasn't any doubt he fought to master the moment as much as she did.

He was huge, thicker than any man she'd been with before, and seemed to continue entering her, treading deeper and deeper. He would hit her belly button if he didn't stop soon. At the same time, she felt her body soak his shaft, wave after wave of pleasure exploding as moisture suddenly coated her inner thighs.

"God damn," she cried, coming in waves while he continued sinking deeper and deeper inside her. When she squeezed her eyes shut, warm lights erupted before her as she felt him split her in two.

"Can you take all of me, sweetheart?" he whispered, his voice rough.

Kylie let go of his arms and pushed herself off the bed, shoving against his chest. His expression changed immediately, growing alert.

"I'll show you what I can take." Her challenge was enough for him to allow her to push him back on her bed.

Then keeping him inside her while damn near being torn in two with the sensations that hit her hard as he pushed against muscles that hadn't been touched in years, if ever, she mounted him.

"Show me, darling," he growled, gripping her breasts.

Kylie got her balance and arched over him, sinking and taking all of him deep inside. She hissed, unable to stop as another orgasm hit her hard enough she would have fallen over if he didn't keep her in place by cupping her breasts.

She barely got a rhythm going when another wave of desire peaked inside her.

"That's it. Come hard for me," he growled.

She stared down at him through blurred vision, pressing her hands against his chest. The solid beat of his heart and the warmth of his skin turned her on as much as the view of his bare chest. She rose and fell, taking all of him and then lifting herself off of him until he practically slipped out before descending again.

His chest was so solid, muscles defined beautifully under a smooth spread of dark, coarse chest hair. When she moved her hands, stroking the corded muscle and feeling it twitch under her fingers, he grabbed her hips and thrust.

"Crap," she cried out, thankful she'd turned off the cameras. Even if they didn't record video in here, the audio in the rest of the house would pick up her cries.

"Take it, baby. Take all of me." He kept thrusting, taking over and driving deep and hard into her.

"Perry," she yelled, scraping her nails over his flesh while her world exploded into warm shades of red and purples. Everything turned vibrant, heat rushing over her furiously while her heart pounded violently in her chest, matching the demanding beat of his against her hands.

She swore everything fell sideways, the room, her world, everything. Wave after wave tore her apart inside as she came harder than she ever had. There wasn't any doubt in her mind. And at the same time he kept thrusting, taking her with him as he fucked her without mercy.

Every inch of him hardened. Kylie did her best to keep her eyes open, aching to watch the level of intensity that created a warm flush on his face and turned his body into steel. She couldn't move, couldn't stop him, couldn't do anything but hold on and take everything he gave her. And as another wave hit her, she felt him swell, tighten, and a low growl erupted deep inside him.

"Kylie," he roared, saying her name as though it was a demand.

He'd reached his limit, and if there was strength inside her to instruct him, order that he come for her, she would. But at that moment, watching him release, all she managed was staring in awe at the most beautiful man she'd ever laid eyes on. She wasn't sure whether it sucked or was a good thing that as he came the only thought surfacing in her fogged brain was that she knew without any doubt she would want this again.

Perry wrapped his arms around Kylie's damp body, feeling her heart patter against his chest. Her nipples were hard pebbles brushing against his flesh, continuing to torture him, even after he'd emptied all he had inside her. She was so damn tight. Or maybe with it being so long since he'd fucked a woman, she simply felt like the perfect glove wrapped around his cock.

Minutes passed before he managed to move his hand and stroke her soft blonde hair. "I'm supposed to bring you over to my sister's house on Wednesday for dinner."

Kylie raised her head, giving him an odd look. If anything, her reaction made finishing the request easier. He moved, lifting her with him easily. She was a small woman, something he forgot with her dynamic personality.

"It's not like you think." He hated sliding out of her and the chill when he was no longer buried in her heat was even worse. "She wants to know you better since the girls are talking about you so much."

It was the line he'd told his sister he'd use. And it was true. There wasn't any point in telling Kylie that Megan loved playing matchmaker. Kylie's silence and cautious expression satisfied him perfectly. She didn't want a relationship any more than he did. Fucking her, keeping an eye on her, and making sure she didn't pull another insane stunt was as far as he'd take this.

Although he'd be honest with himself, when he came over he didn't think he'd take it this far. Something about Kylie made it impossible to leave her alone. She never admitted she left last night to meet someone off the Internet, but Perry wouldn't be surprised if she refused to confess out of embarrassment from being caught doing something she knew wasn't a smart move. Kylie was intelligent. He'd give her that. Whatever compelled her to do what she did last night, he prayed now that they'd fucked each other, she wouldn't try doing it again.

"Give me her number and I'll give her a call." Kylie moved to the edge of the bed and put her feet on the floor, then combed her hair with her fingers.

Kylie would steamroll Megan in a second, something he wouldn't allow to happen. "She wants you to come to dinner."

"Then shouldn't she invite me?" The defiance that sharpened her bright blue eyes added to her flushed expression.

Goddamn she was gorgeous. And she wore that well-fucked look so well. He knew he didn't have sex with her just so he could use that as a tool to demand she listen to him. Kylie would challenge him at every corner, regardless of what kind of relationship they had. As impossible as it had been to keep his hands off her when he first arrived at her house, he knew it would be just as impossible to not have sex with her again. One thing he would be sure of, though. She wouldn't go chasing after other men while she was fucking him.

He grabbed his jeans and then gripped her chin, tilting her head while caressing her moist, smooth flesh. "She is inviting you through me." He made quick work of dressing and headed toward the hallway.

Kylie slipped into her clothes and was right behind him.

"Are there cameras inside the house, too?" It was quite an elaborate surveillance setup she had outside her house, which was a contradiction about her he intended to understand soon. For someone who was so cautious and protective of her home, it didn't make sense she would agree to meet someone under such dangerous conditions.

Perry grabbed the door handle to the middle bedroom and was surprised when she dove at him, using more strength than he would guess she had to rip his hand off the handle. "What's in there, darling?"

"If I wanted you to know, it wouldn't be locked."

He reached for her, but she took a step backward and then pointed toward her living room. "Move," she instructed.

It was a damn shame he never followed orders that well. He grabbed the door handle again and tried turning it, acknowledging that it was locked.

"If you recorded us fucking, I have a right to know."

"If you were worried about that, you should have asked before you fucked me."

He turned the doorknob with a bit more force, fairly confident he could break it if he wanted. Not that he would, but something more than a thesis paper was hidden behind that door.

"Perry, don't make me call nine-one-one."

It was her tone that grabbed him more than her words. She meant it. She would humiliate him by calling Dispatch to keep him out of the room. Letting go of the door, he stalked down the hallway and out her front door, leaving it open behind him. Without turning around he knew she stood in the doorway. Her gaze pierced the back of his neck, making it prickle.

"I'll be here at five on Wednesday to take you to my sister's," he called over his shoulder. By the time he climbed in and started his Jeep, Kylie's front door was closed. "I'm going to learn what you're up to, Kylie Dover," he whispered into the darkness, and pulled away from her curb.

Checking his phone that he'd intentionally left in the car, he pushed the button to hear voice-mail messages. There were two new messages.

"Flynn, this is Bealey," the first message began.

Officer Ron Bealey oversaw the Crime Analysis Department, his frazzled tone proof of the never-ending job he appeared to embrace. Bealey had been with the department long before Perry's sister's husband, David, joined the force.

"We've torn down that hard drive you sent over. There are no chat archives from any program showing she spoke with anyone by the name of Peter. Give me a call in the morning. We'll have the hard drive ready to ship back over. Sorry to offer a dead end, man," Bealey added, and hung up.

The automated voice asked whether Perry wanted to save or delete the message. He saved the message and listened as the second message began.

"Perry, what are you doing, bro? It's Noah. Call me back when you can."

The automated voice offered Perry his options. Glancing to see when the call came in and then what time it was now, he quickly dialed Noah Kayne's number. It rang four times before a woman answered.

"Is Noah there?" Perry asked.

"Sure. Oh wait, you're Perry," she said, her soft voice suddenly sounding animated. "Noah, it's Perry," she called out. "He'll be right here."

Perry didn't wait a minute before his old FBI friend came on the line.

"Screening your calls," Noah teased when he came on the line.

"Got to keep out the riffraff." Perry accelerated onto the interstate and headed toward his neighborhood. His friend sounded relaxed, happy, and shooting the shit with him for a few minutes helped lighten Perry's mood. By the time he pulled into his driveway, he was laughing over an old joke.

"One of these days I'm going to show up on your doorstep and set that woman right about you."

"She's head over heels for me, my friend. Nothing you can say will change her mind."

"I thought you said she was intelligent." Perry laughed easily when Noah defended Rain to the point where he announced she'd agreed to marry him. "And this convinces me that she's right in the head?" Perry envied Noah's happiness, though, and it hit him as odd that he did. "Congrats, man. I'll be looking for my invite."

"Invite, hell. You're going to be my best man."

"Well, hell. I'm honored. And more than willing to give you away."

"The bride is given away, not the groom."

"Damn shame," Perry said, and headed inside and to his refrigerator. Pulling out a beer, he treaded through his dark house to his den and computer. "I tell you what, though. We've got a mess down here that hopefully I'll have cleared up before the wedding. Have you set the date?"

"Rain hasn't decided on a date yet. I'll let you know when she tells me. Don't be surprised if you and I get about a week's notice. She seems to think that even though I'm the one who proposed, I might change my mind if I know the date too far in advance."

"Don't ask me to explain women to you," Perry said, snorting and then taking a long drink of his beer. Relaxing in his chair, he remembered the quick change in Kylie's attitude when he made a show of trying to get inside the middle bedroom. It was like cornering a nervous cat. He swore if he'd pushed her a moment longer, she would have pounced. Although if she attacked, it would have been round two of the lovemaking. Damn if that woman didn't get turned on when he got rough. Thinking about it now got his dick hard all over again. "I've got a little vixen right now who is doing her best to make my life hell."

"Sorry if she won't put out. Can't help you there," Noah said, laughing. "But what is the mess you've got going on?"

Like always, any time either of them got knee-deep in

bullshit, talking it out with each other usually helped. It did for Perry at least. He knew his friend couldn't always discuss cases in depth when he was buried up to his balls in them. But there had been a time or two over the years when he'd unloaded probably more than he should have on Perry.

"Several teenage girls have come up missing. We had one the other day who appeared out of nowhere, raped and beaten damn near beyond recognition. She made it to the back of the grocery store before collapsing and dying. One of the employees there found her."

"Shit. You got leads?"

"I got voice mail right before calling you back. They can't find anything on her hard drive. Another girl who snuck out of her parents' house to meet a guy and got intercepted by her father had been chatting with someone named Peter. I think he's an online sexual predator right here in town. There's a Web site that I found that had the girl we found today's picture on it."

"One of the porn sites you mentioned?" Noah was all business now. "You wanted me to help you figure out how to locate where the Web sites originate, right?"

"Yup. I got put on Kathleen Long's case today, the girl we found behind the store. So hopefully I'll get a bit more cooperation out of the department now."

"What's the Web site that had her picture on it?"

"Are you online now?" Perry moved his mouse, and his screen glowed to life in the dark den. Gulping down more beer, he quickly logged into his chat program and pulled up the Web site.

"I'm logging in now," Noah told him.

Perry waited until he saw Noah appear on his buddy list and then sent the link to the Web site. At the same time, the site opened on the screen. The pictures were different than they'd been the last time Perry looked.

"Damn it, she's not there anymore."

"Big surprise, huh."

"No shit. But I saved the page. Hold on." Perry went to the saved file and then sent it to Noah. "Two girls have disappeared over the past six months. Another would have disappeared if her father hadn't followed her and prevented it. We know all of them were talking to a boy who went by 'Peter.' He claims to be their age, but always says he lives in a town nearby. He lures them out of the house and that's the last we hear of them. I can't prove yet Kathleen Long, or this Web site, is connected to the other two girls. But my hunch is that they are."

"Could be," Noah said, sounding distracted. More than likely he was checking out the Web site. "What else do you got?"

"Not much. My nieces have been talking to a woman who is working on a thesis," he began.

"Okay, and?" It didn't take much for Noah to catch onto a vague line and know there was more to it.

"I've spent a bit of time with her." He wasn't sure why he said that, and paused, regrouping. He didn't know how to explain Kylie. "She's interviewing teenagers so she can write this college paper, but she won't show me the paper and then last night I caught her trying to meet someone in a dark parking lot."

"No shit?"

"I intervened and the guy took off, but then she took off, too. She's got all this surveillance equipment rigged up around her house, and a room that she has locked and won't let me in to see what is in there."

"You think she is Peter?"

"No. Oh, hell no. But I think she's a cop chaser and she's going to get her ass hurt if she tries playing detective, especially with a case like this."

Noah didn't say anything. Perry worked around his thoughts, trying to put into words his gut reaction toward her.

"Dani loves her to the point she even talked to Megan about her. And Dani doesn't open up about her life to any of us."

"Dani is your niece, right?" Noah had met the girls briefly a few years ago, but Perry didn't blame him for not being able to keep names straight.

"Yeah. No student wires her home like Kylie has. The security system she's installed is more sophisticated than most people can afford."

"Kylie Dover?" Noah asked.

"Yeah. Why? Do you know her?" It never crossed Perry's mind that Kylie could possibly be more than a novice detective out to get herself off on some warped obsession with chasing bad guys. Now that he thought about it, if she was connected with some agency it would explain a hell of a lot, except for the part about her intense secretiveness.

"No. Not a Kylie Dover," Noah said, sounding sincere enough to believe. "If she were an agent there would be no reason why she wouldn't tell you."

"True." He stared at his beer bottle and then shifted his attention to his computer screen. "So what can you tell me about this Web site?"

"Rain is checking it out now. I don't think she wants me drooling over all of the pictures."

A wounded female voice in the background made Perry smile, although he wasn't amused. Kylie would tell him if she was FBI or a private detective. There wouldn't be any reason why she wouldn't. Noah was right.

There was another reason she was protecting herself so thoroughly. Which meant that either she was a novice detective or whatever was in that bedroom had nothing to do with the case and she had another secret. It was becoming quite apparent he wasn't going to let it drop until he knew the truth, which meant he needed to push the hot little blonde even harder. Fucking her harder sounded damn good as well.

"Perry, it looks as if you've got quite a scene going on down there. I'll do some checking and should be able to get you a physical address on this Web site's ISP tomorrow. You're right about it being based in Kansas City."

"I knew it. Send me the proof as soon as you've got it."

"Will do. And keep me posted on your new conquest."

"Conquest?"

"Whatever, man. I haven't been FBI all these years to not

recognize the tone in your voice. If you haven't fucked her already, you're planning on doing it soon."

"Either way is none of your business."

"Okay, so you already have." Noah laughed in Perry's ear, undaunted by Perry biting his head off.

Which was a mistake. Perry should know better after all these years. Chewing Noah's ass got him going, and he was ready to spar. Perry leaned back in his chair, growling into the phone. Noah was one hell of a detective and always had been. The only way to keep information from him was to keep your mouth shut.

Another thing about Noah, though: he was loyal to a fault.

"If she were FBI, could you tell me?"

"Sure. As long as she wasn't working undercover."

Chapter 13

Kylie got out of her car at the library when her phone rang. Glancing at the number, she groaned. There wasn't any avoiding the call, but she sure didn't want to take it. Placing her laptop case on top of her car, she took in the cars in the parking lot and who was walking on the sidewalks and coming and going from the library as she answered.

"This is Donovan," she said officially.

"Donovan, I'm going to kick your ass," John Athey yelled into the phone.

"Take a number," she said, and rolled her eyes. She really didn't have time for this crap. "The cameras are on and running properly. I'm headed into the library to meet with some kids and learn if and who might be talking to Peter. Anything else you needed, Chief?"

"Don't fucking patronize me," he hissed, sounding as though his blood pressure would go through the roof any minute. "I've gone through your file. Your level of insubordination won't fly in this town, missy."

"Look through the file again. You'll get your man. I always deliver."

"Many agents deliver," he came back without a breath. "That security system is in your house for a goddamn reason. Don't think I won't pull someone else in on this case if you pull a stunt like that again. See how you like that on your permanent record."

"I could handle a vacation." She hated threats, hated

them more than anything. "You want me to go talk to these kids, or contact my travel agent?"

"Don't fuck with me," he snarled.

"Fine. Oh, and tomorrow night I'm going over to four of these teenage girls' home for dinner. Their mom invited me," she added, and then breathed in deeply. Getting pissed wouldn't help her think clearly when she met the kids inside the library. "I see a golden opportunity to learn more about what's on their home computers. These teenagers are going to become my best friends."

John didn't say anything for a moment and Kylie rode out the silence, watching as the city bus slowed on the street and its doors opened.

"Maybe we will wire you," he said slowly.

"Nope. I'm gathering data right now. Besides, I won't be in the company of any perps. They're all teenage girls."

"Who are these teenagers?"

She rattled off their names, pretty sure she got them right.

"Is the cop they're related to planning on being there, too?"

She scowled, frowning as she looked down at her finger-nails. "Lieutenant Perry Flynn will probably be there."

"Then you have a possible suspect. Kylie, you know your track record is impeccable. Peter is a cop, or someone who works and has access to computers in the police department."

"I already know that." The more time she spent talking to John, the more he got on her nerves. "And I'm still waiting for confirmation on whose computers were used down at the station. Is there a reason we don't have that information yet?"

"I'll check with Paul and get back to you on that one."

When she looked up, Dani and a few other girls were gathered in the grass around the bus stop. Dani spotted her and waved, then beckoned to her friends. The group headed in Kylie's direction.

"The latest murder, Kathleen Long—there was a picture of her on a pornography Web site."

"What?" Kylie's heart lodged in her throat as she quickly processed this information. "Peter has more of an agenda than simply stalking teenagers online and luring them into his trap of rape and murder."

"Can't prove that Kathleen is connected to the Peter girls yet. But we can confirm that Web site is based out of Kansas City. Don't get so close to Lieutenant Flynn that you lose perspective. There very well might be a reason why he's trying to get close to you."

The lump in her throat damn near choked her. "I've got to go," she whispered. "Company. And don't worry. I never lose perspective." She hung up before John could lecture her further, and stepped out of her car as the girls approached.

"That dress is so to die for," a thin blonde said who wore a very short leather miniskirt and halter top that barely covered her well-developed figure.

Kylie glanced down at the figure-hugging dress she wore today. It wasn't much longer than the blonde's, although where the blonde wore black stockings and boots Kylie's legs were bare. She looked up in time to catch Dani giving the blonde a scrutinizing glare.

"Thank you," Kylie said, smiling at the girl. "I'm Kylie, by the way."

"Nancy." Instead of offering her hand, she turned to the girls around her. "Dani says you're doing some really huge research paper on teenagers. I wish I got homework assignments like that."

"As if it would matter." Dani adjusted her backpack on her shoulder. "You don't do your homework now. We going to stand out here or go snag a computer or two?"

"We should go over to the Java Cup," the girl on the other side of Dani offered, whose hair had to be dyed black. It was long and glossy looking and raven black. She immediately shrugged as though her suggestion didn't matter.

"Is James working?" Dani poked the girl in the ribs.

"How would I know?" The girl's expression turned stubborn when she turned away from Dani and hugged herself. "But we can talk easier and they got computers there."

"I'm game, but I'm not walking." Dani looked at Kylie expectantly.

The other two girls followed suit.

"What about your parents?" Kylie wasn't going to take off with girls she barely knew. The last thing she would risk was parents getting pissed at her for driving their daughters places other than where they were supposed to be. "Don't they think you're at the library?"

Dani rolled her eyes, already heading around Kylie to the passenger-side door. "Shotgun," she announced. "And you've got to chill, Kylie. We've got cell phones. Mom doesn't care where I am as long as I'm home when she gets off work."

"All I have to do is call and leave voice mail," Nancy said, lining up behind Dani. "And Mandy's parents never care where she is."

"They just work a lot." Mandy, the black-haired girl, shrugged as if it didn't matter to her.

"Okay. I don't want anyone yelling at me."

The Java Cup turned out to be only a block and a half away from the library, and by the time Kylie parked she decided they would have gotten there faster walking. The coffee shop itself was quaint, though. Kylie liked the atmosphere, with cork walls covered with posters, some of which looked like they'd been hanging there for years. When she saw the young people behind the counter, with their piercings and tattoos, her impression of the place dropped. It was a teenage hangout in disguise.

"I never dreamed of drinking coffee at your age," Kylie mused.

"Whatever, like you are *so* much older than I am." Dani rolled her eyes and breathed in the aroma of her drink. "I can't start my day without a cup."

"Not me." Mandy led the way to a doorway that entered into a smaller room where two computers and then several tables with decks of cards and magazines were scattered. "It's Pepsi all the way, baby."

"Whatever happened to orange juice for breakfast?" Kylie took the chair next to the computer chair, letting the girls decide who would sit at the helm.

"God, I told them you were cool." Dani nudged Kylie. "Don't embarrass me."

"I'll try not to," Kylie said dryly, giving Dani a look to say she should consider herself lucky to be hanging with Kylie.

The look worked, surprisingly, when Dani grinned easily and nudged her way between her friends to take the seat in front of the monitor.

"Mandy, there's James."

"Where?" Mandy spun around with enough force that she almost toppled sideways. She then turned back to face them so quickly it was comical. "Don't say anything," she hissed.

Nancy and Dani giggled and Kylie searched the small room and then looked through the doorway into the larger shop area where a handful of teenagers now huddled in a group, as if plotting their moves while they were at the Java Cup.

It was odd sitting with the three girls, listening to them tease and insult one another and then profess their love in the next sentence. By the time Kylie was fourteen, her teenage years had ended. Kylie didn't have one memory of hanging out with girlfriends like this. Dani and her friends believed Kylie was a lot younger than she actually was, but that was their assumption. Mandy told a joke and Kylie found herself laughing with the other girls. It was easy fitting in with them, their lifestyle so simple and dramatized that it took little effort to act their age.

"Whoa, dude," Mandy said, and laughed, pointing at the screen when Dani logged in. "Look at all of your off-line messages."

Kylie leaned in, staring at the list of messages that appeared over Dani's buddy list as soon as she signed into her chat program. Apparently Dani used Yahoo! Messenger, which offered a list of comments people had sent her while she'd been signed off.

Nancy leaned over the back of Dani's chair and rested her arms on Dani's shoulders. "Who is Pfietterphish?" she asked.

"It's pronounced 'Peter Fish,' and it's Petrie, that exchange student I worked on my German assignment with last semester. Remember?"

Kylie leaned in, noting the spelling of the screen name while her stomach twisted into a cruel knot. She didn't want to think about Peter stalking Dani. But if he was, with her uncle being a cop it would make sense that Peter would disguise his screen name and the name he gave her.

"Where is he from?" Kylie asked, trying to sound unconcerned while she slowly repeated the screen name and how it was spelled in her head, saving it to memory.

"Spain, but he speaks several different languages and he helped me get an A in German." Dani highlighted each message and read it before deleting it.

"Have you met him?" Kylie tried not to be too obvious but managed to catch a few of the messages before Dani deleted them. It looked as if the two of them were rather flirty online. The cruel knot in Kylie's gut rose to her throat, leaving a bile taste in her mouth.

"No, but . . ." Dani turned and met Kylie's gaze. "Oh no, dude. Don't even go there."

"What?" Kylie asked.

"I know you aren't more than five years or so older than me, but sometimes you get this really adult attitude about you. And no offense, but it's really annoying."

"What did I say?" Kylie asked, managing to sound wounded and fighting to stay calm so she could learn as much as possible about Petrie.

"Yeah, man, don't jump her ass," Mandy instantly defended Kylie. "They're planning on meeting, but there's no way you can let her mother know."

"Mandy!" Dani hissed.

"What? You don't trust me to tell me this?" Kylie leaned back, crossing her arms and staring Dani down. It was imperative she knew every detail about this person Dani might meet. What she wouldn't have done for the social skills when she was a teenager that spilled out of her so easily now.

Dani stared at Kylie for a long moment, taking her time

while chewing her lip. She looked as though she wasn't sure how to respond, and the best way to get her to keep open channels was to stay quiet and wait out the silence.

"I'll make you a deal," Dani said, cocking one eyebrow. "Promise you won't come to dinner tomorrow night and I'll tell you about Petrie."

"You don't want me to come to dinner?" That one surprised Kylie.

"You want to come?" Dani sounded equally as surprised.

"If your mom wants to meet me, I don't have a problem with that. I'd be curious, too, if some lady were hanging around with my girls."

Dani snorted and the other girls laughed. Kylie glanced from one of them to the other, sure she'd just missed something.

"What did my uncle tell you?" Dani leaned back in her chair but then snapped to attention when she got an instant message. "We told Mom about you, and my uncle got all bent out of shape. That's all Mom needs to think she can play matchmaker. It will be a totally humiliating evening with her making a big deal over you sitting by Uncle Perry and then scooting everyone out of the room so you are left alone with him. You don't want that, do you?"

Dani didn't want to share her uncle. Kylie believed Dani liked her. Actually, she had no doubts. But there was a line Dani didn't want crossed. Her uncle wasn't available.

"I don't want to upset your mom by declining."

"Just be busy or something. She'll understand." Dani typed a message and hit "enter," sending the message up into the chat box. "Uncle Perry will be relieved if you back out," she added, giving Kylie a knowing look. "He hates it every time Mom tries hooking him up with ladies. It's not like he doesn't have ladies all over the place anyway."

Kylie pressed her lips together to keep herself from asking how Dani might know about her uncle's social life. Did he bring women around his nieces? And if so, Kylie hated the rather possessive sensation suddenly rushing over her when she ached to learn more about all of these women.

She realized Mandy had disappeared and Nancy stood with her arms crossed, watching the interaction between Dani and Kylie with a distracted air of boredom. She looked as though she was trying to decide whether she should remain with them or join the kids in the other room.

Taking an indifferent air would be Kylie's best move. The whole point of agreeing to meet Dani and her friends today was to learn where Peter was striking and to nab him before he captured another girl. If Kylie could do that here more so than at Dani's home, then so be it.

"I'll see if I can think of an excuse to convince your uncle and get out of it," she said, and nodded toward the computer. "Tell me about who you're chatting with."

Dani accepted the arrangement and then began talking about everyone she chatted with. As if they guessed they were being discussed, many started talking to Dani online until she easily chatted with five different people, the computer screen full of chat boxes. Kylie straightened when Petrie instant-messaged Dani.

Homework sucks.

Mandy had returned and she and Nancy pulled chairs around Dani, instantly alert when Petrie sent the message. Kylie glanced at the three girls, realizing the other two knew a fair bit about Petrie. As well, Dani's expression changed and she quickly typed: *BRB* into the other chat boxes and gave Petrie her exclusive attention.

"Tell him you'll help him study," Nancy encouraged.

Dani ignored Nancy, her gaze riveted to the screen, and typed: *No shit. I've got Geometry.*

Same here, and History. Like I care about what happened hundreds of years ago.

Dani appeared to forget she had an audience as she lost herself in her conversation with a boy who obviously she knew pretty well, in spite of never meeting him.

Mandy leaned around the back of Dani and whispered to Kylie, "Petrie is Dani's boyfriend."

"Shut the fuck up," Dani hissed as she continued to type.

"Write about her." Nancy poked Dani in the arm but

grinned at Kylie. "Put in your paper that some teenagers are whacked and commit to boys they've never met."

"I'm going to meet him," Dani said, but then leaned back, pausing from her online conversation, and gave Kylie a furtive look. "We've got a deal that nothing we share with you will be repeated to *anyone*, right?" She stressed the word "anyone" while staring hard into Kylie's eyes. "You've got to swear to that."

"Your mom wouldn't like Petrie?" Kylie decided to play ignorant and hear Dani say exactly what it was she didn't want anyone knowing about.

Dani rolled her eyes and then returned to her conversation. Kylie turned her attention to the chat box as well.

This Friday might work after school.

Dani posed her fingers over the keyboards, not saying anything for a moment, and both of her girlfriends watched her with bated breath. Kylie held her breath, it hitting her that Dani and Petrie had discussed meeting in person prior to the chat.

Dani blew out a breath and typed: *I'll let you know. G2G for now.*

She X'd out the box and quickly closed her chat program. Then pushing her chair back, she grabbed her coffee and stood, walking away from the three of them without saying anything.

Kylie watched her disappear into the other room, noticing she pulled her cell phone out of her backpack when she stood by the front door to the coffee shop.

Nancy moved into Dani's seat and took over the computer. "She doesn't want us to see her talking to Petrie," she pouted.

"Have they been chatting on the computer for long?" Kylie asked, still watching Dani.

"Forever." Mandy rolled her eyes and leaned forward, lowering her voice. "She's scared to meet him but won't admit it."

"Do you all meet guys off the computer a lot?" Kylie asked.

"Oh, sure. All the time." Mandy waved her hand in the air as though it didn't matter. "But Dani's uncle fills her head with crap about stalkers and rapists and bullshit like that who prey off poor little innocent girls like us."

Nancy made a very unladylike snorting sound as she continued typing on the computer. Kylie watched her open the Facebook Web site but kept glancing past the girls to Dani.

"It's not completely bullshit," Kylie said, not focusing on either one of them. "Even I wouldn't meet someone online without knowing a lot about them first. Or at least talking on the phone."

"She talks to Petrie on the phone all of the time," Nancy told Kylie.

Dani pulled open the door to the Java Cup and disappeared outside.

"Still sounds like she should be careful," Kylie said, fighting the urge not to break into a serious lecture. All she would do was chase them away if she did that. "Where's the bathroom?"

The girls pointed to the door leading to the other room. Kylie had spotted the restrooms when she first entered, but it was a good excuse to check on Dani without the others knowing. Neither girl offered to go with her, and Kylie left them hovering in front of the computer, not paying any attention to whether she went into the bathroom or not.

She slipped outside, hoping she hadn't lost Dani. Kylie squinted against the late-afternoon sun at the teenager, who'd managed to make it across the street and leaned against the back of Kylie's car in the parking lot. Watching Kylie approach, Dani repeatedly glanced at her phone in her hand while she text-messaged someone. Her frustrated expression didn't fade when Kylie approached.

"Are all men assholes?" Dani demanded to know, and pressed her lips together as if she'd just swallowed something bitter.

"I don't know all of them." Kylie lifted one shoulder and shrugged lazily, then leaned against her car next to Dani. "Is it Petrie?" she asked quietly.

Dani nodded once. Her cell phone played a happy-sounding jingle and Dani held it in both of her hands, pushing the buttons with her thumbs, when she answered the text message.

"He's going to meet Lanie Swanson. He knows I hate that bitch's guts."

"He sounds like a player," Kylie offered, crossing her arms and staring at the Java Cup across the street.

"No. He's not like that at all," Dani assured her, shaking her head hard enough that her long brown hair fanned over her shoulder and shrouded part of her face. "Lanie is the player. She's a little tramp. The only reason she's chasing him is because she knows I like him," Dani said, her last sentence fading when she lowered her tone to a whisper.

"Do you know anyone else who's met him?" Kylie asked, pushing herself away from her car when Mandy and Nancy walked out of the Java Cup.

"No. And I know what you're thinking. He's not some serial killer." Dani straightened as well. Her phone played its little jingle again and she scowled at the message, then pushed the buttons, answering it while sighing. "I know Petrie is for real."

"How do you know?" Kylie turned when Nancy and Mandy spotted them and hurried across the street toward them. She faced Dani, studying the teenager's determined expression. "Have you actually talked to him on the phone?"

Dani's soft green eyes looked darker with the black eyeliner that was neatly applied. Her pale blue eye shadow and dark mahogany lipstick hid her natural beauty. It could also mislead a person into believing Dani was older than she was. Kylie remembered John telling her about the pornographic Web site and knew all too well how many "barely legal" sites there were out there. Imagining someone breaking Dani's spirit to get her to comply and cooperate for poses used on sites like that made Kylie sick.

"No one talks on the phone," Dani snapped. "You don't get it. You act as though you're all hip and everything, but for real you're no different than Uncle Perry or Mom. I hope I don't turn into a prude as quickly as you have."

"Dani, wait," Kylie yelled when Dani marched across the parking lot to her girlfriends.

"Talk to you later, Kylie," Dani said, waving over her shoulder before forming a quick huddle with Mandy and Nancy.

For a moment Kylie was thrown back in time, the same age as the girls who'd just abandoned her, and feeling so alone the pain threatened to break her in two. She didn't have anyone to turn to, no one to seek out for guidance. Alone in the world without her older sister, who'd been Kylie's resource for all things wise and imperative to know in life, she was consumed with pain that made her eyes burn.

Both girls glanced in her direction before falling in line on either side of Dani and walking away from Kylie. She stared after the teenagers, knowing Dani's indecision had made her snap more than irritation toward Kylie. Dani was smart and for the most part had a fair amount of common sense for a girl her age, proof she'd been raised well. Peer pressure tore at her right now, though. Kylie needed to keep an eye on her and make sure the girl didn't make a very stupid move.

The painful memory of Kylie's youth disappeared as quickly as it had surfaced and a more primal, demanding sensation washed over her.

"You'd better be a pimply-faced kid, Petrie," she said under her breath as she unlocked her car. "Because if you're not, I'm going to kick your perverted ass until you wished you'd never laid a hand on a teenage girl in your life."

Chapter 14

"Do you know where Dani is?" Denise asked.

Perry glanced at the time on the digital clock above his TV on the cable box. Six thirty. "What time is she supposed to be home?"

"We're all supposed to be home by five, Uncle Perry." Denise used her exceptionally sweet voice. "I'm worried. You don't think she's dead in a ditch somewhere, do you?"

"I'll be sure and check all the ditches." He lifted his cell phone from the coffee table when it beeped and glanced to see who else was calling. "She's calling me now, sweetheart," he told her, putting his finger over the button on his Bluetooth to accept the call. "So you can quit worrying over the safety of your sister."

"Okay," she said slowly. "Is that lady coming to dinner tomorrow night?"

"Yup. I'll talk to you soon." He got Denise off the phone, knowing she would go about her business satisfied she'd gotten her sister in trouble. For Denise, that would make it a good night, managing to get one of her sisters punished for something. "Where are you?" he demanded, using his deep baritone when he answered the phone for his niece.

"With friends," Dani said, not sounding worried about the time, or anything else for that matter.

"Where are you?"

"Kylie can't make it to dinner tomorrow night," Dani said, sounding winded and ignoring his question.

Perry straightened on the couch, lifting the remote off his chest and dropping it on the coffee table. "Oh? Why not?"

"She just can't. I'm not her babysitter. I didn't ask." Her defensive tone was enough for Perry to know he was barely getting a fraction of the story.

"I'm sure if she can't make it, she will call and let me know." He was actually pretty positive she wouldn't do that, since she didn't know his cell phone number. And he didn't know hers.

"She can't because you never gave her your number, so she said to tell you. I've got to go. I guess don't worry about coming over tomorrow night."

"Wait a minute." He smelled a rat. "Why aren't you home?" He decided switching subjects would make her talk more. Sometimes gathering any information, trivial or otherwise, out of Dani was harder than pulling teeth. "I do believe your mother's made it clear that you're to be home at five every day."

"I know, but I was busy working on homework with friends." The standard answer that Dani used and believed firmly would keep her out of any trouble. "Have a good evening, Uncle Perry."

"Is Kylie with you now?" He wasn't going to let Dani go that easily. Something was up between her and Kylie. But even if he didn't get answers on that one, his niece was supposed to be home and wouldn't escape from him before he knew where she was.

"We just left her. Walking is good for you, you know."

"Where are you, Dani?"

Apparently she decided it was in her best interest to start answering her uncle's questions. The deep, tortured sigh on the other end of the phone defined her reluctant acceptance of that fact.

"Downtown, okay? I'm sorry it got so late. But I was with Kylie. Mom won't mind."

"Your uncle might, though. What were you doing with Kylie?"

"We were at the Java Cup. That's when she said she can't

make it tomorrow night. I think she mentioned having a date, or something."

A piercing sense of aggravation shot through him from his niece's callous comment. More so, hearing Kylie possibly had a date, in spite of the fact that something told him Dani made it up, didn't sit well with him at all. He wasn't into casual sex. Fucking Kylie when he was pretty sure she'd tried meeting another man the night before might not have been the smartest move he'd made in his life. There was something about her, though, something that tripped emotions inside him he usually managed to keep at bay when around any other lady.

Figuring out what Dani was up to might take hours. He opted for the easier task of learning what Kylie was up to.

"Here is what you're going to do," he said slowly. "You're going to turn around and go back to Kylie and you're going to have her call me."

"I can't, Uncle Perry. She's already left."

"Do you have her cell phone number?"

There was silence for only a moment. "Yeah." She sounded as if it bothered her to relinquish that information.

Perry didn't care. "Give it to me." He stood, headed into his den, and then wrote the number down when Dani gave it to him. "I'm calling your mother. You'll be home in ten minutes, or else."

"Fine," she said, again sighing so heavily it was as though he tortured her. "Talk to you later," she added, and then hung up.

Before he could dial his sister, his cell rang again. Megan was calling him. "Hello," he said.

"Perry, have you heard from Dani?" Megan sounded worried.

"Just hung up the phone with her. She'll be home in ten minutes. Everything okay?"

"Oh, good. And everything's fine," she said, her tone implying just the opposite. "What time will you and Kylie be here tomorrow night?"

"Since you already told me to have her over there by six thirty, why don't we discuss what has you upset?"

It amazed him when she sighed how much it sounded like Dani's sigh.

"I know younger brothers are supposed to be annoying," she began, her usual chipper tone returning. "But annoying and protective make for a bad mix sometimes, you know?"

"I'm sure. What's up?" He hated how hard Megan worked when she had to come home and jump into raising and dealing with teenagers. Megan was the most impressive woman he'd ever known in his life, but he hated how she fought him when he tried shouldering some of the concerns and worries that went along with bringing up her daughters.

"I don't know if anything is up, Perry. And I won't know until Dani gets home. You're not going to start yelling at her until I have the facts straight, and then I get to yell first."

He knew something was up when Dani told him Kylie wouldn't be coming to dinner tomorrow night. Call it a gut instinct, but Kylie wouldn't have canceled. Not only did she want to know the girls better, for whatever reason he still needed to find out, but beyond that, there was a level of interest there. He might not be an expert on relationships, but he recognized the attraction between them. No matter if she tried meeting another guy. Kylie was interested in him.

Perry heaved out a loud sigh. Not only did he have absolutely no interest in a serious relationship, but he couldn't flatter himself into thinking that after knowing him barely a week Kylie would want to set up housekeeping. At the same time, though, it would surprise him if she came up with a lame excuse to get out of going to dinner. If it weren't because of him, she wanted to spend time with his nieces. She had a paper to write, and he had all the research she could ask for in his nieces.

"Is something wrong?" Megan asked.

"Nothing. What do you know?" he asked, keeping his tone neutral. He got a lot further with Megan when he kept his cool.

"Hearsay," she snapped. Denise said something in the background and Megan snapped at her, too, telling her to go unload the dishwasher and quit eavesdropping.

Denise announced in the background that if it weren't for her eavesdropping they wouldn't know right now that Dani was about ready to go do something stupid enough to get herself killed.

"What did Denise tell you?"

"Apparently she overheard Dani on her phone talking to one of her girlfriends about meeting a boy she's been talking to on the Internet."

"What?" Perry turned around quickly in his living room, the sudden urge to destroy something, pick something up and hurl it, or better yet send his fist crashing through anything hit him hard enough that it made him dizzy. "How long have you known this?"

"Since I got home. And I'm dealing with it," she said, using her "I'm the mother" voice on him. "I will not have you reaming her out before I know completely what is going on."

"I can tell you what's going on!" he yelled, his voice bouncing off the walls. "Girls her age are disappearing! I helped peel a teenage girl off the asphalt the other day, beaten damn near beyond recognition, and dead, because of some online stalker."

"Which is why you are not going to talk to Dani about this," Megan yelled right back at him. "You're jaded, Perry. There's no way you can't be with what you do for a living. Dani isn't stupid. I will take care of this."

"She's more than stupid if she's considering meeting someone off the Internet."

"I said I'll take care of this."

"What are you going to do?"

Megan didn't say anything for a minute, proof enough that she didn't know what to do about it. He needed to talk to Dani; the sooner the better.

"I'm going to find out the truth of the matter first." Her tone turned cold. "And then I'll handle it. In fact, she just came home. I'll see you and your lady friend tomorrow night."

Megan hung up on him. She never hung up on him. Perry turned, fisting his hands with enough pressure that he felt the pain in his palms from his fingertips. It didn't help his anger subside. Megan had the power to push him out of his nieces' lives. They were her daughters. But damn it to hell and back, he wouldn't stand around and watch if Dani were about to do something so idiotic it could risk her life.

Stalking into his kitchen, he grabbed a beer out of the refrigerator and returned to his couch and the remote. The beer wouldn't help. Maybe something harder, with a fierce bite, might numb his aggravation and outrage.

"Goddamn it," he grumbled, sinking into his couch but unable to get comfortable. Tilting the chilled bottle, he poured half the brew down his throat. He needed to call Kylie and figure out what the hell was going on with her supposedly backing out of dinner tomorrow night. The sooner he had answers the better. More than likely, Dani would tell Megan the same thing she told him; if anything, his niece would use the topic as a shield against her mother to prevent getting yelled at for talking to boys online that she didn't know.

Megan was one hell of a mother. He'd be the first to admit it. But his nieces were all sharp as tacks. Dani could take Megan on, tell her what she wanted to hear, and have her off her back in a matter of minutes. Perry would bet his paycheck on it.

"It won't be as easy convincing me of your innocence, young lady," he said out loud, and downed more of his beer.

His cell phone started ringing and he glanced around, then realized he'd left it in his den when he jotted down Kylie's number. Once again removing the remote from his belly and pushing himself to his feet, Perry made it to his phone before the caller went to voice mail.

"Flynn here," he said after noticing the caller was Dispatch.

"Flynn, I thought you might want a heads-up." Cliff Miller didn't usually work the night shift, but he spoke quickly, sounding pumped up and riding high on adrenaline, caffeine, or both. "Another teenager has just been reported missing. Her parents are at the station now. Their daughter, Rita Simoli, never came home and didn't show up for her after-school job."

"Is anyone doing a report?" Perry hurried to his bedroom and quickly stripped out of his sweats and got back into the jeans he had worn that day. Missing persons reports weren't filled out until 24 hours had passed. Most cops hesitated in doing even that when it was a teenager.

"One of the clerks is talking to them, but Rad mentioned you were on the Olivia Brown case."

"I'll be there in ten. Keep the parents there."

Barely ten minutes later Perry hurried into the station, nodding when Cliff gestured with his head in the direction of the administrative desks lined in rows in the middle of the station. He pushed the code into the panel alongside the door and shoved it open the moment it buzzed.

Cheryl Parker glanced up at him and looked noticeably relieved when he approached her desk. "Perry, this is Polly and Ricardo Simoli, parents of Rita Simoli." She picked up several pieces of paper and tapped them against her desk, organizing them, and then handed them over to him. "I've taken their personal information but . . ." She broke off, shooting a side-glance at the Simolis'.

Ricardo stood and then put his hand on his wife's shoulder when she slowly rose to her feet as well. "You're going to fill out a missing persons report," Ricardo Simoli didn't make it a question.

"You're going to find our daughter?" Polly asked, her eyes swollen and stained from running mascara.

"Yup," he said, knowing from years on the force that parents asked the impossible questions first and telling them he didn't have a clue whether he could find their child or not wasn't an effective way to begin interrogation. "Thanks, Cheryl," he said, glancing at her long enough to catch her smile and wink, and then turned his focus on the distraught couple.

"Let me know if there's anything else you need," Cheryl offered, never missing a chance to throw shameless suggestive comments in his direction no matter the seriousness of the moment.

He didn't bother answering but gestured for the Simolis to come with him. "I'll need you to help me get a feel of where to start looking," he said quietly. "Do either of you need anything to drink?"

"No, we need our daughter," Ricardo said crossly.

"We'll get her," Perry said without bothering to make eye contact. "Have a seat," he said, moving around his desk in the "pit" and making a mental note of who all was in the building. Other than Dispatch and a couple administrative people, Franco helped himself to coffee and gave Perry and the Simolis a curious stare before taking his time returning to his desk. If Franco was going to rat him out for filling out a missing person's report before the 24 hours was up, he could just go to hell. Perry turned his attention to Ricardo and Polly. "Let's see what we have here."

"Our daughter didn't show up for work. She's never missed a day on the job since she started."

"At . . ." Perry glanced at the notes Cheryl had taken, hand written in neat block letters. "At Simoli's Restaurant." It dawned on him then why their name sounded familiar. They either owned or worked at a family restaurant that was fairly successful, with an unbeatable reputation for incredible Italian food.

"We let her start working there when she turned sixteen. Our daughter is seventeen now and not once has she missed a day on the job. None of our children are slackers," Polly said, straightening. "Something terrible has happened to our Rita."

"Let me ask you this," Perry said, agreeing with Mrs. Simoli but not seeing the point in saying so. "Does your daughter spend a lot of time on the computer?"

"What kind of question is that?" Ricardo snapped. "All of us do. Part of Rita's job is entering tickets on the computer."

"I meant chatting, online chatting. Does she do a lot of that?"

Ricardo looked at his wife, who returned a concerned

expression. She focused on Perry first, her expression sadder than it had been a moment before. "There was a time, not too long ago, when she appeared obsessed with talking to this boy on the computer. It wasn't natural, or proper. Her father and I put an end to it."

"Do you know who she was chatting with? The boy's name?"

"Peter, Peter Rangari. We didn't know his family, and he wasn't from Mission Hills. There are good boys here from very successful families, plenty for our Rita to choose from." Polly straightened, tilting her head slightly while pressing her lips together in a very determined-looking expression. "Why do you ask us this?"

"Peter Rangari," Perry repeated, writing the name down. "I need as many current pictures of your daughter that you can provide, and also, with your permission, I need to look at the computer your daughter used to do her online chatting."

"Our daughter obeys us." Ricardo pushed his chair back and stood, then took his wife's arm and encouraged her to her feet. "Don't even think she would go behind our backs and meet a boy we demanded she sever all communication with. If you want to send a team over to our home, we'll co-operate. But you'd better come up with a better lead than that, or I'll insist another cop be given our daughter's case, one who knows what the hell he is doing."

A couple hours later, Perry walked out of the Simolis' house, a nice two-story country home with a large landscaped yard, his mood more sour than it had been all day.

"Peter is hitting hard," Carl said, scowling when he reached for the passenger door.

Perry looked at him over the top of the car. "She'd been talking to him for months, too. We've got the printed chats, but I think we need to subpoena their hard drive."

"Going to have to. Mr. Simoli didn't like us even going through the computer." Carl slipped into the passenger seat next to Perry. "More than likely he was scared we'd stumble onto all of his souped-up accounting."

Perry snorted, not giving a damn how the man ran his restaurant. "You'd think he'd be more cooperative in finding his daughter."

"At least we know where she went to meet him."

"And we're heading there now." Although arriving at the health-food grocery store where apparently Rita went on a regular basis to pick up vegetables for her family's restaurant hours after she met Peter wouldn't find them shit, and Perry knew it.

Kylie squatted in the dark, frowning at the asphalt in the parking lot as she glanced around at her quiet surroundings. Peaceful and serene, in the wake of a terrible crime. Another teenage girl had been yanked out of her world, taken from the safe and happy life she'd known for seventeen years. It wasn't right that she would be exposed to the nightmares that would follow her abduction. Kylie's heart hurt as anger and frustration bit at her, making the chill in the night air feel more like poison than cooling relief.

Cars drove up and down the main street, even at this hour. She looked in the direction of the intersection and her heart skipped a beat when she saw a city police car. She couldn't risk being seen at a crime scene, even if the police hadn't designated the place as such. When Paul called her, informing her about Rita Simoli, Kylie knew her time was limited before Perry showed up here.

Kylie straightened, not sure what she expected to find here. But a teenage girl had disappeared, possibly where Kylie stood right now, and it always helped her to physically witness where a crime took place. She bet Perry would feel the same way. Which was why she kept one eye on the road and all passing cars.

She looked across the empty parking lot, at the community grocery store and its dark windows. Ads covered the windows promoting healthy food and organic items for sale.

Kylie walked toward the closed grocery store, hitting the wide sidewalk that ran along the building. There was a roof over the sidewalk, and signs on poles announcing no skateboarding allowed.

Kylie started down the sidewalk, her shoes clicking against the paved walk and echoing from the roof over her. There were two vending machines, one offering the standard assortments of soda pops, the next offering an array of juices and bottled water. After that there was a newspaper machine, which displayed today's paper. She glanced at the machine, wondering when a newspaper boy would stop and refill it. Next was a pay phone.

"Interesting," Kylie whispered, staring at the pay phone and the cord that hung from the receiver. It had been cut. Where it should attach to the phone it now hung to the ground, the receiver resting in its holder, but if it was lifted she could actually walk away with it. She wondered when it had been cut.

Walking up to it, instead of lifting the receiver she bent and studied the end of the cord. "Clean cut," she said to herself. If it was yanked out of the phone, someone with some strength did the job.

Looking past the phone toward the next pole that didn't have a sign on it, she noticed something else. Reaching into her pocket, she pulled out a small, flat, little camera. It was a good thing this baby took outstanding pictures in the dark. She snapped several pictures of the sabotaged pay phone and then moved closer to the pole.

It was painted bright red, as were all of the poles. She reached for the pole but instead of touching it stretched her fingers and moved them mere centimeters over the pole where it appeared there were several scratches in the paint.

"As if someone held on to the pole with enough strength that their fingernails dug into the paint." She took pictures of the scratch marks embedded in the paint. "And what do we have here?"

Kylie looked at the curb, then knelt at the edge of the sidewalk. On the other side of the pole was a shoe. She touched her fingertips to the lady's plain brown flat-heeled shoe. It wasn't damp, implying it hadn't been here long. After snapping several pictures of the shoe, moving into the lot and facing the pole and pay phone and shoe on the ground, and taking more pictures, she then pulled out her cell phone.

"Paul, we've got quite a bit of evidence here," she said when he answered.

"What do you got?" It sounded as though there might be laser beams firing in the background and she pictured him sitting in front of his computer, challenging someone's high score or defending his own.

"There's a broken pay phone, indication of scratches on the pole at the edge of the sidewalk next to it, and a shoe. I have pictures of all of it. But if I bag the evidence, we're going to have to go live about being on this case."

"I'd say that's already happening with John talking to the media," Paul pointed out.

"He's doing what?" Kylie ran her fingers through her hair, shaking her head in growing aggravation.

"They're going public with this one. John and the Chief are meeting with reporters and the Simolis' now."

She wasn't surprised, especially with Paul having told her the Simolis' were a prominent family in the community. They were used to a high-profile life and probably would have gone public without the law if they hadn't agreed. "It would have been nice to have a bit more time."

"Want me to send out a forensics team?"

"Yup. The police will probably be here soon and I'd just as soon get a good sweep of the scene before they mess with it."

"Sending them out now." The sounds of explosions and continual laser fire never stopped. "Rita Simoli was talking to a guy named Peter on her family's computer. Your cop, Mr. Flynn, just left there a bit ago and reported in to his Chief. We got the information a few minutes before you called. You need to narrow in on this guy and set up another meeting."

"I'm working on it." She grabbed the evidence bag out of her trunk, then locked her car, which she'd parked on the side street on the back side of the store, and sprinted across the parking lot. "So far we keep missing each other with instant messages, but I'll see if I can lure him out later tonight. If I can, that means he's either disposed of Rita or locked her up somewhere so he can focus on his next prey."

"If the Web site is connected to him, he's locking them up and not killing them." Paul grunted. "At least not right away."

"We also need to consider the possibility that Peter could be more than one person." Her insides churned at the thought of these teenagers being locked up like animals and tortured. "How soon before Forensics is here?"

"You should have a couple agents there in a few minutes. I suggest you take off."

She tried not to breathe too heavily into the phone after running from her car back to the sidewalk. But pulling on gloves and then sliding the shoe into the ziplock bag, she sealed it and grabbed the receiver from the pay phone, sliding it into another evidence bag. "I'm bringing the shoe and receiver in; then I'll see if I can get Peter on the horn and arrange for a meet."

Kylie headed down the sidewalk toward the back of the building when she glanced at the entrance to the parking lot from the main road. A tan sedan, similar in make and model to the ones parked at the FBI field office, pulled into the parking lot. It parked at the end of the sidewalk, but the driver kept the motor running. One of them saluted her when two men got out of the car. She recognized the special agents from when she was down at the office, but didn't know their names.

"I've got confirmation your team has arrived," Paul said in her ear as one guy walked to her and the other popped his trunk.

"That's a ten four," she told him. "I'll brief these two and talk to you soon."

"Roger that."

Kylie walked the two men through the crime scene and helped rope off the scene with yellow tape. A news van entered the parking lot and two other cars, one unmarked and one city police, followed.

"Crap, the circus has arrived."

"You're going to blow your cover," one of the guys warned her.

"Nope." Kylie hated leaving the scene but trusted the two men to do their job. "Time to get out of Dodge."

"You'd better fly," the guy closest to her said, grinning.

"I'm on it, Batman." She bolted down the length of the building, pretty sure no one saw her.

An hour later they had confirmation that the shoe belonged to Rita Simoli and her frantic parents once again turned to the press, offering a large reward for the safe return of their daughter. There were fresh prints on the receiver that matched prints on the pole that had been scratched, but Rita had never been printed. There was no way to make a positive ID other than using the assumption they were hers based on the shoe. Kylie managed to escape the cameras and snuck back to her house unnoticed.

After adjusting the volume on her TV so she could hear the news, she settled in the middle bedroom, keeping an eye on her monitors as well as focusing on her buddy list. Anticipation riddled her insides, like the feeling she got when a case was about to explode wide open. In spite of suspecting she was on to the right guy after learning that Rita spoke to Peter with the same screen name, Kylie guessed her stomach tied in knots for several reasons.

She didn't doubt Perry would be pissed when he learned she hit his crime scene and tagged it before he could, even though he wouldn't know she was the agent who reported to the scene. That wasn't the only reason trepidation ran hot and heavy through her veins.

Dani was speaking with Peter, too. Even though she had told Kylie another girl would meet him this Friday night, that didn't ease Kylie's nerves any. There would be another meet and she knew when. If only she knew where. Somehow she needed to learn where Peter was meeting Lanie Swanson, Peter, or Petrie, wouldn't tell Dani and even if he did, getting

Dani to tell Kylie would be harder than pulling teeth. She'd feel a hell of a lot better if she knew without any doubt Dani wasn't going to meet him.

Kylie continually glanced at the monitors. Something told her Perry would be by tonight, and just thinking about him showing up at her home made her insides swell with expectation. He wouldn't be the only one wound up from working a case. Although she couldn't share with him anything she'd found out or learned, she could show him what to do with all that energy that needed an outlet.

Heading over to the Facebook profile she'd created, she began searching, going from profile to profile, reading every line and checking out pictures and comments posted to each profile. It sickened her how openly teenagers discussed their social lives on one another's profiles, making it so easy to get to know them if anyone wished to take the time and sift through the millions of profiles on the site to find the ones of interest.

She stumbled onto Dani's Facebook profile after finding a profile for the Mission High School drama department. Although Dani's profile said she was ninety-seven years old and lived in Lebanon, there were quite a few references to other kids, and after Kylie checked out each profile she realized who some of them were.

The sound of someone signing on startled her. She was so engaged in what she was doing that she'd even drowned out the TV from the other room. Immediately a chat box popped up in front of the Web site she'd been scrutinizing.

Where were you earlier tonight? I've been bored all evening and no one was online.

Convenient opening line. And an obvious guilty conscience. Peter probably just finished dealing with Rita. There wasn't any reason he should suspect her. Apparently, he felt a need to put in writing he never left the house due to some warped line of thinking that somehow that proved his innocence.

Sorry. I had homework, she typed, and flipped his box behind the Web site to search and see if she could find Rita's profile. She didn't, but there were links on all of the pages she went to for Dani's and some of the other profiles connecting them to a Facebook profile.

Are you done with it now? Talk to me, Kayla. I really need a good friend.

I'm right here. Is something wrong?

Yeah, there is something wrong. It's my birthday and my parents are leaving town.

She didn't get the connection but knew he was plotting a good three or four messages ahead of her. Kylie minimized the Web site behind her so she could focus better on the conversation without distractions.

It's your birthday? she asked, deciding she'd approach the comment about his parents being out of town next. There wasn't any doubt in her mind where he was heading with that one. And from what she'd learned about teenage girls since she started this case, any of them would be sharp enough to guess why he would bring that up.

Not today—Thursday. But both of my parents are going to be out of town on business. I don't get a birthday party.

If they're going out of town, you can have a bash. She cringed after sending it, praying her choice of words didn't sound too square for a teenage girl.

Call me a nerd if you want, but they would kill me if I had a party while they were gone. And well, it's not right.

What the hell was his motivation? Maybe he wanted her feeling sorry for him and agreeing to meet him. Or possibly he believed if he portrayed himself as a compassionate soul, she would like him even more and be more likely to do whatever he suggested.

Then it hit her, and without commenting on what he said, she pulled up the Facebook Web site and quickly went to her own profile. She read what she'd written about herself.

It was right there in front of her, on display for all to read: *I want someone not afraid to do the right thing even when peer pressure pushes for him to do something else. Show me you stand out in a crowd, honest to a fault and not afraid what your friends might say, and I will go anywhere with you.*

"Two points, motherfucker," she mumbled.

He chimed again. She'd waited too long to respond. *Hey, nerds need love, too.*

LOL. Are you going to have a birthday party when they come home? Will I get an invite?

I'll have a party when they get back. But nothing at all is going to happen on the day of my birthday. I'm sure this has never happened to you. You don't understand how sad that makes me.

She understood more than she would tell him. Her fifteenth birthday had gone by unnoticed. It was such a devastating experience she remembered it today as if it were yesterday. Her sister was gone, raped and murdered, which raped and murdered their family, too. Nothing was the same after that. Something as trivial as Kylie's birthday couldn't be dealt with after losing Karen.

Kylie never told her parents they forgot. Even today, when bridges with her mom and dad finally were being mended, Kylie couldn't bring it up to them. There wasn't any point in opening old wounds.

That would suck, she typed, and hesitated, wanting to say just the right thing without sounding too obvious, so he would suggest another meeting. *Maybe you could ask your parents if you could get together with a few special friends.*

You're a special friend to me.

Good. I feel the same way about you.

If my parents say it's okay, you'll see me on my birthday. He didn't make it a question.

"Okay," Kylie said out loud as she typed the one word and clicked "send."

Good. Plan on seeing me Thursday. Tell your parents you'll be at a birthday party for a couple hours. And thank you. You're going to make this birthday one I'll remember for the rest of my life.

Kylie was sure it would be a day both of them would remember for the rest of their lives. At the same time, she noted that Peter just gave himself a couple-hour time frame, which she bet he did with every girl he snatched. And with a couple-hour run time, it made it damn hard for the law to chase him down. Hard, but not impossible.

"This all ends Thursday," she vowed to herself. If she could get Peter to capture her, there would be no worries about Dani, or any other girl, meeting him Friday.

Chapter 15

Kylie sat lost in thought but didn't realize her eyes were closed. Nor did it quite hit her what had brought her back to the present. Twenty minutes had passed since the last entry typed in her chat with Peter. Her thoughts had drifted from Karen to her mother, and her last visit to Dallas and the time she and Kylie had spent together.

Her mom had been friendly, almost loving, when Kylie went down there. There were years of mending for the two of them to go through, and up until the last couple years neither one of them had exerted too much effort to allow the healing process to start between them. But now, with her father sick, something compelled Kylie to return home when she could, even if just for the weekend.

Something her mother said suddenly rang through strong in her thoughts.

"I'm so proud of you." Her mother said it so casually, as if she told Kylie that every day.

Had her mother ever told her that before?

Something pulled her out of her thoughts. She stared at her monitor, but Peter hadn't said anything. She swore she heard something. Maybe her mom's voice in her head came through louder than she thought.

Kylie forced herself to quit daydreaming, or was it night-dreaming since it was now officially after midnight? This time, though, she knew she heard something, and it didn't come from the TV. It was like a scratching sound, like a dog trying to get its owner's attention by dragging its claws down the door. Except Kylie didn't have a dog.

Quickly saving her chat with Peter, she then cleared the box and minimized the Web sites she'd been browsing. Focusing on her monitors, she pushed the button to rewind them ten minutes to see if anyone was outside. A couple minutes of quiet images of her front yard went by before Perry's Jeep pulled up in front of her house. Then it backed up along the curb until it was out of range for the cameras to pick it up.

"Crap," she hissed, jumping up and grabbing her phone. Her gun was in its thigh holster, which she'd worn when she investigated the crime scene earlier this evening. "Sheez, woman, you don't need it against Perry."

But she did need to make sure he didn't see this room. She returned her attention to her monitor in time to see Perry sprint across her yard, running fast enough that the cameras barely picked him up. In a matter of seconds, he was gone from the images playing back for her.

"He ran around the side of the house. Son of a bitch."

Her attention shot to her hallway when the scratching sound repeated itself. Perry knew there were cameras outside and had tried dodging them. Any lesser-quality surveillance equipment probably wouldn't have picked him up. He was trying to sneak up on her.

"Well, two can play this game," she whispered, grinning at the thought of beating him at his own game.

Double-checking to make sure everything was in order in the room, Kylie turned off the light but then turned toward her window. Moving in the dark, she leaned over her computer and moved the closed blinds just enough to peer outside. It was a moonless night and her front porch light hindered her ability to see the car parked in front of her neighbor's house clearly. She assumed it was Perry's Jeep, and she also guessed the blur that had raced across her front yard was him. But what if it wasn't?

Grabbing her gun, she lifted her skirt and strapped the leather holster to her thigh. The cold metal and stiff leather always gave her a sense of security. She closed the bedroom door silently, then locked it. If Perry was in the backyard, possibly at her back door, he wouldn't see her turn off the light. Nor would anyone else who might be out there.

She didn't bother with the hallway light but instead stood silently, her body pressed against the cool, flat wall, and listened. A popular drama and repeat she'd seen one too many times was on TV. It wasn't hard to tune it out and focus on the other sounds in her home.

Kylie moved down her hallway without making one floorboard squeak. She knew how to hunt the predator; in fact, she was damn good at doing it. At the end of her hallway, she paused, not moving while she took in her quiet living room and the glow of the TV that accentuated the dark corners.

Convinced no one was in her living room, which was easy to do because her alarm system would go off if anyone entered her home, she started along the edge of the room toward the kitchen. The blinds were all closed over the back windows, and from where she stood she could see all of them. Her living room opened into her small dining room and then the other end of her house, a small alcove where more chairs could be but where she had nothing. Sliding glass doors were her only view to the backyard, and they were black against the night outside.

Her only advantage was that it was also dark in her house, shy of the glow from her TV. As impossible as it was for her to see outside, an intruder would have as much problem seeing inside right now.

Nonetheless, prickles of anxiety and anticipation rushed over her flesh, giving her chills. Years of experience handling situations so much more terrifying than this helped her remain calm and evaluate her situation carefully before making her next move. And she took her time deciding her best plan of action. Unlike other scenarios where she stalked a killer, this time she was stalking Perry. A smile tugged at her lips. She wouldn't be blowing her cover by besting him at his game. Possibly proving to Perry she wasn't completely helpless would make him back off a bit.

If there was one thing she would change in the man it

was his hell-bent determination to make her submit. She'd have to give him a bit of leeway, since his pushiness stemmed from Perry being a good detective. Something told her even if he knew the complete truth about her, he would still push her harder than she could tolerate. And training him to submit might be damn near an impossible task.

After listening another minute and not hearing anything, Kylie walked quietly into her kitchen. And barely had time to react when a dark shadow leapt at her. Strong arms wrapped around her and she was yanked backward, all the air flying from her lungs with a loud grunt when she slapped against a body of steel.

Try as she would to turn the grunt into something more civilized sounding, a gloved hand crushed over her mouth.

"Why do you have surveillance equipment installed in your home?" Perry whispered against her ear.

Adrenaline hit her hard enough to make her dizzy. Then hearing Perry's voice, his rough whisper that tortured her ear and the flesh on the side of her neck, sent other emotions sky-rocketing out of control.

Instead of answering, she bucked, doubling over and then swinging back hard with her elbow. He was mocking her with the question, showing her no level of security could keep him out of a place if he wanted to enter. It was obvious he didn't like being monitored, which fit with his nature. Perry didn't want anyone having the upper hand. By breaking into her home successfully, he proved to her that she could monitor anyone, but not him. Kylie could show him, instead of tell him, a few things of her own. She didn't need to rely on that equipment as her only means of protection. She was perfectly capable of protecting herself.

There was a moment's satisfaction when her elbow made contact. Although she wasn't sure she hurt him as much as the impact of her bone against rock-hard muscle jarred her. It was her only window, though, and she couldn't dwell on which case might be the truth. Instead, she twisted her body, reaching with her one free hand, and did her best to jump away from him.

"If you break into my house," she snarled, "don't think you can then hold me in your arms."

"Is that so?" He let go of her but grabbed her wrist.

No way he'd have the thrill of watching her surrender. Relaxing for just a moment, she allowed him to pull her toward him. Again, her moment of opportunity was minuscule, but then it had been even shorter when she'd worked in Washington taking down a sexual predator who weighed a good hundred pounds more than Perry.

When she was sure he thought she'd tumble into him, she yanked back, using enough force that she almost dislocated her shoulder. The move was effective, though, and pulled Perry off guard.

"That's what you get for thinking," she snapped, pulling him toward her and then using his grip on her as a brace when she jumped into the air and kicked him hard in the gut.

Perry stumbled backward, howling from the impact. Where her perp on her previous assignment had let her go, hugging himself against the broken rib she'd given him, Perry's grip grew tighter and he pulled her down with him. The two of them went stumbling to the side, hitting the side of the couch and causing it to make a terrible shrieking sound when it scraped across the floor.

"You'd be surprised what I think about," he said, sounding, surprisingly, not hurt at all as his arms wrapped around her.

He pulled her over him so she was draped over all of that steel muscle. It felt a little bit too hard, even for Perry. Relaxing her body and pushing herself off him so she could rest on her elbow against his chest, Kylie ran her hand over the width of his chest.

"What the hell are you wearing?" she asked, and then yanked on his shirt to see for herself. "Body armor," she growled. "You aren't playing fair."

"Want to try it on?" he said, sounding amused. His dark eyes flashed with emotions she wasn't sure she wanted to decipher at the moment.

She hated body armor. It weighed half a ton and itched. "No thanks," she said dryly.

Kylie wasn't paying attention to the drama show on TV, but when it cut to commercial and a news brief started playing she froze, her attention snapping to the screen.

"Earlier tonight, Rita Simoli, a seventeen-year-old junior at Mission High, disappeared from this parking lot," a pretty young woman began, holding a microphone to her mouth as she stared seriously at the camera. "Investigators have confirmed she was chatting with a boy on the Internet that she didn't know, whose name is currently not being released, and agreed to meet here after the grocery store closed."

Perry lifted her, and himself, and resituated them on the couch, pulling Kylie onto his lap. She was so wrapped up in the reporter's story she didn't realize her arm rested on Perry's shoulder, or his hand on her upper thigh, until he had them comfortable. His expression was blank and almost cruel looking as he focused on the set.

"The Simolis, owners of a restaurant here in town, are offering a large reward for the return of their daughter, alive and well. But beyond that, they've arranged to have meetings at their restaurant for parents of other girls who've disappeared in the Kansas City area over the past year. Apparently the number is quite high, and shocking to this reporter that the local law enforcement have kept this so quiet when we obviously have a serial rapist and murderer on our hands. Last October, Maura Reynolds, a sixteen-year-old who lived right here in Mission Hills, was found dead, raped, and beaten. The situation surrounding her murder is so similar to Rita Simoli's, it's eerie. Both girls chatted with a boy on the Internet, agreed to meet him, and then disappeared." The reporter looked at the camera, disgusted. "I don't know about you, Mark, but if I had a teenage daughter, I wouldn't let her chat with anyone on the Internet right now."

The scene switched to Mark, an older reporter sitting in the newsroom. "At least don't let them chat with anyone they haven't already met." He stared at the camera with a serious, remorseful expression. "Take time to learn the screen names of your children's friends, and make sure you know everyone they are talking to," he suggested.

Perry blew out a heavy sigh and then followed it up with several expletives. "Just what I fucking need," he said, his voice rumbling in his chest.

Kylie wasn't sure she had the strength to keep from adding a few words to show her reaction to the idiot reporter who'd just made her job ten times harder than it had been. She would need one hell of a good song and dance now to meet Peter on Thursday. He'd assume she'd be under lockdown after that newscast, which every teenage girl should be until Kylie got the bastard behind bars. But now he'd hide in the shadows even more, and be twice as careful about meeting anyone. Prove too easy or eager and he'd get suspicious, especially knowing the cops were on his ass with recorded chats.

"And obviously I need a better security system." She hated changing the subject. More than anything, sympathizing and having a good rant over media interference hindering investigations sounded a hell of a lot like better conversation than creating a beef with Perry for displaying his abilities to break into her home.

She pushed away from him, but Perry tightened his grip, pulling her to him and then leaning over her. She was forced back on the couch, her legs intertwined with his and his dark, brooding expression inches from hers.

"I'm answering for every move I make these days. I have a perfect track record, and don't deserve the treatment I'm getting," he whispered, his mouth so damn close to hers and his eyes a blur of animosity and lust. "Tonight I arrive at a crime scene only to find out the FBI stepped in and scoured the place before I could get there."

"I'm sorry," she offered, meaning it in more ways than she could let him know.

"Breaking into your home wasn't premeditated. But when I got here, and already knowing those cameras were installed outside your home, I decided to see how well you have yourself protected. Why monitor the front of your house and not the back side?"

"I live alone. Duh," she said, narrowing her gaze on him. There wasn't any point despising not being able to tell him the truth. This was her life, her job, all that she lived and breathed for. That wasn't going to change—ever. "When I can afford it, I'll install more equipment in the backyard. But for now, it's a safety precaution." She couldn't tell him the cameras were there to record whoever she had over, and not for protection.

"Then get a dog."

"Sometimes using something that only requires double A's proves a lot less complicated," she said, and watched his expression darken until it looked as though a thunderhead was ready to explode.

"And maybe something living and breathing would require you admitting that sometimes you need someone else to take care of you." His tone was bitter, challenging.

She bristled under the implications.

Perry lowered his mouth to hers, gentle at first, but then his demands grew, his actions intensifying, until she was panting underneath him and dragging her nails over his shoulders.

"You're starting to get under my skin, darling," he whispered, and continued kissing her.

She was drowning in him, every inch of her tumbling in a whirlwind of lust and need. It was an odd sensation, and one that wasn't completely unpleasant. But when she finally was able to gulp in a breath of air, desperately trying to clear the fog overwhelming her brain, the urgency to ground herself became overwhelming. It would be too damn easy to lose herself in a relationship with this man.

"You're just horny," she said, her voice raspy.

Perry lifted his head, staring down at her as if she'd just said something ridiculous. "Are you trying to tell me you feel nothing for me at all?"

As many times as she'd done it during previous assignments, she hated him cornering her, especially when it forced her to lie. She bit her lip, using the pain to harden her heart. "I'm sure you're a very good cop."

His expression changed, creating a painful sensation that ripped through her heart as if he'd just stabbed her. Kylie couldn't breathe and, worse yet, couldn't look away from him.

"A good cop," he repeated dryly. "That's all you think of me?"

"I've been too busy working on my thesis to give it much thought," she lied, her mouth suddenly so dry she could barely get the words out.

"You keep lying to me and I promise, I'm going to bend you over my knee and spank that perfect ass of yours," he growled into her mouth.

A moment too late she remembered the cameras were on and recording all of their actions and everything they said to each other. Not to mention sending live feed into the field office. Maybe the fact that no one came running to her door when they attacked each other proved no one was watching right now. Or possibly she put on such a good show they were waiting for the finale.

"You lay a hand on my ass and I swear I'll be spanking you right back," she snarled, making sure to keep her voice to a very soft whisper.

Perry lifted her like a rag doll, moving with skills that put all of her training to the test. She was facedown on the couch, unable to outstrengthen him when his hand hit her rear end, creating a cracking sound that forced her pussy to tighten in reaction. The instant warmth that spread over her rear end created a pressure inside her. All of the training she had was no match for the lust Perry ignited inside her in moments.

"Damn it," she cried out, pushing herself to her knees before turning and scowling at him over her shoulder. "You are going to pay for that, Perry. Trust me on that one."

"Tell me the truth and it won't happen again."

"Stop it, Perry." She jumped off him and managed to stabilize her footing before stumbling over her own coffee table. Lord, wouldn't that add humorous undertones to the sexual foreplay at least one agent was possibly enjoying the hell out of at this very moment. If Paul made one crack to her about this, she'd kick his ass.

Perry was pushing her into dangerous territory. Her best move was to get them onto a different subject, one where she wouldn't have to lie so much it cut her to the core. "Tell me how you got into my home."

Perry stood and then pulled off his T-shirt. The body armor was strapped like a girdle around his chest. "Through the window by your kitchen table," he said, thumbing in the direction of the kitchen. "Want to give me a hand with this?"

Kylie crossed her arms, damned if she would record herself helping Perry out of body armor. Even worse, touching him right now would be a serious mistake when her insides were pulsing with need so great it was all she could do to maintain her distance.

"So you climb through my kitchen window. And all because my security system gives you a complex?"

"I didn't feel like knocking." He realized she wasn't going to help him and managed to work his way out of the suit himself.

"Cut the crap." She kept her arms crossed, holding herself, while watching him struggle until the heavy, thick body protection was finally free of his body. It was imperative she keep the upper hand, reprimand him for breaking in, and remain focused—on the conversation and not his suddenly bare chest. "You're a cop, not a criminal."

"A good cop knows the minds, methods, and how to act like a criminal," he told her, his voice low and compelling.

She closed her eyes, all too aware what he said was true. Again, singing his praises for getting past one hell of an advanced security system sounded a hell of a lot more appealing than reprimanding him for doing it.

"Nonetheless, what you did was wrong," she said quietly.

Even with her eyes closed, she heard him approach and stepped backward as she opened her eyes and focused on him quickly. He wrapped his arms around her waist, a relaxed hold this time, and one she could pull free of if she wished. Or at least that was the impression he offered. When she uncrossed her arms, her hands brushed over his bare chest. The heat from his body, his slightly moist flesh, and that perfect spray of chest hair tortured her fingertips worse than she imagined it could.

"I have as much of a problem with a camera spying on me when I want to come see you as I do with your unwillingness to admit you want to see me as much as I want to see you."

There was no way she could comment. It hurt too much lying to him. Sucking in a deep breath didn't do a thing to calm her frazzled nerves. "Then maybe if you called before showing up, I could turn it off just to appease your male ego." She was proud of her flippant tone but couldn't move her gaze from her fingers, which were stretched over roped muscle.

"Where's the fun in that?" he growled.

She shouldn't have looked up. But she did. And immediately drowned in those incredible dark green eyes that swarmed with all the emotions she was feeling. She was sure of it. She saw in Perry what she experienced inside her soul. Most definitely lust. But there was another emotion, darker, primal, unexplored. And it had surfaced in him the same way it simmered inside her. Maybe it was curiosity, or a mutual fascination, a craving to explore and learn more about not only each other's bodies but minds and hearts as well.

"I was informed today that you weren't attending dinner at my sister's tomorrow night."

"So was I."

"I see." That emotion she couldn't label seemed to grow, dilating his pupils and making his hands, which rested on the small of her back, feel hotter the longer they rested there. "So you didn't cancel. I wonder what Dani is up to."

"She's jealous." Kylie didn't mean to let that slip out and lowered her gaze. Staring at his muscular chest didn't help clear her thoughts much.

"Jealous? Of you . . . being with me?" He paused for a moment, but his arm muscles twitched as if he anticipated her moving and didn't want her going anywhere. "Interesting. I guess none of my nieces have ever seen me with another woman."

"At least you have enough manners to keep them away from your family."

His low baritone sent chills rushing over her flesh when he chuckled. And she didn't like the twang of regret when he moved his hands from her back. He continued touching her, though, resting one hand on her shoulder and using the knuckles with his other hand to tilt her chin until her gaze returned to his. "They don't see women with me because I don't date."

"Don't let me disturb your routine." Kylie needed space and pushed away from him.

"Too late," he growled, pulling her back into his arms. He captured her mouth again, his method of attack proving a lot stronger than her ability to fight back.

Kylie wasn't sure how long she'd been returning the kiss, leaning into him with her arms wrapped around his neck and making a feast of him. But a ringing in the background brought her to her senses and made her realize she'd completely surrendered and devoured all he offered.

She quit standing on tiptoes, which ended the intensity of the kiss.

"Who would be calling you after midnight?" Perry growled into her mouth, his question even more proof of how possessive he would be.

That is, if she accepted him as a lover. Which wasn't an option, not to mention, if he learned the secret she kept from him, he wouldn't want anything to do with her anyway.

"I don't know," she said, pushing away from him and hurrying down her hall. She was pretty sure she knew who was calling and had even less doubt why he was calling. "I'll be right back," she called over her shoulder.

As she scooped her phone off her desk in her middle bedroom, frustration and embarrassment made her angry. Part of her believed she'd be smarter to let it go to voice mail. But that would lead to another slap on the wrist from John in the morning. The screen said: *Paul's Desk Phone*, and she answered the call, dreading the chastising she was about to receive.

"Hello."

"Sorry to interrupt," Paul said, his tone not half as amused sounding as she'd anticipated it being.

"I'm sure you are," she said, rubbing her brow.

"You need to send lover boy packing," Paul said. "We've got a situation."

Kylie turned to shut the bedroom door and froze. Perry stood in the doorway, his arms crossed, looking larger than life as he took in the contents of the room. As she turned away from him, realizing how pointless it would be to send him back to the living room now, her irritability grew.

"That's fine, sweetheart," she said, confident her voice sounded calmer than she felt. "You did the right thing. Can we talk about it more tomorrow?"

"He can hear you, can't he?" Paul asked.

"Yes, I do, and that's fine."

"Call me back once you're clear."

"Okay, bye-bye."

Kylie stared into Perry's exceptionally dark eyes as she closed her phone and then gripped it in her damp palm. Suddenly knowing Paul watched Perry kiss her didn't matter as much as trying to figure out the best way to handle Perry now.

"Tell me that wasn't my niece," he growled.

Kylie blinked, and whatever expression he caught on her face relaxed his features somewhat. He started toward her, but Kylie met him before he could walk all the way into the room.

"That wasn't your niece, although I'm not sure what to do about her." Keeping the topic on Dani was safer territory than any other direction it might wander. Kylie pressed her hand against his chest, but he didn't budge. She needed to get him out of this room. "There are other teenagers I'm talking to, Perry. And regardless of how you may feel about it, some of them are starting to view me as a mentor."

"Regardless of how I might feel about it?" he asked, his tone turning dark as he looked past her at the contents of the room. "That implies my thoughts don't matter to you and I doubt you've forgotten already what will happen if you lie to me."

She didn't like his tone, not at all. She hated even worse how his deep baritone sent chills rushing over her flesh and created a quickening in her womb.

"I don't like being manhandled."

Perry grabbed her, lifting her into his arms. "There's a difference between being manhandled and receiving attention."

"Being spanked is receiving attention?" She pushed her hands down on his shoulders, twisting in his arms and trying to slide down his front to the floor. There was no way in hell she'd let him know how turned on she got from that spanking.

"Being spanked can be many things," he whispered, allowing her to slide down his body but then cupping her ass. "It can be erotic, heightening pleasure that I know you already enjoy."

"Yet you imply it's a punishment. And since you don't own me, aren't training me in any way, there is no reason for punishment."

"Let's just say I'm getting your attention." His hands moved over her rear end, and then he squeezed, lifting and spreading her open. "And that I love the way your eyes glow and your cheeks flush whenever I suggest taking my hand to your ass."

"Maybe we should find out what look you get on your face if you're spanked."

"That is something you'll never know," he grumbled.

"And why is that? Is your machoism simply a cover for lack of self-esteem?" she challenged. "Maybe you really are trying to be just another one of those dominating wannabes who don't have the strength within themselves to take in what they dish out."

"And maybe I simply am macho. Maybe my inner strength

is one hundred percent male and I believe with all my heart and soul that I am the protector and you are the one to be protected and cherished."

"If you think I don't have what it takes to protect myself, Perry, you can go to hell. Now back up and get out of this room," she hissed, having had just about enough of his "I'm the man" crap. "I'll have you know that I've taken care of myself very nicely for twenty-seven years."

There wasn't anyway he could research her, especially since there was no Kylie Dover. But if he did do a search on her, it would have said her age was twenty-three, which was what her driver's license said. One look at his face and she knew she'd just blown it.

He wouldn't see her cringe. No way. And she hated that he got her so flustered that she just jeopardized her cover.

"I'm sure you didn't take care of yourself those entire twenty-seven years." Something in his tone, in the way his eyes darkened until they were almost black, was incredibly unnerving.

She'd pissed him off. He made it clear he didn't like being lied to. And with one slip she'd shown him that everything about her quite possibly was a lie. Kylie expected him to turn and march out of the room.

"You know what I mean." Since he didn't confront her, it gave her time to formulate a cover to patch up her mistake. If Perry really believed her to be that much younger than she was and was cool with their supposed age difference, she could always say she had lied about being older so that he wouldn't walk out on her. Because of course she wouldn't think it through that he would research her, since laymen didn't think that way. Or laywomen. "Now please, you know I don't want you in here. This is my personal room."

"I see that. Would you actually let me fuck you in the living room? And if so, would you play it back later and watch, possibly masturbate to it?" he asked, then grabbed her under her arms, once again lifting her into his arms.

"The answer to both of those questions is no," she informed him, narrowing her gaze on his.

He held her, with her feet dangling inches off the floor. "I believe you've told me the truth that time. Possibly for the first time this evening. You know, Kylie, you want to spend time with my nieces, but I'm not sure I approve of the role model you would present to them. And maybe Dani has already picked up on your level of deception. Maybe that is why she conjured up a reason for you to back out of dinner tomorrow night. You want me. You think about me when I'm not around. And then make a show of not caring how your cold comments might affect me when you lie and deny it."

She should let him walk out the door on that comment. Let him think she was less of a person than she was. It would help both of them numb the passion, the friction and fire that sparked to life every time he touched her. Paul needed to talk to her. Perry needed to leave. What was wrong with letting him leave angry? What did it matter?

It wasn't like she needed to go to his sister's. If she could convince Peter to meet her, get a warrant based on the screen name he used, which he also used on Rita Simoli, then she could make her arrest. It would be over.

And she would be assigned to her next case or given downtime, which she would use to go home and spend time with her parents.

"It doesn't usually take you this long to think up a good lie," he growled, and gave her a slight shake.

Kylie felt her gun strap slip just a bit down her thigh. "I don't deserve to be spoken to like this, Perry. I think you should leave."

"Admit you care, Kylie. Tell me you want to be with me."

"I'm not lying. You're berating me, and I don't like it. That's the truth."

He searched her face, seemingly unimpressed by what she had just said. If anything, his serious, focused stare almost made her believe he hadn't heard a word of it.

"Maybe if you're that unwilling to admit your feelings, then you're incapable of having any," he whispered, once again putting her on the floor. This time he did turn and walked into the hallway and then to the living room.

Kylie followed him, her heart swelling in her throat while her eyes burned. She didn't like the tightening in her gut while anticipating him walking out the door and never coming back. And that bugged her. Perry was an incredible man. If she were better at this, she would know how to keep her cover, work the case and solve it, but still be able to keep him in a place where she could get to know him better once this was all said and done. Unfortunately, with his dominating nature, not giving him full reign damaged anything that might come between them before it had a chance to develop.

Perry turned when he reached her front door and she stopped in front of him, clasping her hands behind her back and watching his brooding expression. It was definitely her imagination that he suddenly looked sad. Perry Flynn wouldn't know those emotions. Betrayal, noncompliance, refusal to submit, wouldn't sadden him. It would outrage him. She was certain she misread the way his lips pressed together into a frown as he looked at her with deep green eyes that no longer simmered with passion.

"If you don't want anything between us, so be it," he said, his voice cold and flat. His words stabbed at her with the fierceness of a sharp knife. "But God help you, Kylie, if you know something about Dani that might bring danger upon her and you aren't telling me about it. . . ."

Chapter 16

The night air didn't have the chill to it that it had the past week or so. Instead humidity wrapped around Perry tightly enough that he could hardly breathe as he walked across her dry lawn to his Jeep parked in front of her neighbor's house. Maybe tomorrow, when he'd put his temper, and all other emotions, under lock and key, he'd be able to rid himself of the overwhelming desire to walk back into her home and fuck the shit out of her until she admitted she wanted to be with him.

The sooner he backed out of Kylie Dover's life, the better off he'd be. Focus on this case and nailing the prick who was destroying teenage girls' lives should be all he allowed into his mind these days.

"Proof once again why you don't have time for relationships," he hissed under his breath as he reached his Jeep.

"Perry," Kylie called out.

He held his car door handle, standing in the street, and watched, actually surprised, as Kylie ran across her yard barefoot and stopped when she reached the sidewalk at the front of his Jeep.

"I told you the truth when I said Dani didn't want me to come to dinner because she didn't want her mother playing matchmaker." In the dark, it was harder to see Kylie's face. Dark shadows shrouded a good half of her face, while her blue eyes reflected the streetlight behind him and almost glowed in the darkness. "There's no way to prove this, which makes it speculation, but Dani worries that if we get too close I'll share with you information she's confided in me."

"Why are you telling me this?"

"I didn't mean to hurt you," she said, her voice cracking while she quickly looked away from him down the street, allowing him to see her pinched expression.

"I'm fine." He found it interesting that his walking out on her after basically telling her good-bye affected her as much as it did him. Maybe Kylie did possess the ability to feel. Something twisted inside him, refusing to allow him to shove his growing feelings for her away.

"Good. I'm glad to hear that," she said, her voice soft and sultry. She licked her lips and returned her attention to him, sucking in a breath, which pushed her breasts out and allowed him to see how puckered her nipples were through her dress. "Obviously I don't know Dani like you do," she began, watching him warily. "I see that she's very intelligent. And I see her need to be accepted among her peers, which sometimes allows people, especially young people her age, to refuse to see things as they really are."

"Tell me what you know." He knew he sounded hard and cold, and refused to be daunted when she flinched. He'd never admitted to a woman before that she meant more to him than a good fuck. "If she's done or is thinking about doing anything that could harm her, you'd better tell me."

"I want your word first that you won't let her know I told you."

Like he owed her any kind of promise when she wrapped a cloak around emotions and desire as though it was her fucking wardrobe. Emotions he saw now making her cheeks flush and her eyes glow, even in the darkness.

"If you tell her I told you, she won't confide in me anymore. I won't know if she plans on going through with this if she closes herself off to me—kind of like you're doing now," she added, letting her voice fade away until her final words were barely audible.

"You have my word, and I don't lie."

"There are many different definitions, and reasons for not telling someone everything about you," she said, tilting her chin defiantly. "I guess Dani's safety is more important, though, than what you think about me. I'm worried that she's talking to a boy on the Internet and that she might sneak out to meet him. With teenage girls disappearing right now, and his online name—"

"What is his online name?" Perry barked, interrupting her while every inch of him hardened painfully. He realized he gripped his door handle hard enough that he might rip it off his door and forced himself to let it go. Flexing and unflexing his hands, he doubted there was much he could do to harbor his anger at this point. "Tell me, Kylie."

"It's spelled in such a way that you wouldn't guess it by looking at it, but Dani told me it's pronounced 'Peter Fish.' She's talking to an exchange student named Petrie and has been for a good six months. Now she's outraged that he's meeting another girl who goes to her school when Dani thought that they had some kind of online committed relationship." Kylie walked around his Jeep, pausing at the front end of the driver's side, but then clearing the distance between them and taking his hand in hers. "She's going to go meet him. If the friendship I've created with her is tarnished in any way, I won't be able to stop her."

He pulled his hand from Kylie's and turned to his Jeep; then because the emotions already boiling over inside him from Kylie, the frustrations from dealing with the Simolis, and being terrified that somehow his nieces would be pulled into this nightmare before he could catch the guy, needed an outlet, he roared loud enough to burn his throat when he pounded the roof of his car.

It surprised the hell out of him when Kylie grabbed his arm, pushing him hard enough that he turned to face her, and then moved into his arms. She leaned against him, stretching her hot, sexy body against his, and wrapped her arms around his neck. She wasn't tall enough to capture his mouth without him lowering his face to hers, but when her lashes fluttered over her eyes and once again she licked her lips in invitation he didn't dwell on the very real reasons why he should walk out of her life and stay out of it.

And he needed to. He'd known pathological liars in the past, people who would lie about what they had for breakfast because for some fucked-up reason it was easier for them to do that than tell the truth. They were annoying, exhausting, and he had no time or desire for someone like that in his world today. Refusing to admit to feelings that were as obvious as the nose on her pretty face was damn near the same thing as being a compulsive liar in his book.

Perry broke off the kiss, realizing his hands were on her ass, and dragged his palms around her hips while straightening and then looking down at her.

"I'm leaving," he announced, his voice thick with the emotions that demanded he stay and fuck the shit out of her.

Kylie nodded once, her lips slightly parted and damp and swollen from his kiss. He ran his fingers past the edge of her dress, feeling her warm thigh and something else.

Her pretty blue eyes, turned milky from lust, cleared and grew sharp when he shifted from her, glancing down to see what his fingers had just touched.

"Goddamn, Kylie," he whispered, holding on to the edge of her dress when she tried turning away and backing up at the same time. "You aren't going anywhere. I offered you an out. You came to me. You know I'm not going to accept any lying and I walked away from you, but you came out here."

"To tell you about Dani. I don't want her hurt," Kylie pleaded, grabbing his hand that held on to her dress.

"You kissed me." He kept a firm hold on her dress, raising it slightly while she pushed on his hand, although there was no way she could make him let go of her, or keep him from ripping the damn thing off her if he felt so inclined. "You want this, darling, it's a full package. Tell me right now why the fuck you're wearing a gun strapped to your thigh, and if it's a lie—"

"You broke into my house," she cried out, digging her nails into his wrist in an effort to keep him from dragging her dress up to her hip. "I knew someone was in there. I heard you. But I didn't know—"

"Stop right there. Your cameras picked me up running across your yard. And you're a smart woman; you would have backed up the footage, possibly seen me park my Jeep." That busted look he'd seen way too many times in his life was written all over her face. It was the same expression he saw when she told him she was twenty-seven when her ID said she was twenty-three. "I'm sure you watched me back up when I decided to try breaking in. Make sure the next words that come out of your mouth are chosen very, very carefully."

He hiked her dress up a bit more, barely noticing the pinch from her fingernails when she tried stopping him. The longer she stared at him, remaining stubbornly quiet, the more he feared the truth.

"Are you hiding from someone?" he demanded. "God, Kylie, if someone is stalking you."

She pursed her lips, looking as though she wanted another kiss. On an impulse, he grabbed the gun, quickly unsnapping the strap that kept it secure in its holster, and slid it out. When he let go of her dress, she let go of his wrist but then grabbed the gun.

And not like a novice, inexperienced and ready to fight for a weapon that could go off and get one of them shot. Kylie's smaller hand went around his, pushing the direction of the gun away from both of them.

"You can't take that," she said, sounding deadly serious.

He shook his head, refusing to let the sense of betrayal that bit at him when she still wouldn't open up and tell him the truth.

"You forget, my dear. I'm an officer of the law. I sure the fuck can take this. In fact, you're going to stand right there and not move while I call it in. Let's find out who it's registered to."

"I can't let you do that, Perry." She looked at him as though she possessed the strength to physically take it away from him. "I'm not hiding from anyone. No one is stalking me," she told him, her crisp, cool tone grabbing his attention. She blinked a few times as she chewed her lower lip, as if it took a lot of work on her part to force whatever she might say next out of her mouth. "I am looking for Peter. He's not going to take another teenager. I'm really close to meeting him myself and when I do—"

"Goddamn it. Like fucking hell!" Perry yanked the gun from her and opened his car door, placing the gun on the seat and then turning to her. "And this is why you feed me lie after lie, denying your feelings for me, because you know I'll stop you? Are you that obsessed with playing detective?"

"Perry, give me back my gun. If you call in to your dispatch and run those serial numbers, they will know you're here with me. And I can't allow you to risk your investigation, or mine, by doing that."

"What the fuck?" He stared at her, digesting what she'd just said. "Why would my running those serial numbers hinder my investigation?"

"Please give me back my gun."

Turning from her, he climbed into his car and flipped on his dome light. It surprised him and irked the hell out of him even more when she didn't say anything as he wrote down the serial number. Kylie had just warned him against calling the number in to his dispatcher. But there were other ways to learn who owned this gun.

After writing down the number, he stood, holding the gun flat in his palm, and held it out for her to take. Which she did, and promptly checked to make sure the security on it was in place and then slid it back into its holster, not watching what she did but focusing on his face. Like she'd done it a million times—like a pro.

Suddenly the thought of her being incapable of feeling faded from his mind. Kylie's story went a lot deeper than that, and it was about to get exposed.

"I'll see you tomorrow night at five," he informed her, sliding back behind his driver's wheel. "Wear something nice but casual. No short skirts."

He drove off with her blank, almost hard expression burned in his mind. It was as if she was resigned to something, and he wasn't going to sleep until he knew every detail of what it was.

Thirty minutes later he endured the silence on the other end of the line, about done with people who he thought were his friends not telling him what he wanted to know.

"Noah, man, talk to me," he insisted.

"I'm here, man. Where did you get this gun again?"

"Just tell me who the fuck it's registered to."

The loud sigh on the other end of the line crept over his skin annoyingly, like someone juicing up his nerves, exposing them, and rubbing the wrong way so as to irritate him and piss him the fuck off.

"Damn it, man, I'm sick the fuck of being lied to. I've dealt with it all night and walked away from it once. She came back to me, damn it. I have a right to know the goddamn truth."

"Actually, you don't," Noah said seriously. "And I believe you, man. I would be mad as hell, too. I know it doesn't make any sense to you. I'm afraid you're going to have to leave her alone."

"Excuse me? What? Suddenly you're my mother?" he snarled. "Noah, tell me what the hell you're talking about."

"Man, you've taken on the wrong woman this time. Leave it to you . . . ," he said, pausing and grunting something under his breath that didn't sound good.

"Tell me who she is."

"I can't."

Silence weighed so heavily between them it was making it hard as hell to breathe. Perry wanted to scream. He wanted to reach through the phone and beat the crap out of his longtime good friend.

"She's an FBI agent," Perry spit out, guessing.

But he wasn't ready for the continued silence to follow. Perry felt a cold sweat soak his forehead when Noah didn't confirm or deny his guess.

"Goddamn, son of a bitch." He rubbed his face, his heart

suddenly pounding adrenaline through his system with a fury he could barely hold on to. "No wonder she almost panicked when I suggested calling in the serial number."

"Perry, leave it alone."

"Of course, Noah. I'm sure that is exactly what the fuck you would do in the same circumstance."

Noah grunted into Perry's ear, again not commenting, but not disputing the accusation, either.

"Goddamn good thing I speak Neanderthal. So tell me, she's working undercover and that is why she's lying every time she opens that pretty little mouth of hers."

"You know I'm not going to answer your questions." Noah might as well just have confirmed everything Perry just said. His mind raced, trying to come up with wording good enough to drag more information out of his FBI friend. "I made it to a crime scene tonight only to learn the FBI beat me to the punch. They announced tonight their involvement in this case. But I've worked alongside FBI agents before on other cases. So there's got to be a damn good reason why someone has decided she can't reveal who she is to anyone, not even me."

"Don't push it, man."

"Like fucking hell. I'm going to fucking shove my way into this one. You have no idea."

As he remembered how she ran across her yard barefoot, chasing him down instead of letting him leave her, Perry's insides tightened. His urge to protect her peaked to dangerous levels. He would make sure she didn't get hurt while she pursued a madman, and at the same time vowed to destroy whoever it was who decided she could take on this case by herself.

"This isn't worth jeopardizing your career over, man."

"You have no idea what it's fucking worth to me, man. What if I told you going after that cop lady of yours wasn't worth it a year ago?"

"I would have told you to go to fucking hell," Noah said, laughing dryly.

"Well, back at you, man."

"You take any information you stumble onto, Perry—"

"I know the fucking ropes," he hissed. But the realization hitting him like a brick in the head at the moment was strong enough to knock sense even into his thick skull. "She's on this case, undercover, and can't tell me the truth. I can learn it, though, man. I wouldn't jeopardize her job. All that I need to know is the truth. I'll make sure she understands that I won't blow her cover." There wasn't an ounce of doubt in his mind that once he made her see that he knew who she was, Kylie would quit lying. Then he could protect her properly. And he would get her to admit she was having feelings for him, too, feelings that went beyond craving a good fuck. "I know she won't stop working the case. But you have no clue. Kylie is one hot, petite little number. Whoever decided to send her after a monster all by herself needs his head examined."

"You go right ahead and tell her that," Noah suggested, this time his laughter deeper, louder, as if he'd just heard a good joke. "I know a lady cop who just loves hearing that because she's hot as hell and sexy to boot she shouldn't go after the bad guy. Let me know if your woman can kick ass as well as mine can."

Perry barely listened. He sat at his computer, typing in various versions of Kylie's name, along with the words "agent" and "FBI," until he found what he needed.

"Donovan," Perry said out loud.

"What?"

"She isn't Kylie Dover. Her name is Kylie Donovan."

"Man, let it go. Just go solve your case."

"Do you know her?"

"You know I can't confirm that. Furthermore, this conversation never happened."

Perry knew he had it now. "It's cool, man. What are friends for."

"Uh-huh. Talk to me once you've solved this case."

"Will do." Perry hung up the phone. It was time to read up on Miss Donovan.

Special Agent Kylie Donovan had one hell of a track

record. He wasn't able to find so much on the Internet, other than random newspaper articles, when he did a search on her name. But when he logged onto the special Web site allowing him exclusive access to crime history and a search engine designed to focus on criminal history, Agent Donovan appeared as much as any agent.

She was in fact twenty-seven years old, from Dallas, TX, and the only surviving daughter of Kent and Deirdre Donovan. The password-protected search engine pulled up a lot more articles that were successfully buried in the Internet available to the general public. Government agencies might not be able to curb reporters and different forms of media across the nations, newspapers, magazines, blogs on news channel Web sites, from reporting facts they'd just as soon not have as public knowledge. There were ways, however, to make it hard for names to pop up when a search was done. It was a process that Perry didn't know a lot about. What he did know was that if he truly wanted information on someone, logging onto the Web site offered through his line of work proved the most effective and the least hassle.

"Impressive, Donovan, very impressive," he said, leaning back in his office chair in his den and stretching. It was almost four in the morning, and sleep was a long way off. Especially with adrenaline pumping through him with a vengeance. "You've nailed quite a few sexual predators in your time." In fact, it was obviously her area of expertise.

He opened another file, which was an article dated thirteen years ago. It wasn't about Kylie Donovan but Karen Donovan a teenage girl found raped and murdered in Dallas, TX. Surviving family were her parents and younger sister, Kylie.

Perry blew out a staggered breath, scrubbing his head with his palms while his eyes burned from staring at his screen for so long. He stood, feeling the kinks in his muscles, and twisted his torso a few times while contemplating his next move.

"You've got the facts, Flynn. Now what to do with the

knowledge." He spoke the words, but there wasn't any doubt in his mind what he would do.

There were options. Breaking into her home again was one. He could show up over there and knock on her door, let the cameras record him arriving. Although now it made more sense why they seemed to be set up more for surveillance than protection. It also made sense why she didn't want him in that middle bedroom or running a check on her gun. Kylie worked undercover. But part of her was real. He'd seen some of her true colors. The most recent being her running barefoot across her lawn after him when he walked out on her.

Maybe she couldn't tell him she was working the Peter case, but she was able to show him that she didn't want him walking out of her life.

Perry picked up his phone and scrolled to her number, which he'd recently entered. Then finding his earpiece, he pushed the send button and listened as it rang.

"Hello," she said, sounding out of breath, when she answered on the second ring. Kylie wasn't sleeping.

"Where are you?" he demanded.

"Who is this?"

"Special Agent Kylie Donovan, this is Lieutenant Perry Flynn. We need to talk."

Chapter 17

Kylie tripped over her foot walking to her car. "Crap," she hissed.

"Yeah, crap," Perry said in her ear. "Where are you?"

She sighed, reaching her car and staring at the field office, which was dark and appeared very closed in the middle of the night. Thunder rumbled in the distance. It better rain soon; the humidity was worse than anything she'd experienced in a while.

"Getting ready to head home," she said, feeling a wave of exhaustion hit her.

Sitting with Paul, going over ISPs and listening while he explained how a Web site could be tracked to an "address," basically showing where it was created, didn't help her mood. When, once again, it became apparently clear that whoever Peter was, he was working out of the computers located inside the police department, she got pissed.

Then Paul suggested it was an interesting coincidence that whenever she finished talking to Peter, Perry showed up. That's when she walked out the door. If Paul wanted to camp there all night, that was fine with her. But she wasn't hanging around any longer and listening to bullshit.

"Stop by here. I'm at Three Twenty-seven Elm Street."

Kylie unlocked her hybrid and slipped behind the wheel, feeling a wave of light-headedness hit her. "It's late, Perry." She wasn't sure she could take him on right now. If she went over there, she doubted they would do much talking.

"You can come over here, or I can show up at your place and whoever is monitoring your house will know when I show up, and when I leave," Perry added, letting the last words he said fade into a dark promise.

In spite of how tired she was, her insides tightened with the need he'd created in her earlier when he'd kissed her senseless. "I'll be over in a few." She hung up, unwilling to listen if he started in on her for all of the lies she'd told him. She was doing her job.

Starting her car, she put a shield up around her heart. This couldn't get personal. Once this case was solved she would leave town. It was probably best Perry understood that now, before he started assuming there was more than what she could offer. And regardless of Paul's speculation, Kylie wouldn't buy into Perry being a possible suspect. For years she'd been tracking sexual predators, creating profiles. Perry wasn't a criminal. Most definitely possessive, aggressive, and demanding, but those were very common traits found in detectives. Other men as well, but Perry's nature fit who he was, a single cop with a sister who had daughters. They were his world, and he was their protector. He would slip Kylie under that balloon, too, if she let him. And what a comfortable spot to be.

Kylie punched his address into her navigating device on her dash. The female voice started instructing her where to turn, her soft monotone enough to lull Kylie off to sleep if she dwelled on it. Thinking about Perry and the case kept her alert, though. Perry could blow her cover if she wasn't careful, which was why she agreed to go over there. They would talk; she would learn where he stood, and make her decisions from there. The last thing she wanted to do was pull herself off this case, though. Worse yet, she would die if they took her off the case. In the years she'd been with the FBI, she'd never fucked up any case she'd worked on. Her track record was perfect. It had to stay that way. No matter what.

Her navigation device brought her to a quiet neighborhood where she envisioned older couples, their kids already moved out, yet for whatever reasons their parents hadn't moved into smaller homes. The yards were all oversized and neatly mowed. Trees larger than the houses shrouded the neighborhood, adding to the peaceful setting.

The lady in the navigating device indicated Kylie had arrived at her destination. She paused in the street, staring at the dark home on the corner lot. Perry's Jeep was parked in a gravel drive close to a door she guessed was the back door. Her stomach twisted with nerves when she parked on the street and then walked on the gravel to the door.

Perry opened it before she could knock. One look at the tight, almost angry look on his face and her heart swelled to her throat. He didn't say anything but stepped to the side as she walked in.

"Where were you?" he asked when she walked as far as a kitchen. There weren't any lights on except in a room on the other end of the house. And she knew that only because of the lit windows from outside. "Or wait, let me guess, you can't tell me."

There wasn't pain in his tone, more like resignation. It still stabbed at her heart, the heart that was supposed to be well guarded by walls that would prevent any emotions from getting to it.

"And you would tell me every case you're working on?" she demanded, turning around and facing him.

Perry crossed his arms over his muscular chest and glared down at her, his lips pressed into a thin line.

"Oh, no, let me guess," she said, mimicking him. "It's different because you're a man."

"You're goddamn straight," he hissed, but then stopped, turning and storming past her into his dark living room. He rubbed his hand over his head, barely tousling his short, dark hair, and turned on her. Whatever demons haunted him turned his eyes black as night.

"No," she hissed, pointing at him. "That's wrong. You quite possibly have jeopardized my whole case. I wouldn't do that to you. And your only argument is because I'm a woman?"

"I haven't jeopardized your case," he said, his voice lowering to a dangerous, if not deadly-sounding, baritone. "Not a fucking soul knows you're FBI other than me. And of course whoever you're working with," he said, waving his hand at her but then turning to pace. "I tried walking out on you, and you stopped me, remember?" he continued. "I told myself at first that the only attraction was that you're fucking hot as hell."

"Thank you," she said dryly. But then let the rest of his words sink in. "At first?"

He walked toward the room off his living room where light flooded from the doorway. Kylie stood alone in his living room, waiting for him to answer, or at least suggest she follow. But he did neither. She stared at the extra long and wide leather couch and pictured him sprawled over it, remote in hand, watching his large-screen TV. She guessed even when the lights were on the room would be dark; black leather furniture and dark-stained wooden end tables and coffee tables with equally dark-stained floorboards and doorways gave the room a dominating yet calm and controlled atmosphere. Every inch of the space around her was filled with Perry's aura.

She'd entered his lair. There were pictures on the wall, but she didn't focus on them, instead moving warily toward the doorway with light streaming out of it. Even the air sizzled with his controlling nature wrapping around her, making her flesh tingle. She fought for calming breaths when she reached the doorway and paused. This wasn't the time to search her surroundings and learn more about the man who'd seeped into her pores and created a longing that wouldn't go away. She shouldn't dwell on how he'd arranged his home, or how it gave her more insight into the nature of the man.

Perry stood in a den, a room she guessed was where he spent most of his time, his personal haven. Everything in the room spoke of Perry. From the dark green walls and even darker-stained woodwork bordering the floors and ceiling and doorway to the thick roped circular carpet covering wooden floors. His computer was set up in the corner, and bookshelves that she'd love to explore lined two of the four walls. They were crammed full of so many books, and trophies, more than likely a showcase that displayed his life. But it was the tall, glass-enclosed cabinet that he stood facing, filled with guns of all shapes and sizes, that she guessed summed Perry up. Weapons of power, of control, deadly and dangerous just like the man.

"We've got a problem." He didn't elaborate, although the silence grew between them. Instead, he continued facing his display case, possibly not even seeing the weapons inside. "I don't compete with anyone when working a case. It's my case, or it's not."

"I was called in to work this case. I didn't ask for it." Kylie walked toward him but stopped and faced his back, staring at roped muscle stretching under his shirt. He wasn't going to turn around. Well, let him play stubborn. The facts were simple. "Nothing has changed, Perry. Except hopefully now you understand that I wasn't lying to you by choice."

"Things have changed." He turned around, and the fierceness in his gaze looked worse than angry. A tiny muscle twitched in his jaw as he fought to maintain outrage that made his eyes black. "You're the bait for a madman and I have to stand by and allow this to continue. I'm not sure I have what it takes to do that, Kylie."

"You don't have a choice."

He grew before her. She was sure of it. Muscles flexed under his shirt and it seemed she was forced to tilt her head farther to maintain eye contact.

"I definitely have choices," he whispered, his baritone sending chills over her flesh. "The obvious one was whether to walk away from you, or not. You're here. That choice is made. Now to decide if you're going to bring this guy down alone, or not."

"Wait one minute," she hissed, pointing her finger at him.

He grabbed her wrist, keeping her hand raised between them as his face came closer to hers. "Possibly one minute, but not much longer. You're going to keep me advised on where you're going."

"I can't do that."

The passion, anger, whatever emotions made his eyes glow, seemed to disappear at once. He stared at her, his green eyes flat, closed off to her. Perry nodded once, releasing her wrist. "Okay then. I guess there's nothing else to discuss."

There were things they needed to discuss. If she thought Perry would blow her cover, she was obligated to report in and let John know she'd been revealed as FBI. Policy was very clear on this matter. Kylie crossed her arms, studying the dull gaze Perry offered her and his stance, not confrontational but not intimidated, either. Not that she ever thought he would be by her.

"I need to know what you're going to do now that you know I'm FBI," she said, her heart constricting as she fought to suppress all the feelings she had, pain over how he looked at her, frustration that he was acting like a big baby, and fear that he might do something to make her life hell.

"What I'm going to do?" Perry raised one eyebrow while a muscle twitched over his jawbone. "What I'm going to do," he repeated. Then turning from her, he walked across the room to a doorway shrouded in darkness. "I'm going to bed."

She stood there, confused and suddenly alone in the room. It was either turn around and leave, which was probably her smarter move, or follow him and demand that he talk to her.

"Damn it," she hissed, and stalked after him, fisting her hands at her sides. "You're being a—"

She stopped talking when, even in the incredibly dark room, she got an eyeful of incredibly hard-packed ass. Perry dropped his jeans to the floor and stepped out of them. His shirt came off next. Her mouth watered as her eyes adjusted quickly so as not to miss a moment of viewing roped muscle twitch across his back when he raised his arms, pulled his shirt off, and dropped it on top of his jeans. Then walking barefoot across his bedroom, he turned on the light in an adjoining bathroom and closed the door on her.

Kylie listened when water started running but then looked at his bedroom. Spotting a lamp next to his bed, she turned it on, then sat on the oversized bed. Everything in his house seemed so masculine and large. Just like Perry. His bed was firm and high off the floor. She couldn't sit on it and put her feet flat on the floor, so she pulled her legs up and sat cross-legged, taking in the contents of his room, and waited.

Perry's bed frame was the same dark varnished wood as his dresser. There were a handful of snapshots arranged in frames on the dresser, and after a minute of sitting there, wondering why she waited for him, Kylie got up and flipped the switch on the wall by the door, flooding the room with light, and leaned in to see the snapshots better.

Perry's nieces, at different ages, were posed in each shot. There were a good ten pictures framed and placed on the dresser. She arranged them with her eyes in chronological order, not touching any of them, and noted that Dani didn't wear the amount of makeup she did today in the recent past. Kylie focused in on a picture of the girls, all close to the age they were now, maybe a year or two younger, surrounding a very pretty woman. Her hair was brown, like the girls', and her oval face gave her an air of regality. But it was her eyes, slightly large for her face, that reflected the strong family trait. Kylie knew without a doubt she was looking at Perry's sister. They had the exact same dark, all-knowing eyes. The woman sat with her girls around her, but by the length of her slender arms and her long neck Kylie guessed she was a tall lady. Height must also be a family trait.

Kylie glanced at the papers thumbtacked to the wall. School papers and artwork. One might think these were Perry's daughters instead of his sisters. Kylie wondered why he had never married and started a family of his own; obviously fatherhood appealed to him.

No. It wasn't fatherhood. Kylie knew better. Like her, she guessed, Perry was married to his job. His sister's daughters were safe because he wasn't obligated to show up at the house at a decent hour or risk being called a bad dad. Control appealed to him, manipulating and running other people's lives.

Kylie turned and looked at the closed bathroom door when the shower started. She really should leave. He wasn't the man for her. There wasn't a man for her. Like Perry, her work was her life. Although unlike Perry, she didn't have a ready-made family that she could step into when she needed the fix.

Usually being alone didn't bother her. When she was assigned a case, she submerged herself completely and didn't give anything else any thought. It kept the loneliness away. In fact, Kylie wasn't sure she'd ever felt lonely. She'd felt alone, but there was a difference. Ever since her perfect older sister was ripped out of her life, Kylie had walked through life alone. And being alone kept her strong, kept her moving from one case to another and nailing bad guys. With every arrest, she assured herself that she had saved one more person from the pain she'd endured at too young an age.

Her eyes suddenly burned and she realized she stared at the bathroom door without blinking. And she hadn't left yet. He'd be out of the shower soon, and it would be too late.

Kylie dragged her fingers through her hair, feeling a wave of exhaustion hit her when she tried to get her brain to decide whether her smarter move was leaving or staying and demanding that Perry promise not to reveal who she was.

"He's not going to promise you shit," she mumbled, dropping her chin to her collarbone and feeling the stretch in the back of her neck. All of this would be a hell of a lot easier to figure out with at least a few hours of sleep. If she held out much longer she would lose the entire night, and sleeping tomorrow away—or was it today?—wasn't an option.

There were large wooden blinds closed over two windows in his room. Her eyes still burned as she stared at the one next to his bed. She swore lights beamed against the pane outside. Frowning, she turned and reached for the bedroom light, switching it off.

"Interesting," she whispered, walking to the bed and flipping off the lamp.

When she did, the light shining through the blinds grew quite obvious. Her heart started pounding when she climbed on the bed and crawled across it on all fours, instead of taking time to walk around. Then barely lifting one blind, she squinted outside at what appeared to be headlights, glaring straight at the side of the house.

"What the fuck?" she hissed, sliding off the bed and hurrying out of the room. All other lights were off in the house and she found the closest window in the next room where Perry's computer was.

The headlights weren't shining directly on this window, making it easier to peek outside. She spotted the dark vehicle parked across the intersection facing Perry's house. Why would someone sit there with their car running and headlights glaring at someone's house at this hour of night? Or very early morning, as the case might be.

Her heart thudded in her chest as she patted her gun in her thigh holster. The only way to find out whether someone was up to no good or not was to do a little investigating. She turned toward the living room and stopped in her tracks at the sight of Perry.

"What are you doing?" he asked, standing there with a towel wrapped around his still-damp body and not wearing anything else.

She pointed toward the window, dumbfounded briefly at the incredible view he offered. If whoever was out there was up to no good, Kylie needed to get out there quickly. That thought helped clear her head and gave her the strength to stare at Perry even though he was damn near naked, still slightly damp from his shower, and looking sexier than he did when he was outraged and all pumped up on adrenaline prior to going into the bathroom.

"Someone outside has their headlights pointed on your house," she said, and moved her hand when he lowered his gaze and noticed she was holding her gun through her dress.

"Hold on," he said, disappearing into his bedroom.

Kylie headed into the living room, checking the next window. The window behind his couch offered the best view. The vehicle was still out there, and as she watched, their headlights turned off. But then it started moving, coming down the road without lights until it slowed and idled in front of Perry's house.

"A black Suburban," she whispered, backing up from where she looked out of the corner of the blind without moving it.

She jumped when Perry's hand squeezed her shoulder. "Friend of yours?" There was a dangerous edge in his tone that crept over her flesh, giving her a chill.

"Nope." Kylie turned around, edging around the now-dressed Perry. "Who do you know who drives a black Suburban?" she asked, having to tilt her head to look into his brooding expression when he didn't back up so she could get around him.

"No one." He wore jeans and a blue T-shirt that smelled of fabric softener.

When he turned toward his kitchen she watched him lift a black belt that he'd held in his hand and begin sliding it through the belt loops on his jeans. Kylie hurried after him; damn if she was standing in here when she'd planned on going outside to investigate before he even appeared from the shower. At the door he turned around, and she was ready for his macho crap to start flying. When he looked away from her after only a moment to focus on working the belt through the side loop, she hurried around him.

"Let me do it," she said, not wanting to lose this guy if he was who she thought he might be.

And if he was, then why was Peter following her?

A strange sensation washed over her when she helped slide Perry's belt through the loops while he lifted his arms and allowed her to finish dressing him. His gun was already in the holster, and after she finished, Perry slid his belt through his belt buckle while she made sure the snaps were secure on his holster. It was a simple step, one she had done a million times, but helping Perry, knowing in the next moment they were headed outside for some very simple investigation, created a pressure inside her that swelled throughout her in record time.

This wasn't the time, or place, to get all hot and bothered

about doing detective work by his side. Not to mention, there wasn't a time, or place, to get turned on by this. They weren't partners and never would be, professionally or personally. Kylie let go of his gun and walked around him toward the door.

"Are we assuming this is the same Suburban that drove toward you in the bowling alley a few days ago?" he asked from behind her.

"That's my guess." Kylie reached for the door handle, but Perry put his hand on her shoulder.

He ran it down her back and then cupped her ass. Pulling her to him, he held her while opening the door. Perry guided her outside, keeping her close, and then let go to close the door.

"He's taking off," Kylie whispered, feeling drizzles dampen her cheeks and hair. She swore they sizzled against her already-overheated flesh. Perry kept her close, which didn't help her resolve to not get involved. "We're following him."

"Who is he?" Again Perry took her arm and turned her away from the street. Instead of walking toward either of their parked cars, he led her to his garage. "I'm driving."

"What are you driving?" She glanced toward the street where the Suburban had idled. It was gone now. "You'd better hurry."

"Get in," Perry said once he'd opened the garage door and disappeared inside. "And who is he?"

Kylie walked alongside a sports car. She ran her hand over the cool metal until she reached the passenger door. The interior light turned on when Perry slid behind the wheel and reached to open her door. Kylie slipped into a reclining bucket seat and stared at the black dash with individual round, clear plastic–covered gauges and then down at the gearshift between them. Perry grabbed the ball with his large hands, cupping it and shifting as he started the car. It purred to life with energy and power suitable only for Perry.

She studied his profile when he looked over his shoulder

and backed out of his garage. "If my hunch is right, he's Peter."

Perry took off quickly, reminding her to search for her seat belt.

The smile he gave her when he glanced her way was cruel and determined. "He won't get away from us."

"What is this?" she asked, pulling the belt around her and finding the clasp to secure it.

"Nineteen sixty-nine SS Camaro, Z twenty-eight, five-speed," he said, shifting the car into second but keeping over a block's distance from the taillights in front of them. "It belonged to my brother-in-law."

"Your sister's husband?" Kylie again took in Perry's strong profile, then glanced lower as his arm muscles stretched against his T-shirt sleeve as he gripped the stick shift.

"Yup."

She wouldn't ask him to elaborate. It was personal information, and discussing anything too close to their hearts would create more friction between them. She forced her attention to the road but knew he looked at her as she stared straight ahead.

"He died in the line of duty. Megan gave it to me. She doesn't know how to drive a stick, and I helped David build it," Perry offered.

"He's turning." Kylie pointed ahead of her. "Don't lose him."

"I won't."

She didn't ask any more about the car or Perry's family. Forcing herself to focus on the taillights ahead of her, Kylie knew protocol insisted she call in and let Paul, or whoever answered, know she was in pursuit of a car whose driver might be her perp. But that would mean informing them she was with a local police officer. She wasn't ready to tell anyone Perry knew who she was yet. Not until she knew beyond any doubt that Perry wouldn't betray her.

Something deep inside told her there wasn't any way Perry would rat her out. That wasn't his style. But he had ultimatums. And until they came to terms she could live with, she wasn't ready to talk to anyone about this.

They rode in silence for a few minutes, the rumble of the engine vibrating the seat under Kylie and making it harder to keep her desire for Perry at bay. He turned again, and she watched roped muscle flex in his forearm and hand when he shifted and his grip on the ball at the end of the stick relax.

"We might have a false alarm," he announced when he came to a stop before turning onto the quiet side street. The Suburban had turned less than a minute before, but Perry didn't follow. "We'll give the Suburban a minute to pull into whatever drive it's heading for," he added, edging toward the corner and cutting his headlights until they could lean forward and see brake lights come on. The black SUV slowed and turned as a garage door opened on a house midway down the block. "Crap. What I was afraid of."

"What?" She looked from the Suburban to Perry. "What were you afraid of?"

"Franco."

"Franco?"

"One of the cops on the force." Perry turned the corner, driving with his lights off and crawling down the street. By the time they reached the house where the Suburban parked, the garage door was closed. "I didn't know he drove a black Suburban. I wonder why he came by. Looks as if we just went on a wild-goose chase."

Kylie wasn't so sure. She nodded once, though, unwilling to share her thoughts with Perry. She didn't know what he knew, but she suspected a cop on the force could be Peter and now she had a cop who drove a black Suburban.

"Too bad we didn't get tag numbers," she said instead of voicing her thoughts.

Chapter 18

Perry turned his lights on and shifted into second after taking the corner. He needed sleep, but the thought of taking his baby out on the interstate, cutting loose for a few, and feeling the power of his Z underneath him sounded really good. Something about Kylie sitting next to him just added to his craving to drive for a while instead of returning home. It would be light soon, though, and there was a lot of work to do, work that would be done a lot better with at least a few hours of sleep.

Kylie fought to hide a yawn from him, and he suppressed the urge to reach out and stroke her hair from her face. He wasn't sure what pissed him off more, her cold reaction to him when he told her he knew she was FBI or that he hadn't figured it out on his own sooner. Proof right there that being around her was fogging his thoughts.

Perry stopped at the stop sign, glanced both ways, and shifted into first as he pulled onto the deserted street. A delivery truck idled in a parking lot as they drove by; otherwise the world was asleep. Perry wondered if he'd be able to crash at all tonight.

"You going to be able to drive home?" He glanced at Kylie when she yawned again, this time not hiding the fact that she did.

"I've driven on less sleep than I'm working on now, Officer," she said, and gave him a smirk.

God, she was cute as fucking hell. "You can stay at my

house," he offered, shifting again and making the light as he headed back to his neighborhood. "I'll even take the couch."

"Yeah, right."

"Think I wouldn't?"

"It doesn't matter. I'm not staying the night at your house, Perry. You know as well as I do that I can't do that. For whatever reason, someone checked your house out tonight and my car was in your driveway."

He looked at her. Kylie relaxed in her bucket seat, her seat belt secure and pressing between her breasts, making them look even perkier. Her bare knees were pressed together and she gripped them with her hands, her pink-painted fingernails adding to her youthful appearance. It hit him at that moment that he probably didn't even know the real Kylie Donovan. She was working undercover, playing a part, a part that demanded she appear young, carefree, and a bit on the easy side. He cringed at the blunt reality that easy and available was the way teenage girls looked. On the prowl, in heat—how did Kylie usually dress?

"That's not the only reason, though, right?"

She looked at him, her blue eyes flashing with emotions he doubted she'd share with him. "You know it's the only reason that matters."

He watched her expression turn stubborn as she returned her attention to the road ahead of them. Blonde wisps curled at her neck. Her hair was slightly tousled, which made her look even hotter, although he also saw the level of exhaustion settling in on her.

Driving his Z with Kylie sitting next to him, relaxed, her sultry air obvious even without sleep, exhilarated him. Perry felt the rumble of the engine when he downshifted. This old car would run forever, kicking ass any chance it had, as long as he took care of it. In a way, his car was like him. As long as he kept his head clear, he would take down Peter.

And God help Franco if he was abducting teenage girls and brutalizing them. Perry would dismember the son of a bitch.

Perry turned into his driveway and eased the Z into the garage. Kylie got out before he turned off the motor.

"What do you know about Franco?" she asked, adjusting her dress as she walked out of the garage.

There was still a heavy mist in the air that dampened her hair. In the darkness, it took on a soft, golden brown hue. She didn't look at Perry but stared toward the end of his drive while continuing to run her palms down the length of her short skirt.

"He's been on the force for about five years, I think, not as long as me. His record is okay, I guess." He wasn't sure why he didn't add that Franco was a prick. But until Perry did some further investigation on his own, he would hold back his personal feelings about the man. "He usually goes for the high-profile cases."

"Likes the camera, does he?" She turned, her gaze lifting slowly to Perry's face as a small smile appeared.

"Franco is all over letting the media know how it is." Perry liked talking shop with her. He realized that knowing who she was removed a barrier between them. If he pushed, he could get closer. They were two birds of a feather, investigators. Although the thought of this sexy, petite woman standing before him protecting the community the way Perry would didn't register well for him. She needed protecting, not being put in the line of fire. "I'll find out why he drove by."

She nodded once and pressed her teeth into her lower lip, studying him for a moment. "Perry," she began.

"I'm not going to blow your cover," he told her, letting her hear what he suspected she needed to know more than anything.

"Thank you," she said, exhaling.

"Did you think I would?" he asked before thinking about it. It would start getting light in the next hour or so. He reached for her, touching her shoulder, and led her toward his house. "You're getting soaked," he told her.

"I'm going home." She didn't answer his question.

"You'd do better with some sleep." He stopped at his door, wanting her to come inside but at the same time arguing with himself to let her go.

"I'm sure we both would." She didn't say she was going home to crash.

They'd hit a new level in whatever kind of relationship existed between them. And if he was smart, he'd tell her to drive safely, and head inside for a couple hours of sleep before heading to the station. There was work to do, and a monster to catch. Quite possibly they were given one hell of a clue tonight, and that needed to be checked out.

"Come inside for a minute."

She looked at him warily. "Why?"

"Because you're getting soaked and I want to talk to you without getting wet myself." He ignored the little voice in the back of his head that yelled at him about getting involved with Kylie, with any woman for that matter.

"For a minute," Kylie said, sounding hesitant.

Telling himself that understanding her mind didn't mean they were bonding in any way almost got his conscience to leave him alone. He closed the door behind him and stood against it when Kylie turned to face him. She looked trapped, wary, and curious. It would be a hell of a lot easier to close himself off to her if he didn't see that glint of interest sparkling in her pretty blue eyes.

"Thank you for staying quiet about this," she said, and looked down at her hands.

He guessed she wanted to say more. Possibly like him, a relationship scared her.

"Where are you from?" He understood her surprise when she looked back up at his face, her lips parting although she didn't say right away. He asked her, although he already knew the answer, because putting into words what he really needed to say was damn near impossible. Telling her he regretted having sex with her would be a bold-faced lie. But saying he would leave her alone would be a lie, too.

"Good question," she said, her laugh not sounding too sincere. "I have a post office box in Dallas. Does that count?"

"Where do you stay when you aren't working a case?"

According to what he read she lived in Dallas but her holding off telling him showed her wariness bordered more on lack of trust. Even if he didn't plan on building a relationship with her, he would gain her trust.

"I have an apartment," she offered. "In Dallas."

"I've been there a few times. Huge city." He was stalling. Watching her shift from one foot to the other, lick her lips, and brush a strand of damp hair from her face proved enough distraction to keep him from focusing on what he wanted to say. Although at the moment, he wasn't sure what he wanted to say. *Don't think anything will come of it, but I want you answering only to me.* That would go over well.

Thunder suddenly exploded outside, lightning stinging through the air almost at exactly the same time. Kylie jumped and yelped, then pressed her hand to her heart, looking toward the windows that faced the street. It was still black with night outside, but the sound of rain suddenly pounding on the roof over them created a dull roar.

"Shit," Kylie hissed. "I need to go."

"On no sleep? You want to drive in a downpour?" He shook his head, willing to take her on if she argued with him. "Let me check radar."

Perry walked past her into his home and headed to his computer. If Kylie tried leaving, he would stop her. And he wouldn't fight the fact that the sudden downpour didn't bother him a bit. For whatever reasons, he wasn't ready for her to leave.

When he moved his mouse, Kylie was right next to him. Thunder exploded again and she jumped. He looked at her as lightning briefly lit up his den.

"Scared of storms?"

She instantly stiffened, then glared at him. "No," she said stubbornly.

He hid a grin as he quickly pulled up his weather program. "Okay," he said slowly. Clicking the link to check radar, he straightened while it took a moment to refresh itself and show him current conditions. "Looks as though it might rain all morning," he said when radar appeared. "But the nasty cell is over us right now. That scary thunder will be gone shortly."

He caught her pouting expression, accentuated by the glow of the computer, and watched as her long lashes fluttered over her bright blue eyes. He told himself it was because he was exhausted, that if he were well rested he would have the strength to stop himself. Perry turned, slid his hand alongside her neck, and used his thumb to press under her chin.

Kylie's head fell back too easily, her eyes closing and then opening slowly as she focused on him. "What are you doing, Perry?" she whispered.

"I think you know," he said, his voice suddenly very gruff.

Simply tasting her wasn't enough. Especially when she parted her lips, invitation enough to devour her. He pulled her against his chest, possibly a bit roughly, but it was too much work at the moment to push his desire for her back into a safe place where he could control it.

Perry tangled his fingers in her damp strands and tugged harder. Kylie arched her neck, her head falling all the way back, and offered him a feast with her mouth and her soft, slender neck. He was harder than steel within moments. His cock throbbed in his jeans. Standing like this, with her body pressed against his, grew unbearable in moments.

If she told him no now, he wasn't sure he'd be able to stop. As he lifted her into his arms, thunder erupted outside once again before he carried her to his bedroom.

"This probably isn't a good idea," she whispered against his ear.

He reached his bed and lowered her onto it. Lightning shook the house and the rain pounded louder when he exerted the effort to straighten. He swore he felt the air charge with electricity when he reached for his shirt.

"You're probably right." He ripped his shirt off his body, anxious to get out of his jeans, too. "We're going to do it anyway, though."

He'd never felt more awkward when he stripped out of his clothes. His jeans were damp enough to cling to his legs. He peeled them down and then fought to get his shoes off.

Kylie leaned back on her elbows, one leg bent enough to allow him a view up her skirt. She didn't undress but instead watched him stumble around at the edge of the bed until he was naked. Kylie sucked in a breath through her teeth, and her cheeks flushed, reward enough when she looked at him with complete adoration and need. He quickly forgot about the ordeal of undressing when he crawled over her.

She tried collapsing on the bed, but he grabbed the back of her neck and lifted her to him, then once again captured her mouth. As hard as it was to get out of his clothes, Kylie's seemed to glide off her body. He had her on her knees in the middle of the bed when he tossed her bra to the floor. Thunder and lightning exploded simultaneously, and he swore at the same time her nipples hardened into tempting beacons that made his mouth water.

Her fingers were cool when they brushed over his arms, and her eyes wide open in the darkness. Thinking about her taking down a criminal, carrying a gun, created sensations inside Perry that he didn't know how to handle. As much as he couldn't tell her what to do, he wanted to do just that. But for now, here, just the two of them, he would run the show and she would submit to him.

"I'm going to make you forget about that storm," he growled, taking her hands in his and lifting them above her head.

"It doesn't bother me," she said, her voice raspy.

Perry dragged her backward and moved around her when he had her flat on the bed. Then taking her wrists in one hand, he dragged his fingers down her middle, watching as she shivered under his touch.

"I need to decide what to do about you not telling me the truth." As if to back him on the matter, thunder exploded loud enough that the windowpanes rattled. Kylie hissed out a breath, her eyes growing wide as she looked toward the window next to the bed. "Let me see what I can do to make sure the next time it storms, you think of us making love instead of how loud the thunder is."

"Just because thunder grabs my attention," she said, but then moaned when he latched onto one of her breasts. "You're wrong about me. It doesn't scare me but you're going to have to do a lot more than that to distract me," she suggested, a grin on her face.

Kylie pressed her hand on his head and pushed his face into her breasts. Arching her back, she hummed her approval of his actions. Perry saw that Kylie didn't view these little denials of hers as lies. The storm rattled her nerves more than it did others'. Some people just got jittery when weather got loud. He didn't doubt for a minute Kylie could hold her own under much more terrifying circumstances.

"Trust me, sweetheart, I'm definitely going to do a lot more." He wouldn't voice whether it would be for better or worse. And he refused to think about any repercussions from fucking her again. Right now, she felt and tasted too damn good to think about anything other than enjoying her hot, perfect body.

The storm rumbled outside, lighting the room for brief moments before again enclosing them in darkness. He enjoyed every flash of light and the view offered underneath him as Kylie started breathing heavier while her lips parted.

"I'm going to make every inch of you tingle with need," he informed her, his voice a husky whisper as he left her breasts and kissed a path to her belly button.

She blinked, and he knew the moment she focused on him. The gaze in her eyes burned into him, fiery lust creating a unique shade of blue that glowed when lightning flashed in through his bedroom windows.

"I think you should fuck me," she whispered. Her voice held a sultry, needy edge to it that sounded as fucking hot as she looked when she shifted underneath him. "Now," she added, pressing her lips together and holding his gaze.

"Soon, my dear," he told her, and cupped her breasts as he moved lower.

Perry ran his tongue over her pelvic bone, her smooth flesh warm and feeling very recently shaven. Picturing her paying close attention to shaving her intimate parts, running her fingers over the flesh to make sure it was smooth, got his dick even harder than it already was.

"Relax and enjoy the moment. I'm going to make you come more than once tonight."

"Keep it up, and it will be morning," she whined, squirming and gripping his wrists with her small hands.

She couldn't move his hands if she tried, and she gripped him firmly, but when he lowered his mouth even farther and breathed in deeply, her rich scent made him think she held on tightly to maintain composure and not to move his hands.

When he placed a gentle kiss over her clit, Kylie jumped, shrieking, and dug her fingernails into his arms. He pulled free of her grip and pressed his hands on each thigh, then opened her for him.

"My God, woman. Damn, you taste good." He filled his mouth with her rich cream when he ran his tongue down her soft folds.

"Shit, Perry," she cried out, reaching for him, her head coming off the bed as she almost moved into a sitting position.

"So sensitive. And so wet," he growled, adjusting himself between her legs and holding her in place as he began feasting.

She was so close to the edge. Moisture coated his lips, and its ripe scent filled his lungs. He could get drunk off her. And not only how easily she got soaked for him, but also the smoothness of her skin, the subtle way she shifted her body while he stroked her with his tongue. Kylie damn near purred as he continued licking and sucking. The sounds she made were enough to push him to the edge right along with her.

Every man loved knowing his actions pleased a lady. But it was more than knowing. Deep inside Perry's soul, he accepted that what he did to Kylie affected her so strongly that she melted underneath him, submitting completely. It was more than an ego high; it created an animalistic sensation to protect, claim, and mark the beautiful creature humming her praise over what he did to her.

"Perry!" Kylie cried out at the same time the storm intensified outside. Lightning and thunder shook the house, lighting up the room.

"That's it, sweetheart," he rumbled into her soaked entrance. "Come for me."

She didn't cry out because of the storm. He seriously doubted Kylie even acknowledged the weather. He'd taken her where he wanted her, and knowing so hardened him to steel. Her body quivered, and her leg muscles clamped against him, threatening to smother him in her drenched heat. He was the stronger of the two, though, and grabbed her thighs, keeping her open, and waited the additional moment until she spasmed and came hard.

It was all he could do to move, but he wanted that clenching heat, craved that soaked paradise as much as she ached to have him. Perry crawled over her while she groped at him, tugging and almost fighting him to make him move faster. Her legs wrapped around his waist the moment he was in position and she pulled down on him while at the same time lifting her ass off his bed and meeting him halfway.

Her pussy was like a magnet, pulling his cock deep into her heat until he was positive he would drown in her.

"God, yes! Fuck me, Perry. Fuck me now," she demanded, dragging her nails over his shoulders while almost crawling into his arms.

He was over her, on hands and knees, and thrust inside her, impaling her without ceremony. Their growls filled the night, making the storm outside dim in comparison to the energy and stamina that sizzled inside. Perry was certain he'd never known better sex. As he fucked her, thrusting deep inside her again and again, the only thought that managed to seep through his fogged-over, lust-filled brain was that he had become addicted to Kylie faster than a junkie craved his next fix. Regardless of what labels they wanted, or chose, to put on whatever kind of relationship that existed between them, Perry knew without a doubt that he would fuck the shit out of her. And he'd want her again the moment he was through. Taking Kylie once, twice, several times wasn't enough. He wasn't sure how many times would be enough, or if he would ever have his fill of her.

As his balls tightened painfully and all blood drained from his body and caused his cock to swell larger and grow harder, Perry fought to hold out just a few minutes longer. He'd found paradise and didn't want to leave. Somehow he needed to keep this woman close. In fact, he would do whatever it took to make sure she didn't go anywhere. Focusing on having her in his life, satisfying her well enough that she wouldn't want to be apart from him, destroyed his resolve and the dam holding back his release.

"Kylie," he howled, come rushing from him with enough force that the room tilted for a moment. He was pretty sure he didn't yell anything else, nothing that would reveal the strange thoughts swimming in his head right now.

"Yes, yes," she whimpered, her body spasming around his as she came again, matching his orgasm with the same explosive energy.

Perry felt everything he had unload deep inside her. The release brought some blood back to his brain and helped him think a bit clearer. Even then, as reality kicked in and he knew keeping Kylie around wasn't an option, he still found himself contemplating ways to do just that.

Perry's eyes burned when he walked into the station several hours later. It was still drizzling and his plain T-shirt hugged his body, which itched. The floor was slick and one of the administrative girls walking in front of him with an armful of files slipped.

"Easy there," he said, grabbing her arm and then damn near slipping himself when he helped keep the files from crashing to the floor. "Hey!" he yelled at the janitor down the hall. "Get a sign up here that the floor is wet."

The janitor mumbled something but moved to obey.

"I'm fine. Thank you." The young clerk looked flushed when she clutched the files to her chest.

"Good." Perry was sure he sounded gruff but didn't care.

He never thought twice about most of the women he worked with flirting with him or showing signs of interest or curiosity when they shot furtive glances his direction. Usually, if a woman acted just the opposite, he noticed that faster than the blatant invitations he too often received. But this morning, exhausted, wet, and aching to be curled up under warm blankets with Kylie sleeping in his arms, he didn't care what kind of reaction the young lady he wasn't sure he'd seen before gave him.

He entered the "pit," immediately aware of how loud everyone seemed to be. Heading for his desk, he didn't realize he glared at Barker and Richey until the women quit giggling and gave him curious stares.

"Tough night, Flynn?" Jane asked, giving him the once-over and then nudging her partner with her elbow. "I'd hate to see what the lady looks like."

Both women chuckled and resumed their conversation, an animated gossip session concerning someone in Forensics. Perry wasn't expected to respond, so he didn't.

"Perry, there you are. Come here." Carl gestured with his head and then brought his Styrofoam cup to his lips and downed a fair bit of coffee.

Coffee. That's what Perry needed. Several cups at least.

"In a minute," he said, and turned toward the industrial-size coffeemaker that sat on a table in the corner of the "pit."

Perry helped himself to a cup and blew on the steaming brew as he turned and followed his partner.

"What's up?" Perry asked, enduring how hot the coffee was and practically gulping it down, willing the caffeine to kick in quickly.

"Rad's not in yet."

Perry reached his desk and slumped against it. "Okay, and?"

"Man, you look like shit. Like you've been up all night or something." Carl downed more of his coffee and turned toward his own desk, which was next to Perry's facing it. Grabbing the morning paper off it, Carl flapped it open and slapped it down on Perry's desk. "We're front-page news, man, and not in a good way."

Perry hated having to concentrate so he could focus on the print that glared up at him. The large headline and subtitles underneath were enough to kick-start his brain into high gear—and create a dull headache, which started throbbing as his blood pressure soared.

"Fuck me, bitch," he grumbled, downing the rest of his coffee. The burn down his esophagus did nothing to distract the headache that grew in intensity by the moment. "This is this morning's paper?"

Carl must have viewed the question as rhetorical, since the date was right on the top of the page. "Not only does the fucking reporter dog the hell out of us—the prick—but look," he growled, speaking faster as his temper became more apparent. He stabbed the newspaper with his index finger. "It says here they're turning the case over to the FBI. We're on this case, Flynn. I'll be a goddamn monkey's uncle if we're pulled off this one, man. This is a doozy. We just need a few really good leads. Fucking reporter, what's her name?" He started muttering in Spanish as he dragged his finger down the paper. "Hannah Oswald here announces to all of Kansas City and surrounding suburbs that the online predator could possibly be one of our own."

Perry pushed himself away from his desk and refilled his cup. Carl followed him, ranting and raving, while Perry drank half of the cup, refilled it again, and then turned to meet his partner's heated gaze.

"Let's head downstairs and talk to Pinky. I don't know who the hell leaked the news to the press, but if Peter is using one of our computers to stalk these girls, I want to know right now which computer he's using in our station." Suddenly a few things made sense, Rad's behavior for one. But if the Chief believed Peter was a cop on the force, why didn't he fill Perry in on that piece of info when he gave him the case?

If the motherfucker believed Perry was a suspect, he would hand the man's head to him on a goddamn platter.

Pete Goddard and Franco joined Barker and Richey. Perry wasn't sure which one of them spotted the newspaper on his desk, but the four of them started commenting on it and he watched each of them closely, focusing on Franco and Goddard. He didn't see any reaction out of either one of them that could qualify as odd or suspicious. But then if a cop was abducting teenage girls and using the station to instigate his crime, the asshole would have balls of steel. He'd be cocky—arrogant enough to believe he could pull off horrendous crimes under everyone's noses and not get caught. And so far, he'd been right.

Joseph Pinkman might have possibly invented computers and just stayed on the low about it. Fitting the profile of the classic geek to a T, Pinky glanced up from behind his monitor and pushed his wire-frame glasses up his nose when Perry rapped on the open door to Pinky's office.

"I need you to solve a case for us, Pinky," Perry said, entering the small room lined with filing cabinets and three desks, all smothered with mounds of paperwork. To the best of his memory, no one had worked in this office other than Pinky, but the extra desks had never been removed. Perry pulled the CD that he'd saved all the information he had so far on Peter out of the file folder he'd brought from home and handed it over to Pinky. "I need to know what computer our man is using to talk to the girls he's abducted."

"I've been playing around with that already this morning." Pinky pulled the CD out of the case and slid it into his disk drive. "I'm assuming this is the online predator case? You two going to try and nab him before the FBI come in and take over?"

"Yes and yes," Carl offered.

"This should be pretty simple." Pinky started explaining how every computer had its own specific address and left a trail that was easy to trace. "Several computers are being used. Give me a minute."

Perry walked around Pinky's desk and stared at the computer while Pinky switched screens and clicked his mouse repeatedly until he found the page he wanted. Then pointing at his monitor with his long, skinny finger, he looked up at Perry and smiled.

"Now, match these numbers up to the ones we have on file," he said, again flipping screens. "It's one of the computers in the 'pit.' Hold on; I've got a diagram right here. Wait. This can't be right."

"What?" Perry's headache was moving between his eyes. "Tell me."

"It's your computer, Perry."

Chapter 19

"Give me one solid reason why I shouldn't pull you off this case?" John Athey's silver streak that ran through his brown hair looked more dominant this morning. He watched Kylie with cold steel blue eyes that didn't blink. "You're sleeping with our primary suspect."

"He's not a suspect." She heard herself talk, knew the words coming out of her mouth weren't enough to convince anyone she was thinking rationally. "I've got a meet lined up for tomorrow night. I'll prove it to you."

"What you'll do is march into that station and pull Flynn in for questioning," John retorted.

"I'm not going to do that." She stared at her empty cup, willing the caffeine she'd consumed to kick in, and finally pushed away from the desk she'd been leaning on and headed toward the half-full pot of coffee sitting on the warmer in the corner of the meeting room. "If I blow my cover to the cops here in town there's no way Peter will come out and meet me."

Kylie had her back to John and the police chief while she blew on her fresh cup and organized her thoughts. "Take his hard drive," she announced, thinking her plan through as she spoke. "The one at the station and his personal computer at home. You'll see a man can't be two places at once."

"You're going to confiscate these from him?" the Chief asked.

Kylie turned, seeing immediately the question was more

of a challenge. "You know that isn't possible," she said coolly, matching Chief Radisson's hard expression. Neither man knew she'd blown her cover with Perry. And she wouldn't allow them to bluff any information out of her. "If you need proof that your man is innocent, you're going to have to confiscate them yourself."

There wasn't enough coffee in the pot to wake her up this morning. If she was going to pull this dinner date with a bunch of attentive teenagers off tonight in any way, she needed to head home and get in a good nap. "I'm meeting with several teenagers tonight—"

"Flynn's nieces," John interrupted. "Getting cozy with his family."

"And tomorrow night I have a date with Peter," she continued, ignoring John's comment. "I'll have your arrest for you tomorrow night. Wait and see." She took her opportunity to head for the door.

"If that is the case, then you really don't need to keep this date tonight then, do you?" John asked.

"One of the girls I'm having dinner with tonight," Kylie began, downplaying the fact they kept referring to it as a date. She swallowed, knowing explaining Dani's secret online boyfriend was once again breaking the confidence she swore to keep. "She's talking to a Peter. If I can get more information out of her, it will make the arrest more solid."

Kylie headed out of the conference room and ignored the agents in the outer office as she headed for the door. She'd agreed to meet with John against her better judgment. She was too damn exhausted to play battle of wits right now. More than anything, all she needed was sleep.

The last thing Kylie expected was to sleep for over four hours.

"Crap," she hissed, hurrying into the bathroom and shoving the shower curtain out of the way. Turning on the water, she straightened and stripped, panic washing over her at how little time she had to get ready.

Perry would be here in an hour to pick her up and take

her to his sister's. If four hours of sleep wasn't enough, there wasn't any way of knowing. She made quick work of showering, drying off, and applying makeup. By the time she decided what to wear, it was almost five.

"Maybe he'll be late," she decided, fingering the few pairs of earrings she had spread out on top of her dresser. A firm knock on her front door brought her heart to her throat. "Or maybe not."

Damn it. He was ten minutes early. Still undecided on earrings and barefoot, she marched down her hallway and yanked open her front door. "I'm almost ready," she announced in a form of greeting, and studied Perry's tight expression. "What's wrong?"

"I can't make dinner."

"Oh." Disappointment immediately washed over her, and she hated thinking it was because she'd been excited to spend the evening with him in a casual environment. It had crossed her mind she might learn more about him watching him interact with his family, seeing him in a non-work-related setting. "No problem," she announced, switching gears quickly. "Just give me directions. I'm sure I can find it."

"I'm taking you over there. I'll pick you up in an hour and a half." His gaze traveled down her, and she caught the worry lines at the edges of his eyes. "Get your shoes on," he told her, sounding firm.

Kylie turned, heading down her hallway again. At least this time the middle bedroom was securely locked. Perry might know she was FBI, but that didn't mean revealing all her work would be a good idea. The less he knew about the details of her schedule, the better. Fantasizing about him running backup for her was one thing. The truth remained the same. It would never happen.

She grabbed the closest earrings on the top of her dresser and slid the posts into the holes in her earlobes. "Why can't you have dinner at your sister's?" she asked, not looking over her shoulder but knowing Perry stood in her doorway. His powerful aura wrapped around her, strong and tight, like a leather glove molding to fit and protecting her from everything around her.

"Rad knows we're seeing each other."

Earrings in place, Kylie reached for her brush as his meaning sunk in. She turned, staring into those dark green eyes and damn near drowning in them.

"How would he have talked to you about me?" she asked carefully, her antenna of caution quickly rising.

"If you're asking if I blew your cover, don't." He pressed his fists into his waist, looking pissed. "I didn't."

"Then how was I discussed?"

"Rad had me meet him over at the FBI field office today," he offered, his tone flat. "I met with a John Athey, and after two hours of feeling as though I was being interrogated for a goddamn crime I'm then informed I'm in charge of a meeting at the high school tonight to discuss with parents how to make sure their children aren't talking to online predators."

"They interrogated you?" She didn't have to act surprised. Honestly she believed the Chief and John had pressed her to approach Perry to get her to admit something was going on between them. Kylie moved to her closet and squatted, reaching for white cloth tennis shoes. She was going casual tonight, jeans and a white blouse. Nothing that made any statement of any kind. "What do you mean, interrogated?" she asked, turning and catching him scowling at the floor.

His gaze was haunted, disturbed, when he raised his attention to her. "Peter is a cop, Kylie. Or do you already know that?"

"I don't know anything for a fact until I make an arrest," she answered carefully, watching him. He didn't look pissed, but his emotions were running strong. If he had spent his afternoon being interrogated, he had a damn good reason to be upset, though.

Kylie realized then while she'd slept the afternoon away after being up all night, Perry wasn't offered that privilege. She returned to her bed and slid her shoes on, then tied them.

"What did they ask you?" she asked, honestly curious.

"You didn't know they were going to question me?" he asked, still standing in her doorway.

Pausing with her laces wrapped around her fingers, she met his brooding gaze. Ever since meeting him she'd filled his head with lies. He studied her, waiting out her silence, and she didn't doubt for a minute he was ready for her to feed him more untruths.

"They told me to stay away from you because you could be a suspect," she said, holding on to his gaze and waiting to see some kind of appreciation that she offered him the truth. When his expression remained hard, not one muscle relaxing in his tense stare, she blew out a breath, exasperated, and returned to tying her shoes. "What did they ask you?"

"Not once have I ever been interrogated as if I was a goddamn criminal," he growled.

If he wanted comforting, Kylie wasn't sure that was a good idea. A girlfriend would console, offer reassurance. Not only could Kylie not honor herself with that title, but she also didn't have it in her to sugarcoat the situation. Perry would learn right now that she wasn't the kind of woman who would work overtime to assure him that while he was at her side everything would be peaches and cream.

"You said it yourself. All probability points to Peter being a cop, or at least someone who has access to computers inside your police station."

"The ISPs used to chat with Rita Simoli were on my fucking computer on my desk at the station," he hissed.

"What?" Kylie whispered, her jaw dropping while she watched a small muscle begin to pulse at the edge of his mouth. "Can anyone use that computer who isn't a cop?"

He swallowed and then looked away from her, pushing his large body off her doorway and slowly approaching. Kylie saw his exhaustion in his movements. For the first time since meeting her he didn't approach her like a predator ready to attack. If anything, even with his height and broad, muscular shoulders, armed and still probably incredibly dangerous, Perry looked damn near wiped out.

She stood, ready when he was at arm's distance. He pulled her to him, but not for a kiss. Instead, wrapping his arms around her, he pressed her against his rock-hard body and cradled her, as if she were the one needing consoling.

"I've been ordered to stay away from you," he told her, his rich baritone vibrating through her as he spoke quietly.

Kylie couldn't help chuckling. "You follow orders well."

"I walked out on Rad when he told me that and came straight here."

"Why does that not surprise me?"

"They told me I put myself into the line of suspicion by being everywhere you were when you were waiting to meet Peter. Apparently when you talk to him on the computer, and then quit, I show up here shortly after. Although they are playing with fucking coincidences, that, and the ISP being on my computer, is putting me in a very sticky position."

"What are you going to do about it?" She was very comfortable being wrapped into his arms, his chin resting on the top of her head while she relaxed her cheek against the side of his neck.

"Not my problem. I'm not guilty."

"They didn't pull you off the case?"

"I didn't give them the opportunity. I walked out." He straightened, letting go and walking out of her room, taking his warmth with him.

Kylie hugged herself, hating the ache he left simmering inside her. She grabbed her brush, fighting to put thoughts of fucking him later this evening out of her head, and glanced at her reflection in the mirror over her dresser while doing some last-minute primping.

She stopped in the hallway outside her door when Perry stared at the door to the middle bedroom. He looked as if he contemplated tearing the door down, or just bulldozing through it.

"When I bring you home later," he began with a lazy drawl, "I want you to show me these chats you've had with Peter." Perry pinned her with an all-business stare, whatever emotions he almost released while holding her briefly in the bedroom now very well in check. "We're both working the same case. There's no reason for the two of us not to share information, not as I see it, not now that they've told me you've got the case."

His argument was valid. "We're going to be late."

He didn't budge, didn't take his focus off her. And she hated not being able to tell whether he was pissed or simply exhausted.

"Okay," she said finally. "We'll talk shop after I have dinner with your sister and the girls."

He nodded once, satisfied, but showed no signs of gratitude. Instead, stalking into her living room, he did a quick glance over before opening her front door for her and waiting while she set her alarm, then closed the door and made sure it was locked after she stepped outside.

Megan Vetter didn't appear surprised when Perry dropped Kylie off, explained quickly he still had to work, gave his sister a peck on the cheek, and disappeared. The confusion and chaos that followed swept Kylie right along with it as the four girls appeared to continually surround her while following their mother's calm direction of putting supper on the table. And in spite of being sure she didn't have any appetite, Kylie walked her cleared plate to the kitchen sink along with everyone else after dinner.

"What made you decide on KU if you're from Dallas?" Megan asked when they made it to the living room after supper.

Not once did she scoot the girls upstairs so the adults could visit. In fact, Megan appeared indifferent that Dani, Diane, and Dorine continued hovering around her but simply extended one arm so Denise could cuddle into her on the couch.

Megan sipped her coffee, watching Kylie over the rim with a patient yet attentive gaze.

Kylie found the overstuffed chair facing the couch to be more comfortable than it appeared. The three teenagers collapsed on the floor around her, all finding positions where they could focus equally on her and their mother. Not one of them reached for the remote.

Dani and Diane also sipped coffee, matching their mother's expression while waiting tentatively for Kylie's response. She couldn't help getting the impression her personal interrogation had begun. Kylie guessed the girls remained glued to her side to make sure she didn't say anything to their mother that might require damage control on their part.

"KU is a good school," she offered, wagering Megan didn't really care why Kylie went there but was just opening the conversation. "I've got some incredible professors, but my thesis advisor is the best."

"The girls tell me your thesis will be about them. Will you be using their names? I've heard before sometimes theses get published."

"You're right." Kylie nodded, grinning. Megan needed to see Kylie's enthusiasm about the project if she was going to allow her daughters to continue associating with her. After seeing how Megan easily adjusted to Perry not being able to make supper and knowing she was a cop widow, Kylie prayed her forgiveness would be quick when she finally learned Kylie was undercover. "I don't know yet whose names I'll use, or if I'll use real names. Obviously if I do, I'll have consent forms signed. Since your daughters are all minors, I would seek your signature."

"I'm not a minor," Diane offered quickly, straightening and pinning Kylie with green eyes so similar to her uncle's it was uncanny.

"I'd still want to know if she used your name," Megan informed her, holding her youngest close while placing her coffee cup on the end table next to the couch. "Are you going to discuss this online predator who is all over the news right now in your paper?"

Megan's question surprised her, but the angle was good. Kylie paid attention to the girls' reaction and would give Dani credit for remaining indifferent to the question. Either she was a master at not showing her emotions or she seriously didn't believe her relationship with her online boyfriend fell under the category of "cautious" with all the media screaming caution right now.

"Excellent question." Kylie focused on Dorine, the fourteen-year-old, who straightened while sitting cross-legged on the floor.

Dani remained stretched out on her stomach, propped on her elbows and focusing on her coffee. She didn't look up at the shift in conversation.

"Let me ask you this," Kylie added, returning her attention to Megan, whose thick long brown hair looked as healthy and youthful as her daughters'. "Are you taking any precautions with your daughters with this predator all over the news?"

"My girls get more of an education than most with their uncle so active in their lives. He's quite the family man." Megan looked at Dani instead of Kylie when she spoke.

Her daughter focused on her mother, her smile so damn angelic it merited an award. Kylie's stomach tightened as she ignored the plug for Perry and instead noted how Dani would play her mother to maintain her private online relationship. Maybe Dani really did believe the boy she spoke with online was harmless, which proved to Kylie even more so how much she needed to be protected.

"So you're telling me you don't worry about your daughters' online time?" Kylie asked.

All girls looked at her, their expressions varying from curious to concerned. Kylie focused on Megan. There were similarities between her and Perry, one being the focused look Megan returned to Kylie.

"That almost sounded condescending."

Kylie shook her head, relaxed in her chair and knowing in spite of what the girls and Megan thought her reasons for being here were, she wasn't here to make lasting friends but to save lives.

"Not at all," she offered, keeping her tone soft and watching the wary expressions exchanged among the girls. "Do you know who your girls are chatting with and when?"

"Not always," Megan admitted, stroking her youngest daughter's hair.

Denise cuddled closer to her mother. Kylie did see a close relationship between mother and girls.

"I'm not a mother," Kylie admitted, meeting Megan's knowing look. "And I admit I haven't given much thought to becoming one. It's clear you five are very close. I'm not trying to judge you."

"Good thing," Megan said, laughing easily. "I work two jobs and have to rely on my daughters to help a lot around here. I also have to believe I've raised them well enough that they know the difference between right and wrong."

"We do," Dani said quickly, pushing herself off the floor and bending over her younger sister to give her mother a hug.

"You wouldn't meet someone off-line you didn't know, would you, Dani?" Megan asked when Dani straightened.

"Of course not, Mom."

"You better not," Dorine grumbled.

Dani spun around and Kylie caught the fierce look she gave her younger sister. Kylie tried grabbing Dani's attention, but the girl stalked out of the room and there was the sound of her ascending stairs as the room grew quiet.

Kylie glanced at the front window when everyone else did. A moment later the front door opened and Perry immediately grabbed her attention.

"What's wrong?" he demanded, shifting his dark gaze from her to his sister.

"Nothing." Megan looked tired when she leaned her head back and smiled at her brother. "That is, unless you view teenage emotions as an issue."

"Dani?" he asked, barely taking a second to note who wasn't in the room.

"I don't think she cared for the conversation." Kylie stood, straightening her blouse.

"More than likely because she doesn't want anyone to know she's thinking about meeting someone," Dorine offered, standing as well, and clasped her hands behind her back as she walked out of the room, whistling.

Megan sighed, pushing herself off the couch and leaving Denise to curl into a ball in the corner, simply watching the adults with a look of vague understanding on her face. Diane, however, groaned and patted her mother's arm.

"She won't do it. Don't worry. Dani isn't an idiot."

"She better not," Megan said, crossing her arms and glaring at her oldest, probably because the one she needed to glare at had stormed out of the room.

"Dani has been chatting with him for like forever," Dorine announced, prancing back into the room with a victorious grin on her face. "They are totally in love and she is finally going to meet him for real," she added, clasping her hands over her heart and making a show of swooning.

Maybe only spending half her childhood with a sister and the other half alone made Kylie ill prepared for what happened next. She wasn't sure, and she didn't bother taking time to analyze it. Dani flew into the room, appearing out of nowhere, and bulldozed Dorine over the coffee table. Denise howled on the couch, jumping toward her mother, and Diane screamed, falling backward and landing on her rear with a thud.

"Dani!" Perry roared, grabbing her backside and yanking her backward through the air.

"You little bitch," Dani howled, her arms and legs whaling around her while her long brown hair flew like a cloak blinding her face. "How dare you say such a thing."

"It's the truth!" Dorine wailed, her legs up in the air hanging over the coffee table while tears streaked down her face.

"Perry!" Megan yelled, reaching for Dani. "Don't hurt her."

"Enough!" Perry yelled again, and silenced the room.

Kylie felt like an onlooker, momentarily forgotten in a family dispute that she had no part of. Except that she had instigated the matter.

She clasped her hands behind her back, standing to the side, while her mind now went into analytical mode. Watching quietly, she observed and noted how each of them reacted to an ugly situation. What was said next, though, would possibly prove invaluable.

Dani struggled out of her uncle's arms but then hugged herself instead of walking into her mother's arms. "She's a big fat liar, Mom," Dani said, a sneer in her tone as she shot Dorine a warning look.

"And you're an idiot," Dorine retorted, holding her own.

Dani stood a couple inches taller than her younger sister, but Dorine weighed more. It was the older sibling intimidation that won out, though. Dorine pressed her mouth closed, obviously conceding not to say more.

"I think it's time you share the details about this boy with me," Megan demanded, her focus hard on Dani.

"Not a problem." Dani didn't move. Her uncle remained an overwhelming presence, towering over her backside, while her mother scowled, her arms crossed while glaring at Dani. She stood as tall as Megan, and her attention didn't sway while she explained herself. "Dorine eavesdrops on my conversations and fills in the holes to create her own gossip. It's not my fault she has no life."

Dorine made a snorting sound but again snapped her mouth closed when Dani seared her with a hateful glare.

"Do you really think with all the mess going on in town right now about some serial killer that I would go meet some guy off-line I didn't know?"

"I hope to God not," Megan said softly. She let out a breath and backed away from her daughter. Then as Megan combed Dani's thick brown hair away from her face with her fingers, her tormented expression would have broken a softer person's heart. Her fingers trembled when she reached for her daughter's face. "You've got so much of your father's fiery independent spirit. I look forward to watching it blossom as you get older."

Dani deflated at her mother's words and pulled her in for a hug. Perry glanced her way for the first time but then quickly moved to pull Dorine to her feet. He pretty much pushed her into Diane and with a look had the two of them heading out of the room.

"Denise, head upstairs with your sisters," he instructed, his calm baritone enough to make the twelve-year-old scurry off the couch and dart out of the room, probably grateful to leave the dramatic scene. Then taking Dani by the shoulders, he turned her around to face him. "Swear to me right now you aren't planning on meeting some boy you've only chatted with online."

"I can't believe you'd think such a thing," Dani whispered.

"Then explain why you just attacked your sister, and it better be the truth this time."

"Perry, let me handle this," Megan began.

"I'm not walking away from this, Meg," Perry informed her, crossing his arms over bulging muscle when he let go of Dani. "Talk to her all you want, but after the day I've had, the last thing I'm going to do is walk out of this home before I'm very satisfied that the girls I love aren't anywhere near the monster I'm stalking."

"I am not talking to that murderer!" Dani yelled. "Don't you think I would know if I were?"

Kylie almost said no, she wouldn't know, at the same time Perry did.

"Do you think the other girls who've disappeared were idiots?" Perry challenged her, ignoring his sister when she tried turning Dani toward her. "I've seen the chats he's had with those girls. He's a master at making girls your age believe he's a boy your age. He thrives off that, becoming your best friend, confiding in you, talking about his parents and homework and complaining about tests and acne. Any of that sound familiar to you?"

Dani didn't answer but stared at him with wide, moist eyes. She was an intelligent girl. And God willing, the boy she was talking to online was legitimate and there wasn't anything to worry about.

"Maybe if you promise your mother and uncle you won't meet anyone until this guy is arrested," Kylie suggested, and both Megan and Perry looked at her as if they'd forgotten she was in the room.

"Whatever!" Dani said, waving her hand dismissively in the air. "But there isn't anyone I'm planning on meeting," she added, sticking to her story as she edged around them and headed to the doorway and the stairs. "This conversation is over," she announced, and ran from them, bolting up the stairs loud enough that it sounded as if all of them raced upstairs together, instead of just Dani.

"I'm sorry you had to see that," Megan said, once again playing hostess when she tried smiling politely at Kylie. Worry created deep lines in her forehead and around her eyes, though, and she looked exhausted. "It really was good meeting you, though. Perry, bring her back soon."

"She'll be back," he said, speaking before Kylie could think of what to say. Then as if to seal his words, he pulled Kylie to him, wrapping his arm around her.

The intimate contact, which he held on to when he walked the two of them to the door, would make it damn impossible to convince Megan they were only friends. Granted, Megan didn't know anything about Kylie, but what she believed now brought a smile to her face.

"I'll feel a lot better when you have this guy arrested," Megan said, following them outside but remaining in her doorway. "And Kylie, stop by anytime. I know tonight wasn't proof, but my girls love you."

"Thank you," Kylie said, although it was hard to turn when Perry kept a firm grip on her.

"You won't have long to wait," Perry said, finally stopping and facing his sister when they were halfway down the sidewalk. "I'll let you know the moment the asshole is behind bars."

"Good." Megan shifted her attention between both of them, her fatigue apparent but her expression definitely showing approval when Perry kept his arm around Kylie. "Good night, you two."

Chapter 20

Perry couldn't kick his foul mood, so he didn't say much as they drove in silence. After he had spent the last hour or so talking to teenagers and their parents and listening while the Simolis again addressed the press and warned everyone to keep their daughters under lock and key, it had been all he could do not to toss Dani across the room until he knocked some sense into her head. He would tear through her computer and phone, regardless of what Megan thought, if it came down to it. Dani could be pissed all she wanted, but she would be alive.

"Perry, where are you going?" Kylie pulled him out of his thoughts.

He turned into his driveway. "Home," he grunted.

"What about me?" She didn't take off her seat belt when he put the Jeep in park and then cut the engine. "No way, Perry. You've got to take me home."

He wasn't in the mood to argue. Opening his car door, he stepped out into the muggy night. Another storm was heading their way. "I will soon."

She hurried out her side and trailed him into his home. "I can't stay here. It better be really soon."

"Why can't you?" he asked, turning in the darkness and pulling her to him, then reaching over her and pushing his back door closed. "Your car isn't outside. No one will know."

"But they will know if I'm not at my house all night. And if I'm not, they will know where to look for me."

"Good." He liked believing his house would be the first place they would search for Kylie if she went missing. It meant all those down at the FBI field office believed she was his woman. "We'd hate to have them worrying about you."

"Perry," she said, uttering his name with a soft whisper. She implored him to be reasonable, but her eyes were like a midnight sky, large and sultry and slightly hooded with her thick lashes. "We've both been ordered not to see each other."

"They can all go to hell." He didn't care if he sounded irritated.

"You would lose your job over me?"

"Do you really think you'd lose your job because of me?"

She chewed her lower lip and he hardened to stone. Her silence was answer enough. They both might endure more humiliating reprimands, although he didn't doubt for a moment if Rad tried lecturing him that he'd walk out before he could get started.

He wasn't Peter. The only reason Kylie would need to stay away from him was if she suspected him to be their perp.

He'd help her through her indecision. "Am I your perp?"

That sultry gaze of hers faded quickly as she made a face. "Good grief, Perry."

That was answer enough. He grabbed her arms, dragging her to him. "Then stay with me," he demanded, his voice a vulgar growl but the best he could master.

He wasn't used to his emotions being so exposed. But kissing her, not hearing her hesitate but feeling her hot body relax against his, protected the vulnerability that threatened to rise too close to the surface.

Perry ran his hands down the curve of her back, cupping her soft ass, and lifted her against him. He had his arms under hers, encouraging her to run her fingers up his arms. She opened up to him, deepening the kiss as her fingernails scraped his shoulders.

But the soft sigh she released, while stretching against him, was all he needed to lift her into his arms and walk through his dark house to the bedroom.

"God, we shouldn't—"

"Like hell," he grumbled, picking up his pace until he reached his bedroom. He tossed her to the bed and was on her before she could turn around. Grabbing her shirt, he yanked it up, forcing her arms up until he ripped it from her body. "You need this as much as I do."

"True, but." She bit her lip, her thick lashes shrouding her gaze when he pinned her to the bed.

He was exhausted, damn near spent. It boggled his brain how being with Kylie, feeling her soft, perfect body underneath his, created energy he was positive wouldn't have existed otherwise.

"The only truth here is this is where you belong," he told her, nipping her lower lip and kissing the full, moist flesh he just tortured.

"You know once this is over—"

"So I'm a fling to enjoy while you work a case here in town?" he asked, already knowing from the look in her eyes that wasn't the case. He was prepared for her to admit that as the truth, though, and ready to show her what he would do if she lied. "Is this something you make a habit of doing?"

"No and no," she said firmly, her look intent when she stared up at him.

Perry ran his finger along the edge of her lace bra, watching her flesh bulge against the fabric when she sucked in her breath.

"Then what is this?" He slipped the material away from her breast, exposing her eager, puckered nipple.

He sucked her into his mouth and Kylie cried out, dragging her nails down the back of his shoulders and arching into him.

It sounded as if she forced the words out. "I'm not sure," she uttered, her voice strained.

Perry moved his mouth to her other breast, slipping the fabric to the side and exposing a very hard nipple. "You aren't sure?" he whispered over her flesh.

She smelled good. A mixture of soap and perfume proved she had primped before going to his sister's house. And when she had prepared to go over there, she thought they were going together.

"You tell me," she gasped when he wrapped his lips around her nipple.

Perry bit her, pressing his teeth into her tender, puckered flesh and using enough pressure to make her flip off the bed. Her nails dragged into his flesh, digging in deep enough he was sure she punctured flesh. The sharp pain sent the need inside him to a boiling point.

He grabbed her by the back of her neck, yanking her off the bed to a sitting position, and held her while devouring her mouth. She was everything he needed, fresh and fiery with an energy that ignited something inside him every time he was around her. No matter the circumstances or kind of day he was having, Kylie was the perfect medicine for him.

"All right, I'll tell you," he growled, aching to be inside her. In spite of being exhausted, he wanted to take his time devouring her. Kylie would scream his name and not have an ounce of doubt in her mind what was happening between them once he made her come. "The truth is that while desperately trying to find an asshole and take him off the streets, we've both found something we didn't know we were searching for. We'll solve this case but ending what is growing between you and me might prove more work than either of us wants."

Kylie opened her eyes and stared at him while he pulled his face away far enough to focus on her. Her expression remained serious, although she didn't look as though she would argue with him.

Perry grabbed the top button on her jeans and tugged until it came undone. "From this point forward, you and I are working on this case together."

"Okay," she said offhandedly, as if she didn't hear him or didn't give his statement any merit. She kicked her shoes to the floor and lifted herself, allowing him to pull her jeans and underwear off her.

Perry doubted she would agree as easily as that. But he'd

hold her to her concession. He'd hold a few more things against her, too, easing her back against the bed and pulling her blouse over her head. Her blonde hair fanned around her, softer than silk and such a beautiful shade next to her creamy skin.

He had a hard time picturing her taking down a bad guy, and an even harder time stomaching her working to capture someone as insane and cruel as a man who could desecrate and torture, then kill a teenage girl. Just thinking of Kylie putting herself in that kind of danger, even knowing she'd done it many times before meeting him, made him wonder if he saw her for who she really was at all.

He wanted to possess her, control and take care of her. Feeling her soft hair against his fingertips when he brushed her hair from her face and lowering his mouth to hers caused something to twist inside him. It created a pressure that stemmed from more than a desire to be inside her. It grew hot, smoldering around his heart until he was sure he'd break out in a sweat from it.

Kylie tilted her head, her breathing hard when she fingered the material by the collar of his shirt. "Is there a reason why you wanted me naked?" she purred.

"Most definitely," he growled, dragging his fingers down her front and pausing between her breasts.

Her heart released a hard, steady thumping against his fingers while he lifted his gaze to her face. "You're beautiful."

"And you're dressed."

"In a hurry?" He wanted to take hours to enjoy every inch of her, claim and mark all of her and make sure she never doubted she was now his.

"Maybe I've decided I want to enjoy myself, too." She twisted the top of his collar in her fist, tightening it around his neck, while her expression grew challenging. "I suggest you take your clothes off now," she whispered, the soft inflection like feathers brushing over her flesh.

There was something in her gaze, though, a glint visible even in the darkness that showed defiance and a friskiness in her nature. It grabbed his attention and he moved, adjusting his weight and grabbing her wrist as he pulled her hand from his shirt.

"I don't take orders well," he growled.

Kylie also moved quickly, rolling out from underneath him, and although she made no attempt to free her wrist, she pulled herself to her knees and stared into his eyes. "Do you think stripping me naked renders me harmless?"

"Are you taking me on?" he asked, more than amused.

She yanked her hand free, which he allowed her to do, but then shoved him backward with her hands pressed against his chest. When he didn't move she laughed, and pushed harder, this time showing she wasn't completely defenseless by catching him off guard when he braced himself, and then, instead of shoving, she yanked him forward.

"Such the tough guy," she said, all grins.

Wrapping her arms and legs around him, she reached with her hand and slapped his ass. Perry jerked up, feeling the smack under denim, and although it didn't sting, her defiance turned determined and it was clear immediately they needed to establish a few ground rules.

He grabbed her arms, and although she fought him, gritting her teeth and applying all the muscle she had, he forced her hands above her head and pinned her wrists together.

"Don't do that again," he warned, brushing his lips over hers as he spoke and adjusting his body so he could rub his crotch between her legs. He imagined what the roughness of his jeans against her sensitive flesh would do accurately when she hissed through her teeth. "Patience will bring you so much, sweetheart. Relax and let me take you to new places."

"Are you sure you can show me something new?" she asked.

"Do you think I can't?"

The defiance faded and her features softened. "You probably could." She twisted her wrists against his palms until he released one hand, which she immediately brought to his face. "I still want you naked if I am," she suggested, her tone softer.

Maybe Kylie wasn't used to asking for anything but instead taking what she wanted or needed. He saw that in her nature, and believed possibly it was instilled there from living and working in what was still predominantly a man's field. He wouldn't argue he bordered on the old-fashioned side, but she saw something in him she liked or she wouldn't be here. That realization created a hard, quick urge to please her, give her anything she wanted.

"Not willing to take the patience lesson, huh," he teased.

God, she was fucking adorable when she wrinkled her nose. "I'll take it when you do," she said, her sly smile turning him harder than stone.

Not that he wasn't already sporting a hard-on from sparring and caressing her naked body. "Trust me, I'm already enduring it."

She lifted her hips underneath him, keeping her legs wrapped tightly around him, and rubbed her pussy against his crotch. When she purred, he swore he saw stars explode before his eyes. Kylie had no clue how much she tortured him. And she complained he wasn't being fair.

"You're asking for trouble." He didn't want to be rough with her. In spite of how much he wanted to enjoy her for hours, he was all too aware of his level of exhaustion.

"Trouble?" She sounded disbelieving and ran her foot up the back of his leg. "Do you really think you're trouble?"

"I think you might not like what I dish out if you keep pushing me."

Kylie shoved his shoulders, although this time her expression hardened. "Fuck you, Perry Flynn, if you think I'm so fragile I can't handle it rough."

Perry pushed himself off her to his knees, before untangling her legs from his thighs and standing. Ripping off his shirt, he then undid his jeans, watching her look turn pensive while he stared into her round blue eyes. Her blonde strands tousled around the pillow underneath her head and she licked her lips, then sucked in her lower lip while her attention drifted to where his hands were.

He gripped his jeans and boxers and pushed them down

his legs, stepping out of them and leaving them on the floor when he moved to the bed. "I'm more than willing to find out what you can handle, if you are?"

She licked her lips again, her hooded gaze making it hard to see where she focused. "Bring it on, big guy," she said, her voice rough and tight as her hand drifted down her body and paused over her shaved mound.

"Are you wet?" He grabbed his cock, needing to stabilize himself after the view Kylie offered.

"Soaked." She bent her knees, pressing her feet into his bed, and shoved a finger inside her, hissing as she did.

"Do you masturbate often?" He could picture her lying alone, playing with her shaved pussy until she cried out, alone and in the dark. He preferred that image over one of her doing this for another man, or fucking another man.

"Sometimes," she whispered, stroking herself while her finger disappeared and reappeared, coated with come. "How often do you masturbate?" she asked, her attention focused on his cock as he stroked the loose flesh over steel.

"All the time," he growled, deciding he liked her bold nature. As long as it never got her killed. "But I'm not going to tonight."

"Good thing." Her smile brought a flush to her cheeks.

Maybe she wasn't this bold but trying to impress him. Perry didn't have a problem taking the time to learn who Kylie Donovan really was. If she would give him that time and not disappear once they caught their guy. Her line of work would insist she do so, though. He wouldn't dwell on the future right now but instead enjoy what lay on his bed tonight.

Perry knew he possessed more control than most men, but still letting go of his cock and gripping Kylie's legs, spreading them open, caused all blood to drain from his head.

"I want to taste," he growled, his voice tight.

Kylie pulled her fingers from her damp pussy and held them out to him, offering the cream clinging to her flesh. He moved closer, leaning down and taking the tantalizing treat. Sucking her fingers into his mouth, he tasted her, the thick, rich cream clinging to his tongue and its erotic aroma floating to his brain like a highly addictive drug. He growled his approval and held her fingers between his teeth, scraping her flesh when he slowly moved backward until they slipped out.

Kylie's sharp inhale of breath proved he wasn't the only one affected. And he needed more. "I'm going to make a feast out of you," he told her, grabbing her legs and dragging her to the edge of the bed. Then sliding off so he knelt on the floor, he breathed in the rich aromatic scent of her. "What a perfect pussy," he whispered. "So smooth and creamy. Look at how wet you are, sweetheart."

He glanced up when she moaned. Her eyes were squeezed shut and her hands in her hair, but as he watched she opened them and reached for him.

"Please. Oh, God, Perry," she whined.

"What, sweetheart? Tell me what you want."

"You, please. Taste me. Touch me."

"Like this?" He ran his tongue over her entrance, using his fingers to spread open her pussy lips, and then delved inside, licking the thick cream visible around her smooth folds.

"God. Yes. Perfect," she uttered, still doing her best to drag her fingers into his hair, pin him where he was, and press his face into her heat. "More. I love that. More."

He dipped inside her again, then ran his tongue around her clit before pressing his lips to the swollen ball of nerves and kissed her. Kylie about jumped off the bed. He gripped her legs, keeping her open and right where she was.

"Do you like that, darling?" he whispered against her flesh.

"Yes. Yes," she cried, panting hard. "Love it. More."

"You like your pussy eaten?"

"God, yes."

"When was the last time a man did this to you?"

"What?" She sounded disoriented and brought her hands to her head again, tangling her fingers in her blonde strands. "I don't know. I don't remember."

"Was it with someone you cared about?"

"No," she said, without hesitating.

"So, a one-night stand?"

"I don't know." She shook her head from side to side and reached for him again. "Don't ask me questions right now. I can't think straight. Just don't stop."

Perry chuckled, satisfied she didn't make a habit of seeking men out while on assignment. Her reputation was impeccable, which it might not be if she distracted herself with affairs in every town she worked in.

And her track record was perfect. All of her was. So far, even her demanding nature and struggle for independence, the entire package, appealed to him. Every bit of Kylie was his definition of everything he'd ever wanted in a woman. He just hadn't known it until now. Kylie was the woman for him and somehow they would make this work.

He teased her clit, watching how she shivered and jerked while her body eased its way into an orgasm. He held her like that, keeping her on the edge, until her cries turned louder and she grabbed him, raking his shoulder while moaning loudly.

"Please. Perry," she uttered, her breathing coming hard.

"Does my baby want to come?"

"God. Yes," she wailed.

He stroked her smooth flesh with his tongue, dipped inside, and started fucking her. Then using his finger, he pressed the swollen nub, prepared when she leapt off the bed. But this time her thighs closed around him, hard as steel, and held him where he was while she exploded, every inch of her trembling as she screamed.

Perry pried her legs, which were clamped against his ears, and lazily licked the cream flowing from her pussy. "I don't ever think I've made a lady come that hard."

"Then you've been holding back," she said, breathing heavily.

That, or she really needed to come. A wave of pride washed through him knowing he was the one to force her to let go. She was washed in glistening perspiration, her breasts full and round and nipples pointed into hard peaks. He loved how her chest rose and fell, her ribs perfectly shaped and dipping down to her hard, smooth belly.

Her legs were still bent and spread, and he stroked her inner thigh, her warm smooth skin just as incredibly perfect as the rest of her. Perry couldn't remember a time when a woman completely filled his thoughts, even for a few moments. It dawned on him as he licked her from his lips that while he was enjoying her there hadn't been any other thoughts in his mind—not work, or his sister, his nieces, not anything but Kylie. Even now, as he meagerly attempted to analyze what that might mean, or if it meant anything, no other thoughts dared interrupt his contemplation of the hot female still breathing heavily before him.

Other than his cock throbbed painfully and his balls were so tight that acknowledging them was enough to almost make him come.

"I'm going to fuck you." His voice was scratchy, as if he'd been the one howling and wailing.

Kylie's lashes fluttered over her dark blue eyes, a shade he once believed were the result of contacts and now accepted was her natural color. Even in his dark bedroom there was an intensity to them, proof there was so much to Kylie, knowledge he ached to learn.

"What if I fuck you?" Kylie pushed herself up on her elbows and attempted to roll her legs to the side.

Perry stopped her. She was perfect right where she was. "What if you just stay there," he decided.

She cocked one eyebrow, her attempt, he guessed, at letting him know she didn't want to be told what to do. He was diplomatic. It wasn't as though he were a chauvinist or anything, but he'd brought her to where she was now, and he would keep taking her, allowing her to experience pleasure offered completely by him. Kylie would see life with him was exactly where she needed to be. He'd already decided his life would be a hell of a lot better with her in it. Getting to know her, learning how to tame her stubborn, defiant streaks, and enjoying every inch of her sexy body again and again would be the best gift ever offered.

"What if I don't want to stay here?" Her brow was still arched, but there wasn't any way she'd read his thoughts.

"Then I'll change your mind." While her ass twitched on his bed he grabbed her ankles and knelt before her. Then as he leaned over her, leaving her feet to rest on his shoulders, her heat pulled him to her, his cock finding exactly where it needed to be without instruction.

"I wonder if your incredible self-confidence or sheer bullheadedness has gotten you where you are today," she murmured. Leveling her gaze on his face while pressing her legs against his shoulders in an effort to keep him from leaning closer into her.

"A mixture of both, I'm sure," he told her easily, pressing his fists into his bedspread on either side of her and balancing himself over her while the tip of his cock nestled against her entrance. "Of course there are also my charm and natural good looks."

"Of course," she said dryly, but then grinned, her lips still pressed together as she reached and brushed her fingertips over his hair. "Did you neglect to mention your modesty on purpose?"

"It was an intentional oversight. I didn't want to gloat." He slid inside her then, feeling so many tiny muscles constrict and drag him in deeper while her heat threatened to suffocate him.

"God, that feels good," she purred, still holding his head in her palms. "Fuck me good and hard, okay? Don't hold back. Promise you won't hold back."

"So bossy," he growled, but loved her imploring request. He wasn't sure he could hold back. Although he took his time sliding deeper into her moist heat, every inch of him constricted painfully until it became hard to breathe. But still, he didn't want this to end. He sure as hell wasn't taking her home. "Enjoy the ride, sweetheart," he told her, leaning closer to her face and forcing her to bend in two. "You can file your complaints when we're done."

She chuckled and nipped at his lip when he tried kissing her. "I'll keep a mental list," she whispered roughly, but then groaned into his mouth when he thrust the rest of the way inside her, impaling her and soaking his balls in the process.

Thick cream spread over his most sensitive flesh, making it constrict and tighten. His balls filled to the point where he knew they would burst if he wasn't careful. He fought for control, acutely aware of her muscles massaging his shaft when he pulled out and then dove deep inside her again.

"Kylie," he growled, quickly building momentum while staring at her through blurred vision. "Look at me."

He adjusted himself, getting a grip on his bearings and finding a good, steady rhythm where he could enjoy how tight she was while riding her at a good pace.

She grunted, her boobs bouncing deliciously while her lashes fluttered and she fought to obey him. When she looked up at him, her mouth shaped into a small circle and her breathing came loud. She grabbed his arms, digging in with her painted nails, and stared into his eyes. Her glassy gaze was as erotic as the feeling of stroking her hot pussy while fucking her.

"I want you looking at me when you come."

"Oh." Obviously words now evaded her, sending another wash of pride over him. His sparring partner was finally subdued where he wanted her. Perry made a mental note that any time Kylie tried taking him on, he would simply fuck her into submission.

"Hard and fast. Is that what you said?" he asked, diving deeper inside her, feeling her juices flow from her as he picked up momentum.

"Yes. Crap!" She hissed between her teeth while her nails dragged down his arms.

He felt the sting of her scratches and didn't care if she left a mark on him. He fucked her with all he had, gazing into her face while he breathed harder and his balls constricted until he knew he couldn't hold out any longer.

"Come for me, darling," he told her, barely able to utter the words while he created friction between them that would burn him alive.

"Perry," she uttered, gasping for breath and digging her

nails into his forearms. "Perry . . . I'm . . ." She didn't finish but instead thrashed her head from side to side, causing blonde strands to stick to her face as she cried out and her cheeks turned a dark blushed red.

She didn't have to tell him she was coming. Her pussy got so tight, draining him before he could grab another breath to ease him through his own orgasm. He gave her all he had, his ears ringing while the room got so hot he wouldn't be surprised if the two of them combusted from their love-making.

Kylie drained him so thoroughly it was all he could do not to collapse on top of her. He lowered himself over her, allowing her to slide her legs off his shoulders and collapse under his.

"Are you going to get that?" she whispered.

Her words didn't register at first until his brain kicked back to reality and it hit him it wasn't a ringing in his head but his cell phone.

"Crap," he growled, not ready to move and certainly not wanting out of her yet. "Whoever it is better have a damn good reason for fucking calling."

"They always have a good reason," she groaned, sounding as though she didn't want the moment to end any more than he did.

He rolled off her, certain he would go into shock from the instant cold that surrounded his soaked cock. Then dragging his jeans from the floor, he found his phone clipped to his belt loop and pulled it free to glare at the number displayed.

"It's Megan," he said, wondering what the hell she wanted. "Hello," he said, knowing he sounded gruff.

"Perry," she said, her anxious tone not sounding good. "Dani has run away."

Chapter 21

Kylie wasn't sure she could move. Her legs were like wet noodles and her heart pounded too hard in her chest. She lay there, managing to tilt her head and stare at Perry's perfect naked body in the darkness while he stood in the middle of his bedroom on the phone.

"She did what?" he growled, sounding bewildered.

It took some effort to push herself to her elbows and then even more effort to clear her vision from the blurred state it had been in for the last twenty minutes at least. Every inch of her pulsed and the heat between her legs still smoldered at a temperature she could barely control. In spite of how sated she was, just admiring the well-defined muscles throughout his body created a tingling inside her that grew the longer she drooled over him.

"Okay, Megan, calm down. I don't understand. She wouldn't just run away."

Kylie's attention snapped to his face. Even in the dark she noticed his strained expression, and the heat inside her turned to something more numb. Her antenna went up as reality kicked in with a mean punch. She sat up, easing herself to the edge of the bed, and draped her legs over the side, watching Perry.

"Well, hell. You're positive. . . . Okay, calm down. . . . No. It's fine. Just tell me this. Did she walk out the door or did someone come get her?"

Kylie jumped off the bed, grabbing her clothes and untangling them while her heart started racing all over again. This time, though, it wasn't from passion but panic.

"Is it Dani?" she asked, keeping her voice low, when she figured out what the conversation was about. Megan didn't need to know Kylie was over at her brother's house.

Perry glanced at her as if he'd forgotten she was in the room. He didn't nod or shake his head, though, but instead continued listening.

"All right. I'll head over that way. Have the girls check her room, her computer, anything you can think of. I want all the information you can gather that will help us determine where she might have gone."

"What about her cell phone?" Kylie whispered.

Perry mouthed to her that she had left it at the house.

"Check recent messages and text messages," Kylie whispered.

She barely remembered getting dressed and hurried after Perry when he continued pulling his shirt over his head while heading through the dark house. When he paused in the living room and checked his gun before hooking it in its case to his belt, Kylie patted her waist where her gun would usually hang if she was going out in the field.

"I don't have my gun," she told him, meeting his intense gaze when he turned and looked down at her.

There was something unreadable in his expression, something that caused her insides to quicken as he searched her face without saying anything for a moment. Then without commenting, Perry turned, pulled open the top drawer to a cabinet against the wall next to his gun display, and pulled out a nine millimeter and handed it to her.

She didn't have her security belt, but it wasn't the first time she ran down someone with only her purse and all she needed inside. Quickly checking the security, then pulling it back to see if it were loaded, she met his gaze again when he handed her ammunition.

"Tell me what's going on," she said, feeling an awkwardness grow inside her that mixed with several other emotions she didn't have time for right now. Anxiety crept over her flesh, leaving damp gooseflesh, but the tightening of her gut was usually what she felt when it was time to make the cut. They weren't bringing in their guy tonight but going after an obstinate teenager. At least that was what Kylie gathered.

"Dani and Megan had a fight. My sister is pretty upset right now and honestly she wasn't making a hell of a lot of sense. I guess Dani got mad again when she was accused of agreeing to meet someone online."

"But we already know that is true. Dani admitted as much to me. She's got a guy online she refers to as a boy-friend, yet they've never met in person. And he's got a screen name that is spelled funny but pronounced 'Peter.'"

"You told me." Perry's voice was deep, gruff, almost pissed sounding when he finished putting his shoes on, then grabbed his keys and headed for the door. "Apparently Dani stormed out of the house, calling her mother a few choice names, and when Megan stormed out after her Dani took off running. They can't find her."

"Megan hasn't called in to Dispatch, has she?" Kylie was already around Perry's car, reaching for the door handle on the passenger side when he climbed in behind the driver's wheel.

He met her gaze when she slid in next to him. "Nope. And she won't unless I ask her to. Why? Are you worried about going on a call with me?"

"Are you?" she challenged. The way she saw it right now, he was putting himself more on the line than she was with the two of them leaving together like this. No one on her side would know about this circumstance, especially if Megan didn't call it in.

"Nope." Perry's profile showed his determination and his jaw was set the way he always held it when he was hell-bent on seeing something through.

As he backed the Jeep out of the driveway the quickening returned in her gut with a vengeance. They'd just made in-credible love to each other. She could feel the dampness between her legs, and for the first time since dressing and hurrying out the door she imagined she probably looked like hell—or like a lady who'd just gotten the shit fucked out of her.

Now they were headed out on a call, working together. This was almost as good as rolling over and fucking him again. And if it weren't for the dire circumstance and the possibility that Dani could run into trouble out at night alone and pissed, Kylie would probably be reveling in the moment, inspired by the opportunity to work by his side, even if it was just this one time. She would get to see him in action. Once she kicked Dani's obstinate ass, she might just have to hug her for giving Kylie this opportunity.

"You've got your cell phone," Perry said, not making it a question as he headed down the road with his high beams creating lines on the road ahead of them.

"Yes," she said, again studying the strong features of his profile.

"Good. We won't have radios. If we have to comb the neighborhood it will be the only way we can communicate."

"Works for me."

Perry obviously didn't give any thought to how Megan would react when she learned Kylie was still with him. Megan opened the front door the moment he knocked but then gawked at Kylie before quickly regaining composure.

"Which way did she head?" Perry asked, ignoring Megan's reaction to seeing Kylie.

Megan pointed out the door and down the street to their right. "I followed her for about a block before she lost me, I hurried back home to call you."

"Did she change clothes after we left?" Kylie asked.

Megan searched Kylie's face, as if drawing her own conclusion about something, and took a moment before her face lit up. "Yes. She did change. She's wearing a white T-shirt. Are you going to help look for her?"

"Yes." Kylie didn't hesitate in answering.

Diane pushed her way next to her mother in the front door. Although an older version of Dani, Diane also held strong features very similar to her mother's. Diane focused on Kylie but then glanced furtively from her mother to her uncle.

"I'll help look, too. With all of us we'll have her back in no time." Diane rubbed her mother's shoulder, looking worried.

"No." Perry spoke so firmly all the women looked at him. "None of you are leaving this house. Is that understood?"

Diane looked ready to argue, but Megan put her arm around her daughter and backed her into the house. "Bring her home, Perry, alive and well so I can kill her."

"You've got a deal."

Megan looked so distraught, torn between outrage and pain that created hard lines around her pretty eyes. For a moment, Kylie was ripped back thirteen years and saw her own mother, worried sick while waiting to hear word from the police that her oldest daughter was alive and safe. That message never arrived.

"Here's what I need from you," Kylie said, and both Megan and Diane gave her their full attention. "I want you to go through her computer. Find any chats with this boy she was supposedly going to meet."

"But," Diane began, immediately chewing her lower lip.

"Do as she says," Perry ordered.

"I know you don't want to violate her privacy." Kylie would snap at Perry later for being so gruff with both of them when they were obviously worried sick. "But it could save her life. Call us immediately if you find anything indicating she planned to meet him tonight. Or if you find her agreeing to go anywhere. Do it now. There isn't any time to waste."

Perry turned from the door, taking her by the arm. Kylie hurried down the path with him, not bothering to say goodbye to either of them but hearing the door close behind them.

An hour later, Kylie and Perry had combed the neighborhood and been on the phone with Diane and Megan more than a handful of times. Kylie got stubborn with Perry, aware that he worried about the rest of the women in his life when Dani was missing but insisting they would cover more ground and learn more faster if the two of them split up. Reminding him he wanted to know if she carried her cell phone so they could communicate didn't seem to help much, but when Kylie pointed out she'd taken on many killers in the past, all alone, Perry's gaze darkened over, his expression bordering on violent.

"Fine," he growled.

"Diane is calling Dani's friends now," Kylie reminded him. "I say we head to all hangout spots where she might have gone to regroup and be alone. We check out every one of them that is open at this hour."

"Bowling alley is still open," Perry said. "We can go there together."

Kylie nodded. She needed to get to her car, but they would figure out how to do that if the investigation continued into the night. She stared into the darkness, scanning her attention across the large, empty parking lot. It was the fifth or sixth one they'd cruised around and then through. Dani wasn't anywhere.

Worse yet, Diane couldn't find anything on any of the computers at the house that helped them. "She's password-protected her cell phone," Diane told Kylie in her most recent call.

"Try thinking of her password. Anything you can think of," Kylie suggested.

"Try 'Peter,' " Dorine said in the background, doing what the fourteen-year-old did best, eavesdropping.

"No luck." Diane was obviously trying every password she could think of while they talked on the phone.

"Wait a minute," Kylie said, sitting next to Perry in his Jeep while they drove across town to the bowling alley. "The screen name she was talking to when she told me about Peter . . . it was spelled funny."

"I've got it!" Diane laughed in her ear. "It was Petrie, not Peter. Way to go, Dorine, for being queen eavesdropper."

Kylie didn't smile as she listened to the two girls laugh. She wondered what Megan was doing, and felt her pain as her stomach twisted when they pulled into the bowling-alley parking lot. The building had a sign on it that lit up a lot of the parking lot, and streetlights lining the lot added to the visibility. She remembered coming here when she was supposed to meet Peter, and Perry interrupting the meeting. What she wouldn't do for that to happen again tonight.

"Kylie?" Diane's soft-spoken, serious tone didn't sound good.

Kylie's heart moved to her throat and beat furiously as anxiety created a sheen of perspiration over her body. "Yes?" she asked.

"She went to meet him."

"Crap," Kylie hissed, meeting Perry's dark gaze when he stared at her after parking his car. "Please tell me they discuss where and what time."

"The bowling alley," Diane said, and then paused, her breathing coming hard through the phone. Dorine obviously felt the need to keep her mother apprised of the conversation, as she yelled in the background. "And ten minutes ago," Diane said, her excitement level dropping drastically. "At eleven. You need to get to the bowling alley now."

"We're here," Kylie informed her.

"What's going on?" Perry demanded.

"Dani agreed to meet her boyfriend, Petrie, here at the parking lot ten minutes ago," Kylie told him without ceremony.

"Goddamn it," Perry howled, slamming his fist into the dash hard enough to make the car shake. He jumped out, slamming the door, without another word.

"I'll call you back," Kylie told Diane.

"He won't hurt you," Diane whispered.

"I know that," Kylie assured her, forcing her tone to remain calm. "We're going to go find Dani. You go take care of your mother and sisters and be calm for them. Okay?"

"Okay, Kylie," Diane said, and said good-bye reluctantly before hanging up.

Perry had stormed off in one direction and Kylie opted to take the other, wishing she was more properly equipped but patting her purse and feeling the small handgun inside. She stared into the darkness, her heart pounding so hard it was damn near deafening.

There weren't many cars in the lot at this hour, most of the stores closed except the bowling alley and the donut shop on the other side of the lot in the adjacent strip mall. She could see into the shop through its glass windows, and a few people sat at tables inside while one employee stood behind the counter. The best she could tell, everyone inside eating pastries were men. She didn't see any women or teenage girls. Nonetheless, she sprinted across the lot to the wide sidewalk and then strolled down it, past the donut shop, and confirmed Dani wasn't inside.

Petrie hadn't picked her up and taken her for a bite to eat so she could unload the woes of her home life on him. But then the sickening feeling inside Kylie's gut told her Petrie wasn't who Dani believed him to be.

"Please let me be wrong," Kylie muttered under her breath, combing her hair away from her face with her fingers while staring across the parking lot.

She didn't see Perry. Her cell phone rang, though, and she jumped, then damn near attacked it as she dragged it out of her purse and stared at the unknown number.

"Hello," she said, answering on the fourth ring and praying whoever it was wouldn't hang up, and would be someone she wanted to talk to right now.

"Kylie?" a small voice said, sounding broken and terrified.

For a moment Kylie couldn't breathe. "Dani?" she asked, praying she was right.

"Yes."

"God, tell me you're all right."

"I'm not all right."

Kylie was hightailing it back to Perry's Jeep before thinking about it. Perry must have spotted her, because he appeared out of the shadows at the far end of the bowling alley, and she gestured to him frantically as she raced around the truck to the passenger side.

"What's wrong, sweetheart? Where are you?" She forced herself to remain calm, take deep, soothing breaths. If the son of a bitch had Dani and was using her to lure Kylie in, she was more than game to take the motherfucker on.

"I'm at a pay phone. I need you. Please come get me and don't tell anyone. Please? Promise? I've done a very, very bad thing and my uncle will kill me for sure."

Kylie slid into the passenger side at the same time Perry slid into the driver's side. His wild look was frantic as he stared at her and then her phone.

"What?" he demanded.

"Oh my God, Uncle Perry is with you. Kylie, you've got to lose him. Please." Dani was crying now and harder to understand.

"Where are you?" Kylie asked, remaining calm as she stared into Perry's dark, fierce eyes.

"I don't know," Dani wailed into Kylie's ear.

"Are you hurt?"

"I don't think so. I'm scared. And I'm the biggest fucking idiot."

Perry started the car, continuing to look over Kylie's way. "It's Dani, right. Where is she?" he asked with a baritone so cool sounding it gave Kylie chills.

"She's scared and isn't sure," Kylie told him, hearing Dani hiccup in her ear as she continued crying hard. "But she sounds as if she's okay." Then putting the phone close to her ear, Kylie covered it with her hand, needing only to hear Dani. "You know your town, Dani. Look around you. Tell us where you are."

"You're bringing Uncle Perry. He's going to kill me."

"We were both out looking for you, so we're together, and yes, he is bringing me to you. You have my word he won't kill you."

Perry grunted and she ignored him.

"You don't know my uncle that well then."

"Dani, where are you?"

The sobs continued before Dani finally answered. "On the south side of the bowling alley parking lot. I ran back here. But I think there might be a problem. God, Kylie, *please* come by yourself. I've done something really, really bad and I might be in some serious trouble."

"The south side?" Kylie looked outside, getting her bearings. "I'll be there in a second."

"Okay. Where are you?"

"Don't hang up, Dani. Stay right there and do not hang up the phone." Kylie pulled the phone from her ear just far enough to focus on Perry. "She's on the south side of the parking lot here at a pay phone," Kylie whispered. "She keeps repeating she's done something terrible and doesn't want you to come get her, just me."

"Damn the luck," Perry growled, making a sharp turn back into the parking lot instead of turning onto the street.

"Kylie, I think he's coming back. He's going to see me. I've got to go," Dani hissed into the phone.

"We're right here. Don't hang up," Kylie said frantically, and then heard the hum in her ear. "Damn it," she snapped, tossing her phone into her purse but then quickly reaching for her door handle. "She was on a pay phone on the south side of the bowling alley but just panicked and said she is afraid he's coming back and that he'll see her. She hung up on me."

Perry didn't answer but accelerated hard enough that the tires squealed. He raced across the parking lot but then hit the brakes so hard Kylie slammed her palms against the dash. Making a sharp turn, he drove only a bit slower through the dark side of the back of the building toward the other side.

"She kept saying she's done something really terrible."

"She agreed to meet that bastard she's been talking to online," Perry hissed, sounding mad as hell.

"I think so. But something happened and it caused her to call me from a pay phone crying her eyes out and begging me to come get her. Yet then she hangs up in a state of panic. I think she got away from him and he's coming back for her."

Kylie didn't have to voice her thoughts. Obviously Perry was thinking the same thing. He turned the corner sharp enough that Kylie swore he did it on two wheels instead of four.

"There!" Kylie pointed at a small figure racing down the length of the building.

At the same time another car turned around in the back lot—a black Suburban.

"Drive!" Perry ordered, slowing the truck and undoing Kylie's seat belt at the same time.

"What?" She looked at him, confused.

"Drive!" he yelled. "Go get her now!"

He barely brought the truck to a stop and at the same time dragged Kylie across the seat toward him. She didn't have time to question the madness of his actions before he jumped out of the truck and ran around the back side. The Jeep kept rolling forward and she quickly adjusted herself in the driver's seat, which was set back way too far for her to sit comfortably.

There wasn't time to adjust it. "What the hell are you doing?" she howled, shifting it back into drive and pressing her toes against the accelerator pedal while gripping the large steering wheel.

Perry raced faster than a man his size looked like he could run. And another time she might have admired the view, and easily gotten hot as hell doing so. Even in the dark she could tell how muscular he was, and in shape, as he sprinted toward the Suburban. When she noticed his gun in his hand and that he pointed it at the Suburban, she cursed out loud and gunned the engine similarly to how Perry had a minute ago. It took no time at all to catch up with Dani.

The teenager looked terrified and makeup streaked down her face when she looked at the Jeep and took a minute to register that Kylie was driving her uncle's vehicle.

"Get in," Kylie ordered, easily finding the right button to roll down the driver's-side door window. "Dani, hurry. In, now!"

Dani didn't argue and raced around the front, then climbed in. Kylie grabbed her before Dani could react and used one hand on the side of her head to force her down into the seat.

"Stay low and don't move," Kylie demanded, turning the large steering wheel and making the tires squeal just as a gun went off.

Chapter 22

Perry aimed for the back tire. He pulled the trigger.

"Fucking son of a bitch," he growled when the Suburban made a sharp turn and started coming toward Perry.

Mess with his goddamn family. He didn't give a fucking rat's ass about rules or regulations. He would take the asshole out right here and now.

"Sick bastard," Perry yelled, aiming when the black SUV started at him. "Take me on. You'll die slow and tortuously. I'll fucking see to it."

There was a rumbling behind him as well. Kylie had Dani and was heading toward him and the black Suburban. He didn't budge, though. All he wanted was that fucking SUV to get close enough so he could dive to the side. He needed to see the driver, confirm for himself his suspicions. Then he would nail the fucking bastard to the wall.

Kylie stood on the damn horn behind him and the SUV swerved, squealing its tires and burning rubber when it took off around the side of the building. He noted the license plate numbers as being the same ones they'd taken down before. It was Peter!

"Scoot over," Perry yelled, grabbing the driver's-side door and yanking it open when Kylie slowed.

He was impressed that she had Dani lying on the seat, and didn't bother waiting for either of them to adjust themselves next to him when he gunned the motor and took off after the Suburban.

"It's the same truck," Kylie told him.

"Yup. This time we're going to find out where he's going."

"Watch out," Kylie yelled, her hand going protectively in front of Dani when a car came at them from the front of the building.

"Son of a bitch." He was going too fast and slammed on his brakes, barely missing the other car. "Fucking idiot," he hissed.

Kylie and Dani didn't say a word, which was in their best interest. Neither one of them dared cross him right now. He needed blood, needed to see the asshole suffer who had tried stealing Perry's niece from her family.

"Where did he go?" Kylie asked. She'd taken his gun from his lap when he'd gotten in the car and had secured the safety on it, and now had it pressed in her lap.

Perry's heart beat furiously in his chest when he blew out an exasperated breath, searching the dark lot and the exits. "He couldn't be that far ahead of us."

Kylie leaned against him, but when he glanced in her direction focusing on the exit at that end of the parking lot he noticed she shifted her body to put her arm around Dani. Kylie could cuddle his niece all she wanted. When they got home, the kid would be in more trouble than she'd ever known in her life. He shook from the terror of how close they came to losing her tonight. And he'd be damn sure she understood that before he left her with her mother.

"Over there!" Kylie almost yelled, her entire body stiffening when she pointed in front of them.

Dani yelped but didn't make any further noise when Kylie quickly sunk into the seat and wrapped her arms around the teenager.

"Do you see?" she added, more quietly.

"Where?" He frantically searched the dark, way-too-still parking lot.

"At the edge of the strip mall. There is a car not moving, as if it's hiding."

"Not anymore," Perry growled, cutting across the lot although this time he watched for inattentive drivers. He didn't have lights in this truck that he could slap on the hood to keep civilians out of his way. They were on a silent run, which meant he needed to be as alert for their perp as he was for everyone else around them. "I've got you now, mother-fucker."

Perry drove the truck straight across the parking lot, ignoring the arrows indicating the flow of traffic and cutting across empty stalls until he reached the end of the building. His heart sunk when they pulled up alongside a parked black Ford van.

"I don't understand how he can keep disappearing so easily when he's in such a large vehicle." Kylie voiced Perry's frustration, her own voice tight with emotions he was sure matched his own. "Let's take Dani home. I need to make some phone calls."

"Can I stay at your house?" Dani asked, whispering.

Perry was pretty sure she wasn't presenting that question to him and opened his mouth to give her a piece of what he had to dish out to her but didn't get the chance to speak.

"You're going home." Kylie sounded stricter than he'd ever heard her sound before. Her soft, sultry tone was gone. "Your mother is worried sick."

"None of this would have happened if—"

"Don't even go there." Now Kylie was pissed. She shifted more in the seat, completely facing Dani, with her ass brushing against Perry's thigh. "None of this would have happened if you'd thought like an adult, which you obviously aren't. And until you are, don't you ever storm out on your mother again like that. Do you understand at all?"

"I can't believe you're yelling at me," Dani said, breaking down into a serious sob session.

Perry knew his niece well enough to know when she started crying that hard there wasn't any point in continuing the lecture. Dani wouldn't hear a word of it. Obviously Kylie didn't know this about her.

"I can't believe you left every ounce of your intelligence at home when you ran away."

Dani sniffed and then sucked in a hard, staggered breath.

It was quiet for a moment and Perry chanced glancing over at the women after turning out of the parking lot. Let the two of them battle it out. He was getting some new insight into Kylie, one being that she had no problem speaking her mind when she was pissed. The other being that she obviously cared about his niece.

Kylie straightened, facing forward as Perry picked up speed, keeping his eye open for the black Suburban. He relaxed his arm on the back side of the bench seat, which he often did when he drove in the car, especially when he had more than one passenger. Dani looked at him for the first time; her black eyeliner streamed down her face, staining her cheeks clear to her cheekbones. He met her gaze, daring her without saying a word to even try to comment about his arm being around Kylie. Dani looked away first, pressing her hands together in her lap, and stared at them.

"I thought you would understand," Dani said, stubborn and stupid enough to press the subject.

"When I was fourteen my seventeen-year-old sister stormed out of the house after fighting with my parents. She was running to her boyfriend's house and I knew it," Kylie began, relaxing her head against his arm. Her soft hair tortured his already-overstimulated nervous system. She didn't seem to notice how close they were. "Karen never made it to her boyfriend's house. She was raped and murdered. We didn't find her until three days later. There wasn't Internet back then, or cell phones, or media that is all over everyone's business like they are today. We didn't know there was a rapist in the community who'd already attacked twice. He killed one other girl after my sister and was never caught, at least not that we know. My sister's death destroyed my parents. They never recovered from it. For three years afterward, they forgot my birthday every year. It took me years past that to forgive them for ignoring me after they lost Karen."

"I understand, I think," Dani said, still sniffling.

Perry slowed when they reached Megan's house and realized as he parked that he hadn't called his sister. "First thing out of your mouth better be an apology," he told Dani, opening his door as he spoke.

Dani didn't answer but opened her passenger door and slid out of the truck. Kylie hurried after her, but Perry grabbed her arm and pulled her back against him. "Tell me what she told you on the phone," he said, wrapping his arm around Kylie's waist.

Something soothed the tortured frenzy he'd experienced burning him alive since they left Megan's when Kylie didn't fight him to be free. She leaned against him, tilting her head against his shoulder so that her soft blonde hair tickled his flesh.

"She went and met Petrie. She didn't say what happened." Kylie looked up at him, her blue eyes clouded with her concern and her tone serious, and once again soft and sultry sounding. "I'm going to find out, and I'll do better if you don't go in there fully cocked and ready to tear into her. But my guess is that she had a run-in with Peter and for whatever reasons got away. If she hadn't called me from that pay phone it sounds as though he would have snagged her."

"And then the motherfucker got away." He got away with a bullet nick on the side of his Suburban, something that would make it easier to identify. "I'm going to have to call this in."

"Same here," Kylie added, and then adjusted herself just enough to look him squarely in the eyes. "Sounds as if you and I are going to be in as much trouble as Dani."

He doubted anyone inside was looking out the front window right about now, but he didn't give a damn if they were. Cupping Kylie's chin, he forced her head back just a bit more and tasted her.

Kylie was warm, moist, and breathless as she greeted him with soft, full lips. For the first time since they'd left to search for Dani he smelled his sex on Kylie. They hadn't taken time to shower but had raced out of his house and over here without putting themselves back in order. Under different circumstances, at least one of the attentive women in that house would have noticed.

"If we hadn't been together tonight, we wouldn't be as close to nailing our perp," he told Kylie, moving his mouth over hers.

"Good story, but the truth is if your niece weren't such a willful teenager we wouldn't be closer to knowing who our guy is."

"Speaking of which." Perry let go of her long enough to lock his truck. "Let's go hear what she has to say. We can call in after we leave."

She didn't try getting away when he draped his arm over her shoulder and led her to the front door. Kylie put her hand on the door handle before he could, though, and turned, looking up at him. "Promise me now you won't go off on her."

"I'll tell you the same thing I tell Megan. I don't believe in babying any of them just because they're girls."

Kylie shook her head and it looked like she almost rolled her eyes. If she did, the action was quick enough in the dark that he wasn't sure.

"Their gender has nothing to do with it. Yell at anyone and you get less out of them than if you are levelheaded and feel the situation out before interrogating."

"Telling me how to do my job, Special Agent?" He was poking fun at her, intrigued by her concern that they enter his sister's house as though it were a crime scene. In actuality he'd already viewed the situation as needing just that kind of approach. Perry was quickly learning Kylie wouldn't automatically follow his lead. She would jump in fully prepared to command the situation unless he instructed her otherwise.

"I'm just saying . . . ," she said, licking her lips and shifting her dark blue eyes while searching his face.

Perry put his arms on her shoulders, turning her around, then reached under her arm and pushed open the door. "We'll work the scene, partner, but you'll keep in mind this is my family and you won't undermine anything I tell my nieces."

"I wouldn't dream—" Kylie stopped talking when Denise jumped up from where she was watching TV, her eyes wide, but then grinned broadly and ran to Perry.

Kylie stepped away so Denise could climb him, the last of the four still able to do that. "Dani came home, Uncle Perry. She and Mom are upstairs fighting."

"You're smart to stay down here and watch TV," he told her, pecking her forehead with a kiss before peeling her off him and placing her on her feet.

"Will you watch TV with me?" Denise looked ready to fall asleep, her eyes puffy and her light brown hair tousled, probably from her being half-crashed on the couch.

"I'm going to go upstairs and check on things then I'll be back down." Knowing it would be harder to get away from Denise without her latching her small body to his leg, he escorted her back to the couch. "But I'll fluff the pillows just like I would for me if I were getting ready to stretch out at my house and watch TV."

"You're the best pillow fluffer." Denise crossed her arms, watching him seriously, but shot Kylie more than one curious glance. "Can I have a blanket, too?"

"*May* I have a blanket," Kylie said behind him, and walked to his side with the folded afghan from behind the large corner chair in her hands.

"May I have a blanket?" Denise asked, sounding sleepier when she crawled onto the couch and straightened so Perry could unfold the blanket and cover her with it. "Everyone says Kylie is your new girlfriend," she asked, whispering although Kylie stood next to him. "Are we going to have to start calling her Aunt Kylie?"

"No," he told Denise, not hesitating. That was one response he could give without getting a headache thinking of how to answer. "Now get comfortable and I'll be back down in a few."

"Okay, Uncle Perry. Mom said Kylie would see right through you and she would lock horns with Dani and all of that would be bad. So I'm glad she isn't going to be my aunt."

Denise didn't look at Kylie but snuggled under her blanket and turned to face the back of the couch.

Perry didn't even want to think about what his sister meant by Kylie seeing right through him. He didn't have anything to hide. One look at Kylie's face and he knew she found his niece's comment rather amusing. She was a smart woman, though, and hid the smile he saw glowing in her bright blue eyes. Instead, she turned toward the stairs and led the way up to the bedrooms. At least he had a hell of a view while climbing the stairs.

Megan approached the top of the stairs at the same time they did. Exhaustion lined her face and she was several shades paler than usual. God, he hated how hard she worked. And the added stress of the evening was the last thing she needed.

"Oh, Perry," she cried, reaching for him while fresh tears appeared in her eyes. "Thank you so much for bringing her home."

Perry didn't make it to the top step before his sister wrapped her arms around him. She seemed thinner than usual, and she almost collapsed against him when he gave her a big hug. Glancing over Megan's head at Kylie, who'd moved out of the way for the second time since they entered this house to allow his family near him, she stared at the floor, her expression unreadable. Before he looked away, he caught her glancing toward the one open bedroom door and guessed she itched to go talk to Dani.

"Kylie, would you give us a minute?" he asked, hating to admit she would probably be more successful getting information out of Dani than he would right now. In fact, before he calmed down it was probably a good idea if he let his niece alone. "Dani's bedroom is straight ahead, the open door."

Kylie didn't say anything but nodded once, her expression tight when her gaze traveled down Megan's backside. She left him with his sister and walked silently down the hall, her purse clutched to her side. Kylie disappeared inside Dani's room, closing the door behind her.

"Dani called Kylie. I really don't get any credit for finding her. And she kept me from killing your daughter, so she probably should be thanked twice," he said, still holding Megan tightly in his arms.

"I need to get the girls to bed." Megan didn't comment on what he said.

Perry remembered Kylie's brief story about her sister being killed when Kylie was a teenager and wondered if she wouldn't do better consoling his sister, too. Emotions were running too high in this house, and he wasn't the best psychologist on the planet.

"Denise is tucked in on the couch. I wouldn't be surprised if she's already out. I've locked the front door."

"You know, you're supposed to be a pain in my ass. You're my baby brother," Megan said, shifting in his arms but not looking up at him. Instead she made a fist and pressed it over his heart. "I was so scared, Perry. You have no idea—"

"Yes, I do." He felt her start trembling and knew she held back from a full collapse. "I want you to take a hot bath. I've got your back, Sis. Go soak. Make it a bubble bath. The girls will be in bed tucked in and snoring when you get out."

"Perry, I can't."

"Like hell. Quit acting like your daughters and talking back to me," he growled, putting her at arm's length and turning her around. Then holding on to her, he guided her to her bedroom, which was the only room upstairs with an adjoining bath. "I don't want to see you again tonight," he informed her.

"I'm too drained to fight you tonight." Megan's laugh was dry, but there was appreciation in her tone. "If I ask you a question, will you tell me the truth?"

"Do you know how much men hate hearing that out of a woman's mouth?" He tilted his head, focusing on the dark circles under her eyes and how easily he saw her cheekbones. His sister needed a long vacation, to be pampered. Hell, if he could think of one good man in this town, he would play matchmaker. She was doing way too much on her own, and the girls' acting up, like Dani did tonight, was more than she could bear. "What is it?"

Megan searched his face, worrying her lower lip for a moment. Even when they were kids she got the same look on her face she did now when she thought really hard about how to say something, or approach an uncomfortable subject. He narrowed his gaze on her, wondering what in the hell she was about ready to drop in his lap.

"What is your relationship with Kylie?" she asked, whispering as she shot a furtive glance at Dani's closed bedroom door.

"We don't have a relationship." It was the second time tonight he'd denied anything was going on between him and Kylie. Tonight wasn't the right night to suggest anything otherwise.

"Your hands have been all over her ever since you've been here." Megan crossed her arms over her chest, giving him her shrewd mother look that reminded him so much of their mom. "You are having sex with her."

"Do you really want to know what women I have sex with and when?" He didn't like this conversation but knew how to throw it back in her face so Megan would back off.

"We're a very tight, small family, Perry. And you are the main father figure in my girls' lives. I know you want that role, and I don't have a problem with it. But if you're going to have any kind of relationship, then yes, I want to know when and how often," she said firmly although still whispering. "I should have a right to yea or nay someone else entering into our family."

"You don't like Kylie?" He had a hard time believing that.

"Dani told me Kylie took your gun out of your lap while you were driving and Dani was sitting next to Kylie. She told me Kylie handled the gun like a pro, barely looking at it while checking its safety and ensuring it didn't have bullets in it."

"I noticed that, too." He hadn't given a thought to how professionally she handled the gun. Her actions had made sense at the time and he would probably have done the same thing if their roles had been reversed at that moment.

"The list of qualities and talents you possess is longer than my arm." Megan placed her hand on his shoulder and stared up at him with dark, all-knowing eyes. "We're all accustomed to you handling all matters and seldom making mistakes."

"Thank you," he said, sensing he wouldn't like where she was going with this.

"Kylie is a very beautiful woman. Smart and pretty, with a likeable personality. I can see why you would fall for her." She paused, holding his gaze, and dragging the moment out before continuing. "Is there a chance she might not be being honest with you? Dani told me some of the things she said while in the truck, like how she needed to make some phone calls, and how she easily handled a loaded weapon. Before you left to go look for Dani, Kylie kept her cool while drilling me for information on Dani. Perry, is Kylie a cop?"

Perry saw immediately why Megan believed he would keep information from her like Kylie being a cop. "No, she isn't. And if she were I would tell you," he said, not lying.

Megan let out a long breath, once again exhaustion lining her face and making her eyes look puffy like her daughter's. Perry ran his hand down the side of Megan's head, hoping his smile reassured her.

"You don't have time or energy to worry about me. Nor is it necessary. Go get that bath and relax."

"You'll make sure all the girls are in bed? They all have school in the morning."

Perry wasn't sure he wanted any of them leaving the house, even tomorrow for school. The hit tonight was personal, and he'd be damned if Peter were given another chance to smooth out his failure tonight.

"Bathtime now, young lady. Your girls are in good hands." Perry turned her around and pushed Megan into her bedroom, closing her in when he pulled her door shut.

As outraged as he was at Dani for pulling the most stupid stunt of her life, one that too easily could have cost her life, it amazed him how perceptive she was. Kylie would need to watch her ass or a sixteen-year-old would blow her cover. He pondered this, going back and forth between being proud and furious with his niece while turning out Dorine's lamp when he found her asleep in her bed and then carrying Denise upstairs and putting her in her bed next to Dorine's.

When he opened Dani's door without knocking, three incredibly stunning women turned their attention to him. Diane looked tired like her mother, Dani leery, and Kylie's bright blue eyes were guarded for reasons he wasn't sure of as he entered and closed the door silently behind him.

The bedroom was so quiet he swore he would hear a pin drop on the other side of the house as he walked into the feminine paradise of pink pillows and white lace. Dani sat cross-legged in the middle of her bed facing Kylie, who relaxed in the wooden rocking chair Megan used to have in the living room and where she had nursed all of the girls when they were babies. Diane was stretched out behind Dani on the bed, her head propped up by her hand.

"We're pretty sure the man I saw tonight was the bad guy you're trying to catch with your case, Uncle Perry." Dani offered the information lightly, flashing him a glowing smile as if she were showing off an A on a report. "I can totally ID him for you. I know exactly what he looks like. Caucasian, brown straight hair, shorter than you, probably less than six feet tall."

"None of that information is worth you almost losing your life tonight," he growled, the anger that had burned through him earlier quickly returning. "*If* that man is Peter, he's raped, tortured, and mutilated girls in town already. Would you like to see pictures of what he's done to them?"

Dani shook her head and looked down at her hands, her long brown hair draping over her shoulder and hiding part of her face.

"At least she had the sense to figure out before she got in the car with him that he wasn't the guy she'd been chatting with online," Diane said, pushing herself to a sitting position and rubbing her sister's back.

"Yes, he was," Kylie and Perry said at the same time.

"That's the whole problem and what had me terrified,"

Kylie added, resting her elbows on her knees while staring at the two girls. "All this time, Dani, you've been talking to an online sexual predator."

"That is just so hard to believe," Dani said, although she sounded more defeated than defiant now. As she collapsed back on her pillows, her long thick hair fanned around her face, which had at some point been scrubbed free of makeup. Dani looked younger and more innocent than ever. "We did our homework together, talked about the future, our families and our brothers and sisters."

"If he weren't as good as he is the police would have captured him already," Kylie offered soberly.

Dani turned her head, staring at Kylie without saying anything at first. "I swear you're a cop. I'm going to find a Bible and make you put your right hand on it and tell me you aren't."

Kylie's laughter was melodic. "I would do that for you," she said easily, pushing herself to her feet. "Tomorrow," she added. "It's late and I do believe it's a school night. I can't believe your mother hasn't kicked me out yet."

"Everyone is in bed or heading there," Perry announced. "Diane, call it a night."

Diane didn't argue with him, but then she seldom did. She gave Dani a quick hug, and her sister pulled her into her arms, hugging her fiercely. It was an act he hadn't seen between the two of them in ages, and he hated thinking of where the night could have ended up if events had turned out differently. He would give thanks they didn't, though, and prayed that the reality of the situation would scare some serious sense into his nieces.

Diane crawled off Dani's double-sized bed and straightened her blouse that hung low over leggings, which showed off her thin legs. Then grabbing her hair at her nape and pulling it behind her shoulders, she turned to Kylie but didn't approach her. "Thanks for helping our uncle," Diane said, fidgeting with the bottom of her shirt as if hesitating to say more. "Good night," she added, then walked around her uncle to her room across the hall.

"Yell at me tomorrow, okay?" Dani said, rolling to the side of the bed. "I just want to crash."

"Be grateful you are crashing in your bed tonight," Perry said, wishing he could think of the perfect thing to say that would convince him Dani wouldn't ever seek out a stranger online again. "And we will discuss this in great detail tomorrow. I'll be over to get a full statement from you."

"Like the real deal?" Dani's eyes lit up, as she once again saw all of this as a great big adventure.

"No," he barked. "Not *like* the real deal. This *is* the real deal, young lady, so damn real you better never forget it."

"I won't, I promise." She dropped her feet off the side of her bed but then sat there instead of standing. "I need to go to the bathroom and get ready to go to sleep."

Kylie headed toward the door, pausing when Perry didn't move and hugged herself. Perry looked at his niece, who met his gaze, suddenly looking very sad.

"I guess I wanted someone to care for me and want me for me so badly, Uncle Perry, I refused to look at the obvious. Kylie and I went through a lot of the text messages Petrie and I exchanged and it was kind of obvious he wasn't who he said he was. Kylie pointed out some things I'll be sure and check for in the future."

Perry knew how proud Dani was. She was just like him in that sense. Being wrong sucked. But getting killed over stupidity sucked even more. He still wanted to knock some serious sense into her, but the way she looked at him right now, appearing more defeated and so incredibly innocent with all of that crap washed off her face, Perry was around Kylie before he thought about it and pulling Dani into a huge bear hug.

Lifting her off the floor, he wrapped his arms around her slender, firm body. She was the perfect sixteen-year-old, her future ahead of her and so many doors open and waiting for her to choose. No one would rip her out of his life. This family already had lost a good man, Megan's husband and the girls' father. It had nearly destroyed them, and only time and a lot of love kept them from falling completely to pieces. No one would do any more damage to Perry's girls.

"I love you, Dani," he said, his voice thicker with emotion than he cared for it to be.

"I love you, too, Uncle Perry," Dani said, a sob catching in her throat.

Perry did a final walk-through of the house, making sure everyone was in bed and checking all doors and windows. It crossed his mind to take Kylie home and then come back here, camp out on the couch for the night. Then it also hit him to just keep Kylie with him and both of them crash here.

Although he didn't really like what Megan had to say, she had a point. Bringing a lady around the girls, if that lady wasn't going to hang around, didn't help create a healthy environment for any of them. He couldn't do that any more than Megan could have men coming in and out of her life. Parenthood had some fucking steep criteria.

Chapter 23

Kylie glanced at the clock on the wall and again at her cell phone as it rang for the third time. "Hello," she said, and adjusted her Bluetooth in her ear. "Did you stay home from school today?"

"Mom said I could." Dani sounded like her usual happy self. "I drew a picture of the guy in that black SUV last night. Would you like to see it?"

Kylie perked up, hoping more would come to Dani today. Any information Dani offered would only bring Kylie and Perry closer to arresting the asshole. "I'd love to see it," she said, not hiding her excitement.

"I figured you would, although I find it interesting that a picture I drew of a guy who tried to kidnap me would appeal to you so much if you aren't a cop." Her tone was victorious, as if she'd just busted Kylie.

Kylie didn't sleep for shit last night, waking up several times and reaching for Perry only to realize he wasn't sleeping next to her. Nor would he ever be sleeping next to her. He'd made as much clear last night when he told his nieces, on two different occasions, that he and Kylie were not a couple. If thoughts of pressing whatever it was between the two of them further truly appealed to Perry, he would prepare his family for the fact, get them to accept her. Perry took what he wanted and made the world accept him for who he was.

It just wasn't meant for the two of them to be together,

other than possibly to share some mind-blowing sex while working an investigation. That was enough to depress her through the day, and it was a fight to keep her spirits up.

Kylie managed to laugh. "You got me. I'm busted."

"You are? I knew it," Dani said, and made a whooping sound through the phone.

Kylie laughed even harder.

"What?" Dani demanded.

"You're funny. I'm not a cop."

"Damn you. That isn't funny." She didn't sound as if she pouted too hard. "Why were you so thrilled to see my drawing?"

"Because it would make you happy," Kylie explained, thinking quickly, on her toes. "A very traumatic experience happened to you last night, something many people never have happen to them as long as they live. You need to work through it, and if drawing the guy you saw helps you, then I very much want to see what you've drawn."

"Well, you know where I am," Dani said. "I'm not allowed to leave the house or even unlock the front door. I don't think Mom meant you couldn't come over, though."

"Call her and get permission and let me know," Kylie told her, and glanced up when John Athey paused in the doorway of Paul's office, where she'd set up camp this morning while Paul was at a doctor's appointment. "I'll talk to you soon, Dani." Kylie said good-bye and pulled her Bluetooth from her ear. "Good morning," she said, again looking at the wall clock and confirming it was still morning. It seemed as though it should be almost five.

"You mind filling me in on the excitement you had last night?" John asked, crossing his arms as he leaned in the doorway.

Kylie was convinced John simply wasn't a happy man. Either that or he really didn't like her. He scowled at her now as if whatever it was he'd heard about last night didn't impress him, or pissed him off.

"You already knew I had plans to have dinner with Perry—Lieutenant Flynn's sister and her daughters," Kylie began, ignoring the frown that created more lines on John's face as he watched her.

"And you knew I told you not to go," he informed her dryly.

"It's a damn good thing I did go. We're closer to Peter than ever now. And we've got a witness who can ID him."

"Do you really think Flynn will allow his niece to be used as bait to bring the perp in?"

"Of course not. I would never ask him to do that. She's only sixteen."

"You make it sound like he would do anything you would ask of him."

"Do you want to discuss my personal life or this case?" Kylie snapped, and stood to refill her coffee.

"Tell me what happened last night."

"I ate dinner with Megan and her daughters and then Perry picked me up to take me home."

"To take you home?" John interrupted. "Why didn't you drive there?"

"I'd planned on it." She needed to choose her words carefully, without tipping John off that she'd fucked Perry. And that she couldn't wait to fuck him again. "He insisted. I think he wanted to be there when introductions were made."

"Cut the crap," John hissed, walking into the office and stopping when he loomed over her. "Do you have any idea who you're talking to?"

Kylie stood, glaring at him even though he was a good six inches taller. "I know exactly who I'm talking to," she sneered. "And I'd like the same respect. I'm getting damn close to cracking this case wide open, and your going on about my private life is distracting us from the issues."

"Your private life becoming a distraction is the issue." He narrowed his gaze on her. "Not to mention you were specifically asked to stay away from anyone who could be a suspect."

"For crying out loud!" Kylie threw her hands up in the air while turning and pacing the length of the small office. "His own niece was almost abducted last night. Do you really think he's a suspect?"

"Mighty damn convenient that she was *almost* a victim."

"Would you rather have had her raped and killed?"

"What I would rather have is an agent who does as she's told." John stepped in her path, preventing her from pacing. "You can date a cop, or you can solve this case."

Kylie froze. Anger attacked so hard she damn near shook from it. John didn't have the authority to fire her, but his word would carry a lot of weight if he filed an official complaint about her performance. As much as she ached to say a few choice words to him, Kylie stepped around him, grabbed her purse, and stormed out of the office.

"I've got a job to do," she sneered, grinding her teeth while the bilious words fought to slip out.

"I'll take that as your answer."

"I don't do ultimatums," she growled, storming out of the building and into the parking lot.

Her outrage hadn't subsided when she pulled up in front of Dani's house. As Kylie parked behind Perry's Jeep, mixed emotions hit her that he was here, too. She'd forgotten to call Dani to make sure her mother was cool with Kylie being there, and pulled out her cell phone to place the call while staring at the back end of his car.

Perry wasn't worth losing her job over. She scrolled down her list of numbers to Dani's number while repeating that mantra inside her head. What pissed Kylie off more than anything was that field supervisors seldom cared what she did in her downtime while working in their cities. And not that it happened that often, but she'd seen men before on the side while handling a case. Nothing ever that serious. Other agents did it, too.

"Dani, I'm here," Kylie said when Dani answered the phone. "Did your mother say it was okay?"

"My uncle is here, so I know it is okay. I'll unlock the door." Dani hung up without saying anything else.

Kylie dropped her phone into her purse and shut off her

car, putting her keys away, too. Grabbing her door handle, she paused when a black Suburban drove by. She froze, certain she'd seen wrong, but her wits returned quickly and she jumped out of her car, squinting to catch the letters and numbers on the tag.

XLS519.

"I know those are the same," she grunted, dragging her phone out and feeling the cool hardness of her gun brush against her knuckles. Kylie snapped her purse shut and pushed speed dial on her cell phone, pausing on the walk leading to Dani's home. "This is Special Agent Kylie Donovan," she said quietly, glancing at the house and then back in the direction the Suburban headed. "I need you to run a tag for me, Kansas, Johnson County, XLS five-one-nine."

She fidgeted, waiting while the dispatcher at the FBI field office chatted with her about nothing while pulling up the tag. Paul was out of the office, and the last person Kylie wanted to speak with was John, so the dispatcher would do.

"Are you sure you got the tag number right?" the dispatcher asked. He cleared his throat before she could answer. "I mean, if you did, it's a fake."

"I'm sure, and thank you," she said, telling him good-bye and snapping her phone closed. One more quick check of the side street in front of the house and she turned to the front door. Following the Suburban crossed her mind. Something told her she knew where it would head. If Franco was Peter she needed more proof. Nailing a cop was tricky business.

As if her emotions weren't already all screwed up, now adrenaline pumped through her. Peter had just driven by the house. And there he found her car and Perry's. More than likely Peter knew Perry, if he was Franco, or at least knew who he was, and would recognize his car. Kylie gave Peter credit for being on top of his act, which would include knowing all law enforcement in town, especially since he was probably one of them.

She would wager he also knew Dani wasn't in school today. Most serial killers learned everything there was to know about their victims, bonding with them, in a sense, before killing them. It made the attack more personal, and some, although not all, got off on that moment of death when their victim quit breathing. It was a sense of victory, of claiming a life they'd become so close to. Sick. So fucking sick. Kylie wasn't aware of any rehabilitation that had been successful in curing this type of mental disorder. But after seeing what this monster was capable of, she would get off with his death.

The front door opened when she stepped onto the first step leading to it.

"What were you doing?" Dani stuck her head around the door but was pulled back as Kylie approached.

"I didn't want to be rude and come to the door while on the phone," Kylie offered, smiling easily at the teenager.

Perry had a firm hand on Dani's shoulder and pulled her farther back into the house as he opened the door wider so Kylie could enter. He shut it the moment she was inside and slid the dead bolt into place.

"It looked as if you were looking for someone. Not that I could see all that well with my personal bodyguard haunting me worse than a stalker."

"You've got it so bad," Perry said, rolling his eyes and glaring at Dani. "I've been waiting on you hand and foot."

"That's because you love me the most." Dani wrapped her slender arms around her uncle's waist and smiled up at him. When she shifted her focus to Kylie, she swore she saw a bit of territorial possessiveness going on in the glow of Dani's eyes.

"Don't push your luck." Perry looked stern and his face was lined with worry or stress, although probably both. "Go get your picture you drew for Kylie."

"I didn't just draw it for her," Dani said, and pouted, reluctantly dropping her hands when her uncle peeled her off him. "And you really want me to go upstairs alone?"

"Hurry," Perry ordered.

Dani's attention shifted from one of them to the other. "Don't worry. I will." She damn near ran out of the living room and pounced up the stairs.

Perry didn't move in for a kiss the moment Dani left the

room. Kylie wasn't sure how she felt about that, and her indecisive emotions irritated her as much as being unable to piece the puzzle of this case together.

"Did you see the Suburban drive by?" he asked, keeping his voice low. He'd showered recently and his dark hair almost looked black as strands covered the top half of his ears and turned in small curls at his collar.

"Yes." She recited the tag number to him, admiring his green eyes that were also exceptionally dark today. He was wearing jeans and a T-shirt, and it wasn't often she got to admire all of that roped muscle out of uniform. "It's the same tag number you called in when you chased him out of the bowling alley last week. It's a fake."

"That makes it the third time this morning he's driven by," Perry announced, walking past her to the window and clasping his hands behind his back while staring outside. His jeans were faded and looked very comfortable, as well as providing eye candy that made her insides swell with instant need as she studied the roped muscle flexing in his thighs.

"Good thing you're here then," Kylie said, her mouth too moist after drooling over Perry. She was certain it wasn't the only part of her body now soaked. "She's going to need to be watched over twenty-four-seven until we catch him. Why are you out of uniform?"

He pierced her with a hard stare as he turned his head and captured her gaze with his. "I took a personal day. It was that or kill Rad when he implied I could get a thirty-day suspension without pay if I didn't stay away from you."

Was that why he didn't touch her? Or was there another reason? She ached to ask but wouldn't. There wasn't any reason to open up that discussion in spite of her heated craving to know the answer.

"I got a similar speech," she offered.

Dani came bounding down the stairs holding a piece of typing paper she'd used to draw Peter's face. She'd used colored pencils, and at first glance it was obvious she'd labored over the task. Kylie stared at the picture, willing recognition to kick in. Who was Peter?

"Your job or a relationship?" Perry asked, his soft baritone doing a number on her almost as bad as when his dark eyes caressed her soul.

"What?" Dani asked, pausing in between the two of them and staring from one to the other.

"Pretty much." She stared over Dani's head into those compelling eyes of his, and her insides twisted into a knot of anticipation. There was an overwhelming urge to walk into his arms, to say to hell with supervisors and threats of job security.

"Uncle Perry doesn't like it." Dani lifted her drawing to eye view for Kylie.

Perry pulled his gaze from hers first, shifting his attention to his niece. "I never said I didn't like it," he said in that low, soothing voice of his.

"Fine. He said it wouldn't help."

Kylie pulled her attention and her focus to the drawing, then took it from Dani, staring at it. "You were pretty upset last night; maybe if you tell me again exactly what happened." She stared at the drawing, understanding Perry's comment. The cartoon caricature could be anyone.

"I've already told Uncle Perry twice," Dani groaned.

Perry moved over to the couch, his expression serious and unreadable when he looked out the window. Then reclining, stretching his long legs out before him with cowboy boots making them look even longer and more muscular, he rested his arm on the back of the couch and looked at Kylie.

Every inch of her tingled when she once again lost herself in his dark, brooding stare. If she was going to learn anything during this meeting, though, she needed to keep her thoughts off how his hands felt when he touched her.

"This is a good picture," Kylie said, turning her attention to Dani and trying to reassure her. "Is this a ball cap?"

Dani walked around the coffee table and sat right next to her uncle, sitting cross-legged and brushing her long brown hair over her shoulder. "Yes. I don't remember what it said on it, but I think it was red, so that is what color I made it."

Kylie nodded, taking the other end of the couch and lean-

ing against the side so she faced Dani. Her gaze shifted to
Perry's long fingers, relaxed behind Dani's head on the back
of the couch, but she diverted her attention again to the picture.

"So his hair is dark and his eyes are blue?" That much
information eliminated Perry from any line of suspects, not
that she believed his chief suspected him or he wouldn't
have put Perry on the case. His eyes were definitely not blue.
"Can you describe his build?"

Kylie already guessed John would be wary of any statement coming from Perry's niece. She wasn't sure why John
didn't like Perry, but it was obvious he didn't.

"Now you're asking questions like my uncle." Dani narrowed her gaze on Kylie. "How much time are you spending
with Uncle Perry?"

Kylie wasn't sure why a wave of relief washed over her,
but she grinned easily, grateful the smart and attentive teenager didn't bust her for being more than a college student
and friend. She focused on Dani's soft green eyes. Of all his
nieces, Dani probably looked the least like Perry.

"You know, you look a lot better without all that eyeliner." Kylie meant it, too. Dani was very beautiful and minutes away from looking like a young adult instead of a child.

Especially when she narrowed her gaze and made a tsking
sound with her tongue. "And you suck at avoiding answering questions," she retorted, lifting one eyebrow and looking rather haughty. "What are your intentions with my uncle?"

"Dani!" Perry exploded, coming forward on the couch
and practically knocking Dani onto the floor.

"It's okay." Kylie held her hand up, grateful for his outburst so the focus wouldn't be on her while she struggled for
an answer. *I just want to fuck him as much as I can before I
leave.* That wouldn't be an answer Dani would tolerate.
Hell, Kylie was having trouble tolerating that conclusion.

"You want information from me. Well, I want answers,
too." Dani adjusted herself on the couch, facing forward now
so she could look at her uncle before returning her attention
to Kylie.

"You're out of line, young lady," Perry said, his tone cool and reprimanding. "You will answer any questions we have. They are imperative for an investigation and you know that. As for—"

"I've already lost a father and I will not lose my uncle," Dani cried out, jumping off the couch and trembling. She balled her hands into fists at her sides, obviously a lot more upset about this than Kylie originally thought.

Kylie hurried off the couch, pulling Dani into her arms, in spite of Dani stiffening at first. "You won't lose your uncle, not ever."

"You can't swear to that," Dani said, suddenly very quiet. She'd been traumatized and now was on house arrest. It made sense she would strike out in the only avenue that appeared safe.

"I can swear that you won't because of me."

"But you like him."

Kylie sucked in a breath, all too aware of her backside tingling from Perry keeping an attentive watch on both of them yet remaining quiet and observing.

Kylie nodded, unable to lie to Dani any more than her job required her to. "Yes, I do," she whispered.

Dani pulled out of Kylie's arms, wiping her face and brushing her hair behind her shoulders as she straightened and stared Kylie in the eye. "If he got a girlfriend he wouldn't be over here all the time. Mom couldn't raise us without him. She wouldn't ever admit it, but it's true," she whimpered as tears streamed down her cheeks.

"I don't have any family, not like you do," Kylie said, the words spilling out of her before she gave them much thought. "If, someday, I committed to a relationship, having a guy with a ready-made family would be pretty cool." She straightened, sucking in a breath and keeping her focus on Dani even though she felt the heat burning her alive from Perry watching intently behind her. "But there are complications," she began, swallowing the lump in her throat. They were thoughts she would swear were on Perry's mind as much as hers.

And they needed to be voiced. She would take advantage of his niece's outburst and say out loud what needed to be said. "So many complications they might not be able to be overcome."

"Like what?" Dani's face lit up.

Kylie stared at her for a moment, the silence in the room growing. Perry wasn't going to jump in and help her here at all. Exhaling, Kylie decided she could go out on a limb fairly safely. She wouldn't insult Dani's intelligence but felt safe that her next comment wouldn't jeopardize anything.

"The FBI have ordered me to stay away from your uncle," she said quietly.

"What?" Dani howled, her milky green eyes growing as large as saucers as a slow smile spread over her face. "You're breaking the law being here? And why would anyone care if you saw Uncle Perry?"

"I'm not technically breaking the law," she conceded, just risking her entire future. That wasn't something she would explain, though. "The FBI is involved with this case, too, apparently. And like you, I've been questioned. They believe the man who is kidnapping teenagers in town, Peter, might be a cop."

"No way!" Dani jumped back as if Kylie just slapped her, and gawked at her and then her uncle. "My uncle isn't guilty of shit!"

"Watch your mouth," Perry growled, speaking for the first time.

Kylie jumped to the side, too, unaware that he'd moved off the couch and stood behind her.

"You're right. I'm not," Perry said, his voice still low and menacing-sounding.

Kylie risked looking into his face and lost her breath when she drowned in his smoldering gaze.

"I never would have pictured you as a bad girl, Kylie." Dani was grinning from ear to ear now, no longer shaking and noticeably calmer. Painting herself as a rebel made her cool in the teenager's eyes.

"I didn't know he was here when I headed over here," Kylie announced.

"Would you have stayed away if you knew?" Perry demanded, his baritone sending chills rushing over her flesh but at the same time creating a heat inside her she ached to have him take care of.

"Probably not," she said truthfully, still staring at him.

"God, you don't need to feed his ego." Dani rolled her eyes and walked around her uncle, returning to the couch. "You know a guy gets off when a girl breaks rules to see him."

"And how would you know that?" Perry was wound tighter than usual when he snapped his attention to Dani.

She seemed to notice that as quickly as Kylie, because she didn't throw her usual smart-mouthed comment in his direction. "Everyone knows that, Uncle Perry," she said softly.

"No rules are going to stop me from seeing Kylie," Perry announced, facing Dani, who sat on the couch again staring at him wide-eyed. "And furthermore, you're not going to bully her into not coming around."

Kylie wasn't going to wait for silence to build between her and Perry again. Especially with him standing so close she could feel the tiny hairs on her body standing at attention. Even with the words he had just stated ringing in her ears, she fought desperately to move the conversation over to something that wouldn't cause her heart to race so fast she couldn't breathe.

"Dani, would you tell me what happened last night? You were so upset I didn't want to press, but I would love to hear the details." She followed Dani with her eyes when she jumped off the couch and headed out of the living room.

Kylie started after her when Perry grabbed her arm. "Give her a minute; she doesn't do well when embarrassed," he said, almost whispering.

"Dani embarrassed?" Kylie said, hoping she wouldn't blush when she offered him a sly grin. "I'm not the best at laying my feelings out on the table, either."

"It was so hard for you to admit you like me?" He moved his rough fingertips over her pulse on her wrist.

"I guess not." She straightened but didn't have the strength to pull her hand from his. Worse yet, the urge to walk into his arms and stretch against that body of steel also made it impossible to move.

"What complications were you talking about?" he asked, keeping very little distance between them as he stared deep into her eyes, while continuing to brush his thumb over the inside of her wrist.

She swore she would break out in a sweat, start salivating or even panting with the close proximity between them. The distance she would need to clear to touch him was driving her crazy. Bad enough she could barely organize her thoughts to answer his question, it was on the tip of her tongue to deny any complications.

"You know what I was talking about," she said, biding time and finally looking away from his face. Staring at his muscular chest didn't help matters much, though. He didn't say anything and she knew he was staring down at her. Something told her pulling out of his grip wouldn't be as easy as it appeared. She sucked in a breath, filling her lungs with him, and fought for an answer that would sound relatively coherent. "I think we both like being employed," she muttered.

He took her chin with his free hand and lifted her face so she was forced to look at his face again. Kylie closed her eyes, knowing it would be a hell of a lot easier taking on a mouthy teenager than it would be Perry.

"If you want to be with me, we can make this work." He brushed his lips over hers.

Kylie melted right there on the spot. No man had ever suggested he would fight the system, not only local law enforcement but also the FBI, just to be with her. Perry's statement scared the crap out of her and created an excitement inside her that had her floating in the air.

"Dani is going to come out here and throw a fit," Kylie whispered, her voice cracking from too many emotions swirling around inside her.

"She needs to get accustomed to seeing me kiss you." He

pressed his lips to hers again, taking his time and tasting her.

Kylie couldn't help feel that the kiss was a challenge. Not only was Perry staking claim, in his sister's home, as to what would be allowed and tolerated from this moment forward, but he was also putting Kylie on the spot, giving her this one chance to accept the conditions or push him away and negate them. She hated ultimatums.

"This isn't the time, or the place, to lay out the terms of our relationship," she whispered, her lips moving against his while her lashes fluttered over her eyes. She couldn't focus on him clearly with their noses damn near touching.

Perry straightened and let go of her hand, then backed up before turning to the couch. She stood there, watching him, feeling a sense of doom twist around her heart when she feared she'd just pissed him off. But damn it, there was too much at risk to just announce how it would be and believe it to be so. He sat slowly, taking his time stretching out his long, muscular legs, before crossing one cowboy boot over the other. Fire burned in his eyes, a mixture of lust and anger, which with Perry she anticipated could be a very dangerous combination.

"Is there anything to discuss?" His question came out of nowhere.

"Well, of course," she stammered, answering without clearly understanding what he meant.

"Then we will discuss it," he said with firm resolution.

Kylie headed to the kitchen, feeling numb from head to toe. This was why she steered clear of relationships. If she let her guard down for a fraction of a second, the pain and anxiety would wash over her worse than a tidal wave. And she knew without a doubt her heart wouldn't be able to handle it. Kylie gave up loving a long time ago when she lost Karen, and then her parents. She'd barely started reconciling that relationship. How in the hell would she find the strength to start another relationship? Especially one she knew without a doubt would kick her ass and inevitably break what little heart she had left. Perry would take everything she had and destroy her, unless she gave all of herself to him.

Both of them knew there wasn't any way she could do that.

Chapter 24

Perry doubted anyone would question his being at the station at night. Hell, he'd been here around the clock more days and nights than he cared to think about. He mulled over a believable story in case questioned as he walked through the "pit" to his desk.

There wasn't anyone in the "pit," which was probably for the best, since his mood had gone from sour to downright pissy after he left Megan's house earlier tonight. Kylie had hung out, spending most of her time with Dani, after he confronted her about their relationship. But she had slipped out after Megan got home, in the midst of the chaos that always followed when all the women in his family descended in one room after the end of their day. He'd driven by Kylie's house twice, and she hadn't been home, which damn near made him decide to stalk her until he found her, instead of coming here and doing what he had planned on doing after leaving his sister's.

Rad's office door was closed and no light streamed out from under it. Everyone had gone home. The evening shift were cruising their beats and would be in and out throughout the night, but mostly downstairs by the holding cells or in Booking. There wouldn't be as many people here at their desks, although anyone who needed a computer or a space to do reports could always show up and take advantage of the space.

Or at least they could before Rad password-protected all the computers and enforced strict policy that everyone only use the computer at their own desk. Perry understood now why Rad had implemented these new precautions. The Chief was under pressure to prove none of his cops were Peter. Although it appeared from the ISPs they'd narrowed it down to that one of them was Peter. And whoever it was had used Perry's computer to talk to those girls.

Motherfucker!

Everyone in the department who was innocent would abide by the new policy. Only Peter would go out of his way to not use his own computer when talking to the girls. When he struck again, Perry would be ready for him.

Sitting down at his desk, he glanced around the "pit" one more time, then stared at the doorway and the lit hallway beyond it. Voices echoed down the hall, probably from the stairwell. Someone was being brought in for booking. Perry doubted anyone would head up this way, but either way he needed to hurry. He didn't feel like explaining why he was downloading a program onto his work computer.

Taking the CD he'd used to download the program he had bought online at his house, Perry slid it into the disk drive and waited for the box to pop up, introducing him to the ultimate computer protection.

Record every keystroke. Know what Web sites your loved ones go to. Read every chat conversation they have while online. The "Online Undercover Detective," was designed to appease parents who felt a need to watch what their children were doing online and for spouses to catch each other cheating. He clicked on the button to download and then tapped the edge of his desk while the bar slowly slid across the screen, showing the extent it had downloaded so far.

Perry read each box as it popped up on the screen before clicking next. The software was undetectable once installed. No icons or programs would appear anywhere on the computer to clue anyone into the fact that it had been downloaded. The program would record every document opened, any file downloaded or uploaded even if it came from a CD put in the disk drive. It would take screen shots, and best yet, it would send all the information it logged to Perry's computer at his home.

It would be interesting to find out if Pinky could detect the "Online Undercover Detective." Hopefully Perry would bust Peter before Pinky proved the advertising for the program wrong, if it was wrong.

He quickly typed in the password he'd chosen, "Kylie," and clicked "save." One last box appeared, announcing he had successfully installed the software. It flashed an announcement telling him which keys to press down simultaneously to pull the program up and suggested Perry write down this information for future use, and then the box disappeared. He was done.

"Trap is set," he murmured, standing and reaching for the disk drive on the tower to remove the CD.

Footsteps sounded on the stairs and Perry quickly slid the CD into its sleeve and then tucked it into his inside jacket pocket. He barely sat back down before Rad and the agent Perry had seen at the FBI field office entered the "pit."

"What are you doing here, Flynn?" Rad demanded, narrowing his gaze on Perry and then shifting his attention to Perry's screen. "You took a personal day today, didn't you?"

"Yup. Hung out with my niece until my sister came home this evening." Perry looked pointedly at the man standing silently next to Rad. He was tall, in a suit, and possibly somewhere in his fifties. There were silver streaks through his brown hair, and alert blue eyes studied Perry in return. "She was pretty shook up after last night. The whole family was," he added, returning his attention to his Chief.

"Might be a good idea to bring her in for questioning. I'll have Barker or Richey talk to her."

"I've questioned her thoroughly and can type up the report for you tonight if you need it."

"I'm not saying you haven't," Rad said, his expression serious and unreadable. "But it would be a good idea for her to be debriefed on the situation by someone who doesn't know her. You don't have a problem bringing her into the station, do you?"

"Nope." Perry would even go as far to agree it was a good idea. Someone who wasn't family might pick up things from Dani he might miss. He wouldn't tell Rad that Kylie had already recorded the conversation she had with Dani earlier today at the house. "She even drew a picture of Peter."

"You don't say?" the man in the suit said.

"Flynn, you remember John Athey."

"Lieutenant," Athey said, not smiling or changing his expression but nodding once.

"What are you two doing here?" Perry asked, returning his attention to Rad.

"We came down to go over the files on the Peter case, figured we would use my computer to see if we can find any more similarities we've overlooked." Rad looked past Perry at his computer. "And what are you doing here?"

"Just logged in. Figured I'd take a look at what fun I missed out on today."

"It was relatively quiet. Go ahead and type up that report on what happened the other night when your niece was almost abducted." Rad started toward his office. "I also want a copy, or better yet the original, of that picture she drew of her abductor. And bring her down tomorrow after school or as soon as you can. We'll have either lady talk to her. What was her name again?"

"Danielle. She goes by 'Dani.' "

"Good. Dani. Bring her in tomorrow and get me that report." Rad walked away from him without saying anything else.

John Athey gave Perry a final appraising look before following the Chief. "I've heard a few things about you," Athey said gruffly, his comment sounding anything but complimentary.

He would learn now Perry wasn't easily intimidated. "Can't say I've heard a thing about you," Perry told him.

"How good of a look did your niece get of this guy?"

"She ID'd him pretty well." Perry leaned back, crossing

his arms, and stared into John Athey's face. Something dark passed over the man's expression, a tightening of the lips, a narrowing of the eyes.

If the man hated Perry that much for seeing Kylie, he would get over it like everyone else. Athey wasn't Kylie's father. And even if he were, Kylie was a grown woman, free to make her own decisions, and Perry knew beyond any doubt she wanted him.

"You think you could ID him if you saw him?" John asked.

Rad turned, before reaching his office, and listened, shifting his attention from John to Perry and waiting for his answer. Perry wouldn't let the FBI man make him look like an ass. Standing slowly, he sized the man up, noting he was a good inch or so shorter than Perry. John didn't have Perry's build, making him look a lot smaller than Perry, although in truth he wasn't that much shorter.

Tugging on his T-shirt, Perry let his arms fall to his sides, relaxing his body but keeping a shrewd look in John's direction. The man wasn't easily intimidated, but Perry would have been surprised if Athey was, considering his position.

"Like with any victim who offers a description of a suspect, there are cracks that needed to be filled in," Perry said slowly, not caring if his tone sounded a bit condescending. The motherfucker wasn't his boss. "He never got out of his SUV, so when she tells me he is tall, I appreciate the fact that she never saw him standing. He wore a baseball cap, so when she tells me his hair is dark, I don't know if he's got a thick head of hair or is damn near bald. The only thing she was very adamant about is that he had blue eyes. Hell, for all I know Peter could be you," Perry added, searching John's face and noting the dark hair and blue eyes.

John's expression twisted quickly as he puffed out his chest and growled, as if he would attack.

"Flynn, get that report typed up for me now," Rad bellowed.

Perry squared off, ready for anything John might dish out at him. He didn't take his gaze from the man when Rad approached, touching John's arm and nodding toward his office.

"We've got things to discuss," Rad growled, indicating John should come with him. Then giving Perry a look that would kill, he turned when the FBI man did and the two of them headed into Rad's office, closing the door behind him.

"FBI motherfucker," Perry grumbled, and slouched into his chair to fill out the report.

An hour later, well after Rad and John Athey had left without a word of good-bye, Perry saved the report and clicked to print it out. This was the worst part of his job, the computer work. He leaned back, stretching, and itched to get out of there. His trap was in place on his computer and when he got home, he could test it since everything he'd typed should have been sent to his home computer via e-mail.

The sky was a heavy black velvet blanket, stretching out beyond the businesses lining either side of the street. Perry bet it would be full of stars if he were home and not in the middle of town, with streetlights blinding his ability to truly appreciate the night. He headed over to his Jeep, feeling the cool night air on his face as he unlocked his car and slid in behind the steering wheel.

A quick drive by Kylie's showed she was home this time and all lights in her house were off. At least she wasn't out offering herself as bait to a madman. Picturing her cuddled under her blankets, sleeping soundly, made it damn hard to keep driving. There was one thing he wanted to do, though, and it would be best to do it alone. Driving past her house, he told himself he would go over there later. Like any FBI man or his Chief would keep him away from Kylie.

Turning off her street, Perry focused on his headlights beaming on the road ahead of him as he headed across town toward Franco's house. Then parking down the street, Perry cut the lights and motor and stepped out into the calm, cool night air. He breathed in the scent of freshly cut grass as he walked slowly down the quiet street. Very few houses had any lights on, and he guessed those that did left those interior lights on all night. It was almost midnight, and middle-class homes such as these were filled with people who would get up at the crack of dawn, dragging themselves out the door for another day at the job.

It was people like these, just like Megan and the girls, whom he'd vowed to protect with his life. For those reasons, and especially after the death of David, leaving his sister alone with four children to raise, Perry always believed he would never settle down with a woman. His job required taking risks, stepping into the line of fire and protecting citizens of his town so they could go about their lives without interruption.

So what changed? Perry neared Franco's house, checking out the neat yard and the dark windows, then glanced up and down the street. Not so much as a dog announced Perry's presence. It was almost too quiet. Which left his thoughts to torture him as he neared the garage.

What was it about Kylie that made him want to risk hurting another person? Let alone take the chance of getting hurt if he turned his heart over to her. In all his years, he'd managed to keep any relationship he'd entered into with a woman casual, consensual, good sex, and that was it.

The sex with Kylie definitely qualified as better than good. Hell, it was damn near the best sex he'd ever had in his life. Was that the reason he wanted to push their relationship to the next level?

Perry reached the side of the garage and stood there, leaning against cool brick, and didn't move, letting the peaceful night sink into his pores and listening for any sound of intrusion. He didn't hear anything other than crickets. Relaxing against the wall, he studied the side door to the garage that opened to a cobblestone path, which led around to the back of the garage and backyard.

Kylie was more than any other woman he'd met before. Maybe it was because her line of work was so similar to his. She would leave town once this case was solved. There wasn't any changing that. He would never ask her to quit what she did for a living any more than he would tolerate being asked to give up being a cop. Kylie was gorgeous to a distraction, sexy as hell, but smart as a tack, too.

Even when he thought of how she challenged him, didn't listen very well when he told her what to do, those traits in her didn't turn him off. Perry shook his head, afraid he might be a goner where she was concerned, and stepped toward the side garage door. Franco would have an alarm system installed. He was a cop. It was in their nature to protect what was theirs. But as Perry studied the structure of the garage, let his gaze travel along the roof and guttering system, he didn't see any sign of an alarm installed. Not that many alarm systems were visible from the outside. Few were as elaborate as what Kylie had installed at her house. Perry moved in front of the door, putting his hand on the doorknob, and stared into the glass pane, seeing his reflection stare back at him.

Something creaked around the back side of the garage and the crickets grew silent. Perry froze, knowing he was working off duty and getting caught in this compromising position would be his ass. Looking around quickly, he didn't see as much as a bush or decent-sized tree to hide behind. He looked down the length of the cobblestone path, his eyes burning from not blinking as he fought to see better in the dark.

His heart pounded so damn loud he wasn't sure he would hear another sound if there was one. Taking in a slow, silent breath, he willed his heart to quit thumping in his chest and cleared his mind, forcing thoughts of Kylie out of his head so he could cover his own ass. There wasn't backup on this assignment.

When a cricket sounded, Perry damn near jumped out of his skin, and managed a smile as other crickets joined in and returned to their middle-of-the-night symphony. Whatever made the sound out back wasn't a threat to them. But, Perry pointed out to himself, he stood here and that didn't bother the bugs, either.

Perry didn't doubt for a moment he could take Franco on if confronted. Granted the man could press charges since

Perry was on his property, but if he used every ounce of his training, he wouldn't be discovered. Nonetheless, it was best to check out his surroundings before returning to the task at hand. Testing the cobblestone path, he put one booted foot down on it and proceeded slowly, silently, pressing his palm against the cool, moist brick wall as he walked to the back of the garage. If there was someone there, the element of surprise would be in Perry's favor. He'd never been one to run from a fight, but he knew he could outrun Franco.

Perry gripped the corner of the garage, wrapping his fingers around the rough edge, and took that final step. Bushes lined the back of the garage, neatly trimmed and creating a border between the cobblestone path and backyard.

Perry didn't breathe. He didn't move. Standing, listening to the crickets, he still swore he heard something else. Anyone wandering around in the yard after midnight wouldn't be up to any good. Not that he was, either. But at least his cause was justified. He wanted sound confirmation the black Suburban in the garage was the same one he and Kylie had spotted every time Peter came around. Fake tags or not, if they matched the tags on file for Peter, then Franco was their man.

Perry would take Franco out, limb by limb, if the bastard was stalking Mission Hills, torturing, raping, and murdering teenage girls. His blood boiled just thinking about it.

Standing against the garage, Perry glanced behind him toward the street. It was so dark where he stood, he barely saw to the end of the driveway. Beyond that was a black abyss, quiet and serene. Too damn quiet. He focused on the bushes in front of him, which stood about as tall as he did. The branches moving would give him away. But Perry wouldn't chance entering the garage and taking a picture of the license plate until he knew the area was secure.

The last thing he needed right now was to run into a cat burglar trying to break into one of these houses while Perry was snooping around, off the clock. He didn't want to have to decide whether he would run a common crook down or let him be the ultimate distraction so Perry could fight for a higher cause. Stealing physical possessions didn't rank as high of a crime in his book as taking lives, let alone young ones.

He heard something again. So did the crickets. Silence fell over the yard as if the black velvet blanket draping across the sky fell to the earth, enveloping all around it with an eerie quiet that sent chills rushing up his spine. Someone was in the yard. Perry was sure of it now.

The best thing to do at this point was become invisible. Mentally calculating the space between the tall bushes and the back of the garage, Perry pushed himself into the narrow space, enduring scratches on his arm and face while struggling not to move any more branches than necessary.

That's when he saw her. At least he guessed it was a woman. A person had raised one of the upstairs windows in Franco's house and was climbing out. The dang fool would break her fucking neck. And if she turned in Perry's direction, she would spot him hiding behind the bushes from her elevated vantage point. Fortunately for both of them, she was intent on her mission and not paying attention to bushes or trees in the yard.

Perry watched, somewhat amazed, as the person shimmied down a drainpipe and jumped the last four or five feet to the ground. She rolled over the grass, then came to her hands and knees, frozen for a moment until the crickets started singing again. Then she sprinted to the edge of the yard and jumped the four-foot fence, disappearing in the yard behind Franco's. In the next minute she was gone, leaving Perry and the crickets alone in the yard.

What the fuck had he just seen?

Perry stared at the spot where the girl had vanished, positive she was female now by how she ran and the shape of her body when she climbed the fence. Returning his attention to the window on the second floor, he stared at the open window, watching a curtain move in the breeze. Someone had just fled from the house. From what Perry knew, Franco wasn't married and didn't have any kids. Perry wouldn't swear to it, but from what he could make out in the dark, and the shape and movements of the person who had just darted through the yard, he would guess she was young, possibly a teenager.

His blood pressure skyrocketed as his imagination fueled the images that popped into his head as to possible reasons why the girl would take off running. He returned his attention to the spot at the fence where she'd jumped free and disappeared. Should he go after her?

No one appeared to be following her. The way she boogied across the yard and over the fence, he doubted she was hurt, at least not seriously enough to slow her process. She disappeared quickly. Perry weighed his options and turned toward the side garage door. He would inspect the Suburban. If he found anything suspicious around it, he would seek out a warrant. Possibly inspecting the inside of Franco's home was in order, too.

Once again Perry put his hand on the doorknob to the side door of the garage. He stared at his reflection in the clear, dark glass but didn't focus on it for long. This time, pushing his face up to the glass, he shaded it with his hand and stared inside the garage.

There was no vehicle in the garage. It was empty.

Too much time had passed to chase down the girl. Nonetheless, Perry drove around the neighborhood after returning to his Jeep, searching yards and looking for any sign of anyone. There wasn't as much as a single soul walking along the sidewalks.

The clock on his dash told him it was almost one o'clock in the morning. He turned at the next intersection, realizing he headed toward Kylie's home instead of his own. His cell phone rang and he jumped, grateful it hadn't rung while he'd been alongside the garage. He'd forgotten to put it on vibrate.

"This is Flynn," he said, his voice sounding scratchy when he answered the call from Dispatch. He was off duty and it was the middle of the night; there couldn't be anything good coming from this phone call.

"Flynn, Lieutenant Goddard asked me to call you." Cliff Miller, the dispatcher, spoke quickly and sounded out of breath, which he often did when he was upset. The guy never moved out of his chair at the station, but when an urgent matter came through the man would sound as if he'd just run a mile. "They found another teenager over on Antioch, near the mall."

"Fucking hell," Perry growled, understanding now why the Suburban wasn't in the garage. Peter had been busy. "What is the exact location?"

Miller gave him the address. "Flynn, there is a situation, which is why Goddard wanted me to contact you personally."

"What's that?"

"He asked you to get there ASAP. He said it's personal."

Perry didn't have a hard time finding the crime scene. After he turned onto Antioch, flashing lights from several police cars and an ambulance grabbed his attention. He pulled up and parked not too far from the crime scene tape and hopped out of his car. No one said anything when he climbed over the tape and walked over to Pete Goddard.

"What do we have here?" he asked Goddard, a decent cop who'd been on the force about as long as Perry had been.

Pete Goddard was fair complected, with strawberry blonde hair that was closely shaved to his head. He was tall and lanky and his uniform always looked as though it was half a size too big.

"It's pretty ugly." Goddard shifted his attention to a body, which lay crumpled up against the side of the building. "She had ID on her."

"Oh, yeah?" Perry walked up to the girl, who didn't look a day older than Dani, and stared at her half-nude and bloody body. "Who reported her?"

"Anonymous nine-one-one call." Goddard moved in next to Perry, holding a clipboard and staring grimly at the dead girl. "We've cataloged all the personals found on her, which were basically a purse, a wallet with seventeen dollars on her, and makeup, along with a cell phone."

"She wasn't robbed." Perry followed Goddard over to the back of Goddard's squad car where Baggies were spread out in an open briefcase, already tagged and numbered and ready to be taken to the station. "What was her name?"

"Elaine Swanson." Goddard sifted through the evidence Baggies and picked one of them out, then held it at eye level. "This letter indicates she went by 'Lanie.'"

Perry glanced past the hood at the crumpled body, another teenager robbed of life before given the opportunity to really start living.

"And look at this—grades." Goddard sounded disgusted, but it wasn't from the report card he held up in another bag. Elaine, or Lanie, made all A's and B's. "She was a sophomore. My son is a junior, still a virgin, hasn't been out on a real date yet. That girl was a child. To kill someone like her."

His tone registered the anger radiating from him. Perry looked at Goddard, whose reddened complexion made his strawberry blonde crew cut stand out and look more white than light red. His light green eyes darkened as he met Perry's gaze.

"This whole thing turns my stomach."

"It's fucking sick as hell," Perry agreed.

After glancing at the case filled with evidence bags, Perry walked around the patrol car, leaving Goddard to talk to his partner. Perry noted Goddard didn't have blue eyes, not that he would have guessed the cop was Peter. Goddard was a churchgoing man, with a good-sized family and a sweet little wife who adored him. Criminals came in all shapes and sizes, though. Perry knew from many years on the force that attending church every Sunday didn't mean a man wasn't capable of murder.

"You got an extra pair of gloves?" Perry asked the officer squatting next to the body.

She glanced at Perry and then straightened, interest or at the least acknowledgment that she liked what she saw registering on her pretty face. "Sure. I know you, don't I?" she asked, standing and making a show of smoothing her uniform before walking over to the forensics kit sitting on the asphalt not too far away.

Perry noticed how she bent over, took her time pulling out

a spare pair of latex gloves, and how she straightened. She had a nice ass, narrow waist, and mousy brown hair cut short in a pageboy. Although she wasn't his type with her tomboy figure, small breasts, and petite frame, another time Perry would take time to talk to her. He wasn't sure he'd seen her before, but she wasn't ugly and Perry never discriminated against a lady just because she didn't meet his definition of a perfect 10.

"I don't think we've met," he said, accepting the gloves and donning them, then turning back to the body.

"Gracie Pierre," she offered, making a show of offering her hand to shake but then laughing and pulling back her gloved hand, which was soiled with blood.

Something about the fact that she could make jokes and be so carefree and flirtatious while the two of them squatted over a mutilated, murdered teenage girl's body didn't sit right with him.

"Nice to meet you, Gracie," he said, but then turned his attention to the body. "Any speculation on the cause of death?"

"Oh," she said, squatting next to him, her leg brushing against his as she leaned forward and lifted the girl's arm, which had been over her face. "I just gather any evidence off the body. I'm not a doctor and I don't play one on TV." Again laughing easily, obviously finding herself very amusing.

"Regardless of your role in this crime scene, you'll learn what evidence to gather if you focus on the whole picture," he snapped, wondering how long she'd been on the force. "The evidence you seek out would be different if someone was attacked by a dog than if they were brutalized and murdered."

He didn't bother checking out her reaction to his biting her head off. But the silence that grew between them told him she probably thought him a little less attractive than she had a few minutes before.

"I might just be a rookie," she finally said, sounding more hurt than mad. "But I looked at the big picture well enough to suggest to Goddard he contact you after tagging the picture that was rolled up in her hand."

Perry did look at Gracie then. She frowned at the dead teenager, her lips pressed into a thin line. He would guess Gracie was in her early twenties, younger than Kylie, and not as well built. It wasn't just that her breasts were smaller; everything about her was smaller. Possibly that made her look younger. If anything, he thought, returning his glance to Lanie Swanson and reaching with his gloved hand and attempting to cover her exposed breasts with her torn and dirty shirt, Gracie didn't look much older than their victim.

"What was rolled up in her hand?" Perry asked. "And which hand?"

"Why does it matter which hand?"

He didn't take the question as sarcastic, even if that was how she meant it. "I don't know if it matters or not. Was her other hand always here?" he asked, sticking his index finger into her curled fingers resting at her side.

"Yes, and her right hand was above her head, her forearm resting over her face. I'm sure it was just the position she was in when she finally gave up on life."

"Or how she stopped moving after being tossed out of a car."

"Tossed out of a car?" Gracie asked, standing when the medics walked over to them with a gurney.

"Why would she die up alongside a building like this?" Perry stood as well, facing Gracie and watching her chew her lower lip and study his face. It was as if he could see her brain churning, struggling to come up with a believable answer that might impress him.

"Well, maybe she couldn't walk very well from her injuries and started walking alongside the building, using it to hold her up."

"Good." Perry nodded. Maybe Gracie wasn't as self-centered and cold to the line of work she was in as she first appeared. "If your theory is right, though, with the amount of blood covering her body, if she walked along the building there would be blood on the bricks. Have you checked?"

"No. Do you think I should?"

"Yup. If your theory is right, it would tell us which direction she came from. If there aren't any blood trails on the wall, then my theory might be right." He decided Gracie had a pretty smile, although he missed the glow that Kylie would get in her eyes when challenged.

"I'll check," Gracie said, as if she'd just decided she would do so. "If I'm right, though, you have to take me out for a drink," she added, winking at him. She didn't take his comments as instruction but almost as a game.

"We'll see," he said, watching when she again walked to her case and pulled out what she needed to search for blood samples on the brick wall. "What was this picture you mentioned?"

Gracie stood over Lanie's body, facing the wall. She looked over her shoulder, grinning at him, her gaze traveling down his body shamelessly, and the sparkle he had missed in her eyes when he challenged her was there now as blatant interest brought out color in her cheeks.

She licked her lips and arched her back slightly, reminding him of a hungry feline, or possibly a feline in heat. "I've already tagged it as evidence," she said, and turned from the wall and walked up until she stood close enough that she needed to tilt her head to look at his face. "It was a picture of another girl. It looked like it was taken with a camera phone possibly and blown up and printed. But I think I've seen the girl in the picture before down at the station. You might know her."

Taking his arm, Gracie wrapped hers around his and escorted him to Goddard's patrol car. Perry freed himself, frustrated with her unprofessional behavior, and the curious look Goddard gave him when he and Gracie rounded the car to the trunk.

"Where is that picture?" Gracie asked Goddard. "The one the girl had in her hand?"

"You didn't see it already?" Goddard frowned at Perry but then sifted through the evidence bags and pulled out a piece of typing paper in a bag with a picture printed on it. Then grabbing his flashlight, he turned on the beam and handed the picture to Perry.

If the thing were alive it would have bitten off his hand. Perry gawked at the picture, his stomach churning so furiously while bile moved to his throat. He stared, his hand shaking, at the picture of Dani, taken in the dark, with her staring slightly above the camera, as if possibly she didn't know the shot had been taken. Over the picture, written in block letters with a red marker, it said: *Guess who is next?*

"Fucking son of a bitch," Perry roared, needing to hit something worse than he'd ever needed to before.

"What's wrong?" Gracie asked, once again touching his arm.

He didn't try to prevent her from touching him this time. If she wanted to mess with his boiling outrage, that was her own stupidity at work.

"It's a goddamn picture of my niece," he roared, turning from both of them and staring at the dark parking lot. It took him a minute to register what he saw, but he did a double take on the car turning in the parking lot and heading toward the exit.

It was Kylie's hybrid.

Chapter 25

"Okay, I think we're ready." Paul walked around the conference desk and looked at the recorder in the middle of the oblong table. "Next time you want to record something, though, let me know. I can hook you up with much better equipment than this."

"It was a consensual recording. I wasn't worried about trying to determine back-down noise, or anything like that." Kylie rubbed her left temple, where a dull throbbing headache had been nagging her since she woke up this morning. It hadn't surprised her that Peter was a no-show the night before. She hadn't talked to him or seen him on-line since he'd suggested they meet Thursday night. The media had spooked him, putting her back to square one. At least she had Dani's testimony to offer.

"Let's hear what it says," John said, sitting across from her. "As long as it picked up what the two of you said to each other, we're fine."

He scowled at the handheld recorder Kylie had owned for a couple years now. She used it any time she wanted to record an interview and never had problems with it. But with her headache, not enough sleep, and feeling grouchier no matter how much coffee she downed, she didn't feel like arguing with them.

Reaching for the recorder, she pushed "play," turned up the volume, and reclined in her chair. Static popped for a moment but then stopped. Kylie relaxed her elbows against the armrests and held her cup with both hands, watching the steam twist and evaporate above her fresh cup.

The recording began, Kylie's voice sounding tinny but audible.

"This is a recorded interview conducted by Kylie Dover," she said through the small speaker, using her undercover name and the front that she was recording this in an effort to show the reaction of a teenager to a traumatic, terrifying, event.

Dani stated her full name and age; then Kylie announced the date and time. After the usual formality of asking Dani if she would willingly participate in the interview and consent to it being recorded, the questions began.

Kylie had listened to the tape several times already but knew her presence was advantageous while playing it back for John. Paul was present for two reasons. One, he was very good at deductive reasoning and two, because Kylie knew if she was left alone for too long with John, she'd kick his ass. The man just rubbed her wrong every time she was around him.

And this morning wasn't a good time to be around anyone. After showing up at the crime scene last night, keeping her distance, and observing, she immediately wished she'd stayed home and in bed. More than once she had stopped herself from marching across the parking lot and throwing that little runt of a cop as far away from Perry as she could.

It had been impossible to fall asleep after that. She'd even gotten dressed and gone over to his house, hell-bent and determined to give him more than a piece of her mind. Driving across town to his house didn't calm her down, but she did manage to stop herself from barging into his home when it was mere hours before dawn. It would be better to take him on after a good night's sleep. Except she didn't get one.

It was bad enough that she tossed and turned once she finally crawled back into her bed, but she woke up with a headache. And it appeared to have no intention of going away.

"After walking out of your house, you text-messaged Pe-

trie, your online boyfriend whom you hadn't met yet, and told him you'd fought with your mother and left home?"

"You make it sound really bad," Dani said, but then cleared her voice. She mumbled something inaudible. Kylie ignored John's and Paul's inquiring looks. Dani had mumbled under her breath, begging Kylie not to make her out to look like a fool. Kylie remembered Dani later admitting she felt like an ass for committing the most stupid stunt of her life, and hugging Kylie and thanking her for saving her life. That wasn't information John, or Paul, needed to know, though. Dani continued, *"But yes, I texted Petrie. He told me it wasn't safe walking around alone at night and that he would pick me up. He offered to take me to get a pizza."*

"Where did he tell you he would meet you?"

"At the bowling alley."

"Do you know why he suggested the bowling alley?"

There was silence for a moment. *"Probably because he knows I hang out there with my friends a lot. He wanted a place where I would be comfortable."* Dani's voice cracked and she coughed, trying to cover up emotions over a boy who had turned out to not be who she thought he was. *"Or at least that is what I thought."*

"Okay, so you go to the bowling alley. Did he tell you what car he would be in, or how to find him?"

"He said he would meet me there. I figured he meant inside."

"What happened when you got to the bowling alley?"

"I never made it inside. I was walking across the parking lot when this big black car showed up. He pulled up so quickly behind me I thought he would hit me, but then his driver's-side door opened and he tried grabbing me."

There were shuffling sounds and murmurs that Kylie remembered being Dani crying. Kylie slouched in her chair, stroking her coffee cup with her finger, while the tape continued playing. Dani had endured so much, and Kylie worried for her life, especially now that she had successfully escaped the grip of a killer. After the murder last night, it possibly being the fifth life Peter had taken, his craving for blood, for death, would grow. It was stereotypical of a serial killer. Kylie's thoughts went also to the other girl whose father had followed her and prevented her from meeting the boy online. Sally Wright's father had reported there was no boy at the meeting site but a man. Would Peter go after Sally and Dani again?

"Did he ever talk to you?"

"He said, 'Dani, get in the car.' But it wasn't Petrie. It was a man. He wore a baseball cap, but I would know him again in a second if I saw him. He had really blue eyes and dark hair and he was white."

"Arrange a lineup for her," John suggested. "I'm skeptical that her memory is as strong as she suggests, but we can do a lineup of the police officers downtown."

"Do you really think that would work?" Kylie raised her gaze to him lazily. She needed to get out of here, although if she did, the first thing she would do was track down Perry, and that wouldn't be pretty. "Dani knows most of the officers who work with her uncle."

"How do you know that?" John challenged. "Has she told you that? Or has Flynn informed you his niece is well acquainted with everyone he works with?"

"No to both," Kylie snapped, the throbbing in her temple intensifying. She slid her chair back, deciding maybe a search for aspirin would help. "Her uncle has been on the force for seven years. It goes without saying, since he is so involved in her life, that she would know at least a handful of police officers in this town. Not to mention she is a sixteen-year-old who was born and raised here. That alone would make many of the faces familiar to her."

"I have to agree with Kylie on that one," Paul interjected. "I also think this kid needs some serious protection, possibly more than her uncle can provide, just being a cop."

Kylie leaned forward and paused the tape. "We know Peter drives a black Suburban, late model."

"With forged tags that can't be traced," John interrupted. "Honestly, Kylie, you don't have shit to nail this guy."

She stared at him, her head pulsing all over. If it didn't

hurt so badly, she would give John a piece of her mind. Bringing up Perry, arguing that the two of them could nail this guy if just given a little more time, would start a full-fledged fight that any other time she would welcome. In spite of no sleep, she still felt like she had energy to burn.

"I'm a hell of a lot closer than I was a week ago," she said, biting her lip to prevent from saying more.

She would save her energy, and her head from exploding, for a battle she actually wanted to fight. When she found Perry, there would be words. Maybe they hadn't voiced out loud where their relationship stood, but he'd made it damn clear he wanted something between them. For him to say that and then flirt with another woman, and at a crime scene no less, was beyond unacceptable. Kylie couldn't wait to kick his ass to kingdom come. Attack first and listen to explanations later. That is if she decided to hang around to hear any lame excuse he might have. She knew what she saw. She might look young, but she wasn't born yesterday.

John slapped the table, standing when Kylie did. "There's only one solution." He leaned forward and popped the tape out of the cassette player, then fingered it as he walked toward the door. "You're going to set up another meeting with this Peter guy. But this time, you're going to go with him. The only way we're going to nail this guy is to catch him in the act. Even if all we bring him in for is assaulting you, we'll get the confession out of him for the others."

John walked out the door and Kylie slumped back into her chair.

"Nothing better than finding out you get to be assaulted first thing in the morning." Paul tried to make light of it, but there was compassion in his eyes when he looked down at her.

"I've endured worse." She sipped her coffee, willing herself to get back up out of the chair. "I didn't get a lot of sleep last night. I had a second meeting with Peter. He no-showed and hasn't been online. If I could have made him meet me last night instead of Elaine Swanson, I would have." Maybe I'll go home and crash for a few hours and then see if I can connect with him."

"Sounds as if last night was pretty nasty," Paul said, grabbing the tape recorder and unplugging it from the wall. "That picture they tagged as evidence has got to have your cop friend pretty pissed off."

"Picture?" She frowned, realizing she hadn't taken time to read the reports Paul would have prepared for her. "What picture?"

Paul finished winding the cord around the recorder and stared at her. "You doing okay?"

"Yup. Just tired. I haven't read the report on last night yet. What is this picture you're talking about?"

Paul shook his head. "There was a picture in the victim's hand when she was found. It was printed on typing paper. The picture was of one of Lieutenant Flynn's nieces that had a message written across it in marker. It said: 'Guess who is next?'"

Kylie was out of her chair before she realized it. "I've got to go," she said, waving her hand over her shoulder and bolting for the door. She had to find Perry.

It was worse than she thought. Kylie wasn't even sure which way she drove. Perry wouldn't be home. She couldn't go to the station, although she had half a mind to do so. She wanted to see that picture, and by all rights she could demand to see it. She had the proper credentials. No one would deny her access once she flashed her badge. But agreeing to work undercover meant just that. Kylie couldn't just go and blow her cover because she was pissed, and because it would be convenient to do so at the moment. Paul would arrange for her to see it, or at least a copy.

As she turned at the next light it dawned on her that she was headed to Perry's sister's house. It wasn't even lunchtime. There wouldn't be anyone there, unless they kept Dani home from school again today. If so, someone would be with her. Kylie couldn't imagine Perry's Chief allowing him to become her personal bodyguard. Although she could see him telling his Chief where to stick it if Perry felt protecting his niece was of paramount importance. And of course he would think that.

"God. You need to quit being a chickenshit and just call him." Kylie had vowed repeatedly over the years if she was anything, she wasn't a procrastinator. If something needed to be done, she jumped in and dealt with it. "Well, something needs to be done about us, mister," she grumbled, fishing through her purse next to her and pulling out her cell phone.

The moment she held it in her hand, it buzzed, kicking her heart into overdrive. Taking a gulp of air, she glanced at the number.

"Well, hell," she said, recognizing the Dallas area code. It was her supervisor, and she would probably get her ass chewed for not checking in sooner. Although she could just imagine John had touched base with Susie Parker, and what he might have said.

"Donovan here," she said, switching lanes and signaling to turn into the nearest parking lot. Her brain was too sore to take this call while driving. And it was high time to check in and run everything she knew past Susie. In the past, oftentimes when the two of them brainstormed, Susie offered good input.

"It's about time I reached you. I was getting worried." Susie's soft-spoken voice misled many people. A good-looking lady, in her thirties, Susie had used her appearance, as well as her intelligence, to climb the ladder to where she was today, and she had no regrets for doing so. Kylie both admired and despised the woman for her efforts. She wouldn't take advantage of a man's weakness for a pretty lady to get what she wanted in life. Although more than once, other than arguing it was scruples, she wondered why she wouldn't. "Where have you been?" There was concern in Susie's voice.

Kylie pulled into a stall outside a Mexican restaurant, where the lot was starting to fill up with the early lunch crowd. Leaving her car in drive, she cranked the AC and reclined in her seat.

"You've been trying to reach me? I haven't had any missed calls from you."

"I tried calling your cell a week or so ago and then tried the field office there in Mission Hills. They told me there you weren't getting a good signal with your service there in that town. I was promised a new number for you, but no one got back to me."

"That doesn't make any sense. I haven't had any problems with my cell." Kylie frowned, watching a young couple enter the large restaurant while her stomach growled. It hadn't dawned on her until now that she hadn't eaten since yesterday afternoon. "Someone must have gotten their wires crossed."

"Well, I have you now. How are things going?"

"I'm on the verge of discovery."

Susie's laugh was melodic, relaxed, and reminded Kylie that before long her stress would be directed toward a different case, in a different world, and the problems in Mission Hills, Kansas, would once again be resolved and those living here would get on with their lives. Would she ever see any of them again? The thought left her feeling empty and she sighed, her gaze drifting to a car that parked near her and several ladies who were all laughing and talking, got out and headed to the restaurant.

"That's my line, and you're reminding me why you're one of my top agents. Fill me in on the details."

Kylie put a neutral tone in her voice, offering the facts and fighting to keep her emotions and feelings for the people involved in this case at bay.

"Perry. Now who is Perry?"

Kylie smiled, although she felt anything but happy, and looked down at her lap as she realized how much she had just failed in keeping her emotions out of this case.

"Lieutenant Perry Flynn is with the police department here in Mission Hills. He is also working on this case."

"Total hunk, huh?"

"He's not bad." Not bad in bed. Not bad at stealing her heart. "John Athey hasn't contacted you?" she asked, changing the subject from Perry. Although talking about John, and what he might have told Susie, wasn't a conversation Kylie wanted to have, either. Best to get it out of the way.

"I haven't talked to him," Susie said. "I've left messages, but he hasn't returned them."

"Really." That didn't strike Kylie as quite right. Usually supervisors kept in touch, especially when a field agent was sent from one location to another. "I'm sure there've been reports, though, right?"

"Nothing." Susie didn't hesitate. "Why? What's wrong?"

There wasn't any point hedging around the situation. "We don't exactly get along."

"Although that's odd for you," Susie said, sounding serious, "I've had agents before who clash with local FBI. You do what you're there to do and move on. You know how to do your job."

"I know." She hated the emptiness that seemed to spread inside her.

"You know, oftentimes an agent gets involved with the community, especially when doing undercover work. It isn't a bad thing," Susie offered.

"I know where you're going with this," Kylie said, breaking off the inevitable pep talk about how this, too, would pass. "And you're right. I think it's just the timing with your call," she lied. "I just left the field office after having it pointed out to me very clearly that I have absolutely nothing to nail this guy with. I have a clue who he is," she admitted, and felt even worse as failure wrapped around the emptiness inside her. "But I really don't have any proof."

"Let's break it down. What do you have?" It sounded as though Susie was typing in the background, her nicely painted nails she was able to grow sitting in an office these days instead of working out in the field tapping over the keys while she talked on the phone. "You have a description and a common location."

"Yes. It appears he agrees to meet the girls at the bowling alley or at shops nearby. The bowling alley is a local hangout for a lot of the teenagers here. He met one girl at a grocery store she went to on a regular basis."

"He meets the girls at locations they're comfortable going to," Susie suggested.

"Yes. The grocery store was closed when Elaine agreed to meet Peter. Later in the evening, there is hardly any traffic around the bowling alley. The parking lot isn't well lit other than the marquee from the local businesses' lights. There are some streetlights in the parking lot but not enough to cover the dark patches where it's easy for cars to park without being noticed. Dani met Peter there after dark."

"So a secluded location where each girl wouldn't hesitate going."

"Exactly."

"And the description?"

"One of the girls who agreed to meet Peter, the name we've given our killer since that is the name he is using online, or variations of it," Kylie reminded her, "saw him and drew us a picture. It's not a lot to go on but we know he's got dark hair and blue eyes."

"I've pulled up the local newspaper there. Sounds as if you're battling the press and concerned parents as well."

"It's become too high profile for it to be otherwise. Fortunately, working undercover, I haven't had to deal with either myself."

"Which is how it should be. Leaves you open to focus only on your killer. What is your current objective?"

"I'm going to set up another meet and let Peter take me with him."

"Should I send in backup?" Susie sounded concerned. "I think I'll get in touch with the local chief of police there. I'll try calling John Athey again, too."

Kylie didn't understand why John hadn't talked to Susie. Unless he was one of those agents who believed their city was their own domain and didn't care for outsiders intruding on their space. She'd run across other agents like that when traveling from city to city, those who tackled crime in their town and balked at outsiders, even when their intentions were good. She could see John being the one who would want credit for taking Peter down. Suddenly John's behavior made more sense. He didn't like her because she posed a threat at stealing his glory if she and not John received credit for nailing Peter. By sending her in, informing her she would go with the perp, John would get glory for rescuing her.

Kylie blew out a loud sigh, resting her head on the back of her seat and staring at her visor. It wasn't the first time she was the bait, entering the line of fire, only to be rescued and the bad guy taken out. For some reason, allowing John that credit rubbed her wrong. It would be so much better, so much easier, to part ways when the painful moment arrived, if Perry was the one who made the arrest.

"Stay focused," Susie said, her tone serious again, as if she were reading Kylie's thoughts. "There's nothing wrong with caring about the people you're working with as long as you keep it business, and make sure those who need to know understand why you're there."

Kylie didn't say anything. Susie was right. Kylie had botched it up big-time, and as she searched her memory, replaying events since she arrived here, she tried focusing on the moment when she'd fucked up. Had it been the first time she met Perry? The first time she made love to him? A physical, almost animalistic passion had hummed around them, charged in the air, from the moment they met. Although she was coming to believe he didn't act this way around all women, what she had witnessed last night at the crime scene made her wonder. Why would she be the only woman so strongly attracted to him? And wouldn't he be better off finding a nice, local girl, who wasn't going to leave the moment the case was solved?

That acknowledgment weighed so heavily inside Kylie it burned her eyes as well as made her heart hurt so badly she could barely breathe. Adjusting the key in the ignition, she rolled down her window, suddenly needing air.

"That's what I'm doing," she lied again, unwilling to let Susie see how badly she was handling this particular case.

"Good. And just so you know, the situation in Nicaragua is about ready to explode. You've always wanted one of the seriously high-profile cases, and I haven't forgotten that. Wrap this up and I'll get you on a plane down there. After that, I promise I'll get you some downtime."

Susie's words hit Kylie hard. As focused as she was on this case, she had just been reminded of the big picture. Less than a month ago she was in Washington, doing everything in her power to nail a sexual predator who'd already raped, tortured, and mutilated several women by the time she arrived on that scene. Nonetheless, she'd jumped in, made the case her own, and solved it. Once this case was done, she'd been on a plane leaving Kansas City. Where would her thoughts be a few months from now?

"Thanks, Susie. That means a lot to me," she said, meaning it, although she couldn't get the excitement into her voice.

"I'll be in touch." Susie said her good-byes and hung up, probably to make another call to another agent somewhere else in the United States and to hear their personal situation.

It was the job Kylie had signed up for. The life she had craved and the dream she was seeing fulfilled. Solve this case and move on. Probably within a month she'd be trekking around in a jungle, dealing with people she would call friends whom she didn't even know right now.

And Perry would go on with his life.

Chapter 26

Perry let himself into his sister's house that evening. He couldn't remember the last time he'd been wound so tight. Stress had the muscles in his shoulder blades burning, and the pain crawled straight up his spine to his head. He stared at Dorine and Denise, lying in the living room watching TV.

"Mom, Uncle Perry is here," Dorine screamed, rolling onto her back and letting the words wail so that they vibrated off the walls and pierced his already-throbbing head.

"Dorine, was that necessary?" He scowled at his niece, who looked at him upside down from the floor before rolling back and resuming watching her show without answering.

There was a pounding down the stairs and Dani flew into the living room and into his arms. Ever since her almost abduction, she'd been clinging to him. And he couldn't pull her tight enough into his arms. If he prayed for anything, it would be that he be given a thousand more chances to hug her like this.

"Kylie won't answer her phone for me," Dani whispered, still clinging to him when Megan walked into the living room, wiping her hands with a dish towel.

"There's supper left if you're hungry," Megan offered.

He hadn't given thought to food all day. "Thanks," he said, nodding to Megan. Possibly some food would recharge him. He lowered his head, breathing in Dani's strawberry-scented shampoo. For a moment he was thrown back to the little girl who would cry in Megan's arms when she scraped her knee or when she fell out of a tree. Fixing those aches and pains had been a hell of a lot easier than taking care of the pain and fear that had Dani trembling in his arms now. "She's not answering my calls, either," he said into her hair.

Another reason he knew he was wound tight. He hadn't been able to get over to Kylie's last night and today she'd been MIA. He had half a mind to drive over to the FBI field office and demand to know where the fuck she was. Not knowing twisted his gut and left him convinced there was only bigger trouble looming just ahead. If things were okay, Kylie would be with him.

Dani pulled away, remaining at arm's length, and stared up at him with sad green eyes. "Did you two have a fight?" she asked, almost whispering.

"No," he said, shaking his head and wrapping his arm around her as he headed for the kitchen. "What's for supper? Anything good?" he asked, changing the subject from Kylie.

"I made cheeseburgers," Megan announced, leading the way to the kitchen. She handed him a plate that she'd piled with a mound of fries next to two burgers. "Of course they aren't as good as when you make them on the grill." Even her smile showed her exhaustion.

His family was suffering from this case. The sooner he wrapped it up, found the prick who had also ripped five other families in Mission Hills apart and also made it clear his intentions to stalk Perry's niece, the better life would be for all of them. Perry almost felt guilty accepting the seat Dani pulled out for him and the food Megan put in front of him.

"Where's Diane?" he asked, grabbing one of the burgers as his stomach growled.

Megan took a seat next to him, and Dani slid into the chair on the other side of him.

"She's got some term paper," Megan explained, dipping a tea bag into hot water and looking noticeably more worn-out than she usually looked. "I told her to be home by ten, but she's at the library with some friends."

"She's got forty minutes," Dani announced, leaning back

to see the wall clock. "Shouldn't those two go to bed?" she asked her mother, jabbing her thumb in the direction of the living room.

"Yes, they should." Megan gave her daughter a pleading look.

"Get your sisters up to bed," Perry told Dani, talking with his mouth full of burger. He gave her a look, ready for her to argue, but obviously the stress that had descended on the household took the fight out of all of them.

Dani sighed heavily and scooted the chair back from the table, forcing it to scrape loudly across the floor. Megan cringed and dabbed her tea bag with more energy when Dani left them alone.

Perry put the first burger away and stared at his sister, noting the lines at the edges of her eyes and the dark circles underneath. Megan was a pretty woman, overworked and determined to raise intelligent young women. He was proud of her but knew at the moment she wasn't doing shit to take care of herself.

"Why don't you head up to bed, too?" he suggested. "You look like shit."

Any other time Megan would have been ready with a comeback, but when she sighed he almost felt bad for picking on her. Putting his hand over hers, he didn't move it when she gripped his larger hand with a fair amount of force.

"I'm scared, Perry," she whispered. "Did you see this morning's paper?"

"Yup." He hated how the media was making it a hell of a lot easier for Peter to do his job than it was for Perry to do his. Although that was the way it was most of the time. But the paper announcing the most recent murder, recapping the disappearance of the others, and labeling Peter as the high school girl murderer, was throwing the community into a panic. "We'll nail him."

"I'm scared for Dani," Megan whispered, her eyes moist when she looked at him. "He's already targeted her. What if he tries to take her again?"

"He won't succeed," Perry said firmly. Thankfully, the press didn't get ahold of the fact that a picture of Dani was left in Lanie's hand when she was found. "What do you think of sending her—"

"No!" Megan interrupted, yanking her hand from Perry's and lifting her teacup. She stared hard at Perry over it. "I'd be scared to death he would snag her from anywhere I sent her," Megan stated. "I did talk to the principal over at the high school today. I know they've put several cops on permanent duty over there to protect the kids while they're switching classes or out in the parking lot, but I am still scared something could happen."

"Nothing will happen."

"You can't swear that to me," she pressed.

He stiffened. The day his sister didn't have faith in him would be the day all hell would break lose. "Like hell I can't," he growled.

The girls paused at the bottom of the stairs, peering into the kitchen, their innocent faces full of curiosity as they stared from their mother to their uncle. It wasn't often he and Megan argued about anything. And they weren't arguing now.

"Go to bed," Megan instructed, trying to sound firm, but the life was gone from her voice. "I love all of you," she added, her voice softening.

"Love you, too," each of them mumbled.

"Upstairs. Now," Perry emphasized, getting the three of them to jump and hustle up the stairs. He looked earnestly at his sister. "There is no way in hell that monster will get anywhere near Dani again. You have my goddamn word on that one, Meg, and if you doubt me for a fucking minute—"

"Quit cussing and I believe you," she said, leaning back in her chair and bringing her cup to her lips. "Eat your supper. You're no fun when you're grouchy."

Perry swallowed a bite from his second burger. "The food is good." He knew he was grumpy but didn't see it going away anytime soon.

His phone vibrated against his hip and he grabbed it,

feeling his mood sour even more when it was his partner, Carl. "What's up?" he asked with a mouthful of food.

"Are you planning on pulling the night shift tonight?" Carl asked, apathetic to Perry's curt manner.

"Probably."

"Just checking. Give me an hour, okay? Mom is cranky tonight and I'm going to chill with her until she settles in, but then I'll hook up. Any word from Blondie?"

"Her name is Kylie, and no." Perry ignored the interest in Megan's eyes when she shifted her attention to him and suddenly made a show of listening. He dropped his burger on his plate and grabbed a French fry. "It doesn't feel right, though, man. I've got a sensation I can't kick."

"Just because you haven't heard from her?" Carl didn't pause to let Perry speak. "Go with your hunches, man. They're usually right."

It wasn't the first time Perry had heard that from his partner. Any other time Perry would advise Carl on listening to his own hunches, paying heed to the electrical charges in the air when he felt them. But tonight Perry didn't give a damn about coaching his partner.

"Yup," he said, shoving the fry in his mouth and swallowing after barely chewing. He slid his chair back, managing to make less noise than when Dani shoved her chair from the table and headed to the refrigerator. He didn't need a beer, especially if he was returning to duty, but damn, he wanted one and almost growled when there weren't any in his sister's fridge. Grabbing the gallon of milk, he placed it on the counter. "Meet me over at Megan's when you head out. I'm staying here until I return to duty."

"Gotcha, man," Carl said, and hung up.

"Why haven't you talked to Kylie?" Megan asked before Perry could put his phone back on his belt.

"Because she hasn't answered my calls," he snapped, knowing his sister didn't deserve him being a pain in the ass.

Perry grabbed a large glass out of the cabinet and filled it with cold milk. He downed half the glass, refilled it, then returned the gallon to the refrigerator.

His sister watched his actions. "You really like her, don't you?"

"Doesn't matter. She's not sticking around."

He hated the way his sister studied his face whenever she decided he wasn't telling her everything she seemed to feel she had a right to know.

"Is she really a college student?" Megan asked.

Perry didn't answer but set his cup down and sat, returning his attention to his food.

"Seems to me if she were, you would be willing to say so," Megan said, apparently content to carry on the conversation on her own. "I haven't seen you worked up like this in a long time." She held up her hand, as if he would actually comment. "And I know you're worked up over this murderer. We all are. But more than that has you bugged, Perry. You forget how well I know you."

"I told you it doesn't matter. She'll be leaving."

"How soon?"

"I don't know."

Megan nodded, placing her cup on the table and leaning on her elbows. She stared ahead, letting the silence grow for a few seconds. "There are days when I really miss David."

Perry wasn't ready for that one. She hadn't mentioned her husband in ages. Perry knew the love between the two of them was something unique and special that few ever got to experience. He leaned back, studying her for a moment.

"He was one hell of a guy," Perry said finally.

"Seems to me, if someone has a chance at what David and I had, they should go for it, no matter what stands in the way."

Perry should have known she was setting him up. He returned to his food. "I'm sure you're right," he mumbled, knowing she would press until he said something.

"I like Kylie." Megan was watching him. He could feel her gaze burning into the side of his head. "The girls like her, too. Dani doesn't think she's a student, though. She's pretty perceptive. You've said so yourself."

"Yup."

"Fine." Megan stood, moving behind him in the kitchen as she started acting busy, although it was her way of preparing for her next attack. "Let's say she isn't a student. Just for the sake of argument. And let's say she is going away, for whatever reason, from here soon," Megan mused, obviously content again to carry on the conversation by herself. "I bet if you made your feelings known, and I know you, Perry, I bet you haven't told her how you feel about her, the two of you could work something out."

Perry stuffed the last French fry into his mouth and stood with his plate, bringing it to the counter. Then downing his milk, he set it next to his plate. Grabbing his sister's shoulders, he turned her around, staring into her concerned expression. "Thank you for supper. You're a jewel to feed me like that. I'm going to go watch TV and try to calm down a bit. This conversation is over."

She nodded once, looking anything but done with what she might want to say. Footsteps sounded on the stairs.

Perry let go of his sister and tapped her nose. "Enough talk of this, okay?"

His phone rang again as Dani appeared in the doorway, looking at both of them as if she suspected they had quit talking because she joined them.

Perry shifted his attention to his phone and looked at the small screen. Kylie's name glared at him. He flipped the phone open, turning from the two of them and heading into the living room.

"Why the hell haven't you been answering my calls?" he demanded, hissing into the phone although too aware of Megan and Dani following him.

"I've been busy." Kylie's cold tone twisted his stomach into a mean knot. "There's a meet behind the bowling alley at ten o'clock. I'm supposed to go with him this time. Be there. I want this bust to be yours." She hung up before he could say anything.

"Goddamn it," he howled, hurling his phone at the couch.

"Perry," Megan said cautiously.

He sprung around, glaring at them. Dani edged closer to her mom, looking wide-eyed at him. Megan's expression wasn't much different.

"Sorry," he grumbled, turning his back to them and pacing the length of the living room, dragging his hand over his hair. "What time is it?" he asked, but then walked over to the couch and picked up his phone to check the time.

"Quarter till ten," Dani said. "What's wrong, Uncle Perry?"

"Megan," he said, adjusting his gears quickly. It wasn't the first time he'd been sent out without knowing shit about the scene. And he'd done just fine under those circumstances. "Call Diane. I want her home now."

"She's supposed to be home at ten." Megan tilted her head, this time looking as though she wouldn't press.

Damn good thing.

"Call her and tell her to get home now," he ordered. "I want all of you upstairs. No matter what, you will not answer the door or come downstairs. I'll lock up before I leave and I have a key. I'll come back when I'm done."

"Are you going to go catch him, Uncle Perry?" Dani asked, her eyes suddenly moist when she took a cautious step toward him.

"I sure hope so, baby." He reached for her, pulling her into a tight hug.

Megan hurried into the kitchen and he heard her talking to Diane in the next minute.

He'd driven over to his sister's in his squad car, and took off toward the bowling alley a few minutes later. After putting a call in to Carl, filling him in on what was going on and struggling to answer his questions about Kylie being FBI as quickly as possible, he could get off the phone. Perry slowed and turned into the small strip mall parking lot across the street from the bowling alley. It was almost ten.

Parking alongside of the narrow, long brick building, Perry cut his lights but left the squad car running as he got out and popped the trunk. He grabbed a flashlight, continually shooting furtive looks across the street where he had a decent view of the entire lot on both the front and back sides of the bowling alley. It was set off the road far enough, though, and the parking lot surrounding it large enough and not well enough lit that movement could occur in the shadows and he might miss it. His position was temporary.

With his hood as a shield, Perry placed his flashlight on the edge of the car and pulled out the bulky body armor. Memories of wearing it over to Kylie's, of the look on her face when she first realized he had it on and then her failed attempt to appear uninterested when he stripped out of it in front of her, came to mind as he ran his fingers over the thick, heavy protective wear. He didn't bother putting it on under his shirt this time. This wasn't undercover work, and he wasn't trying to impress anyone.

Was he out to impress Kylie that night?

God, it seemed centuries ago when he broke into her home. At the time he'd thought only of proving to her that no alarm system would keep him away from her. He was pulling macho bullshit, which now almost proved an embarrassing memory. It had proven effective that night, though. What he wouldn't do to turn back time, remove himself to a period when his heart didn't weigh so heavily in his chest. If they played their cards right, even though he hadn't seen the entire deck, tonight was the night.

Kylie could very well be on a plane tomorrow heading out to her next assignment.

Perry fought the overwhelming urge to hurl the protective armor across the dark lot.

"Focus, motherfucker," he growled. Shut down. Turn all emotions off. He'd pulled off not feeling for years, acting like a machine, taking care of his family and his city. He would keep doing just that.

Something stirred behind him and he grabbed his flashlight, unclipping the holster snap on his belt that secured his gun at the same time as he turned around. Two teenagers, a boy and a girl, appeared from behind the adjacent building, squinting and covering their eyes when he flashed the beam in their faces.

"Head home, now," he growled.

"We weren't doing anything wrong." The boy had his arm draped around the girl, both of them looking not much older than Dani.

Perry ached to knock some parents upside the head for allowing their kids out this late, and obviously unchaperoned enough they could wander this far from a residential area or any business that was open.

Perry breathed in the smell of pot and lowered the beam enough to allow them to focus. The teenage girl wouldn't meet Perry's gaze, but the cocky boy, obviously thinking his idiocy would impress his girlfriend, stared at him boldly with bloodshot eyes.

"You don't do as you're told right now, that will change." Perry made a show of taking a step toward them, which was obviously enough to break the bravery in the boy. He hesitated. Perry nodded toward the street. "Head home and walk along the sidewalk instead of in the shadows. Or do the two of you not know about a killer who loves little girls like your girlfriend there?"

That snapped the girl's attention to Perry's face. She looked shocked and then tugged at her boyfriend. "Let's go," she whispered.

"I'm not scared of the asshole," the boy announced, but was already heading away from Perry to the street.

"But you better be scared of me," he muttered under his breath.

He needed a fucking vacation. When did he get it in his head that bullying children protected them? Probably when they started acting like morons.

Shrugging into the bulletproof vest, he pulled the Velcro tight around his front as a patrol car slowed in front of him and signaled to turn into the parking lot across the street. The two teenagers started walking faster away from him and the other police car. Perry ignored them and focused on the number on the squad car.

"Franco, I'm going to take you down, motherfucker," He

scowled and reached inside the vest into his shirt pocket to pull out his Bluetooth. Perry placed a call into Dispatch while closing his trunk and walking around to the driver's side. "This is Unit Number Seven. I'm returning to duty."

"Ten four," the dispatcher said. "Please hold, will advise."

He started to tell her he'd received a tip but was put on hold. He shifted into drive and pulled out of his semi-secure hiding place, glancing at the clock on his dash. It was just after ten. If Franco was Peter he couldn't believe the guy would use one of the city's squad cars to commit such a heinous crime.

"Unit Seven, what is your ten twenty?" Dispatch asked when Perry pulled out into the street and cut across to the bowling-alley parking lot.

As he turned in, he spotted Kylie's hybrid entering from the side entrance at the other end of the lot.

"This is Unit Seven," he said, searching the lot for Franco's squad car. "I'm at the bowling-alley parking lot. I received a tip earlier—"

"Unit Seven, report to the station, please," she told him, cutting him off.

"Is Unit Six on a call?" Perry asked, ignoring her request. He wasn't going anywhere.

"Stand by."

His phone beeped in his ear, and he picked up the handheld, checking the screen to see who the caller was. Then not waiting for Dispatch to return, he switched over.

"Tell me what's going on," Perry demanded, relieved as hell Kylie was calling him.

"Get the hell out of sight," she hissed.

"Where is your meeting point?" He turned and drove along the side of the building, cutting his lights and crawling toward the other side.

"I called you so you could get your arrest. You deserve that much. So just stay on your toes." She sounded so cold, so distant.

He hated thinking she had shut down because she knew

she was heading out. It was one thing knowing he needed to shut down just so he could handle her leaving. But for some reason it hurt like fucking hell knowing she was capable of the same coldheartedness.

"Kylie," he growled, creeping around the building and spotting Franco parked on the other end, his lights also cut. At Perry's distance, he couldn't tell if Franco was even in the squad car.

"Save your speeches for your lady cop friend," Kylie snapped, the coldness in her tone increasing and so noticeably bitter that Perry brought his car to a stop.

"What lady friend?"

"The one you were hanging all over last night at the crime scene. You know, I thought I knew you better. Funny how well I can profile, yet I nailed you so wrong. Personally, I can think of a lot more romantic locations to flirt with someone than a scene where a young girl was killed." She hung up on him.

"I wasn't hanging on her—" Perry slammed his dash when he heard the click in his ear.

Suddenly it was clear as glass why Kylie hadn't answered his calls all day. He had seen her leave the crime scene last night and apparently she had seen more than he wished she'd seen. Fucking little mousy bitch. Perry was disgusted by the female cop's behavior as much as Kylie was. And any other time he might have found some warped amusement in learning Kylie got so pissed when she was jealous.

At the moment, though, he didn't find any fucking humor in it.

His phone beeped in his ear again and he accepted the call. "I want to know right now—"

"Perry, this is a secure line," Rad growled into Perry's ear. "What are you doing?"

"Rad, I got a call earlier from Kylie."

"I just got a phone call, too. Why the hell are you horning in on Unit Six's beat?" Rad demanded. "He's got backup in place and calls complaining you're running with lights and messing up their game plan."

"Like hell I am."

"Report to the station now. We'll discuss this when you get here."

Perry frowned when he got close enough to Unit Six to tell there was no driver in it. A quick glance around the parking lot showed no other cars, marked or unmarked, anywhere around him.

"There's no backup. Unit Six is unoccupied."

"Flynn, report in now or I swear to God I'll—"

Perry would take his reprimand later. He hung up on the Chief, red flags popping up all over the place as he pulled up behind Unit Six. Franco was moving in on Kylie. Perry didn't know what the hell the bastard had told Rad to convince him to yell at Perry, but he had to be pretty damn convincing. And a psychopath getting ready to make the cut could convince God to his knees if he wanted.

Perry had thrown his car into park, opening his door, when his phone made another sound, informing him he just got a text message. Reaching over and grabbing the phone, he pushed the button to take the text and read the block letters on the screen.

If I call again, start recording. Kylie had sent him the message.

"Crap," he hissed, impending doom closing in around him as he dove at his glove compartment and yanked everything out of it until he found the small device he could hook up to his phone to make it record conversations. Then snapping it to his phone, he jumped out of the car. As he gripped his phone in one hand, sweat drenched his palm. He slapped his gun at his waist and sprinted around Unit Six.

His phone started ringing in his ear again. Perry glanced at the screen in his hand. It was Rad calling him back. Perry knew it wasn't the first time he'd been insubordinate when he sent the call to voice mail, and if he was wrong, he would take whatever disciplinary action Rad wanted to dish out to him, but if he was right, he was about to take down Franco. It would get really fucking ugly before it got better.

Perry reached the front of Franco's car when he spotted

Kylie's hybrid. She was parked where she'd been parked the last time. Again a flashback of interrupting her meet, not understanding what it was she was about, hit him as hard as if a flood had just released. It didn't knock him off his feet with the clarity of it. This time Perry saw the reality in the situation. Kylie sat, planted as bait, ready to take on a monster. And it appeared she was fucking alone while doing it.

There better be FBI agents sitting and waiting, or he'd take down that field office, starting with fucking Athey.

A dark shadow appeared in the bushes behind Kylie's car at the same time sirens sounded in the distance. Hell, maybe Rad was quicker than Perry gave him credit for. The chances were strong the sirens were unrelated, but Perry would love an audience when he nailed Franco to the fucking wall.

The shadow moved quickly, coming up alongside Kylie's car at the same time the black Suburban appeared at the other end of the parking lot.

"Fucking hell! There are two of them." Perry barely grunted out the words when he heard Kylie cry out. Whoever was alongside her car had just dragged her out of it as the Suburban pulled up alongside her car.

Her cry was stifled quickly when the person in the shadows shoved Kylie into the back of the Suburban and slammed the door shut. Perry damn near ran backward when Franco bolted to his squad car. The motherfucker had just abducted Kylie and would now run to his car and make a show of trying to catch her.

Perry turned, hauling ass back to his car. His phone rang before he reached it and he pushed the button, willing it to be Kylie.

"Why are you doing this?" he heard her wail.

"Shut the fuck up, bitch." The outraged male voice sounded too fucking familiar.

Perry leapt into his car at the same time that Franco squealed out of his hiding place. His phone beeped, indicating another call, and Perry cursed. He couldn't take a call while recording. Glancing down, he saw it was Carl.

"Where the hell are you, man?" Perry asked the darkness

of his car as he left his lights off and followed Franco around the corner of the building. He could really use his partner right now, or that supposed backup to truly exist. This was going to be one hell of a bust, and witnesses were always good, especially when taking down a cop who'd been on the force for as long as Franco had.

Perry would kick himself in the ass later for not noticing an insane child molester walking among them, right under their fucking noses, all these years.

Carl pulled into the parking lot in his own car when Perry made it around the corner. Franco was ahead of him and the Suburban was leaving the lot. Perry struggled to listen to the noises he heard in his ear while cutting across the dark lot and pulling up alongside Carl. Fortunately, he knew to ask questions later. Carl parked his car, jumped out, and climbed in on the passenger side, barely managing to shut the door before Perry hauled ass after Franco and the Suburban.

"What the hell is going on?" Carl demanded, struggling with his seat belt.

"Kylie just got picked up. The Suburban is ahead of us and I just witnessed Franco yank her out of her car and throw her into the backseat of the Suburban. I've got her on the phone now, recording it, but she isn't saying anything."

"Put it on speaker," Carl suggested. "Is that Franco?"

"Yes, and the motherfucker is mine," he growled, merely glancing when Carl picked up the handheld between them and pushed the button to send it to speaker. "What the fuck?" Perry howled when Franco didn't turn out of the lot but instead squealed to a stop and turned his car sideways, completely blocking the exit.

"What the hell is he doing?" Carl yelled.

"You won't get away with this, John," Kylie said through the phone.

"John?" Perry and Carl asked at the same time.

Franco stopped his squad car, completely blocking the exit as Perry slowed. Perry turned on his headlights, blinding Franco, whose face was twisted into a determined scowl as he glared at them.

"I don't fucking believe it," Carl said, his accent growing thicker. "What does he think he's doing?"

"Get the camera out and start snapping pictures," Perry demanded. "And then hold on tight. We're going for a ride."

Carl yanked the digital camera out of the glove compartment, pulling it out of its case quickly and holding it up in the air as they slowed in front of Franco.

"Smile pretty for the nice man," Carl said, a sneer in his tone.

"Keep taking pictures," Perry ordered, and accelerated, bypassing Franco's squad car and running his own car over the curb and onto the grassy median toward the street.

"Oh, crap!" Carl yelled. "He got out and is pointing a gun at us."

"Keep taking pictures," Perry yelled.

"He's aiming a gun at us!"

"Then take pictures and duck!"

A shot exploded into the night and Carl howled just as the car bounced over the curb and hit the street.

"Son of a bitch," Carl swore, bouncing sideways next to Perry as he tried turning around and ducking at the same time.

"Come on, sweetheart," Perry whispered, searching the street ahead of them for signs of the Suburban. "Tell us where you are."

"How in the hell do you think you're going to get away with this?" Kylie asked, her voice tinny through the speakerphone.

"Are you kidding?" John Athey laughed. "We've got the perfect setup, darling. You've got no backup, and your police lover is grounded. I saw to it. Kind of has its advantages when you can tell the cops in the town what to do. Not to mention a Suburban that can't be pinned to anyone." His laugh was sinister. "Got to love a car auction and then never registering the vehicle," he added as if he were telling a good joke.

"You killed all those girls," she accused. Kylie wasn't laughing.

"Not your problem anymore."

It wasn't exactly a confession. Perry prayed she would get him to say exactly what they needed to nail the bastard to the cross right alongside Franco. He couldn't believe this. Not in a million years would he have guessed John Athey and Franco were in this together. They did have the perfect setup.

Only one problem. There was no such thing as perfect, and Perry would see them both dead before the night was over if he couldn't successfully pull off an arrest. First he needed to find them, and before Kylie got hurt.

"You're wrong, John. This is my problem, and even more so now that I know you're guilty. This is the same SUV that tried abducting Dani and I bet we'll find where Perry shot at it. You're Peter. You might as well admit it. I've got to take you down. Do you realize how serious a punishment you'll face for this?"

"Are you seriously as dumb of a blonde as you come across?" John demanded. "You don't get it, sweetheart. There is no one coming to save you. Do you think you can simply say, 'You're under arrest,' and I'll pull over?"

"There is someone coming to get me. He's right on your ass as we speak. And I'll give him the honors of slapping the cuffs on you."

"What are you talking about?"

Kylie squealed and Perry gripped the steering wheel so hard the car swerved and Carl gave him a nervous glance.

"Keep it cool, man," Carl said, his voice calm as he watched Perry.

"I'm cool." Perry would take the bastard's life with his bare hands. If the son of a bitch laid as much as a finger on Kylie . . .

"Don't say a fucking word," John yelled through the phone. "Not a goddamn word."

"Why are we pulling into a car wash?" Kylie asked.

"I said shut the fuck up!" John bellowed so loud it distorted through the phone.

"Car wash. Car wash," Perry repeated. "Where the fuck is a car wash?"

"Are you sure we headed the right direction when we left the bowling alley?" Carl asked. "There are several car washes up and down this street."

Perry didn't want to think they were losing her. John was right on one thing. There wasn't any backup. He did hold the power to eliminate any help for Kylie. Or he did up until he made the mistake of messing with something Perry viewed as his. He would fight for Kylie's life, and then he would fight for her. His sister's words picked an odd time to pop into his brain, but he agreed with her advice now. Kylie was worth laying his heart on the line for. She would become part of their family, one way or the other.

As soon as he found her.

"If you're wired . . . ," John hissed. "You fucking bitch. I was just going to make you disappear. No offense but you're a bit too old for my tastes. But if you've screwed me, I swear to God the last thing that fucking cop prick of yours will hear are your screams as I torture you until you die. He can live with those memories while he rots in prison for the murders of all those girls."

"You're going to do that in a car wash?" Kylie asked. "That convenience store will have witnesses all over the place. And I bet the drive-through at McDonald's across the street will offer at least one or two people who will see you, too. And why would Perry go to prison?"

Kylie screamed at the same time that the sound of flesh hitting flesh made Perry's blood boil.

"McDonald's," Carl yelled. "We're going the wrong way. McDonald's is in the other direction."

Perry pulled a U-turn in the middle of the street, forcing a couple cars to a screeching stop, and turned on his lights while gunning it. He hauled ass down the street, yelling at Carl to call Dispatch.

"Whatever it takes!" Perry demanded. "Get backup on the scene now. Tell them whatever you have to tell them."

Carl didn't argue or ask for advice on what to say but fumbled with his phone while the digital camera fell to the ground at his feet.

Perry focused on the golden arches when they appeared ahead of him and Carl. He saw the convenience store Kylie had mentioned and then spotted the car wash. There weren't any sounds coming through the phone anymore, which made Perry's blood curdle. He didn't want to think about what John might have done to her to make her quiet.

Perry squealed to a stop in front of the car wash, slamming the car into park before it had fully stopped. He spotted the Suburban and the open driver's-side and passenger door didn't look good at all. His heart swelled into his throat and he trembled when he grabbed his gun, pulling it free as he climbed out and headed around his squad car.

"Cover me," he yelled to Carl, and held his gun out, aiming it toward the ground, while he searched for Kylie. "Athey, where the fuck are you?" he yelled.

"Perry!" Kylie howled, her high pitch sounding full of fear and panic.

At least she was alive.

Perry ran through the stall, looking both ways on the other side of the car wash, until he spotted them at the edge of the lot.

"Stay right there," John ordered, gripping Kylie against his chest while walking backward, the gun in his hand pointed at Kylie's head.

Her hair was messed up and her expression looked panicked, but otherwise she didn't look hurt.

"Are you okay?" Perry asked her, an overwhelming sense of calm hitting him. Something told him John wouldn't kill her. It would be murder one, and there wouldn't be any way out of it. Perry was convinced the man was too much of a survivor for that.

"I'm fine," she said, also sounding too calm.

"Get back in your car," John ordered, taking the gun from Kylie's head and pointing it at Perry.

"It's over," Perry told him. "Franco is under arrest. The FBI has been contacted."

As if to back Perry, sirens approached, growing louder by the second.

"Backup is here. Put down the gun."

"Like hell." John pushed Kylie forward, causing her to trip and fall to the ground.

Perry lunged for her just as the shot rang through the air.

Chapter 27

Three months later

Kylie's eyes burned, and she wondered for the third or fourth time since leaving Dallas if she had any sense in her head to start the trip to Kansas City this late at night. It was an eight-hour drive and it was damn near three o'clock in the morning. She wasn't even sure there was a reason to rush back there.

Her leg cramped, the bullet wound she'd taken while in Nicaragua pretty well healed but still giving her grief from time to time. The humid night air, with summer kicking in hard and fast, seemed to make her leg act up. She didn't mind the injury, other than it had hurt like fucking hell getting shot, since her return shot took out the leader of the cartel they were after. Her orders had been to bring him in alive, but arresting and escorting the cartel leaders' number one in command had satisfied Susie, and Kylie's government. She was awarded a two-month respite once she checked out of the hospital in Dallas, for her efforts and a job well done.

Kylie passed another mile marker and squinted when her brights reflected against the road sign ahead. Five miles to Mission Hills. Already buildings lined the Interstate as she got closer to her destination.

It had been two months since she last talked to Perry. Once she was buried in the Nicaraguan jungle, Internet access was limited to a "must have" basis. Chatting online with a man who'd changed her life didn't qualify as a "must have."

And as she'd done throughout her career, she'd engrossed herself in the community, what there was where she was located down there, and taken on her assignment with everything she had. But even after being wounded and her time in the hospital, nothing she'd done managed to get Perry out of her mind.

Was he the one?

It was a question she'd fallen asleep asking herself too many times over the past few months. Now, with a slight limp she was promised would go away with continued physical therapy, thoughts of moving to a desk job had crossed her mind. It wasn't the most appealing thought, but there was a job opening. Susie, her supervisor, was a bit too attentive to the needs of her agents at times, and had mentioned it while visiting Kylie in the hospital.

After being released, spending a week with her parents, she looked up the job opening online. John Athey's position, supervisor of the FBI field office in Mission Hills, still hadn't been filled. Paul qualified for the position but had turned it down. More than likely because he wouldn't be able to sit and play his computer games as much.

"God, am I doing the right thing?" Kylie groaned.

When she'd mentioned to Susie she might come back up here to see how everyone was doing, her supervisor set up an appointment for her to meet the area field supervisor. There were no obligations, but it was more or less a job interview. "A desk job," Kylie muttered, wondering if she could handle it.

Her mother didn't have the insight to see it; there was still so much mending to do between the two of them. Kylie wasn't sure if they would ever return to the closeness many mothers and daughters shared, especially now that her father was ill and most of their conversations and actions stemmed around him. But her supervisor questioned Kylie's motives. She hated admitting her consideration of the job was based on where she might stand with Perry.

The night John Athey took a bullet to his head and Lieutenant Franco was arrested appeared a blur in her mind.

Franco had ranted about Perry being the one, that all they had to do was check his computer at the station. Perry was too calm when he announced how he'd bugged his own computer, making it clear to everyone around them that he was innocent. He had set it up so anyone typing on his computer at the station would send all keystrokes to his computer at his house.

It was the days that followed that were clearer in her memory. Learning how the two men had worked together, capturing girls, torturing them, building a Web site where people could pay to see the atrocities done to many of the teenagers which they'd run out of Franco's house. Perry had a friend in the FBI, who never blew her cover, but verified the ISP location. Athey had prevented anyone in his office from gathering the information. Rita Simoli and Maura Reynolds' bodies were found in shallow graves on land John Athey had owned. Franco had started spilling his guts, especially after he learned his partner in crime had killed himself, anything to lessen the charges. Kylie doubted anything he said would get him anything less than life in prison. She wouldn't be surprised if he still got the death penalty. And after it was all wrapped up, the flight out of Kansas City, talking to Perry on the phone a few times before leaving the country, and then after that a handful of times online.

Kylie accepted his story about the lady police officer at the crime scene the night she watched her grope Perry, that her actions weren't reciprocated. Perry stressed that over and over again, his story never changing, nor his disgust for her indifference to the grotesqueness of the scene. Like Kylie, Perry was leery of any law enforcement officer who, so early in their career, wasn't affected by the blood and gore they were sometimes exposed to.

Remembering how he had tried calling her several times a day the first couple days after she left Kansas City and how their phone conversations had changed from confrontational to friendly, and even intimate, gave Kylie hope. She had held on to the words he'd shared with her over the phone for quite a while. The phone calls ended after she left the country.

Kylie stared at the sign that welcomed her to Mission Hills as she passed it. The very next sign showed her the speed limit.

"Crap," she hissed, hitting her brake, but it was too late. Lights flashed in her rearview and side mirrors. "Damn it. This is the last thing I need." Like the potentially new FBI field office supervisor needed to enter the town with a speeding ticket.

She slowed quickly, watching the speedometer go down and knowing she'd been doing a good 20 miles per hour over the limit. There wouldn't be any getting out of this, and she doubted she could use knowing one of the local cops intimately as an excuse to get the officer not to write her a ticket.

Kylie pulled to the side of the road, hit her hazards in her newer-modeled Toyota that had been in her parents' garage for a few years now. She'd finally taken it out and decided to drive it instead of renting a car. The officer who pulled her over would run her tag and know exactly who she was. If Perry was working tonight, he would hear her name over the radio. This wasn't how she wanted him to know she'd returned to town. Hell, she'd even thought of approaching his nieces, since she knew where they hung out, or at least where they hung out a few months ago, and paving the way to learn if approaching Perry would even be worth it. For all she knew, he'd moved on by now.

She turned off her radio, which was barely audible. Pressing her finger on the button on her door she moved her side mirror slightly to better see the officer who got out of the patrol car behind her. Red and white lights flashed in the darkness, creating the surreal image that made it harder for suspects at night to focus clearly and see their surroundings. Being accustomed to emergency vehicle lights didn't help her get a better image of the officer who took his time closing his door and strolling patiently toward her.

More than likely he'd already run her tag.

His flashlight washed over her car, the back of her head, and then along the outside of her car while he moved closer.

Kylie watched his long muscular legs, his strides controlled and confident. He was tall, muscular, his broad chest well outlined in the darkness. As he neared she moved her finger, pushing the button to lower her window.

"Get out of the car, miss." That deep baritone sent chills rushing over her.

Kylie's mouth went dry when she cranked her head around, but she was unable to see his face from where she sat. Her fingers were suddenly too damp when she reached for her door handle, managed to pull it and then push open her car door. Right now would not be a good time for her leg to act up and make it more difficult to get out of her car.

"Do you know how fast you were going?" he asked, his hat shading his eyes and the top part of his face.

Kylie stood, staring at Perry's rugged facial features, noting a day's growth, which made it harder to read his expression. She could barely see his eyes, which appeared cold, distant, and stared down at her without offering a glimpse into what he might be feeling.

"Obviously too fast," she offered, but didn't smile. She rested one hand on her door, not sure she wanted him to see, or know yet, the extent of how badly she was injured, or how far she still needed to go to full recovery.

"Are you in a hurry to get somewhere?" He didn't ask for her driver's license and registration.

Not that she was opposed to the ticket. It was obvious by watching her speedometer decelerate that she'd earned it. But this was why she'd come here, to see him. Kylie wished she could see his face better, read his facial expression. But, unless he'd moved on, he probably was guarding his feelings as much as she was guarding hers.

"I don't know if I was in a hurry, but I was obviously not paying attention to how fast I was going. I've been driving all night," she admitted, aching to take his hat off. It was as bad as if he wore dark sunglasses late at night. "I'm sorry I wasn't paying attention."

His lips pressed into a thin line, and a moment of silence passed before his deep baritone brushed over her again, causing every hair on her body to stand at attention and her insides to tighten, creating a heat she was sure he must be able to notice.

"I find it hard to believe a special agent with the FBI wasn't paying attention," he accused. "Why are you here, Kylie?"

His cold words were a stab to her heart. He didn't want her here. She could barely answer from the lump that threatened to close her throat. Worse yet, she didn't know how to answer. And if she did, her voice would crack, her leg would give out, or something else would happen to make this moment turn from bad to worse.

As a warm breeze wrapped around her, a damp sweat spread over her body and her heart pattered furiously in her chest. Lately panic attacks were hitting her without warning. The psychiatrist she'd been forced to visit after being shot told her they were possibly a reaction to the medication she'd been on in the hospital. Not to mention, being shot was a traumatic experience, not only physically but also emotionally. Everyone handled it differently.

Kylie wasn't sure she agreed either of those was the reason for her sudden erratic emotions. "I have some time off," she heard herself say.

"So passing through again?"

Maybe it was for the best that she not even make it into town before learning she wasn't wanted here. If she continued with this conversation she would break down, right here on the side of the interstate in the dark. Stability would return to her in time. And her own mental counseling told her that once she put closure where closure belonged and understood if there was anything between her and Perry, she would have better control of her emotions. As before, she would be able to keep them in check, under lock and key.

First, though, she feared, she needed to get that key back, because someone had stolen her heart.

"Let me get my driver's license. You need to write your ticket." She couldn't take him standing there, not moving, his dark, cold manner eating her alive. "I promise not to speed again."

He didn't stop her, or comment, when she turned her back on him and leaned into her car. When the muscles in her outer thigh, around the mending wound, quivered as she shifted her weight, she braced herself, putting her hand on her opened door. Perry didn't say anything, or stop her from getting her purse and registration out of her car.

An emptiness consumed her when he took her information and returned to his car. He didn't tell her to wait in her car or follow him to his. She saw his partner sitting in the passenger seat, although she didn't take time to note his reaction to her being here. She'd never had time to know Carl Ramos, but more than likely he would know something about her. At least Perry's opinion of her being here when he returned to his patrol car.

Kylie felt as though she floated without direction all of a sudden. While recovering and then after spending time with her parents, she knew without a doubt she would return here. All that was on her mind throughout her recovery was seeing Perry. Maybe she should have exerted the effort to pick up the phone and call him. Why had she thought returning here would be like it was in movies, with the two of them running into each other's arms and promising to be together forever?

Forever didn't exist for her.

Although it seemed like forever, barely eight minutes passed before Perry returned, handing her personal information back to her, and a small clipboard for her to sign for the speeding ticket. Her hand was so damp and she was so shaken, she doubted the signature was legible. It didn't matter. He tore her copy for her, handed it to her with his gloved hand, without bending down to see her better as she sat in her car. Another plus, tears threatened to fall and a pending pity party would release soon enough.

"You didn't say how long you would be here," he said, his tone still flat, unwelcoming, while he stood outside her car door.

With her window down, the temperature inside her car rose drastically. Sweat beaded over her flesh under her clothes, adding to her discomfort.

"I . . . I'm not sure," she said, admitting to herself it was the truth. In spite of her two months off, did she really want to stay where she wasn't wanted? There wasn't any point in going to the interview. She couldn't stay here, or work here. This was Perry's town. If she wasn't welcome, she wasn't welcome.

"Where are you headed?"

That much was a simple answer. "I have reservations at the Holiday Inn."

"I'll follow you there."

Kylie turned to look up at him, confused why he would suggest doing so. But he'd turned already, returning to his car.

Way too aware of his headlights beaming in her rearview mirror, Kylie was so sick to her stomach when she pulled into the hotel parking lot she couldn't think what to do. Her luggage was in the trunk. But should she haul all of it in?

Perry parked at the edge of the parking lot, not getting out of his car, and possibly doing paperwork. He watched her when she walked into the lobby and checked in, and Kylie felt his eyes boring into her backside when she moved her car in front of her motel room door. Did he want to see how much luggage she'd brought? That would clue him in on how long she planned on staying here.

He didn't approach her, didn't offer to help with her luggage, and didn't pull out of the parking lot when she finally decided on her overnight bag and laptop, then disappeared into her room and closed her door. Like she would be able to sleep with him sitting out there.

After pacing the room for fifteen minutes, sitting on the edge of the king-sized bed when her leg started throbbing and peeking the closed curtain half a dozen times to see him still sitting there, she finally opted for a hot bath. When she got out, still nervous and feeling more out of sorts than she had when she climbed into the hot water, Perry's patrol car was gone.

A part of her left with him. Kylie climbed into the too-large bed, cuddling into a fetal position, and let the tears fall.

On Wednesday, Kylie had been in Mission Hills for two days. Her laptop was online, available for instant messages, but none came. Her cell was fully charged, and she got several phone calls. None of them were from Perry. She'd forced herself to go to the mall, trepidation over running into one of his nieces bringing on another of her annoying panic attacks. But when she saw no one she knew, even when she drove to the grocery store and purchased a few things to eat in her motel room to give herself a break from restaurant food, the overwhelming emptiness threatened to consume her.

Perry couldn't make his message clearer if he yelled it in her face. He was no longer interested. No matter the intimate words they had shared on the phone a couple months ago before she lost service and spent two months in the jungle, enough time had apparently passed that he no longer felt that way.

"So what to do now?" she asked her reflection, standing with her hair in a towel and her bathrobe hanging over her naked body. She'd lost a lot of weight. "That appointment is this afternoon. You go or cancel."

Her reflection stared back at her dumbly, not answering. She shifted her attention to the phone in the room and the phone book she'd put underneath it when she'd ordered delivery the other day. Maybe she was just more bullheaded than most, but this wasn't enough closure. It could be that she was more of a masochist than she cared to admit. She needed to be yelled at in the face to get the truth to sink in. And there was only one way to make that happen.

Sitting on the edge of the bed with the phone book, she flipped through it, surprised but pleased that Megan Vetter, Perry's sister, was listed in the book. Using her cell phone, while a small part of her insisted that seven thirty in the morning wasn't the best time to call a household with children when they were probably all scurrying to get ready for school, Kylie dialed the number before she lost her nerve.

She had no idea where the powerful special agent, with nerves of steel, had disappeared. But she wasn't anywhere near while the phone rang once, twice, and a breathless girl answered with a cheery hello.

"Hi," Kylie said, licking her dry lips. "Is Megan there?"

"Who is this?"

"This is Kylie."

Silence. Kylie waited it out.

"Kylie who?" the girl asked.

Kylie sucked in a breath. "Kylie Donovan."

"I knew you weren't a college student and you insisted you were. You lied to me." Dani hung up on her.

"Crap," Kylie said, hanging up on her end and dropping her head into her hands. Her towel fell forward, twisted around her hair, and weighed heavy as it hung to the floor.

Her cell phone rang and she struggled to untangle the towel, then tossed it on the bed as she grabbed her cell and stared at the name on her phone. She'd never deleted Dani's cell phone number and it was calling her now. Apparently the teenager felt she had a right to chew Kylie out more.

"Hello," Kylie said, and headed to the bathroom for her brush before her hair dried in a tangled mess.

"Why did you lie? And you left without even saying goodbye? Do you have any idea how badly you hurt my uncle?"

"Dani, I came back here for him. But he won't come see me. Do you have any idea—"

"You came back here for him?" Dani interrupted.

Kylie swallowed, realizing she was dumping everything she had held in the last few days on the teenager, or at least was ready to until she'd been interrupted. "Yes," she admitted.

"Then why are you calling here?"

"Dani, he knows I'm here. He knows what hotel I'm at and what room I'm in, and since the night I arrived he hasn't sought me out. He talked to me the night I arrived and he was so cold to me. I thought I could talk to all of you. If it is true that he isn't interested, I'll leave."

"You need to tell my uncle that. He's stubborn but not stupid. I have to go. The bus is here. Bye-bye." Dani hung up without waiting for Kylie to tell her good-bye.

It took a teenager telling her what she knew all along. Kylie dressed quickly, keeping it simple with a pair of jeans and a sleeveless blouse, and left her hotel before she lost her nerve.

It was already hot outside but she wasn't ready to show off her scar yet by wearing shorts. Hiding in her room wouldn't resolve anything. She had an appointment at four o'clock this afternoon. Time was running out on determining her future.

A calm came over her as she pulled into Perry's driveway. One way or another, very soon she would be able to lay out plans for her future, maybe even the rest of her life. No more riding in limbo. No more hiding and trembling. Her resolve returned to her as if a dam had broken inside her, returning her confidence and determination. She'd gotten this far in life reaching out and taking what she wanted. There was something else she wanted, and now was the time to take it.

Kylie parked her car, turned off the engine, and got out. His Jeep wasn't in the driveway. She looked at her watch: eight AM. He either had left for the day or wasn't home yet. She hoped it was the latter. It would suck if she had to break and enter and wait for him for eight hours. Kylie smiled, imagining a concerned neighbor calling Dispatch to inform them that the good cop Lieutenant Perry's home was being broken into.

Testing the doorknob on the back door where he'd entered with Kylie before, she wasn't surprised that it was locked. The garage was locked, too, as was the front door. Kylie would have been surprised to learn otherwise, but checking helped her kill time. She walked around to her car again, glancing at her cell phone to see the time. Fifteen minutes had passed. If he worked the night shift, he would be here in less than half an hour.

Unless he had someone else in his life now and possibly would go to her house.

Kylie kicked the thought out of her head. The connection they had was too strong. From the moment they'd met up until her leaving, the feelings between them were so intense they created charged currents in the air. It was more than a sexual attraction. At least she knew it was for her. More than once while she was in the hospital, the last thing she could have done was made love, yet she still craved being with him. Too many times she wanted to call him. And she'd chickened out.

Her chickenshit days were over.

Kylie leaned against the back of her Toyota, crossing one leg over the other, and watched large green leaves rustle in the trees, as a warm breeze seemed to bring everything around her to life. Why was she just now noticing how gorgeous this part of the country was?

Eight fifteen passed, then eight twenty. She studied her fingernails, the way her shoes looked on her feet. She stared up and down the quiet street. Maybe he did work the day shift, even though he'd worked the night shift a couple days ago. She would give him five more minutes.

She heard the engine before she saw his Jeep. Perry came around the corner slowly, their eyes locking immediately. Her stomach twisted into so many knots she couldn't breathe. But nor could she take her eyes off his. Perry wasn't wearing a hat any longer. He didn't have on sunglasses. She locked gazes with his, drowning in that dark, commanding stare that never left hers.

He parked behind her car. She wouldn't be able to leave until he moved it. Was that a good sign?

Kylie dragged in a deep breath, which got stuck around the lump in her throat. Perry turned off his car but then sat there, staring at her, his long fingers wrapped around his steering wheel. She'd come this far. She wouldn't go any farther. Perry would get out of his Jeep and come to her. She wouldn't walk to him.

Maybe he read her mind. When he stepped out of the car, his uniform clinging to him as if he'd sweated a lot during his shift, or for some reason had been wet, she couldn't help dropping her gaze and appreciating the bulging muscle easily viewed through the taut material.

If anything, his dark hair seemed a bit longer, with slight curls covering his ears and looking sexy as hell. His green eyes were so intense they stole her breath, but his slow, quiet way he stalked her reminded Kylie of a predator moving in on his prey. It was almost too much. She felt her wounded leg quiver and worried if she stared much longer she'd drool down her jaw while her legs gave out and turned her into a puddle of pent-up desire at his feet.

Perry stopped within a few feet of her, crossing his arms over his chest and taking his time letting his gaze travel over her. Kylie's skin prickled. There wasn't disapproval on his face. If anything, his relaxed features looked less guarded than they did the night she drove into town.

"Did Dani call you?" She broke the silence.

"Nope."

Kylie nodded. He wasn't going to make this easy. But then she already knew not a damn thing about Perry Flynn was easy. "I need some answers, Perry."

His green eyes darkened, causing her insides to tremble with nervous anticipation.

"I need a shower." He jingled his keys in his hand. "And I haven't eaten since yesterday. We can talk in a bit."

Perry started to the door and she walked as far as her car door, not sure whether she was invited inside or not. But when he unlocked his door, he stood to the side, looking her way. Kylie did her best not to limp toward him.

"What happened to you?" he asked from behind her, closing the door and then following her into his kitchen.

Obviously her limp was more noticeable than she wished. "I got shot."

"Where?"

She didn't know if he meant where as in where had she

been when she got shot or where on her body. She placed her hand gently over her outer thigh just below her right hip. "Right here while I was in Nicaragua."

"How bad was it?"

"I was in the hospital for two weeks." She wasn't sure if telling him more would open up the conversation or simply make her appear the damaged goods she felt like she was half the time now.

When he didn't say anything and she turned around, he lifted his gaze to her face. Kylie wasn't sure whether he was looking where her injuries were or somewhere else.

"I'm going to take a shower. Make yourself at home." He walked through his house, leaving her standing in the kitchen.

And he had told her to make herself at home.

Half an hour later, when Kylie heard the water turn off in the shower, she had bacon ready, coffee brewed, and toast buttered. Since she didn't know how he liked his eggs, she held off on making them, but the carton sat on his counter. She wiped the counter and turned when he appeared from the other room, his hair almost black from being damp, and wearing only boxers.

She was sure her admiration was written all over her face.

"You made me breakfast?" He sounded impressed.

She forced her gaze from his rippling chest muscles to his face. "You said to make myself at home." She pointed to the eggs. "I don't know how you like your eggs."

"Kylie, why are you here?" The look he gave her made it appear he'd been torturing himself trying to learn the answer.

Maybe she wasn't the only one enduring a personal hell.

She put the washcloth on the counter and rubbed her hands down her jeans. It was time for reckoning, laying her cards on the table and seeing where it got her. No more waiting. No more praying things would work out to her advantage without her making an effort to make it happen.

"I'm afraid I left something here when I left a few months ago."

"What was that?"

Her mouth was suddenly too dry when she lost herself in those sensual dark eyes of his. "My heart," she whispered.

She couldn't breathe when he simply studied her, not saying anything for a moment and not moving from where he stood damn near naked several feet away from her.

"So what will you do? Get it and leave again?"

"Well, that depends."

"On what? Are you leaving the FBI?" He sounded incredulous, clearly understanding she could no more leave her line of work than he could his.

She shook her head, not taking her focus from him. "I came back to see you." Her voice cracked. For whatever reasons, telling him she had a job interview would make it sound as though she was begging for his attention. If he wouldn't come to her now, she'd taken all the steps she could to make something happen between them.

Perry walked to her and she didn't dare move. When he was inches away, he took a slice of bacon from where it lay on a paper towel, draining. She watched him slide it into his mouth and then chew. His jaw muscles constricted. Roped muscle spreading from his shoulders flexed when he turned. But when he lifted his hand and brushed a strand of hair behind her ear, she closed her eyes, afraid to breathe.

"There's been a lot of loss in this town over the past few months," he said, his deep baritone gentle, quiet, but still sounding distant and serious. "My nieces, who have already endured the loss of their father, went through the pain of losing friends in their classes." He paused for a moment. "And you."

"I know. I got an earful this morning," she admitted, focusing on the spread of dark curls that traveled over his tanned chest. "You know I couldn't tell them who I really was."

"Yup." He picked up another piece of bacon and then walked to his refrigerator.

Kylie focused on his back, deciding he'd lost a few pounds, too, over the past few months. Her attention shot to the red mark that stretched over his shoulder blade, bright and puffy and shaped like a bolt of lightning. She cleared the distance between them, touching the puffy skin and acknowledging the fresh wound.

"You're hurt."

Perry spun around, his eyes on fire when he grabbed her wrist, pinching her skin as he held it firmly against his heart. "I helped pull a couple out of a car that capsized in the river earlier tonight when we couldn't reach a diver," he explained. "The pain from it will go away before long. I'm not worried about it. What I am worried about are the girls, me, what is mine," he said, his fierceness unleashed on her.

Kylie looked up at him, her lips parted and her breath coming hard. Emotions he'd apparently managed to keep at bay, possibly as long as she'd been gone, suddenly tumbled at her like an avalanche. And he held on to her, refusing to let go and staring down at her with a hard stare that bordered on violent.

"It hurt when you walked out of my life, hurt really fucking bad. And I knew you were leaving. But then I had to deal with the girls, who were not only recovering from the hysteria and trauma involved with a madman stalking one of them, and with girls they knew having been brutally murdered, but also with a sense of betrayal they felt from you."

"Perry," she breathed, knowing nothing she could say right now would take away the pain and heartache he had to deal with.

"So if you've come back to stay, we'll talk. But if you're here for a short while, only to leave to start again in another town, then there isn't anything for us to say." He let go of her wrist, opened the refrigerator, grabbed a beer, and walked out of the kitchen.

Hell. She didn't know if she had come back to stay unless she knew where things were with them. He wanted it just the opposite, and she wasn't sure how to give it to him like that.

Taking a moment, finding one of his coffee cups and pouring herself coffee, she then found a plate, poured the stack of bacon onto it, added the two slices of buttered toast, and followed him. She walked through the masculine-looking living room, which appeared almost dusty from lack of use, to the den where his computer was. He sat in front of it, not looking at her, with the glow from the monitor creating a shiny texture in his hair. His bedroom door was open, the lights off in there and the lingering smell from his shower drifting toward her. It didn't seem so long ago she had been here, although then her concerns had been so different.

Kylie placed the plate of food next to the keyboard. Then nursing her coffee, she walked around his desk to his gun case, the only item in the room that appeared dusted and well maintained. She stared at the expensive collection of weapons housed behind the glass.

"I've been injured, Perry," she began, not knowing where to start in bridging the gap between them. She did know she wanted to, more than she'd wanted anything in her life; she would sweat out this conversation until they found ground to coexist on.

"I can see that," he said, his mouth full of food. When the silence drifted between them again, he chewed and swallowed. "Thanks for making me breakfast. It is really good."

"You're welcome." She didn't turn around, unable to stare into those all-knowing eyes and say what was in her heart. "I was promised a month's vacation after Nicaragua, but after injuring myself, I've now been given two months off."

"So you're here for two months?" Perry asked, sounding very matter-of-fact.

Kylie couldn't turn this into a mathematical equation, giving him figures and making everything cut-and-dry. Her thigh pinched with pain when she shifted, finally facing him and balancing herself against his desk. "I don't know how long I'm here for, Perry. It isn't all black and white. There are gray areas. And I doubt one conversation between you and me can clear all those areas up."

"I'm not going to endure the pain," he said firmly.

"Relationships are about pain," she argued, fighting not to lose her temper with his insistence they create some kind of damn contract that neither one of them would ever stray from. "They are about love and happiness, too. But I can't promise never to hurt you any more than you could make me the same offer."

"I would never hurt you," he hissed.

"You're hurting me right now," she yelled. "You hurt me the moment I laid eyes on you when I was coming into town. And for the past two days I've been dying inside, desperate to know where I stood with you. But that didn't send me running."

She put her cup down too hard on his desk and some of it spilled onto her hand. Bringing her burnt flesh to her lips, she closed her eyes, willing herself to calm down and say what needed to be said to get them past this point. She jumped when strong arms grabbed her, pulling her from the desk.

"Sit down before you fall down," Perry said, his bare chest brushing against her arm and then her back, as he guided her into his bedroom. "So you're here for two months. Are you staying at that motel for two months?"

He stood in front of her and Kylie's heart started pounding when she realized she sat on the edge of his bed. He'd moved her so quickly, obviously more in tune with her movements and how standing for long periods or walking was still difficult to do. She stared at his strong body, at his sleek dark hair, and then into his gaze that was damn near sinful with the intensity that glowed there.

"I checked out," she admitted.

"And you came here. Are you leaving?"

"No," she whispered.

Perry leaned over her, pushing her backward until she lay sideways on his bed. Kylie wrapped her arms around his neck, his damp hair torturing her feverish flesh as she pulled him to her, needing to taste him, to feel him against her. If only she knew in her heart what she felt now would last, forever.

His kiss wasn't gentle. But she didn't want that. He pressed her lips open, moving in and demanding she give him all she had.

Kylie dragged her fingers over his shoulders, feeling his

muscles twitch where she touched him. The heat from his body sunk deep inside her, filling the void that had grown to its painful size the longer she'd been apart from him. As she opened, sighing into the kiss, Kylie experienced the overwhelming sensation that she'd come home, for the first time in her life.

And as quickly as the sensation hit her, the need also attacked her to have him inside her. Talking all of this out no longer seemed as important as making love to him. It had been three long months.

"Perry," she whispered, moving her lips against his.

"Kylie," he responded, making her name sound better than anything she'd heard him say since she got here.

"I need to get out of my clothes."

"Yes. You do." He moved his hand between them, pushing her shirt up over her breasts with a quick thrust. Then his fingers tortured her belly as he worked the snap loose on her jeans and unzipped her zipper. "What is the best way?" he asked.

She didn't understand his question until he lifted himself off her, taking her shirt with him and sliding it over her head. He tossed it to the side and looked like a starving man as he stared at her. Kylie never felt more beautiful in all of her life, and she doubted seriously she was looking her best these days.

"The best way?" she asked.

He pulled her to her feet, keeping her close with his arms around her as he slid her jeans down her hips. "I don't want to hurt you," he whispered against her neck, placing gentle kisses along her collarbone.

She realized he meant because of her injury. "I'm not sure. I haven't had sex since—" She broke off, looking up into his sensual green eyes. "Since I've been with you," she finished her sentence, growing incredibly warm under his heated stare even as she shed her clothing.

"Good." He said the one word so firmly Kylie didn't doubt anymore that whatever their issues, they would work them out. "Neither have I."

"Good." She couldn't help grinning.

Taking a moment to kick off her shoes and step out of her jeans, she then wrapped her arms around his shoulders, leaning into him and kissing him.

When he placed her once again on his bed, it felt better than she remembered it feeling having his flesh touching hers. Her thigh was tender, and she was aware of the gash stretching down his back when she kept her exploration to his shoulders and arms. In spite of neither of them being in perfect condition, Kylie was positive their lovemaking was hotter, filled with more passion, and more intense than it had been before she left him.

His kisses went from gentle and tender to needy and demanding. When he scraped his rough fingertips against her flesh, the tingles that rushed over her were almost enough to make her come. Perry scraped his teeth over her nipples and sucked first one and then the other like a starving man. The pressure that built inside her as he administered his torturous attention to her body filled her with desire to have more of him. With every touch, every kiss, Kylie knew she was right where she belonged, and understood now why she felt so unsettled until she returned to Perry's side.

He was her soul mate, her other half. Regardless of their lines of work, they would make their relationship last. She didn't doubt it for a moment. Perry was her man. And she was his woman.

"I love you, Kylie," he whispered against her mouth when he finally glided deep inside her.

His words along with the pressure he applied took her over the edge. She ignored the pang in her thigh when she arched underneath him, gripping his arms and actually panting as she fought to catch her breath.

"Oh, God, Perry," she cried, feeling another emotional roller coaster hit her, and worried she might start crying in the middle of making love to him. "I most definitely love you, too." And she had for quite a while now, possibly well before leaving him.

"Don't leave me again." It wasn't an order, although not quite a request. And he didn't wait for a response.

Perry impaled her, and when she howled from the depth he reached, he devoured her mouth, taking all she offered and giving as much in return. Her world tilted, all anxiety, the panic attacks, her worries and pain vanishing as their bodies became one. She exploded, the dam of passion releasing and her orgasm pushing her to a new level.

He continued fucking her, bringing her to a hard orgasm several more times, obviously not exhausted in spite of working all night. When he finally released, deep inside her, pumping all he had until his body was covered with a shiny sheen of sweat, his bulging muscles appeared larger and more defined. It was definitely the sexiest view she'd ever witnessed in her life.

Kylie relaxed slowly, taking time to catch her breath while running her fingertips over the tight, dark curls in the middle of his chest. "This afternoon at four I have a job interview," she told him, knowing the time was right.

"Oh?" He didn't roll over next to her when he slowly pulled out but instead moved to a sitting position, pulling her into his arms and cradling her with her injured thigh away from him. He moved his finger slowly around the still-tender scar and slightly puffy flesh where the bullet had entered her. "I thought you weren't leaving the FBI."

"It's an interview for the supervisor's position at the field office here in town."

His gaze shot to hers, one eyebrow tilting slightly as his gaze narrowed on hers. "Why the hell didn't you tell me this sooner? You have come back to stay."

His excitement was so noticeable it was impossible not to smile. "Perry, I needed to know you wanted me here no matter what."

"You knew I did," he growled.

"I thought you did until you were so cold toward me when you pulled me over for speeding." She spoke easily, relaxing in his arms and letting her head rest against his arm. "Then I wasn't sure what to do. I almost left, but couldn't without talking to you first."

"I didn't want to endure the pain of you entering my life again only to leave."

"There is a possibility I might be here for good." She studied his face closely and saw only the love he'd professed to her while making love to her.

"Do you want a desk job?" He surprised her with the question.

When she was sure he would be excited at the prospect of her remaining in Mission Hills, Perry knew her well enough, even after being apart for three months, to know the thrill of solving the case, being on the streets and piecing together the puzzle pieces, meant more to her than anything else in her life. Although she was beginning to believe Perry meant as much to her.

"It's going to take a while before I'm completely healed," she admitted, noting how easy it was to share that information with him when only a few weeks ago the knowledge had made her sick to her stomach. "And there is no insurance I'll get the job here in town, but my supervisor in Dallas arranged for the interview with the area field supervisor. I have a feeling the job will be mine if I want it. I've put in my time, and since I've been injured, they know my experience and knowledge of solving cases can still be put to good use with me running the office here in town."

Perry glanced at his dresser, where a clock radio glowed with digital numbers. It was already almost ten in the morning. "I need to get some shut-eye, and have to be at work at five. But I'll take you to that interview."

She could drive herself, but the thought of having him take her, wishing her luck, and being there afterward so she could share what had happened sounded really appealing.

"Have you had enough to eat?" she asked.

Perry was already pulling the blankets back on his bed, keeping her in his arms while adjusting their bodies until they lay next to each other in his bed. "I have for now," he growled, nipping at her ear. "You should take a nap, too.

You're going to need to be rested. I have a feeling I'm going to wake up a starving man."

"There will be plenty for you to eat when you wake up." She cuddled in next to him, the warmth of his body enveloping her and assuring her once again she was home, for good.

Home was where her heart was, and she had known she'd find it if she came back.

Greg King loved not having to worry about getting a warrant. But if he shot to kill, he would face murder charges. He really did hate some of the laws on the books.

Keeping his Glock pointed to the ground, he hit the street, humidity causing his shirt to cling to him like a second skin. It wasn't even light out yet. It would be another scorcher, tolerable only if he nailed the fugitive they'd been tracking since two AM before the sun got too high in the sky.

And they said life would be boring once he retired from the LAPD.

"Marc, you in place?" he hissed into his Bluetooth.

"Yup," Marc whispered in his ear, sounding somewhat winded. "Stationary and ready for fireworks."

"Jake, what's it like out front?"

"All quiet. He's still in there." Jake's anxious tone sounded as if he were running high on adrenaline.

But then, weren't they all. It had been one hell of a night.

"I'm going in," Greg informed his sons.

Marc and Jake both loved the kill, although technically no one died. Or they weren't supposed to. Greg and his sons were only paid when they brought their prey in alive. A dead fugitive was no good to the bondsman who'd hired them, or in this case, bondswoman.

Greg knew the craving to make the bust, bring down the fugitive, and slap on those cuffs, ran strong enough in his blood that both of his boys would get high from the adventure just like he did. Pulling all-nighters like this never got old. Dealing with the bureaucratic red tape that forced him to wait on judges' signatures and stalling until he got the go-ahead from his senior officers got old as hell. Those days were behind him now. Being a bounty hunter allowed him freedom to do exactly what he planned on doing right now, and would have killed to do for the past twenty years.

Greg cut between the dilapidated house and the house next door where Charlie Woods supposedly lived, moving silently in spite of his size. Size did matter. No one would convince him otherwise. But Greg knew how to move his over-six-foot-tall body—six foot four inches to be exact—without disturbing a soul. There wasn't any reason to wake the entire neighborhood simply because Pedro thought he could jump bail and make a run for it. Charlie was a known member of the Hell Cats, a gang Pedro Gutierrez had once belonged to. According to reliable sources, Pedro was hiding out at Charlie's. Greg wouldn't learn the truth by simply knocking on the door.

He reached the backyard and hurried across the lawn, slowing when he reached the metal screen door. He kept his gun down, pulling the door open with his left hand, then braced it with his body as he turned the handle on the door.

"Are you in?" Jake demanded, his whispered question sounding as if he stood right behind his father.

Greg took his hand off the doorknob and adjusted the earpiece so his son wasn't yelling in his ear.

"It's locked," he growled, having half a mind to shoot the fucking doorknob off the door. "I'm trying the windows."

"We're coming in through the front," Marc decided, breaking in on the conversation.

"Like hell," Greg said, keeping his voice to a barely audible whisper. "He's fucking armed and dangerous. We're working against a ticking time bomb. You two wait for my go-ahead."

Already he was around the back of the house, edging his way to the nearest window. It was probably a bedroom window and quite possibly where their guy might be hiding out. Greg stared at the dark window, blinds, possibly curtains, or even a mattress, that were making it impossible to see inside. The storm window was up, though, and the window wasn't so high off the ground or too small that he couldn't haul his rather large frame through it if he moved quickly. The element of surprise was his only advantage right now.

"Go ahead and call in backup," Greg told Marc.

"I'm on it," his son announced.

Greg didn't bother asking if that meant they were already on their way or not. They would get here when they got here. Greg wasn't waiting.

Sliding his gun into his holster, Greg pulled out his pocket-knife and flipped it open. It wasn't the kind of knife most fathers carried around with them. The razor-sharp blade would cut through the metal of the screen frame if he wanted it to. Instead, he sliced the screen, imagining their fugitive would probably try suing if he owned this dump and charging him for breaking and entering plus vandalizing his home. It wouldn't be the first time.

Maybe he didn't get the protection offered when he wore the uniform. He had to be careful how he went about making his arrests. But at least today red tape was something he would slice through with his handy little pocketknife. Greg ran his own show these days. All that mattered was that the bonds company got their fugitive and Greg got his check.

He sliced the screen, starting in the top left corner and gutting it down the middle, then cutting along the bottom until the screen peeled to the side for him. Greg reached through it, feeling it scrape his damp flesh above his leather glove, and pushed the window up. It lifted with a whiny squeak, obviously complaining from lack of use.

"I'm heading in," he whispered to his sons. "Move now!"

Greg King wasn't a small man. More than once in his life, living in Los Angeles, people had asked if he was a professional wrestler. His size didn't bother him, and it wouldn't slow him down now. Snapping his pocketknife shut and sheathing it into the leather case attached to his belt, Greg hoisted himself through the window, feeling the wooden frame of the window rake over his shoulders and then his legs. He fell to his side on a dirty wooden floor and immediately pulled his gun, forcing his eyes to adjust quickly to his surroundings as he looked around.

Other than a box spring and mattress that didn't have a sheet or blankets on it, there wasn't any furniture in the room. Crumpled fast-food bags and crunched beer cans gave the room the appearance of being one big trash dump.

"Did you hear that?" a man asked from the other room.

"Sounds like we have company." The thick Hispanic accent sounded just like Pedro Gutierrez, a well-known drug lord and arms dealer who'd been arrested last month and yesterday afternoon failed to show up for court. His probation officer couldn't find him and the bondswoman was getting nervous.

It was a stupid move on Pedro's part. He obviously didn't check the statistics before deciding to run. No criminal ran from Los Angeles and got away. This was his town and Greg was too good. His track record spoke for itself.

"Who the fuck is back there?" the man roared, obviously not afraid at all of the boogeyman being in a dark bedroom.

Nor did he turn on the bedroom light as he stormed in, which was just fine with Greg.

"Hello, Pedro," he said calmly, pointing his gun straight at the man's face.

Pedro apparently had no manners. He didn't return the greeting but instead hauled ass toward the other end of the house. Greg charged after him, feeling the house shake from the two of them running through it.

It wasn't a long hallway, but Greg didn't catch the shadow in time that appeared from the bedroom across the hall. He saw the baseball bat, heard the whooshing sound when it sliced through the air.

"Son of a bitch," he wailed, turning and raising his arm. He braced himself for the pain he'd experience in the next moment as he planned on smacking the bat out of his assailant's hands.

Intense pain shot across his shoulder and down his spine. The bat hit the side of his neck, just above his shoulder, with enough driving force to knock Greg against the hallway wall.

"Fucking hell," he roared, although the words damn near caught in his throat when his windpipe smashed closed, stealing his breath, and racking every inch of his body.

Hitting the wall with the other shoulder didn't make matters any better. The intense headache he'd probably have to deal with the rest of the day slammed into his brain instantly.

A dark, burly-looking man bellowed something in Spanish that didn't sound very friendly and Pedro responded, their guttural slang difficult for Greg to translate. Especially when pain ransacked his body and a ringing started in his head as he slumped against the wall. The burly motherfucker shoved him out of the way, causing Greg to lose his footing, and then bounded after Pedro, leaving him to hold up the slimy wall.

At least he hadn't been shot. Maybe the two men weren't armed. The pain hurt like fucking hell, but he'd have to worry about that later. Reaching for his neck, he cringed from the intense pain that shot down his arm. There wasn't any blood, though.

"I didn't give up a night's sleep so you could give me a migraine and get away," Greg cursed, using the hallway wall to push himself to his feet. It seemed his legs were heavier than usual when he tried running after them, and he damn near fell on his face. "Tough it up, King," he ordered himself.

They couldn't get far. His boys were out front and on the side of the house. Unless they'd already entered. He was in the living room, staring at the open front door when he heard gunfire.

"Son of a bitch!" he hissed. Haley would never forgive him if one of the boys were seriously injured, or worse, while working a job.

He ignored the pain and ran out of the house, not having to worry about his eyes adjusting this time. It wasn't much lighter outside than it was in the house, but the pain made everything blur. Flashing reds and whites gave the front yard a surreal look. It was odd that moments like this caused him to think of his deranged wife.

"You have the right to remain silent," a young rookie Greg didn't recognize said as he continued shoving Charlie Woods toward a squad car. His tone was harsh and full of himself, as if he'd been the one chasing Pedro all night.

"Dad!" Jake yelled, hurrying across the yard.

Greg noticed Marc talking to Margaret Young, one of the bondsmen, or to be politically correct, bondspeople, that the Kings worked with on a regular basis. Jake reached Greg's side, grabbing his arm on his injured side.

"Where's Pedro?" Greg demanded, grabbing his boy's arm and holding on to it tighter than he probably should have when he pulled his son's hand off him.

"We got them," Jake said, not complaining even if Greg's hold on him was painful. "Are you okay?" he asked, as Marc headed across the lawn to join them.

"I nabbed Pedro," Marc announced, giving his dad a quick once-over. Although Marc was the oldest at twenty-five, Jake stood an inch or so taller. Both were built like their old man, although at the moment, Greg didn't feel incredibly intimidating as many claimed the three of them appeared when standing together. "Charlie Woods was with him and they're reading his rights to him right now. Margaret has one more. Apparently this one was nabbed at the same time as Gutierrez and missed his court date yesterday afternoon, too."

There were squad cars up and down the street, their lights flashing and lighting up the whole block. Greg and his boys might have done all the grunt work, but the uniforms loved being there for all the glory. It didn't surprise him the moment they called in for backup that it was a race to get here so one of the men on the force could make the arrest. Greg had years of putting more of these hoods behind bars than he cared to count. He didn't need to slap handcuffs on some punk to know he was good. But he'd run his ass off throughout the night and the officers now on the scene weren't giving him the time of day. Now if any of the older boys had been here for the bust, they would have treated Greg differently. It was these young punks in uniform who didn't know how to show respect.

Another time he might have grumbled that he didn't make the arrest after doing all the grunge work but suddenly none of that mattered. Something distracted him.

Greg barely heard his son. He stared at a woman who stood down the street, partially hidden in shadows. His head and shoulder were pounding, causing a ringing sound in his head that damn near drowned out anything his boys said. But it was as if tunnel vision had kicked in and all he saw was the woman, returning his stare while standing a good distance from the crowd of officers around the house.

As crazy as the scene was becoming, she stared at him as if it were just the two of them there. She wore a pale pink jogging outfit, tight spandex that hugged her small waist. Her skin was tanned and her light brown hair cut short, shorter than he remembered it, her natural color that he hadn't seen since high school, and it was kinky from the humidity.

Six years might have passed, but he would know Haley if it had been sixty years and a hundred people stood between them.

Did someone say HOT?

Don't miss the first two novels in
this sizzling series

LONG, LEAN AND LETHAL
ISBN: 978-0-312-94343-1

TALL, DARK AND DEADLY
ISBN: 978-0-312-94341-7

Available from St. Martin's Paperbacks